Hugh Charles McKeown

The Life and Labors of Most Rev. John Joseph Lynch, D.D.,

Cong. miss., first archbishop of Toronto

Hugh Charles McKeown

The Life and Labors of Most Rev. John Joseph Lynch, D.D.,
Cong. miss., first archbishop of Toronto

ISBN/EAN: 9783337426514

Printed in Europe, USA, Canada, Australia, Japan

Cover: Foto ©Raphael Reischuk / pixelio.de

More available books at **www.hansebooks.com**

THE

LIFE AND LABORS

OF

Most Rev. John Joseph Lynch, D.D.,

CONG. MISS.,

FIRST ARCHBISHOP

OF

TORONTO.

BY

H. C. McKEOWN

———

JAMES A. SADLIER,

MONTREAL AND TORONTO.

1886.

PREFACE.

THE writing of a preface is usually a mere conformity to one of the conventionalities of literature; but in the present instance a few words may not be out of place, to explain the apparent anomaly of writing a man's life while he is still living. Such biographies, although not common, are not without precedent, and we think the publication of the following pages will be justified by the peculiar circumstances under which they were prepared. To explain these, some personal details must be pardoned. On the approach of the twenty-fifth anniversary of Archbishop Lynch's elevation to the Episcopal See of Toronto—which, as it will be remembered, was made the occasion of a grand demonstration in December of last year—the writer was requested by a number of His Grace's friends and admirers to prepare a short sketch of his life, to be published for that occasion. This he agreed to do, providing the Archbishop's consent could be obtained, which proved a rather difficult matter. His Grace raised numerous objections to such a publication, chief among which was that he did not consider himself individually of such importance in the Church as to warrant the writing of his life, and that the appearance of such a volume during his lifetime, and with his consent, might lay him open to the imputation of assuming a position in the Church in Canada, to which, on his personal merits, he could lay no claim. His friends, however, were not prepared to take this view of the matter. They attributed these objections merely to His Grace's natural humility. They pointed out to him that, on the occasion of the celebration of his silver jubilee, there could be nothing out of place in publishing a short biographical sketch to commemorate the event, and such other arguments were used as finally induced him to yield to their earnest solicitations to allow such a publication to be issued. The author's design extended no further, in the first instance, than the preparation of a mere monograph. His Grace had but few memoranda, and he had kept but very meagre records of his early life. Such material as he had, however, he kindly placed at the writer's disposal. From many conversations, however, which we had with His Grace, in which, in the freedom of unrestrained conversation, he spoke of his early life, and especially of his labors and, what might with truth be called, his "adventures" as a missionary in Texas and elsewhere, the writer thought that it would be a misfortune if all record of these events should be lost, as inevitably they would be in case of His Grace's death, and he was induced, upon reflection, to believe that a plain account of the life and labors of the Archbishop, continued to the present time, and embodying selections from the most important of his pastorals, lectures, sermons, etc., would make a not uninteresting volume. He, therefore, after having written enough to make such a volume as at first intended, gave up the idea of publishing a short biography in time for the celebration, enlarged his original design, extended the scope of the work, and the result is now in the hands of the reader. Those who will do the author the honor to read the book will, we think, admit that the events here recorded are worth preserving in a permanent form. Had they not appeared at this opportune moment, they would undoubtedly have been lost to the Catholic public. Such as they are, they may possibly form a small contribution to the history of the Catholic Church in this country, and be of some slight service to the future historian of that Church. The life of a Catholic bishop, above that of most men, should be deeply interesting to Catholics, and the study of such a life will not be without its lessons. It will be found that, in the vast majority of cases, the careers of these men present all the elements that go to secure success in any path of life requiring real ability, profound learning, together with perseverance, a large capacity for work, and unwearied industry. The bishops of the Catholic Church in Canada and in the United States are, essentially, what are known as self-made men—men who would most undoubtedly have succeeded in any profession. They owe nothing, as a class, to the adventitious circumstances of wealth, birth, or family influence. Ability and administrative talent, joined to zeal and piety, constitute the chief factors of success in the Catholic Church in America. The strongest and most pronounced opponent of the Church in this country is constrained to admit that, at all events, so far as the hierarchy is concerned, the Holy See shows wonderful foresight in the appointment of its members, and that in making his selections the Holy Father usually puts the right man in the right place. In this respect the Catholic Church is really the most democratic institution on the face of the globe, and looking at it even from a purely worldly and human point of view, we are safe in saying that under no form of government now in existence, nor in any of those professions in which a high order of talent and exceptional powers of intellect are demanded for success, is real ability more fully recognized and more readily rewarded than in the Catholic Church. The life of one of her bishops will, therefore, be found interesting for many of the same reasons that make the biography of a successful statesman, diplomatist, lawyer, or literary man such pleasant and instructive reading, and hence this book. The author has only to say in concluding these, perhaps rather desultory, remarks, that he has made no attempt at artistic skill or literary finish in the presentation of his facts. He has not attempted, even if he were competent, anything like " fine writing." His only aim has been to tell his story in a plain, popular style, suitable to the intelligence of the ordinary every-day reader. He has tried to write the life of a church dignitary without becoming insufferably dull. How far he has succeeded, he leaves it to the reader to judge, as well as to such of the critics as can find time to glance over a few pages of the book before reviewing it. Perhaps he ought to say that he alone is responsible for the opinions, political or otherwise, expressed in the course of this work. Neither the MS. nor the proofs were submitted to the Archbishop, with the exception of a few pages of copy, and therefore he is not to be held as endorsing anything contained in these pages, put forth as the mere personal opinions of the author.

I cannot close these prefatory remarks without acknowledging my obligations to my friend, the Very Rev. Dean Harris, of this city, for the valuable assistance rendered me during the course of this work, especially in that portion of it relating to the Ecumenical Council. The Very Reverend gentleman—then a student—accompanied the Archbishop to Rome as his private secretary, and was present at the assembling of the Council. The opening scene is given as nearly as may be in his own graphic language. He may not be pleased at this public reference, but I feel that I cannot pass over in silence the debt I owe him for the help given me in the preparation of this volume.

H. C. M.

ST CATHARINES, ONTARIO,
Feast of the Immaculate Conception, 1885.

CONTENTS.

CHAPTER XIII.

LIFE AND LABORS

OF

ARCHBISHOP LYNCH.

CHAPTER I.

YOUTH AND EARLY EDUCATION.

Childhood and Youth—Early Piety—Primary Education—Is sent to the Academy of St. Mary's, Clondalkin—On the Point of Death—Recovery and Continuation of Studies—Enters the Lazarist College, Castleknock—His Industry—His Studies—Distinguished Graduates of Castleknock College—Meeting of Old Students as Bishops of the Vatican Council—The Universality of the Church and the Ubiquity of the Irish Race.

JOHN JOSEPH LYNCH, the present Archbishop of Toronto, was born near Clones, in the County Monaghan, on the sixth day of February, in the year 1816. His mother was one of those pious, God-fearing women, so numerous in Ireland among the Catholic population, to whom religion is the most important affair of their lives, and the salvation of their own and their children's souls the chief and supreme object of their solicitude. She came from a family that had given many priests to the Church. She was profoundly religious, and a constant and devout reader of the lives of the saints. Most men who have become distinguished in the world, or have risen to eminence, attribute their success to the influence and early training of their mothers, and nowhere, perhaps, are the results of such influence and training more clearly seen than in the lives of those men who have become eminent for their zeal in the cause of religion, not only in the Catholic Church, but also even in every other religious community. This is strongly exemplified in the case of the subject of this memoir. From his earliest infancy his mother instilled into his mind the principles of morality and religion. As a child he was highly imaginative, and very fond of reading. His mother supplied him with books, particularly the lives of the Fathers of the Desert. The example of these holy men seemed to impress powerfully the imagination of the boy, and to have for him a very strong fascination, and one of his boyish devotional acts was to build an oratory in an adjoining wood, whither he would regularly resort for the purpose of prayer. His mother was also extremely careful in the selection of his companions, knowing well the pernicious influence of bad companionship. She never allowed him to play with any boys except two, whom she chose to be his companions and playmates, and hence the boy grew up entirely ignorant of the vices to which youth is exposed in the promiscuous mingling of our large public schools, and in the evil example of the bad and the vicious. He had from his earliest boyhood the idea of one day becoming a priest, and this always had a restraining influence upon him, as he thought that if he should be guilty of any sin, this hope could never be realized, and thus he was continually upon his guard. Besides this, his mother strongly impressed upon him the nature of sin and the immediate presence of God, and so vividly did he realize, even as a mere child, that God's eye was upon him and saw his every action, that he would often ask his mother if the sun, moon, and stars were not God, for they always seemed to be watching him. He began to serve Mass when quite young—in fact he was too small to remove the book at first, and was obliged to wait some months until he grew strong enough to do so with safety. He received his first Communion and Confirmation from the hands of Archbishop Murray. That prelate made some objections at first to admitting him, on account of his youth, being then only in his ninth year, but after examining him in his catechism, and finding that he was well instructed and fully aware of the importance of the sacrament, he allowed him to pass. From that time forward the boy became a monthly communicant, as well as on all the feasts of the Church, and especially on those of the Blessed Virgin, to whom he has always had a very special devotion.

His primary education was received at a school in Lucan, kept by a graduate of Trinity College, Dublin. During his school years it was his delight to roam amid the ruined abbeys and castles of the neighborhood, and muse on the struggles of his ancestors for faith and fatherland. In his day, however, the political education of the Irish people, which has since resulted in the agitation for Home Rule and a reformation of the land laws, had not yet begun, and he has often been heard to say that it was only in France that he learned the history of his own country. At the age of seventeen he was attacked by typhoid fever, and for many days his life hung by a single thread. He was given up by the doctors and prepared for death. Providence, however, had other designs, and the hour of the future Archbishop had not yet arrived, although he had, as it were, stood on the very verge of the abyss of death. The awful solemnity of the moment when he thought 'he was about to be called before the judgment-seat of God, there to render an account of his whole life, made a deep and powerful impression on his youthful mind, which all the subsequent years of a busy and eventful life have never obliterated.

Resuming his studies, after his illness, for a year and a half at the Academy of St. Joseph, Clondalkin, he entered the College of the Lazarists, then lately established by that order at Castleknock. He was the first student who slept at the new college, which opened in 1835. The learned and pious professors reaped a rich harvest of consolations from their labors. Many of their pupils became bishops of the Church, and many attained to high positions in the world in other walks of life. Had the original founders of the college at Castleknock been present in Rome during the Ecumenical Council in 1869, they would have seen five of their old pupils re-united for the first time since their college days, coming together, after years of separation, from the four quarters of the globe. Parting as humble students of a small Irish college; meeting after the lapse of years as bishops of the Catholic Church, summoned by the successor of St. Peter to attend the most august and most important assembly of modern times—the Vatican Council. From Europe came the Right Reverend Dr. McCabe, Bishop of Ardagh; from Asia, the Right Reverend Dr. Finnelly, Vicar Apostolic, Madras; from Africa, the Right Reverend Dr. Grimley, Cape of Good Hope; from Australia, Most Reverend Dr. Moran, Bishop of Dunedan; from the United States, the Most Reverend Dr.

Feehen, then Bishop of Nashville, now Archbishop of Chicago, and from Canada, the subject of this memoir. Could anything be more indicative of the universality of the Catholic Church and the ubiquity of the Irish race? In order to celebrate this meeting, four of the prelates made a pilgrimage to the Church of St. Paul's Extra Muros and to the chapel of Tre Fontane. It may well be imagined what the subject of their conversation was, and how interesting it must have been. Their college days; their dispersion, one to the wilds of Africa, another to the backwoods of America; one to the jungles of India, another to the forests of Canada. The Irish race are certainly the pioneers of the Catholic faith in these days, and although millions have been driven from their native land by the evil effects of misgovernment, it is nevertheless a strange and suggestive fact —the irony of fate, it would seem—that wherever the British flag has been planted throughout the world, in India, Africa, Australia, or America, there is to be found established the Catholic Church, supplied with priests and governed by bishops of the Irish race. The Catholic Church in the British colonies and dependencies is, in fact, composed almost entirely of Irish or their descendants.

Our young student remained at the Castleknock Seminary for two years, and in that time laid the foundation of a good solid education. The study in which he at that time took the most delight, and in which he excelled, was logic. Knowing that his future career as a missionary priest would be almost entirely devoted to preaching, he founded a small club in the college, composed of four students only, who met once a week for the purpose of practising extemporaneous preaching, from which they all derived great benefit. He was also made prefect of the boys, and thus at a very early age, began his experience in the government of others, a faculty which he has since converted to a noble end in the very exacting and responsible position of a bishop of the Catholic Church.

CHAPTER II.

ST. LAZARE.

THE young student having finished his collegiate course at the College of Castleknock, was sent in 1837 as the first postulant from the college to the Seminary of St. Lazare at Paris. As he had now made up his mind to join the Lazarist Order, and as he became afterwards one of the most distinguished members of a community which has given many eminent men to the Church, a slight sketch of the history of the Order may not be out of place.

The Lazarist Order, whose official name is " The Congregation of the Priests of the Mission," was founded by St. Vincent of Paul in the year 1624. Vincent being employed as a tutor in the family of the Countess of Joigny, was summoned one day to attend the dying bed of one of her well-to-do vassals. He found that the man was a hardened sinner, and he had much difficulty in bringing him to a sense of his condition, particularly as he had been making bad confessions for many years. Vincent finally succeeded, and the man repented, declaring that he owed to the saint more than his life. The countess, on hearing of the circumstance, prevailed on St. Vincent to preach in the church of Tolleville, where most of the congregation were her vassals, which he did with so much success that large numbers were converted. From the success attending his preaching, the countess conceived the idea of founding and endowing an Order for the purpose of preaching missions in the country districts. She desired Vincent to obtain, if possible, the services of the Jesuits, or the French Oratorians; but neither of these Orders was able to undertake the work at that time. Finally it was arranged that Vincent, aided by some secular priests, who had been for some years associated with him in his various works of mercy and instruction, should commence the missions; that the institute should be established in the College des Bons Enfants, offered for that purpose by the Archbishop of Paris; and that the countess should endow it with forty thousand livres. The institute was thus founded in March, 1624, and the countess died the same year. The Congregation was confirmed by a bull of Pope Urban VIII. in 1632. It had a threefold object—the sanctification of its own members, the work of the mission, and the training of priests. As a rule eight months of the year were devoted to preaching missions, which were conducted nearly on the same plan as Passionist missions are conducted at the present day. St. Vincent having lived to see twenty-five houses of the new Order founded in France, Italy, and Poland, died in 1660, being in his eighty-fifth year. A few years after the foundation of the Order it was established in the College of St. Lazare in Paris, which had previously belonged to the regular canons of St. Victor. It was a spacious site, and the third superior-general, Edward Joly, erected on it the vast range of buildings still seen there. St. Vincent was beatified in 1729, and canonized in 1737. At the revolution, St. Lazare was twice plundered by the mob, several of the fathers were massacred, and those who would not take the prescribed oath were banished from France, and their property confiscated. The *maison St. Lazare* was turned into a prison for women, and still remains one. Under the first Napoleon, the congregation was allowed to re-enter France, and under the Restoration a grant was made to it of a house in the Rue de Sévres, in lieu of St. Lazare. The missions left vacant in China and the Levant on the suppression of the Jesuits in 1773 were transferred to the Lazarists.*

The chief seminary of the Order is St. Lazare, in Paris, and thither are sent students from all parts of the world to go through their novitiate. Except the Propaganda in Rome, the seminary of St. Lazare is the most cosmopolitan institution of the kind in the world. As missionaries are to be here trained for service in all parts of the world, so here are to be seen gathered together, and mingling in common, natives of almost every nation under the sun. On one occasion the Archbishop says he remembers seeing in one of their country houses, to which they were accustomed to resort to spend their vacation, a game of billiards played by a Turkish and a French student against a Greek and a German, while an Irishman was keeping the count. The diversity of character displayed in this co-mingling of so many and so different nationalities afforded an opportunity to the young student to study character in all its varieties,

* Catholic Dict., Art. "Lazarists."

and it was here that he gained his first experience and knowledge of men and human nature. He is accustomed to say that, after all, there is not so much difference as is generally supposed between men of different nations in those essentials which go to make up the real foundation of all character. Human nature is pretty much the same in every clime and among all races. Very early in life, especially after his experience at St. Lazare—which was only confirmed by a longer and more extensive experience as a missionary among many peoples and in many different lands—he made up his mind to judge every man as an individual on his own merits, and independent of race, creed, or religion. He says, in all his long experience in the world, he has found that good and bad men are to be found in all nations. The good, honest, and virtuous man is pretty much the same the world over, while the wicked and vicious, whatever nation they may belong to, have the characteristics common to all the children of Satan. Thus he has always made it a rule through life to judge men, not according to their nationality, or even their religion, but according to their real worth as he found them.

The seminary of St. Lazare contained a very fine library, of which our young student made the best use. It was impossible for him to pursue as extensive and thorough a course of reading at that time as he would have desired. He, however, managed to read most of the standard historical works, and of nearly all the books of any authority upon liturgical and ecclesiastical subjects contained in the library; he carefully and frequently noted the indexes, and thus got a general idea of their scope and object. This he found was of immense service to him in after life, and in the treatment of any subject he might have under consideration, he has been always able to know exactly what books he requires, and where to put his hands upon his authorities. During the vacation the students were allowed to visit the public libraries of Paris, the galleries of paintings and statuary, museums, monuments of art, and places of national and historic interest; in the outward life and gaiety of the great metropolis, however, they took no part, but pursued, from day to day, the regular order of their studies, unaffected by the political changes of the times, thankful only that they were allowed to do so in peace and security. As stated above, St. Lazare had once before suffered from the violence of revolution. Situated as it is in the hot-bed of modern revolutionism, the chief house of the Order is more or less exposed, at periods of political excitement, to the fury of the Paris *canaille*, whose brutal passions, when they escape from the control of law and order, fiercely attack the houses and members of the religious communities.

Thus passed three happy years in the life of our young neophyte. Happy because he lived in anticipation of a career as a missionary in some foreign land where he might, with God's assistance, scatter the seed of the Gospel, and bear the light of Christianity to those who sat in the dark shadows of the valley of death. In due course of time he received minor orders, and was ordained subdeacon by the late Monsignor Affre, the saintly Archbishop of Paris who was shot at the barricades during the revolution of 1848, while endeavoring to prevent a conflict between the troops and the citizens, thus laying down his life in the cause of peace and charity. The period of young Lynch's novitiate having expired, it was determined by his superiors to send him back again to Ireland for ordination, with the intention of putting him on the Irish mission. To this the young man strongly demurred. He had entered the Order principally from a desire to devote himself to foreign missionary work, either among the heathens, or else in those countries whither his own countrymen had emigrated, and where they were in many cases without priests, churches, or religious instruction of any kind, and where there was great danger of their descendants losing their faith and forgetting the Church of their fathers. "No child," he said when discussing the matter with his superiors, "will go unbaptized in Ireland, nor is there much danger of any one dying without the sacraments; but thousands of my countrymen I know to be in a sad condition in America and other parts of the British Empire. These are the people who need our services, and to these I would rather be sent." He always had a very high idea of the importance of America as a missionary field, and had eagerly anticipated the time when he might receive permission to go there. He did not care particularly where. Whether to work among his exiled countrymen gathered in the great cities on the Atlantic coast, or scattered over the prairies of the West, whether to the Indians of the Northwest or to the savannas of the South. He eagerly read all the letters received at the seminary from the foreign missionaries, and receiving once a present of four volumes of correspondence from missionaries engaged in North America, he entered the fact in his journal, and then added, "Seed for the foreign missions."

The Superior, however, would not hear of his

being sent to America. He pointed out that there was a great work to be done in Ireland ; that missionary labor was only beginning in that country, and that the Order required as many priests as possible to carry on the work. Finding, therefore, all his entreaties in vain, he sadly and reluctantly gave up the dream of his boyhood and youth, and prepared to return to Ireland in obedience to the command of his Superior. He bade good-bye to the scene of so many happy and studious days, and returned once more to Ireland. He came by way of England, and his first experience of the custom officials was anything but pleasant. It was about the time that the great mass of the English middle-classes were beginning to be somewhat alarmed at the spread of " popery " in England. Everything, therefore, relating to, or having any connection with, Rome or Catholicism, was looked upon by the English officials pretty much as a package of dynamite would be if found in the trunk of an American at the present day. There was no mistaking the fact that the young man was either a priest or a theological student coming from France, and so his baggage was carefully overhauled, and among other things brought to light were his Latin classics and a few dozens of cheap religious pictures. On the former he was obliged to pay duty as prayer-books, for although he tried to persuade the intelligent official that Virgil's Æneid and Cæsar's Commentaries were not Catholic prayer-books, the fact that they were in Latin was quite sufficient evidence to convince the latter that they were certainly " popish," and so he was obliged to pay the duty. As for the pictures, he was compelled to pay a penny on each one, although the whole couple of dozens only cost a few sous in Paris. However, he had some little revenge on the stupid official. In one of his travelling-bags he was carrying home a wreath of locust thorns gathered from the trees in the grounds of one of the Order's country houses near Paris. Into this bag the official wildly thrust his hand to search for other contraband property, but he soon withdrew it again with an exclamation more emphatic than polite and with fingers bleeding. The crowd laughed, and the disgusted official, not knowing exactly how to class the article in question, allowed it to pass free of duty. It seems that the custom officials had strict orders at that time not to allow any objects to be brought into England from the continent of a religious nature—that is Catholic—without paying the heavy duty imposed on them. The consequence was that the most trivial articles of this kind, such as beads, crosses, medals and such like, had to pay a duty usually much greater than the actual cost of the articles. At the present day these devotional objects are not so strange to the eyes of Englishmen as they were some forty years ago.

CHAPTER III.

FIRST MISSIONARY LABORS.

ON arriving at the college at Castleknock, the subject of our memoir was again employed as prefect of the boys, and at once began to prepare himself to receive holy orders. In the month of June of the following year, 1843, he was ordained deacon, and a few days after, at Maynooth, he was raised to the priesthood by the late Archbishop Murray, of Dublin. His father and mother, brother and sisters were present at his ordination, and had also the happiness of assisting at his first mass, which he celebrated on the feast of Corpus Christi.

The young priest did not long remain idle after his ordination, but was at once taken from the college and placed upon the mission. The spiritual condition of the Irish people at this period was well calculated to enlist the sympathies and invite the active help of Father Lynch and the saintly members of his Order. For three hundred years the people of Ireland had endured a persecution to which, in its duration and intensity, the history of the world offers no parallel. The people were not only deprived of their schools, colleges and institutions, but they and their ample endowments were seized upon by the British government, and in its hands perverted to proselytizing purposes. The Catholic people were deprived of their rights, their goods confiscated, their churches despoiled and taken from them, and all that power, superadded to satanic malice, could effect was done to force the people into apostasy, or, failing in that, to reduce them to the most abject poverty and ignorance, and to crush out their manhood. They were able to hold fast to their faith only at the sacrifice of all else, only in bonds, confiscations, fines, imprisonments and death. The Catholic religion was proscribed. The education of Catholics in Ireland was made a felony by statute; and if Catholic parents sent their children abroad to be educated, they rendered themselves liable to the same penalties. The Catholic religion, the religion of the people, was proscribed, and no Catholic could for ages in Ireland practice it except by stealth. All priests were banished the country and forbidden to return, and if they did re-enter it, and were convicted of having exercised any sacerdotal functions, the "priest-hunter" was on their track and they were hanged, drawn and quartered as traitors. They were obliged to resort to all manner of disguises, to live in secret, to conceal their character and to take all possible precautions against capture, as criminals hiding from the officers of justice, in order to minister for a short time to the spiritual wants of their people.

The Lazarists were no strangers in Ireland.

They were the first Order that preached missions in the island, and we find that at the siege of Limerick in 1691, shortly after their establishment, they were engaged in their holy work in the city while it was beleaguered by the English army. Father Lynch and five other priests commenced their labors in 1846. They arose at five in the morning and celebrated a first mass at six o'clock, at which they gave catechetical instructions on the commandments, sacraments, etc. This mass was for the benefit of the workingmen. Another mass was said at nine o'clock, especially for the benefit of the children. As Father Lynch was the youngest of the band of priests, to him was assigned the duty of conducting this portion of the work. The task of instructing the young, and of explaining the truths of Christianity and the doctrines of the Church in language and illustrations suitable to the intelligence and capacities of children, was a very congenial duty to him, and the experience gained in this way during his first mission he found ever after of immense practical advantage in dealing with young and tender souls. It exercised him in clear, simple and intelligent explanations of the doctrines of the Church, and although these were given in simple language, and the illustrations used, homely in their character, yet he found that in after life this simple method of explaining the doctrines of the Catholic Church in an unstudied colloquial style was more effective, and the ideas sought to be conveyed were better understood and more easily grasped by the mind than dry and abstract theological or doctrinal disquisitions more suitable to the professorial chair than to the pulpit.

This first missionary work upon which the young

priest was employed proved successful beyond his fondest hopes. Such a spiritual awakening was very much needed at the time in Ireland. We, in this country, who enjoy all the advantages of large and commodious churches in which to worship God, and convents, colleges and schools for the education of Catholic children, can scarcely realize the condition of the Irish people in these respects some forty or fifty years ago. The long night of political oppression was beginning to give way before the dawn of a new era, but nevertheless the cruel and oppressive laws under which the people had groaned for centuries had wrought their effect. As has been truly said by an eminent English writer, after having been subjected to such misgovernment as the Irish people had been obliged to submit to for such a long period of time, and the diabolic ingenuity with which it was systematically attempted to degrade and debase them by making their education a penal offense, the only wonder is that instead of being what they are, confessedly the most moral and religious people in Europe, they are not the greatest rascals on the civilized earth. In many parts of the country the people were as badly off with respect to the accessories of religion as are the Catholic population of our back townships. They were frequently without the necessary religious instruction, and the sacraments were very irregularly administered, except in the cities and larger towns. These missions had a great effect in rousing them from this spiritual lethargy. Crowds flocked to the churches to hear the preaching and to prepare for receiving the sacraments. The confessionals were crowded. In many of the country places the people came long distances, and, as there was no other accommodation for them, they were

obliged to sleep in the churches. The churches were
kept open night and day, and in them the poor people
were allowed to rest their weary limbs and enjoy
such sleep as under the circumstances they could.
One poor man being told by his confessor about
one o'clock in the afternoon that he had better
go home for that day and come again on the
morrow, anxiously replied to the good father:
"Ah, your reverence! won't you let me stay in
the church again to-night. I'm living far up in the
mountains, and if I went home I'd have to start at
four in the morning to be in time for mass. I'm
now three days and three nights in the chapel." In
order not to keep the people waiting in the church,
the missionaries finally adopted the system of issuing
tickets, which were distributed to the people in the
order in which they came, and numbered accordingly.
In this way the inconvenience of keeping them waiting was in some degree relieved. In one parish between Dublin and the mountains of Wicklow a mission was given, and the Archbishop not having time
to give confirmation during its continuance, it was
postponed for a month, and the missionaries, six in
number, returned to their labors. Ten more priests
were sent to their assistance, and before the arrival
of the Archbishop seven hundred and fifty adults had
been instructed and properly prepared for receiving
confirmation, besides the hearing of thousands of
confessions, preaching and administering the sacraments.

This was Father Lynch's first missionary work.
Not among the Indians of America, or the negroes
of Africa, but among the people of his own country,
and in his own native land. After concluding his
first mission he returned exhausted to the college at

Castleknock for a short respite. From that time forward, and until he left Ireland, he was almost constantly engaged in the kind of work we have just described. The labor was hard, and trying to mind and body. Short hours for sleep, long hours in the confessional; preaching, catechising, instructing, advising, cheering and encouraging the penitent, inspiring with fresh zeal the hearts of those Christian soldiers who are manfully fighting the good fight—such is the life of the missionary priest, even on the home missions. Ten or twelve years of such arduous and trying labor often leave the seeds of permanent ill health. Nothing but the strongest constitution can stand such a strain for any length of time, and it is well known that the lives of such men are usually short. Young men who enter these Orders and undertake this laborious work are well aware that they are sacrificing their health, and shortening their lives, but they voluntarily offer themselves as sacrifices for the good cause. If, however, the pains and hardships of the zealous missionary are great, his consolations not unfrequently repay him for all. To be instrumental in bringing the hardened sinner to repentance; to heal the wounded soul; to encourage and strengthen the sad and sorrow-stricken heart, these are all heavenly consolations known only to the missionary. If during the course of a mission he be successful in saving even one soul, in bringing back one stray sheep to the fold, he feels that all his labors and all his pains have not been incurred in vain.

But much as the young priest loved his native land, and great as was his devotion to his own people, he was still dissatisfied with his lot, he still longed to join the ranks of that small missionary army which was doing such good service in the cause of Christianity and the Church in the new world. He never ceased pressing the matter upon his superiors, and as he gained but little ground for hope from them, he turned more ardently than ever to God, and earnestly prayed that, if it were His divine will, this fondest wish of his heart might be gratified. His desire was even then on the eve of its accomplishment, although he little suspected it at the time. In 1835 Texas, having rebelled against Mexico, and having succeeded in establishing herself as an independent republic, was assigned by Pope Gregory XVI. to the Lazarist missionaries as their field of labor. Father Timon, afterwards Bishop of Buffalo, was at that time the Visitor of the Congregation of the Missions in America. He was at once ordered by the Pope to proceed to Texas, report upon the condition of the country, and recommend such measures as he might deem advisable for opening up this new country to the pioneers of the Church. Father Timon went to Mexico, accompanied by Father Odin, afterwards Archbishop of New Orleans, traversed the whole country and carefully examined the condition of the new republic. The result of his examination was his recommendation that a vicar apostolic be at once appointed and sent out to Texas. In answer to this, he himself was named by the Holy See, but he declined the honor, and advised that Father Odin, also a member of the Lazarist Order, who had accompanied him in his tour of inspection, and who had become thoroughly acquainted with the country, should receive the appointment. Father Odin was accordingly appointed, and at once consecrated bishop. There was, however, great difficulty in obtaining priests for the Texas mission in America, and therefore in 1846 Bishop Odin went to Europe to obtain priests for this new field of labor. Among other countries he visited was Ireland. At the time of his visit Father Lynch was engaged with others of his Order in giving a mission in a place called Black Rock, near Dublin. Descending from the pulpit one evening after preaching, and kneeling in the sanctuary to make a short prayer, he was startled from his quiet, and somewhat astonished by a gentleman throwing his arms around him and whispering in his ear, "For God's sake, come with me to Texas." He started up with surprise, and turning round found himself in the presence of Bishop Odin, who happened to be in the church on that evening. The voice at first seemed a command from heaven, and a direct answer to his prayers. The bishop and the young priest spent the greater part of that night in talking of Texas, discussing its then present wants and future prospects. It is hardly necessary to say that the bishop found a willing volunteer in the young priest, providing the consent of his superiors could be obtained, and this the former undertook to secure. It was, however, a rather difficult matter. The Order in Ireland had not at that period any priests that it could very well spare. It had inaugurated the preaching of missions throughout the country, and the force of priests, even as it was, was altogether too small for the work in hand. But Bishop Odin so eloquently set forth the deplorable condition of Texas, the sad want of priests for such an extensive country, and the grand prospect that was open for the future of the Church in that new land, that they finally yielded, and gave their consent.

CHAPTER IV.

A MISSIONARY TO TEXAS.

THUS, after so many years of waiting and watching, and when his prospects of being sent on
the foreign mission seemed more hopeless than ever,
the young priest at last saw his earnest wish about
to be accomplished. Still, it was not without some
feeling of regret and anguish of mind that he prepared to leave home, kindred and country for an
unknown land; to expose himself to the dangers of
a wild and lawless country, such as Texas then was,
perhaps never to see his own land or family again.
But such feelings were merely transitory. He knew
that the priest who joins any of these great Orders
of the Church, whose especial mission it is to preach
the religion of Christ to all nations and in all lands,
must give up and forever renounce father and
mother, sister and brother, kindred and country. He
therefore set about making preparations for his departure to this new field of labor. He had already
gone through considerable training in such a career
since his ordination, in his own country, and among
his own people; now he was about to enter a differ-

ent field, and certainly there could scarcely be presented a stronger contrast than that between Ireland and the Texas of 1846.

There was no time to lose. It was desirable that he should start at once by the first ship sailing from Liverpool. A missionary outfit was hastily obtained, but it was impossible, in the short space of time at his disposal, to purchase all the articles necessary for the altar and the celebration of Mass. He got together, however, such articles as he could, and such as he could not buy, were given to him. In one place he procured an altar-stone, in another the necessary linen; vestments from one, a chalice from another. Father Dooly, the then Superior of the Order in Ireland, gave the young missionary a chalice, oil-stocks and other articles, but there was not sufficient time to have them consecrated. Fortunately, however, he found, when he arrived in Liverpool, that Bishop Brown was at home, who kindly performed the ceremony of consecrating these articles, and this having been done, Father Lynch at once repaired on board the ship which was to conduct him to the scene of his future labors. The anchor was weighed, and the vessel was passing on her way down the river, when a small boat was seen hurriedly rowing toward them. It turned out to be a boy to whom Father Lynch had, in the early part of the day, given some money to purchase wax candles for the altar, and who was endeavoring to catch the ship before she got away. The boat rowed alongside, the candles were hastily thrown aboard, and the ship proceeded on her course.

There were only three passengers on board, Father Lynch, Father Fitzgerald, full of zeal, who had offered his services to Bishop Odin for the Texas mission, and a doctor. Father Lynch suffered a good deal from seasickness, but he made an effort and crawled on deck as the ship was passing round the coast of Ireland, to get a last sight of his loved but unfortunate country. Already, before leaving Ireland, he had, from the top of Sugar Loaf Hill in the County Wicklow, said good-bye to the green hills and misty valleys of his native land, and now, with feelings of profound emotion, he bid them again farewell, and took his last look at them from the deck of the ship. The voyage occupied several weeks, and was performed without meeting with any unusual adventure. They were becalmed for a few days in the Gulf of Mexico, but finally reached the Mississippi in safety and proceeded up the river to New Orleans. On their way up, the two missionaries visited several plantations in company with the steward when he went ashore to purchase provisions for the vessel, and here Father Lynch had his first view of slavery. What impressed itself upon him was the general comfort of the slaves' surroundings. Although he had always been opposed to the institution of slavery, yet he has often declared that, in his experience in the South, where the institution prevailed, the slaves were much better housed, clothed and fed, and were, so far as mere material comfort was concerned, much better off than the majority of small farmers and cotters in Ireland or Scotland.

They arrived in New Orleans on the 29th of June, 1847, and here an event occurred that came near cutting short the future course of the young missionary. His ship was moored outside two other vessels, which lay between it and the wharf on the further side. Being anxious to get ashore immediately after their arrival, the two young priests climbed over the decks of the two intervening vessels and reached the wooden wharf on the other side. Finding himself on boards, Father Lynch thought the wharf was a gang-way, and was about to step on to what, in his near-sightedness, he believed to be the pavement, but which was in reality the river, when he was caught by the arm by Father Fitzgerald and prevented in time. The cur-rent was very strong, and falling, as he would have done, between the hulls of the boats, he would in-evitably have been drowned. This was the first of his many providential escapes from accidental death during his missionary career in the South. The two missionaries were kindly received by Archbishop Blanc, of New Orleans, and the morning after his arrival, Father Lynch said his first mass in America. He was astonished, on first looking around, to find that the congregation was composed entirely of negroes. He thought at first that the ship must have made a mistake and landed him in some part of Africa instead of America, but he soon found that they were not savages; they were the slaves of Catholic masters, and had been brought up in the Catholic Church and taught the doctrines of the Christian religion. They assisted with great piety and devotion at the Holy Sacrifice, and, slaves though they were, yet, for the time being, and while before the altar of God, they were their masters' equals even in this world.

The two young missionaries were destined for Houston, to which place Father Lynch had been assigned, with Father Fitzgerald as assistant. They were anxious to reach there as soon as possible, but were very much disappointed to find on their arri-val at New Orleans that there was no boat plying between there and Galveston, to which place it was necessary for them to proceed in order to meet Bishop Odin. They determined, however, to make no delay, and as there were no other means of reaching that city, they took passage in a small river steamer which was employed in carrying United States troops from New Orleans to Vera Cruz—the war between that country and Mexico having not long before begun. The soldiers were a pretty rough-looking set; but, nevertheless, they treated the two priests with every respect, and their presence on board had some effect in keeping the unruly spirits among them in decent order. The boat put into Sabine City, on the Sabine River, which divides Louisiana from Texas, and here our two new comers had their first sight of a crocodile which swam leisurely and quite unconcernedly across the bow of the boat. They also saw in Sabine City one of those imaginary "cities" then so common in the newly opened States and Territories in the West and Southwest. They had already seen Sabine City on paper, and it certainly looked very fine. There were duly laid out its broad avenues, parks, sites for churches, school houses, post office, and everything else in beautiful order, but the reality consisted of a building used as a custom-house, and a few houses occupied by the officers and soldiers of the garrison stationed there. Finally they reached Galveston early in July, and were kindly and affectionately received by Bishop Odin. Galveston was the city selected by the Pope for the Episcopal See, to which Father Odin had been appointed bishop. It had a beautiful and picturesque appearance from the water, but sadly disappointed them on landing. They said mass the next morning in the cathedral, which consisted of a small wooden building some thirty feet by sixty, the walls of which, in lieu of plaster, were covered with cloth. The good bishop, as may be supposed, was delighted to receive his two young volunteers. He had preceded them to America, and was highly pleased at the promptitude they had exhibited in preparing for their journey on such short notice, and their safe arrival on the scene of their future labors. He at once accompanied them to Houston, where they arrived in the latter part of July, 1846.

CHAPTER V.

TEXAS.

THE immense tract of country lying between the State of Louisiana and the Rio Grande, a territory covering an area nearly as large as the whole of France, called Texas, was for many years an almost unknown land. Nominally belonging to Mexico, it was at too remote a distance from the centre of government, and the government itself was so feeble and uncertain that very little, if any, authority was exercised over it, and the whole country was, in a large measure, still in its primeval state of wildness and savagery. A few Mexicans, anxious to escape from the incessant political broils of their own country, had crossed the Rio Grande and settled in this new land. Some half dozen towns had grown up along the eastern bank of the great river, and some few settlements had been made further in the interior; but beyond these there was very little evidence of civilized life, or anything to indicate that the country belonged to any civilized nation.

Such was the condition of this magnificent portion of the North American continent, when several American speculators, having visited the country and made themselves familiar with its resources, and well knowing that, lying as it did contiguous to the United States, the tide of immigration which, even fifty years ago, was beginning to set in from the North and East towards the West and South, would sooner or later reach Texas, obtained large grants of land there from the Mexican government. Chief among these speculators was Stephen Austin, who made such efforts to induce immigration into this newly opened territory that soon a large number of Americans, English, and some Germans had settled there. The American immigration had become indeed so large that it alarmed the Mexican government, and a law was passed prohibiting it, but this law was totally ignored by the Americans, and the political condition of Mexico at that time prevented its enforcement. The condition of Texas being such that the want of a regularly organized government was keenly felt, and the population having increased to such an extent that the establishment of a State government was considered desirable, Stephen Austin proceeded to Mexico with a petition to the Mexican Congress for the admission of Texas, as a State, into the Mexican Confederacy. Santa Anna, who had then lately overturned the Mexican government and established himself as dictator, paid no attention whatever to the petition, and Austin seeing no prospect of obtaining the admission of Texas as a State, wrote a letter to his fellow-Texans, advising them to organize a government in spite of the Mexican authorities. This letter was intercepted by Santa Anna's government, and Austin, very soon after his return home, was arrested and carried back to the city of Mexico, where he was imprisoned a year in solitary confinement. This aroused the indignation of the Texans and their sympathisers in the United States, and when, in 1830, the Mexican General Cos entered Texas for the purpose, among other things, of enforcing the law against American immigration, he was attacked and defeated at Gonzales, on the Rio Grande, by a party of Mexicans.

Thus commenced the war for Texan independence. In November, 1835, Texan delegates assembled at San Felipe de Austin, and issued a protest against the action of the Mexican government. The war was thenceforth carried on, with varying success on either side, until April 21, 1836, when the Mexicans under Santa Anna were totally defeated by the Texans at San Jacinto, and Santa Anna himself taken prisoner. On the 2d of March previously the Texan delegates, assembled at Washington on the Brazos, had formally declared their independence, and Santa Anna was required, as a condition of his release, to acknowledge the independence of Texas and to use his power and influence with the Mexican government to have such acknowledgment ratified. This the latter refused to do, and the war was renewed, but it degenerated into a mere banditti warfare. The Texans then made overtures to the United States government to be admitted as a State of the American Union. This was at first refused, as Mexico had officially declared to the United States government that the annexation of Texas would be considered a declaration of war; but by the election of President Polk in 1844, who had strongly declared himself in favor of the annexation of Texas, a new turn was given to affairs, and one of the first acts on the assembling of Congress was the passage of a joint resolution of both houses giving their consent to such annexation. Thus was inaugurated the war between the United States and Mexico, which resulted in the annexation to the former of the territory of Texas, New Mexico, and California.

Texas, in 1846, when Father Lynch arrived there, bore an unenviable reputation for lawlessness and violence, which it has retained to a great extent even to the present day. It was then the great rendezvous of all the desperate characters, criminals, and fugitives from justice from the United States. These men were a terror to the peaceful portion of the community, and for the purpose of preserving life and property the latter were obliged to organize themselves and in self-defence take the law into their own hands, and execute summary justice on these outlaws. This course was necessitated by the lawless condition of the country, the absence of regularly organized courts, and the great danger to which life and property were exposed in places situated far from towns or populated districts where legal officers appointed to execute the law might be found. Immediately after the close of the war a great many soldiers received their bounties in Texas land grants, and consequently a great many settled there. At the time of Father Lynch's arrival, in 1846, the population was very sparsely scattered over this immense tract of country, and was principally to be found along the banks of the rivers and streams. The Catholic population of the whole State did not exceed ten thousand, including Mexicans. The Methodists and Baptists were very numerous, and a few Church of England people were to be found here and there. The majority, if not all of the English speaking Catholics, who had settled in the State at this period, were either Irish, or of Irish descent, and the first thing that struck the young missionary was the number of people bearing unmistakably Irish and Catholic names who were either Methodists or Baptists. This was easily accounted for. There were no priests in the country, and the only churches in their neighborhood being Protestant churches, in most cases, as they had no other places to go to, they attended them, and gradually either gave up their own religion, or, if they themselves did not actually become Protestants, their children were pretty sure to do so. Many were found who amidst all their surroundings had still preserved their faith and had taught it to their children, sighing for and anxiously looking forward to the time when a priest should come among them, and perhaps hoping to see one day a Catholic Church in their midst. In these cases Father Lynch would find that the mother or father had taught the children their prayers and catechism and the general doctrines of the Church, so that he never had much difficulty in preparing them for baptism. But still the numbers lost to the Church in the early settlement of the new States of the West and Southwest must have been very large, and these were mostly Irish. In most cases the Catholic emigrants from other countries, especially from Germany, were accompanied by priests of their own race, but this was seldom the case with the Irish. There were very few priests of their own nationality to be found outside the large cities and towns in the East, and this, no doubt, was one of the chief causes that led to so many settling in towns and cities, especially the large centres of population on the Atlantic coast, which, if it has been largely the means of establishing Catholicity on a sure foundation in these places, has not been without its disadvantages from a Catholic and moral point of view.   Bishop England of Charleston, South Carolina, in a letter to the directors of the Propagation of the Faith in France in 1838, declared that the loss of Catholics to the Church in America might be counted by millions, and that in his own diocese he estimated the loss to the Church, up to the year 1838, to be fifty.thousand.   As to the general loss sustained by the Church by the defection of her own members and through other causes, the estimate of the illustrious Bishop of Charleston may be somewhat exaggerated, but that such loss has been very large, there can scarcely be any doubt, and principally through the causes above stated.   Often, in travelling through the State, Father Lynch would hear of families whom, by their names, he at once assumed to be Irish Catholics.   What would be his surprise when calling upon them to find that their owners were staunch Methodists or Baptists.   Often, in passing through a town, he would see names on the signs, such as McCarthy, O'Brien, O'Doherty, and others of the same kind, and would be much surprised on calling on these gentlemen to find them Protestants.   They would usually admit that their parents had been Catholics, but that there being no churches of that religion in the country, they were gradually drawn into some other religious body.

CHAPTER VI.

MISSIONARY LIFE IN TEXAS.

THERE was, therefore, a good field for missionary labor in Texas, and Father Lynch had at length found work which he felt called upon especially to undertake, and which he believed himself fitted to perform. The labor was great, and the work laborious and dangerous. The chief duty of the Catholic Missionary in Texas in those days was to go through the country and find out where Catholics were located. His principal outfit was a horse, or where a horse could not be procured, a mule, a saddle, and a pair of saddle-bags containing his vestments and other articles necessary for the celebration of mass or the administration of the sacrament. Thus equipped, he started out to traverse the boundless prairies, penetrate the dense forests, and, in many cases, swim the broad rivers that lay in his course. It was literally and in truth looking for the lost sheep. Whenever he heard that a Catholic, or a supposed Catholic, lived in any part of the country, he went in search of him to find him as best he might. If he were overtaken by night on the prairies, and found that he could go no further, he dismounted, unsaddled his horse, turned him out in the long grass to feed, and with his saddle-bags for a pillow, and the broad canopy of heaven above him, lay down and slept soundly till morning. Once while thus sleeping on the prairie he was partially aroused by a snake crawling over his face, but so tired and fatigued was he after a ride of more than forty miles on horseback, and so overpowered with sleep, that he could not summon up sufficient energy to get up and change his position. Often he would lose his way in the forests with nothing to guide his course but the stars and nothing to disturb the stillness of the night but the occasional howling of a cayote. During the summer the heat on the prairies of Texas is intense—not a tree to cast a shadow or under which one might for a few moments find a friendly shelter from the glare of the noonday sun. Troops were often met passing to the seat of war. When he encountered a body of troops on the march he would make inquiries as to whether there were any Catholics among them. If so, he would seek them out and urge them to make their confession before facing the dangers of battle. In these cases, as no delay was permissible, he was obliged to ride along with them and hear the poor fellows' confessions on horseback; when finished they would halt for a few moments, dismount, the penitent

would kneel, and the priest would pronounce absolution. The penitent would then remount and join
his comrades while the priest would go through the
same form with another, and so on until he had
finished with all, when he would bid them a God-
speed and resume his journey.

Houston, to which place Father Lynch had been
assigned, had at one time been the capital of the
Texas Republic, was a small town at that time containing about three thousand inhabitants, and was
named after the Texan hero, General Sam Houston,
who had been so prominent in the war for independence, and whose soldierly qualities contributed
so largely to the Texan success. Father Lynch met
the General shortly after his arrival in Houston, and
was not a little surprised to learn that the celebrated
hero had Irish blood in his veins, his mother having
been a Belfast lady. Although the city had from time
to time been visited by priests, yet, until the arrival
of Fathers Lynch and Fitzgerald, there had been
no priest regularly stationed there. There was only
one small wooden church in the place and the
Catholics were very few. The two priests at once
entered upon the discharge of their duties, and
when everything had been put in order, both in
spiritual and temporal matters, Father Lynch prepared to set out and visit the surrounding country.
He first visited Spring Hill, where a few Catholic
families resided, and from there went to San Jacinto,
where General, then Captain, Sherman was in command, whose wife and family are Catholics. He
made excursions along the large rivers which run
from the northern part of the State and empty into
the Gulf of Mexico, and along the course of which
the settlements were most numerous. He preached

in hotels, court-houses, or in such other places as he could find most convenient for his purpose.   He was always very well received and courteously treated. Wherever he preached all came to hear him, and, of course, the great majority were often Protestants, principally Methodists and Baptists.   They had heard a great deal of priests, but they never had, in most places, seen one in the flesh.   Amongst those who came to hear him were Catholics who were not known among their acquaintances to be such.   These would frequently introduce themselves to him, and would bring their children to be baptized.   The excuse they gave for their course was that, as there were no priests or churches in the country, and as the people were intensely prejudiced against Catholics, they thought it most prudent to say nothing about their religion.

However, the prejudices of the people against the Catholic religion did not prevent them from extending their hospitality to one of its ministers, and Father Lynch never found the least difficulty in getting along.   In Austin, the capital of the State, he was most kindly treated.   There was no Catholic church in the city, and he was obliged to say mass on Sunday morning in the house of a Catholic gentlemen.   In the evening, however, the legislative chamber was kindly placed at his disposal, and the governor and most prominent citizens of the place attended to hear him preach.   The governor pressed Father Lynch to make his home in Austin, offering him the position of tutor to his sons, and promising to raise sufficient funds to build a Catholic church; but, of course, this he could not do, and after baptizing the children of such Catholics as resided in the place, and hearing the confessions, and administering the sacraments to such adults as were prepared, he continued his tour through the State.

The first sick call that our young missionary attended, after his arrival in Houston, was one which gave him much concern, and caused him great pain. He was sent for to visit a man who it was thought was dying. On arriving at the place the priest found that the man was unwilling to make his confession just then, saying that he did not consider himself in any danger, and that he intended, as soon as he recovered, to go to the church and perform his religious duties which he had neglected for a long time. Father Lynch thought the man was in great danger of death, and urged him by all the arguments he could command not to delay this important matter and endanger his eternal salvation; but it was all in vain. Alas! as he afterwards ascertained, there was a woman in the question, and this man was a sad example of a relapsed sinner. Once before he had been on the point of death, and Bishop Odin had traveled over one hundred miles to see him. He then expressed his sorrow for the life he had been leading, and promised to give up the woman who was the partner of his guilt, but recovering he continued his evil course. The woman was at his bedside when Father Lynch arrived, and finding that he could not accomplish anything then he retired, hoping that by morning the sick man would be disposed to yield. The good priest prayed earnestly for him, and returned early the next morning to see him, but he had just died a few moments before Father Lynch's arrival, and the lips that refused to confess were forever closed in death. Father Lynch withdrew in great anguish of mind at the sad result of this his first sick call in Texas. He felt as if Satan had come off victorious in this, his first, encounter with him in this new field of battle, for the possession of an immortal soul.

The first St. Patrick's day after his arrival in Houston he had the happiness of receiving the wife and family of a Protestant minister into the Church. The husband had retired from active work as a minister, and had settled down as a planter upon a large ranche. He himself, as he said, was convinced that as a religious organization the Catholic Church was superior to all others, and he would have joined her community, but he could not accept some of her doctrines, which seemed to him contrary to reason, especially the Catholic doctrine of transubstantiation. He was a very honest man, and sincere in his belief. He said he had prayed for an increase of faith, and that he might be led to believe all truths necessary for salvation. He had, however, no objections to his wife and family joining the Church, and as they were convinced of the truth of her doctrines he would not in any way interfere with their freedom in the matter.

Shortly after his arrival in Houston he heard of a Catholic woman who lived up the country, and who, as doctors were scarce in Texas in those days, acted as a midwife. She was evidently a Catholic who believed in the teachings of the Church, for he had been told that she had often baptized children when she thought them in danger of death, cases of which would, of course, often occur to her in the peculiar position she occupied. He therefore determined to visit her, and arriving at her house he entered, and after a few words, asked her if she had any children to be baptized. Thinking he was a Methodist minister, she replied that she had children who were not yet baptized, but that she was a Catholic, and that she was waiting until she could have them baptized by a priest. "Well," said Father Lynch, "you have a priest here." "What!" she exclaimed, starting up in amazement, "are you a priest? I did not think there was one in the country." He assured her that there were priests in Texas now, and even a bishop, and then he showed her a crucifix he was accustomed to wear suspended from his neck. When the poor woman saw this, convinced that he was indeed a priest, she laughed and cried by turns, exclaiming, "Thanks be to God! I often had my hand in a basin of water to baptize one of my children when I thought it was in danger of death; but God has preserved them all, and now I have a priest to do it." The woman had emigrated to Texas from New York some eighteen years previously, and in all that time she had never seen a priest. She called in all her children, and made them kneel down and receive the missionary's blessing. He then proceeded to examine them in the catechism, and was glad to find that they were all well instructed, as the poor woman had taken good care not to allow them to grow up in ignorance of their religion. He had no difficulty, therefore, in preparing them to receive baptism. The good mother then prepared herself and made her confession. He gladdened her heart by informing her that he would say mass there in the morning. The poor woman replied that she was afraid the place was too poor and wretched for such a purpose; but the priest assured her that it could be made to do with a little fixing up. They all proceeded to help and prepare the room. Clean linen was hung on the walls, an altar erected, and everything prepared in good order. By decorating the room with a profusion of green branches and wild flowers, it was made to look like a rustic bower, and in this manner a beautiful little chapel was improvised for the occasion. The next morning, when the poor woman saw the priest with his vestments on and prepared to celebrate mass, she was so overcome with joy that she nearly fainted. He waited for some time until she had fully recovered, and then said the mass, at which she received communion, the first in eighteen years. The eldest boy made, at the same time, his first communion, and Father Lynch left them full of joy and gladness.

Of course the majority of those visited by Father Lynch were English-speaking Catholics, but although he could not speak Spanish, he invariably sought out and visited such Mexicans as were in the country. One day, while travelling, he was overtaken by a man on horseback, and, as usual in such cases, after a few minutes' conversation, he asked the man if there were any Catholics in that neighborhood. The stranger replied that there were a few Mexican families living near by, and volunteered to bring the priest to them and introduce him, although he himself was a Methodist class-leader. He found the woman of the house at which they called able to speak a little English, but as he had been brought there by a Methodist class-leader, she thought he must be a Methodist minister. He asked her if her children had been baptized, and she replied in the negative. He then told her he was a priest and would baptize them, but she shook her head incredulously, apparently in considerable doubt. She evidently could not get over the fact that he had been brought there by a Methodist. However, to test the geuineness of his priestly character, she asked him if he could bless crosses, and she pointed to a row of crosses, each about a foot long and painted black, which were hanging against the wall. Father Lynch then showed her the crucifix he usually carried about him, at the sight of which, with an exclamation of surprise, she jumped up, and snatching down a large horn which was hanging on the wall, blew a loud blast. In a few minutes five or six men came running up, followed by several women from the neighboring houses. They were delighted to find that instead of danger being the cause of the summons, it was the arrival of a priest. The poor fellows dropped on their knees, and affectionately kissed his hands. They had left Mexico years before to get rid of the revolutions and bloodshed which was then as now the chronic condition of that unfortunate country, and had emigrated to Texas, where they had settled on land, and were engaged in cattle-raising, in which they had been very prosperous. They were good, honest, and pious people, and although there were no priests in that part of the country, they still kept up such practices of religion as they could. The crosses they were accustomed to carry with them to the fields or prairies, plant them in the ground, and say their prayers before them. The mothers set to work to wash and dress the children and to prepare them for baptism. About six or seven were baptized, and during the ceremony the men and women kept singing hymns and reciting prayers in Spanish, while one man sang the *Veni Creator Spiritus* in Latin. Father Lynch was highly edified at the sight, for he had seldom witnessed so much religious fervor as was exhibited by these poor people. After baptism he blessed the crosses, and then each of the godfathers and godmothers, producing a little bag of Mexican silver, presented him with a small donation, at the same time kissing his hands and overwhelming him with thanks for having come so far to see them. They were very anxious that he should hear their confessions, but he did not understand enough Spanish for this, so he promised to send a priest to them as soon as possible, who could speak their language, and who would hear their confessions. They then desired him to go further down the Rio Grande, as there were many other Mexican settlers there who would be glad to see him. He left them all much happier for his visit, and indeed he himself had rarely enjoyed such a day of consolations as he had in ministering to these poor, simple Mexicans and witnessing their trusting faith and ardent piety. Such a day repays the missionary for much labor and many disappointments.

CHAPTER VII.

MISSIONARY LIFE IN TEXAS—(*Continued.*)

EVEN at the period of which we are writing,
the Indians had nearly all disappeared from
Texas. The Comanches of the North and a few
other wandering tribes were all that remained, but
occasionally, in his wanderings, our missionary would
encounter them, and in all cases he would try and
visit them. The first time he heard that he was in
the neighborhood of an Indian camp, he determined
to pay it a visit. It was, he was informed, located
in a neighboring woods. He struck into the woods
alone, and without a guide, and wandered for several hours without being able to find any trace of
the camp, shouting at intervals to attract attention.

At length he heard the welcome bark of a dog, and soon after two Indians came up. They spoke a little English, and he made them understand that he wished to see their chief. They nodded their heads and made signs for him to follow them. He found the chief sitting cross-legged on the ground, the only sign of royalty about him being the peculiar way his hair was dressed, which was wound into a large knot on the top of his head and tied with a red string. He spoke Spanish and, fortunately, a little French, so the priest and he were able to understand each other pretty well. He had been taken when quite young from his tribe and brought up and educated in a Franciscan monastery in Mexico, but when he grew up to manhood, his Indian instinct was too strong for him, and he abandoned civilized life and returned to his native tribe and to savage life. He was a man of about sixty-five years of age, of fine physique and venerable appearance, and very dignified in his bearing. The tribe had just met with a very serious accident in the total destruction of their camp by fire, and they were in great distress. The priest shared his scanty wardrobe with the chief, and the latter was highly delighted and quite proud at receiving a long white night-shirt, which he accepted with a profusion of thanks. Of course he had been brought up and educated as a Catholic at the monastery, and although he had abandoned the Christian religion, he had not by any means forgotten the teachings of his youth. Father Lynch told him that, as he had been brought up a Christian, and knew the doctrines of the Church, it was his duty to teach them to his companions, and he asked to be allowed to baptize the young children of the tribe. To this request of the priest, the old chief replied that he could not do this without consulting the tribe, but if he would wait, he would at once call a council and place the matter before them. A council was accordingly called, and permission was granted to baptize the children, which was accordingly done. The next day the chief called on Father Lynch at the place where he was staying, to return his visit, and his salutation was very beautiful and impressive. First he took hold of the priest's hand and kissed it; then he pressed it to his head, and then to his heart, and desired the former to do the same with him. The salutation meant that he honored him in his mind, loved him in his heart, and would defend him with his life.

In his travels through such an extensive country as Texas, and at that time so little inhabited, he not unfrequently lost his way, and often spent hours and sometimes a whole day in trying to find a human habitation where he might be able to gain some information as to his whereabouts. Once in making his way to the Brazos River, he lost the trail in the woods, and was overtaken by night. The moon did not rise until very late, and it was intensely dark, with nothing to relieve the profound gloom but the incessant flashing of the fire-flies. At length he struck the river, but could find no ferry, and after skirting the bank for some distance, shouting to attract the attention of any one who might be on the other side, he made up his mind to stay where he was until the rising of the moon, and then search for a convenient spot to swim his horse across. He dared not think of sleeping in the woods, as the bears and wolves were incessantly prowling about. An occasional howl from the depths of the pine woods was anything but agreeable music to his ears, and he determined to keep moving and renew his endeavors to find a ferry. After an hour or more travelling along the river bank, he heard an answering whistle on the other side; then he heard the rattle of a chain as it was thrown into the bottom of a boat, and soon a skiff emerged from the darkness, rowed by a stalwart man and a young girl, and put into the shore. He found the man very obliging, and after explaining his position, the former invited him to his house to spend the night. On being informed of the character of his guest he was much pleased, and said that he himself was a Catholic, and that his wife was a good Irish Catholic. He had been born in the woods, but had been baptized some years previously by a Catholic priest who happened to be passing that way. He had never seen a Catholic priest before or since, and had never been inside a Catholic Church, but his wife had taught him his prayers and catechism, and had instructed him in the Catholic religion, and all his children had also been similarly taught; the young girl who accompanied him was his daughter. The priest was most kindly and hospitably received by the wife, and a bed was at once made up for him on the kitchen-floor. He was soon sound asleep, but was awakened in the middle of the night by the entrance of the man of the house with an old sword in his hand. He thought at first that the house was attacked by burglars, but the man told him not to be afraid, that snakes were very plentiful in that part of the country and were very troublesome. "Get up," he said, "and I will show you some fun." Two large snakes, called by the people "egg snakes," from their fondness for that article of diet, which they will sometimes swallow whole, had got into a large dry goods box in which a goose was hatching. The snakes were trying to capture the eggs, while the poor goose was making a desperate fight to protect them. The man came to her assistance and succeeded in killing one of the reptiles, while the other escaped. The dead snake was a very formidable looking specimen of the reptile tribe, and must have measured at least six feet in length.

The next morning being Sunday, the priest prepared to celebrate mass and to administer communion to the man and his wife, whose confessions he heard. It was his first communion, and for his wife the first for many years. As there was no one who could serve mass, the man requested Father Lynch to wait until the arrival of the stage, informing him that the stage-driver could serve the mass; but on being further informed that the aforesaid stage-driver was a local Methodist preacher, he concluded to say mass without his assistance. He was rather puzzled to account for the rather singular phenomenon of a Methodist preacher being able to serve mass, but on talking with the driver the matter was made quite plain. The fact was the man was a Catholic, or at least had been brought up one, but as he had a pretty fluent tongue, he thought he might as well add to his pay as a stage-driver the emoluments of a local preacher. They paid him fifteen dollars a month for his services as a preacher, and he thought he might as well make this as not. However, he said he had never preached anything against Catholics, his discourses being, as he termed them, " moral sermons."

In many parts of the country up to that time, a priest had never been seen even by the oldest settlers, and among the Protestant portion of the community who had never in their lives come in contact with any Catholics except a few of the worst and most ignorant specimens of Mexicans, the prejudice against the Catholic religion was very strong. Father Lynch tried to overcome this prejudice as best he could, principally by delivering lectures through the country on the doctrines of the Catholic Church. On one occasion he visited Washington, on the Brazos, in company with a Catholic gentleman who was known in the neighborhood by the title of Colonel. They put up at the principal hotel in the village, and Father Lynch, as usual in such cases, was cautiously feeling his way and making inquiries as to what religious denominations there were in that part of the country. He was told by the keeper of the hotel with whom he was talking that there were Methodists, Baptists, and a few Church of England. "Any Catholics?" said the priest. "Catholics?" replied the hotel-keeper, laughing; "oh no! We are pretty bad 'round here, no doubt, but we haven't come to that yet." The priest replied that he was not much surprised to hear it, but that after all he did not think the Catholics were all very bad or very ignorant; that he had seen a good many in the large cities, and they seemed to be as intelligent and industrious as any other portion of the community. "Oh, well," replied the hotel-keeper, "that's some argument in their favor, certainly." He then went to the colonel and asked him what kind of a preacher that was he had brought with him. The colonel replied that he was a Catholic priest. At hearing this he was quite taken aback, and said, "Well, if that is so, I have insulted him, and I would not do so for the world. It is the first Catholic priest I ever saw in my life, and the first that ever came into this part of the country." He was very sorry for what he had said to the priest, and desired the colonel to go and apologize for him. "Come on," said the colonel, "let us both go." The matter was explained, and Father Lynch assured him that he was not in the least offended, as without doubt he merely said what was believed about the Catholics, and as he did not know what was his religious belief, of course, no offence could have been intended, and none was taken by him at his remarks. It turned out that the hotel-keeper was himself a local preacher, and combined the two offices of preaching the word and hotel-keeping. The priest told him that if due notice were given to the people, he would deliver a lecture that evening in the dining-room of the hotel. The good man very kindly undertook to do so, and sent out his negroes to announce to the people of the village and surrounding country that a Catholic priest had arrived at Washington and would deliver a lecture in the evening in the hotel. When the time arrived the room was crowded. Father Lynch chose for the subject of his lecture, " What Catholics do not believe, and what they do believe." The lecture was very well received by the audience and listened to with great attention. The next day being Sunday, he determined to say mass. He awaited the arrival of the stage, which brought a Catholic gentleman and his wife, whom he had been expecting. They were both good Catholics, and the husband was a man of influence in that section of the country, although not known to be a Catholic. He had purchased a large tract of land in the neighborhood of Washington, and he was considered a great acquisition to the place. The people were therefore considerably surprised when they saw

Mr. —— serving mass, and more astonished still to learn that he was actually a Catholic, for they evidently thought it impossible that such an intelligent man could really belong to that church. From that time forward they began to have a different opinion of Catholics and of the Catholic Church. They thought that if Mr. —— and his wife, who were the most respectable, and certainly the most intelligent and best educated people in that part of the country, were Catholics, the Catholic Church could not be so bad after all. This good gentleman was the means afterwards of having a priest sent to Washington, and before long a very flourishing congregation grew up.

There is but little doubt that, not only very many of the descendants of Catholics who had become Protestants, but even many other Protestants might have been brought into the Church in Texas in those days, if there had been a sufficient number of priests to have gone through the country, visited the out-of-the-way localities, and lectured to the people on Catholic doctrines and practices. On one occasion, after having preached as usual in a certain village in the interior—or rather lectured—upon the subject of Catholic doctrine and beliefs, Father Lynch was waited on by the head men of the village, who wanted him to become their " preacher." They were all Methodists, but said that for many years they had been without a minister, and that after hearing him preach they thought Father Lynch would suit them, and from his explanation of his religion they would be satisfied to adopt it, as they thought it came nearest to their reading of the Bible. He expressed his sorrow at not being able to remain among them, as his mission was to go through the country in search of Catholics, but promised them to have a priest sent to that neighborhood as soon as possible.

About this time a large number of German immigrants were brought out from Germany by a society which had very little knowledge of the country. The company had bought what are known as bottom-lands, lying along the rivers, very fertile, but exceedingly unhealthy. The poor immigrants, unaccustomed to such a climate, died in large numbers, and when Father Lynch visited them, he counted forty-seven newly-made graves. They had with them a most respectable and learned priest, a German, who had been a professor in the University of Vienna, and had at one time been a candidate for the archbishopric of that city. He was, at the time Father Lynch saw him, past seventy years of age; a venerable, good and holy man, who had left everything, and had given up all the comforts of civilized life in Europe, to accompany this band of German immigrants to the wilds of Texas. He did not long survive his arrival in this country. The labors and fatigues he was obliged to undergo in the new life he was compelled to lead, so different from the quiet and regularity of the life he had been accustomed to for many years, proved too much for one so advanced in years, and he soon found a grave in his new home.

Of course, as was natural to suppose, our missionary often lost his way while travelling, but he always remarked, that invariably in these cases he stumbled, as it were, upon the very people for whom he was seeking. On one occasion, while on his journey through the State, he was caught in a fearful storm—thunder, lightning, and rain. The lightning flashed in his face, followed by bursts of thunder like the crash of artillery. Every now and again a tree would be shivered by the lightning, and he was in momentary dread of being himself struck down by the thunderbolt. Night came on, and his tired horse refused to go any further. He himself was completely worn out, not having had anything to eat since morning. He dismounted and led his horse by the bridle. He was afraid to sit down or rest in his wet clothes, and so he wandered through the woods, following the bridle-path as best he could, and eagerly looking out for some friendly light to indicate that shelter was near at hand. At length he came upon a herd of cattle lying down, a welcome sight, as he knew that a habitation could not be far away. He soon reached a house and roused the inmates. It was near morning, but the proprietor, who was a Methodist class-leader, received him very kindly, put up his horse, and taking his son out of a small trundle-bed, in which he was sleeping, gave it to the priest. It was a pleasant exchange, and he slept soundly until morning. The kind owner had a good, substantial breakfast prepared for him, and did everything in his power to make him comfortable. He found that there were a number of Catholics in the village who had immigrated to Texas from Missouri. He stayed for a couple of days, visited all the families who were Catholics, baptized their children and heard their confessions, said mass for them, and gave them holy communion.

The mishaps and adventures he sometimes met with were somewhat ludicrous, if often dangerous. He was once quietly sitting on his horse at a ferry-crossing on the Colorado River, waiting for the ferry-boat to come over, when his horse approached the edge of the stream to drink. He allowed him to wade out some little distance, when suddenly the horse and rider were beyond their depth, and were both swept down the stream. At first he thought it was all over with him, and he earnestly recommended himself to God. Fortunately, however, the animal proved to be a strong swimmer, and carried him in safety to the opposite shore, a long distance below. Of course he was completely saturated, and the saddle-bags containing his vestments and books were filled with water. He rode into the woods some distance, dismounted, and tying his horse to a tree, proceeded to dry his clothes and his vestments. But misfortunes never come alone, and to add to his disaster, while thus engaged, his horse broke loose and ran away. He had now plenty of time to dry his clothes, and also to say his office, which he accordingly did. Towards evening, gathering up his saddle-bags and his other little effects, he put them on his back and set out for the nearest village. Here he met a number of men, to whom he told his story, and begged them to lend him a horse to return to the place from whence he had that morning set out, about eighteen miles distant, but the men only laughed at him. They said they would sell him a horse, but that there were too many preachers who borrowed horses and never returned them. He was turning away in great distress, when a boy, who evidently took compassion on his sad condition, came up to him and said, " I will lend my horse, sir." "Is it your horse?" said the priest. "Yes," replied the boy, "it is mine. It is my birthday present,"—for in Texas it was customary in those days to give as a birthday present to boys the first colt that was foaled after the birth of the child. The priest was highly delighted at thus escaping from his dilemma. He thanked the boy heartily, and offered him some money, but the latter refused to take any, and would only consent to accept a little book containing pictures of events in the life of Christ, with which he seemed highly delighted, especially when Father Lynch explained to him the meaning of the engravings. Fortunately he was enabled before very long to return the boy his horse. His own horse had returned home, and the owner, fearing that an accident had happened to the priest, sent his servant in search of him, who met him as he was returning. He at once went back to the village, and found the boy and the men in about the same place he had left them. He felt quite proud and glad to be able to give the boy his horse again, and to prove to them that all "preachers" were not as bad as they imagined. The boy seemed very proud of his act of generosity, and the men looked as if they felt ashamed of their conduct in the affair.

He was travelling on another occasion, and not being able to procure a horse, he was obliged to mount an animal then comparatively little known outside of Texas, but now having a world-wide reputation, a "Texas mule," which is by common consent the embodiment of everything vicious and stubborn. He had not gone far when the mule threw him. Fortunately the lasso which the rider always carries fastened to the pommel of his saddle to provide against such contingencies was in his hand, and then commenced a struggle to capture the unruly animal and mount him again, which, after a hard fight, he succeeded in doing. Just as he had got on the ugly beast's back, a gentleman came riding up, who said that he had seen him thrown, and had watched the struggle to capture the mule again. He knew from his dress that he was a priest, and asked him his name and where he was going. Father Lynch replied that he was going to the next village, a short distance ahead, where he intended to preach the next day. "Well," said the stranger, "I must go and hear you preach. I always thought you priests were a kind of half women, but I see you can manage a Texas mule, and I must go and hear you preach." The man did come the next day to hear him, and afterwards called upon him, when they had a long conversation on religious matters, and especially upon the doctrines of the Catholic Church. This was the beginning of his conversion, and Father Lynch learned that he afterwards became a Catholic.

The prairies of Texas are as boundless as the sea, and the traveller, if he does not know the trails, must provide himself with a compass, or he will surely get lost. The first experience Father Lynch had of this, was in crossing a prairie about thirty miles wide. The day was excessively hot, when suddenly the sky darkened and he was caught in a thunder shower. He took refuge in an "island of timber," as they were called, and after the rain ceased he continued his journey. He could not find the trail on which he had been travelling, the sun was hidden by dense clouds, and he unfortunately had forgotten to provide himself with a compass. He therefore took the course he thought would lead to the point to which he was travelling, and towards evening arrived at a house. He rode up to the door and inquired as to his route. The woman to whom he addressed the question looked at him keenly for a few seconds and then said, " Were you not here this morning ?" Sure enough, when he came to look at the place more closely, he remembered that he had called at the house early in the morning to inquire about the way, and here, after all his day's wanderings, he was back at the very place from which he had started, so that this was one day lost.

It often seemed to him as if Providence had actually thrown in his way the very lost sheep for whom he was so anxiously searching. On one occasion he stopped a rather rough-looking individual, and inquired of him how far it was to the next village. The man at first answered him rather brusquely, but when he was about to go on he looked sharply at the priest and said, " Stop, I know you; you are a priest." Father Lynch admitted that he was, and at once they entered into conversation. It turned out that the man was a Catholic, and had been educated for the priesthood at Maynooth, but like many others had given up the idea of entering the ministry, and had immigrated to Texas. " I have not seen a priest for many a long year," he said. On coming to Texas he had followed the profession of a surveyor, and then became a school teacher. Whenever he found the children of Catholic parents he taught them the catechism, and gave them such other religious instruction as he could, and said that he had baptized children when in danger of dying. Father Lynch and he retired into the woods, and there the priest heard his confession, and gave him communion the next morning at the neighboring village, in which the man lived, and where he was conducting a small school.

At this period the great terror of the Texan farmers were the horse-thieves. They were a thoroughly organized body and had their regular stations all through Texas, from the Rio Grande across the State to Louisiana. It was against this body of outlaws more than even murderers that the community was most incensed, for in many cases, indeed in all cases, the horse, or the mule, was the most important member of the family. There were no railroads in those days, not even ordinary highways, and all travelling had to be done by horse or mule, besides the value of these animals in the ordinary work of the farm. Of these thieves Father Lynch had some experience. In the course of his wanderings he came to the house of an aged lady, who owned and lived on the farm on which the battle of San Jacinto was fought. She was a good Catholic, very old, but in the full possession of all her faculties. Here he thought he would remain for a few days and make excursions into the surrounding country. It was his practice to either hire a horse to carry him to the next village and have it sent back, or, as in most cases, he would borrow one from some of the Catholics among whom he was laboring. In the present case he borrowed a horse from the old lady—the only one she had—telling her that he was going to visit a settlement several miles distant. She told him to take good care of himself, and off he started, as he afterwards found out, right into the headquarters of the horse-thieves in that part of the country. It was near dark when he arrived at a house and asked for lodging for the night. The man of the house and his wife were not inclined to accommodate him, and he almost forced them to keep him for the night, as darkness was coming on and he could go no further. They gave him a scanty supper and put his horse in a very good enclosure, but in the morning it was gone —stolen, of course. There was nothing for it, however, but to shoulder his saddle and saddle-bags and trudge on to the nearest village. The day was intensely hot, and he was often obliged to sit down and rest from sheer fatigue. At last he reached a house, got some refreshments, and succeeded in borrowing a mule to carry him to the next house. After proceeding a few miles, the mule suddenly began to rear and kick, broke the girths, threw the rider, and made off for home. Here was a worse plight. He again shouldered his saddle and saddle-bags, and after a weary journey, about nightfall reached the next house. Here he spent the night, and the next morning the farmer lent him a horse to return again to the old lady. He was in great distress of mind, and hardly knew how to break the sad news to her, especially as he had no money to pay for the horse, but when he told her of the disaster that had happened him, and the loss she had sustained, she did not seem to be very much surprised. "Well," she replied, "I almost expected this. I knew you were going right into the settlements of the horse-thieves, but I didn't want to say anything about it, lest I might prevent you from doing some good among them." The old lady took her loss very philosophically. She seemed more anxious that the priest should say mass and give her communion, "for," said she, "it may be the last I will ever receive." The next morning he prepared to say mass, but unfortunately his wax-candles were exhausted, and the good old lady had no such articles in the house as either candles or lamps. What was to be done? The poor woman was very anxious to receive communion, and the priest had not the heart to refuse her. He asked her what kind of a light she usually made use of. She went out and brought in an oyster-shell containing a little grease, and a piece of wick stuck in one end of it. He considered for a few moments as to whether he might say mass with such lights, but never having remembered to have read, in the course of his study on church ceremonial, that oyster-shells *might not* be used in such circumstances, he took the responsibility of getting another oyster-shell, saying the mass, and giving the good and pious old lady the consolation of receiving communion. He had the happiness to hear afterwards that she had recovered her horse. The animal had broken loose from its captors a few weeks after, and returned to the house of its owner.

CHAPTER VIII.

LEAVES TEXAS.

IN the fall of 1847 Father Lynch returned to Houston pretty well tired out. He had travelled over the greater part of the State, had gone north as far as the Indian Territory, and had thoroughly explored the country between the Brazos, Colorado and Trinity rivers. The labors and fatigues of this life necessitated the taking of a short rest, and for this purpose he returned to Houston. His missionary work, laborious though it was, gave him much pleasure, and he had even begun to enjoy this out-door mode of life. As for sleeping out of doors at night, he became so accustomed to it that he often preferred this manner of spending the night to sleeping in the close and suffocating rooms of the hotels in the towns where he was obliged to put up, or in the houses or ranches in the country. Often, on coming in sight of a village late at night, if the weather were fine, and there was no appearance of a sudden change, he would prefer spending the night in some neighboring piece of woods, if there were any near, where he would at least get plenty of fresh air, to sleeping under a roof. He has often remarked that never since in his life has he enjoyed the luxury of such refreshing slumber as was wont to visit him in the woods and on the prairies of Texas. The drowsy god needed no coaxing—he came of his own accord.

But much as he enjoyed, and heartily as he entered into the labor in which he was engaged, it nevertheless had seriously affected his health, although he was not aware of it at the time. It was hardly to be expected that a young man brought up from his youth in a college, and being accustomed for years to the regular and methodical manner of life which obtains in Catholic seminaries, could with perfect impunity brave the dangers incident to such a life as Father Lynch was then leading, and a few days after his return to Houston he was suddenly stricken down with what was at first thought to be yellow fever, but which was most probably a species of typhoid. The doctors were not very skillful in their treatment of the disease, whatever it was, and before many days the patient was brought to the point of death. Father Fitzgerald, his assistant, with many tears anointed him and administered the last sacraments. He was kindly and tenderly nursed by the warm-hearted and generous people of the parish. By degrees he recovered, but very slowly, and in the course of a few weeks was able to go about, and had the happiness of being once more in a position to perform his spiritual duties and say mass. Father Fitzgerald was removed by Bishop Odin to another field of labor, and Father Lynch was, therefore, left alone. This, of course, meant an increase of labor on his part, and this before he was sufficiently strong to undertake even a moderate amount of the ordinary work of the parish. One day, shortly after Father Fitzgerald's departure, he was called in great haste to attend a dying man. The place was at some distance from his residence, and in his anxiety to reach the dying man in time, he ran at the top of his speed. He returned perspiring profusely, and as he had not fully recovered from the effects of his late severe illness, the consequence was a relapse, and again he was brought to death's door. He was in great anguish of mind at the prospect of dying without having the consolation of receiving the last sacraments, for there was no priest within one hundred miles of him. But, resigning himself to God, he said: "Lord, I am here to do Thy work; Thou knowest if my labors be finished. I tried to do Thy will. If Thou callest me hence, when I have but commenced my labors, Thou seest all; Thy will be done." Again he recovered from his illness sufficiently to once more move about, but the disease finally settled into chills and fever, which kept him in a very weak and debilitated condition, and rendered him unfit to perform any of his ecclesiastical functions. Bishop Odin came to see him, and finding him in such a condition of health that he had grave fears lest his malady might end fatally, took him back with him to Galveston, hoping that a change of air and scene might prove beneficial to him. He lingered there a couple of months, but no change for the better taking place, the good and generous Archbishop Blanc, of New Orleans, invited the invalid missionary to spend a few months with him in that city, where he proposed to place him under proper medical treatment and give him the benefit of the best nursing. Father Lynch went accordingly to New Orleans, and was placed under the care of those pious and charitable religious, the Ursuline Nuns, and lived with their chaplain, Monsignor Perché, who afterwards became the successor of Archbishop Blanc.

Here he remained for several months, but still subject every alternate day to a low, distressing fever, which kept him in a more or less weakened condition. From time to time he attended the Military Hospital, on the banks of the Mississippi, where a great number of wounded soldiers from the war in Mexico were being cared for. Troops were continually passing through the city on their way to the front, and Father Lynch, whenever he was able to go about, always made it a point to seek out any Catholic soldiers there might be among them, and hear their confessions. A surprisingly large number of the rank and file of the American army of that day were Irish, and, of course, the great majority of these were Catholics. Many a poor fellow's confession did our zealous missionary hear, sitting on the steps of some of the houses lining the streets through which they were marching, and while a short halt was being made to give the men a little rest. The scenes in the hospital were most distressing and heartrending, and the young priest for the first time in his life realized the horrors of war in all their intensity. He anointed many, baptized more, and did all he could to soothe the last moments of many a poor soldier who was breathing his last on the banks of the Mississippi, far from home and friends, and with no friendly hands but those of that angel of mercy, the

Sister of Charity, to cool his burning brow or moisten his parched lips.

On such days as he was free from the enervating fever which still clung to him, he attended the hospital, as has been said, and he also heard confessions in the church. The many wonderful conversions which a young missionary witnesses, after a short experience in missionary labor—conversions in which the hand of God seems unmistakably to show itself—at first astonishes him, but after a greater knowledge of the ways of Providence as exhibited in His dealings with man, such conversions seem in no way surprising, but appear as special manifestations of God's love and tender mercy towards those who manifest any inclination to reconcile themselves to Him.

Any missionary of large experience could tell of numberless instances of remarkable conversions, and the extraordinary manner in which they are brought about seem so miraculous to the ordinary intelligence, that even Catholics are often inclined to smile incredulously at their recital. But in the mind of the missionary there is no doubt whatever as to the character of such conversions. He knows that they are much more frequent than is generally suspected. He believes them to be the result of special emanations from the abyss of God's mercy, and so far as they are sudden and unaccountable ; so far as they transcend our ordinary experience and cannot be traced to the usual operations of the human mind, and so far as the revolution they accomplish in the human soul is wonderful and lasting, so far may they be said to be miraculous. He is quite convinced that if the skeptic or the scoffer could only see what he has seen, could know what he knows of

God's wonderful dealings with fallen human nature, even he, skeptic though he be, would have to admit that such conversions are unaccountable on the ordinary principles of human action ; that they must be supernatural; that they are striking examples of a special providence, and that the circumstances accompanying and surrounding them have not been unduly exaggerated through the magnifying lens of a religious enthusiast's excited imagination.

Father Lynch had many experiences of wonderful conversions, whose recital would fill a good-sized volume. One instance which occurred at this period of his life, during his stay in New Orleans, will serve as an illustration of what has been said upon this subject. One day, while hearing confessions as usual in the church, he noticed a man come in who seemed to be a stranger to the place, and evidently not a Catholic. He gazed around the church for some time, and then approached the confessional, in which the priest was sitting, as if to listen. Father Lynch came out of the confessional and ordered him away, but the man did not leave the church, and when the priest returned to his residence after having finished his duties, the man followed him and introduced himself, saying that he wished to become a Catholic and to receive instruction in the Catholic religion. This instruction, of course, Father Lynch willingly undertook to give him. The man was a well-to-do mason, and evidently sincere in his desire, but the priest soon found out that he was addicted to the bottle. One evening when he came for his instruction, Father Lynch said to him kindly, but firmly, " My good man, I am sorry I cannot receive you into the Church. Unfortunately we have too many of your kind already among us, and we do not want any more. If you honestly desire to become a Catholic and be baptized, you must first prove your sincerity by becoming a sober man." The man seemed very much grieved; he went away, and Father Lynch did not see him for several days. One day, about a week after dismissing him, he was sent for hurriedly, the messenger stating that the mason was seriously hurt. He hastened to his assistance, and found that he had been crushed under a falling scaffold and was dying. The priest whispered words of hope and consolation into the dying man's ear, and asked him if he desired baptism. He pressed the good priest's hand in sign of acquiescence, and Father Lynch baptized him. He died a few minutes afterwards. That very morning, as the priest afterwards learned from his wife, for the first time in years he refrained from taking his morning dram. He was accustomed to bring his bottle with him to his work. This morning, however, he told his wife that he intended to stop drinking, be a better a man, and be baptized by the priest, and as a pledge of his sincerity, he went out and broke the bottle. It was his last good resolution on earth. God accepted the sacrifice and took him to Himself without exacting its complete fulfilment.

Father Lynch remained in New Orleans until the approach of summer, but failed to gain his former strength, and was almost continually subjected to the chills and fever, a disease which is as depressing to the mind as it is debilitating to the body. He was failing rapidly, and the good Bishop Odin strongly advised him to go North, hoping that a complete change of climate would effect a cure. He accordingly went to Missouri in March, 1848, and paid a visit to one of the institutions of his Order, St. Mary's of the Barrens. Here he intended to remain only for a short time, but it was destined to be his home for many years, as he was appointed its president in September of the same year.

CHAPTER IX.

PRESIDENT OF ST. MARY'S OF THE BARRENS.

Appointed President of St. Mary's of the Barrens, Missouri—Distinguished Graduates of St. Mary's—A New Régime Established—The Discipline of the College Conducted on the Monastic Plan—Abolishes the Office of Prefect—Means taken to Preserve the Morality of the Students—Trusting to the Pupils' Honor—Sent as a Deputy to the General Assembly in Paris in 1849—Visits the Pope—Visits Ireland on his Return—A Pious Irish Mother—His Missionary Labors while President of St. Mary's—Is Struck Down with Paralysis—Is sent as a Delegate to the General Assembly at Paris, 1854—Receives Permission from the Superior General to found a Seminary in the Diocese of Buffalo—Closing of St. Mary's of the Barrens.

IN January, 1848, Father Lynch was appointed to the presidency of St. Mary's of the Barrens, a college of the Lazarists Order, which had been established for many years in Perry county, Missouri, and many of whose students and professors became bishops of the Church, among others Bishop Rosette, the first Bishop of St. Louis; Bishop Deneker, of New Orleans; Bishop Timon, the first Bishop of Buffalo; Bishop Odin, first Vicar Apostolic of Texas, and afterwards Archbishop of New Orleans; Bishop Dominick, of Pittsburg; Bishop Ryan, the present Bishop of Buffalo; and Archbishop Lynch, the subject of this memoir, all of whom were members of the Lazarists Order. Besides these, among many of those who studied there for some time were Bishop Fitzgerald, of Little Rock, Arkansas; Bishop Mora, of Los Angelos; and Bishop Cosgrove, of Davenport, Iowa.

When Father Lynch assumed the presidency of the college, he at once established a new *régime*. He tried, as far as circumstances would permit, to model the discipline of the house on the plan of the old Benedictine monasteries of the middle ages. He held a meeting of the students soon after his arrival, and proposed that the office of prefect should be abolished, and that there should be no eye-servers in the house. Next, to protect the moral integrity of the students, and to prevent the lewd and vicious, if any there should be among them, from corrupting the others, the boys promised to report any pupil among them who should be guilty of immorality, either by word or action, when the culprit was at once to be expelled. These rules were most religiously observed, and as a consequence the morals of the college never suffered, and the instances in which the students were obliged to denounce their companions were extremely rare. The office of prefect being abolished in the study-hall, Father Lynch having determined to trust to the boys' sense of honor, and believing that too much watching tends to make boys cunning, and impair their manliness and sense of honor, it was determined to place a statue of the Blessed Virgin in the hall to remind them of the honorable compact they had entered into. It was an appeal to the religious sentiment of the students, which proved very efficacious in keeping them in order and constraining them to study.

In 1849 Father Lynch was elected as a deputy by the Lazarists Fathers in America to the General Assembly of the Order held in Paris in that year. He hardly thought, when leaving Ireland in 1846, that he should so soon recross the Atlantic. After the adjourning of the assembly, he visited Rome, and had an interview with the great and good Pope Pius IX. His Holiness was very much interested in his account of the situation of affairs in Texas, and especially charmed with his description of St. Mary's College, its mode of government, and the new rules which had been adopted. "Is it possible," said the Holy Father, "that you could enforce such rules in the United States, where they are so fond of liberty?" Father Lynch replied that Americans, as a class, were truthful and very honorable; and that there was no better way of governing them than by appealing to their sense of honor; and that those of Irish descent were extremely pious and conscientious. The Holy Father then wrote with his own hand a few sentences granting an indulgence to the students of St. Mary's every time they should study under such a prefect as the Blessed Virgin.

His visit to Rome had shortened the time at his disposal, in order to arrive home in time for the opening of the college in September, and he had reluctantly come to the conclusion that he should be obliged to return to America without visiting Ireland or seeing his mother. On leaving Ireland and bidding her good-bye, she had asked him when she might expect to see him again. In order to ease her mind, he had replied perhaps in about five years. This was said at random, for in reality he did not know if ever he should see her again, or at least did not expect to for many years to come. He wrote to her from Paris, stating that he could not go to Ireland, as he wished to be in Missouri for the opening of his college on the first of September. However, on mentioning the case to the Superior General at Paris, the latter strongly advised him to go and visit his mother. After the first salutations were over, she begged her son to come into the garden, as she wished to say something to him. When they were alone she said: "Now, my son, that you have come, I rejoice at it. I always ask the assistance of the Blessed Virgin in anything I ask from God, and I always obtain it. I did not ask for you to come and see me; I was afraid to ask lest my prayer should be granted, and thus be the means of taking you from your duties to God and your people." Such was the simple faith of this good, pious Irish mother.

Father Lynch was President of St. Mary's for seven years, varying his duties as president with giving occasional missions in the surrounding country. He built an addition to the college for the accommodation of the professors, and another addition to serve the purpose of a new novitiate. During his presidency over fifty novices were entered. He held regular conferences and impressed upon the students the necessity of constant prayer and frequent communions. But, above all, he did not neglect the physical wants of the students. They had plenty of exercise and recreation. One day in every week the boys spent near a small stream, on which the seminary mills were built. Here they fished, swam, boated, roamed in the adjoining woods, and cooked their meals, returning to the college in the evening much refreshed and invigorated by their day's enjoyment. Unfortunately there was one great drawback to the success of the college, and that was the annual visitation in the spring of that bane of the Mississippi valley, the chills and fever, caused by the spring overflow of the river. The college did not escape the effects of these overflows, although it was situated some twelve miles back from the river, and the miasmas arising from the deposits left by these inundations proved so disastrous to the health of the students that it was found necessary at last to close the college, as the location was altogether too unhealthy for an educational institution.

Although Father Lynch performed the duties of President of the College, he did not give up his missionary work, but, as has been said, continued to give missions throughout the surrounding country. Often he would ride miles on horseback in order to be at the seminary on Sunday, and would frequently say mass at eleven in the morning, after having passed the previous night on horseback or on the deck of a river steamer. He had not then, nor in fact never has, even to the present day, recovered from the effects of his severe illness in Texas; and while at St. Mary's imprudent exposure and over-fatigue resulted in paralysis of one side, his recovery from which he firmly believes he owes to the prayers of the priests and students of the college.

Being again elected to the General Assembly of his Order in 1854, Father Lynch obtained permission from his Superior General to accept an invitation from Bishop Timon, of Buffalo, to found a seminary in his diocese. His idea was to locate it, if possible, at or near Niagara Falls. This idea was not a new one on the part of Father Lynch. He had for many years been considering such a project. Even as a boy, when reading of this monarch of the cataracts, or when listening to the descriptions given by those who had visited it, his imagination was fired with the thought of what a magnificent spot this would be for the erection of a Catholic Church. The dim outline of a project for founding an institution of his Order had haunted him for years, and how such an idea finally developed into the reality, will be told in the following chapter.

CHAPTER X.

FOUNDING THE COLLEGE OF THE ANGELS.

The College of Our Lady of the Angels—The Site—History of Its Foundation Related by the Archbishop—Buying the Site without any Money—Trusting to Providence—Ten Thousand Dollars to be Paid in a Year, and not One Dollar in the Exchequer—A Providential Donation—The Purchase Completed—The College finally Established in an Old Tavern—Turning a Bowling-alley into a Chapel—The Personnel of the House—The First Examination—Opposition to the Seminary—Days of Trial—Progress of Studies—The Church in the New World—Occupations of the Alumni—The College a Success.

A COUPLE of miles below the great Suspension Bridge, on the American bank of the Niagara River, stands the College of the Angels, a large stone structure, overlooking the whirlpool and commanding a fine view of the surrounding country. From its tower may be seen the Suspension Bridge and the Falls above, while below the winding river stretches away to the right until it empties into Lake Ontario, whose blue waters bound the distant horizon, serving as the background for what the Duke of Argyle declares to be the finest scene on the American continent. It is certainly a most charming and picturesque spot, nor could there on this broad continent be found a more suitable site for a college. It is only about fifteen minutes' drive from the Suspension Bridge, where railway communication may be had with any part of the United States or Canada. The " Seminary of Our Lady of the Angels " stands as a monumental evidence of the zeal and undaunted energy and perseverance of the present Archbishop of Toronto.   Its erection was commenced, and the purchase of the land was made without one cent in the pockets of the promoters of the scheme.   The story is simply and graphically told by its remarkable founder in an address delivered on the twenty-fifth anniversary of the opening of the college, as follows:

A DISCOURSE, NOVEMBER 20, 1881.

"*A Domino factum est istud et est mirabile in oculis nostris.*"—Psl. 117.

Most reverend bishops, venerable clergy, and respected fellow-Catholics, the text which I have chosen, not of a sermon nor of a lecture, but of a simple narrative, you will find most appropriate when applied to the occasion which calls us together.   God has done a work which could not be effected by the weak power of man.   He makes use of simple instruments that His own power may be the better perceived in the grandeur of the work.   Look round you here and behold the magnificent prospect.   The mighty Niagara River thundering as it winds its course through the huge gorge below, with its mountain banks draped, not with tiny grass, but with enormous trees; Lake Ontario spreading out its placid bosom in the distance—a lovely landscape of hill and dale and blooming country at your feet.   Then when you behold this magnificent seminary, crowning the highest eminence of Mount Eagleridge, with the cross on its dome appealing to heaven, you must cry out in the depths of your soul: "*Domine, Domine noster quam admirabile est nomen tuum in universa terra.   A Domino factum est istud et est mirabile in oculis nostris.*"

To trace the history of the seminary we must go back to seek its beginnings of life in a little embryo, as it were, from which the idea was sprung and was brought into a sturdy reality by the gentle and strong hand of God.   A picture of Niagara Falls was presented to a little boy in Ireland.   He was enamored and enchanted with it.   He gazed on it again and again with astonishment and delight, and raising his heart to God, he anxiously inquired were there Catholics living round that place where they could so well adore God, the Creator of heaven and earth, and of all things? This image, this thought, and this inquiry pursued him through life, till at length he beheld multitudes of Catholics around the Falls with their temples of true worship, and with a college and seminary to train priests in a heavenly vocation; to offer up the most holy sacrifice of the new law, to give honor and praise to God for ever and for ever. This is the work of God; the conception came from Him, and the means and the perfection of the work. This boy became a priest of the Congregation of the Missions and yearned to cross the ocean to follow his countrymen, lest, in seeking a home for their children from the oppression of the stranger, they might lose treasures above all others, their great faith, and the sacraments that give eternal life.

The young missionary was destined for Texas, given in charge of the Congregation of the Missions under the presidency of Monsignor Odin, Vicar Apostolic, afterwards Archbishop of New Orleans. He landed there in 1846. Texas was far away from Niagara Falls, yet the strong power of God will work out His designs, with poor and simple instruments, *suaviter et fortiter*. In the course of time, Monsignor Timon became Bishop of Buffalo, and our young missionary happening to meet this venerable prelate, remarked to him that he had the privilege of having Niagara Falls in his diocese. Were there Catholics around it, and had they a church? "There are a few Catholics," was the reply, "but there is no church." "Come to us and we shall have a church, and a seminary also." A heavy sigh was the only response. The history of the various ways and little steps that blindly led the young missionary, after a lapse of years, to Niagara Falls would not be uninteresting, yet the narrative would be too long for the present occasion. He became afterwards Superior of the Seminary of St. Mary of the Barrens, Missouri; was sent in 1855 as delegate to a General Assembly of the Order at Paris, and there procured from

the Superior General of the Congregation, Very Rev.
Fr. Etienne, permission to found a house of the Order in
the Diocese of Buffalo. On his return to America, he
was invited to give a retreat to the clergy of Buffalo, and
during that time agreed, with the permission of the then
visitor, to accept a farm and a small house on the lake
shore some miles from Buffalo, there to commence a
seminary. Niagara Falls could not be thought of. Land
there was very dear, and little to be sold, and even if there
were, sufficient money could not be raised to purchase it;
yet the young priest would turn from time to time towards
Niagara Falls and say, " Thy will, O God, be done." An
addition was at once built to a small farm-house on the
lake shore to fit it for the commencement of a seminary.
In the meantime the missionary was giving missions
single-handed, preaching three times a day, and hearing
confessions almost continually, even far into the night.
He was prostrated by sickness, superinduced by fatigue
and cold, and his old malady, the chills and fever, returned. He went to the bleak farm-house on the shore
to recuperate, but Bishop Timon soon came on to see him
and ordered him to the Sisters' Hospital, and henceforth
the lake shore project was abandoned. It had been undertaken through pure obedience and under the pinch of
poverty; but was always considered as not being the place
while there was a hope of procuring land at Niagara
Falls for a seminary. At last a new idea came up. There
was a good building then vacant in the environs of Buffalo,
where the zealous Father Early had a home for orphan
boys. It was proposed to open the seminary in this pro-
visionally for the winter, and to wait on the holy providence of God for a better place. Accordingly, on the
21st November, 1856, the feast of the Presentation
of the Blessed Virgin Mary,—an appropriate festival
for young ecclesiastics, and on which our missionary
made his vows in the Order,—a half-dozen of students were
collected together. These few boys could not occupy the
time of two priests, so the good Father Monahan was
teacher, director, procurator, and factotum of the embryo
college and seminary; whilst Father Lynch, the present

Archbishop of Toronto—we name him now—occupied himself in giving missions and collecting funds for the future establishment. During the Christmas vacation the idea of seeking a place at Niagara Falls was ripe for expression, and a visit was made to the place by the two priests. An obliging cabman told them that he knew of no land to be disposed of around the Falls, but thought that land could be procured far down the river towards Lewiston. Thither they directed their course, and found the Vedder Farm for sale on the banks of the Niagara River. The view from it was grand and sublime. There was a magnificent grove of trees then on the spot, since ruthlessly cut down. Returning, they called on Mr. Vedder near Suspension Bridge, and under his veranda—whilst the snow was falling thick and fast— a bargain was concluded for a farm of a hundred acres at seventy-five dollars an acre, payable cash down in one year. The purchasers were now indeed children of Providence. They had no money to speak of, and seven thousand five hundred dollars were to be paid in one year. This indeed was the folly of the cross, yet there was joy and gladness all around. A place was temporarily secured near Niagara Falls, where God would be worshiped in spirit and in truth; where the incense of sacrifice and prayer would ascend from the depths of pious hearts to a good and merciful God. The year was passing rapidly, but money came in very slowly. To make matters more gloomy, Vedder was reported to have regretted his sale. Yet Father Lynch continued to give missions and to visit the seminary occasionally. In the course of this year it was found that the trustees of the Devoux College had over two hundred acres of land for sale adjoining the late purchase, and by the aid of Mr. Thomas—a very respectable merchant of Buffalo—this too was purchased, and thus the debt was more than trebled. There was need now of confidence in God and prayer. On this new farm there was a brick house used as a hotel. To this the seminary was moved on the first of May, the month of Mary; for every move and undertaking was commenced on one of the festivals of our good and

Immaculate Mother. The seminary was called after her, under the title of "Our Lady of Angels," that thus the inmates might be, as it were, her angels in purity and fervor. The bar-room of the hotel did very well for a sacristy, and a ten-pin alley with some improvements and extra blessings was fitted up for a chapel. Thus did our Lord take up his abode in another shelter attached to an inn. But the money must be found within a year to secure the purchase of the Vedder farm. The terms of the other farm purchased were easy. Now a stronger effort must be made, more earnest prayers must be offered up to God to secure and perfect His own work, for it never came into their heads for one moment that they were tempting Him by what the world would call their mad purchases, as they were convinced that God had chosen this spot, the most famous on this continent, that His name might be glorified, and the gospel truth go forth from a place which exhibits such grandeurs in the temporal order. Masses and prayers for the souls in purgatory were the usual devotions of the day, and earnestly was this duty performed both by priests and students. Beads and visits to the Blessed Sacrament were added, and became, as it were, the lightning-rods that attracted the mercy of heaven. Souls released from purgatory are powerful intercessors before the throne of God.

Father Lynch, strong in his confidence in God, continued to give missions and retreats in the convents, and to collect funds for the seminary. The cathedral of Buffalo subscribed a large sum, as did other places. All the subscriptions were not, however, paid in full. There were many kind and good friends, and liberal ones too. Bishop Timon gave the commencement of a good library, and Father Gleeson often gladdened the heart of the poor missionary, especially at one time on the cars; he first emptied his purse, and then his pockets, and only kept what brought him to Waterloo. Mr. Maurice Vaughan was very generous and kind. The ladies of the Sacred Heart Convent, of Rochester, made large presents to the seminary. We must omit many other names, but not that of Father Early. We must hurry on to mention one of the great marks of our Blessed Lord's holy Providence. Whilst giving a mission to the young men at the cathedral of Buffalo, Father Lynch was struck down with what appeared to be erysipelas of the head. Many thought it was all over with him, that he had run his course; life and death were in the balance for a few days; the doctors and sisters had little hopes; he had been already on the point of death three times; he was anointed once; at death's door another time, and not a priest within a hundred miles of him, and still recovered. When the malady was at its height on this occasion, Rev. Father McGinness, formerly of Brooklyn, came to see him, but the patient could not speak. The next day the priest returned, and Father Lynch was able to say a few words.

The priest told him a very pleasant story—that he was saying masses and was praying to God for about three months to know His will as to what good work he should apply ten thousand dollars; that he was inspired to come to consult the saintly Bishop Timon for advice, and that the bishop had sent him to Father Lynch. This good news hastened the cure of the sick man. What thanksgiving and gratitude to God pervaded all hearts! But then another difficulty lay in the way—the ten thousand dollars was locked up in a second mortgage on a Brooklyn church, and very serious reasons were adduced for leaving it there. In fact, the case was very embarrassing. The good, zealous, generous-hearted, the Columbkill or church-builder of America, Bishop Loughlin, chased away all difficulties, and the money, after much trouble, was obtained; hence the first Bishop of Brooklyn can be justly looked upon as joint founder of this establishment with Bishop Timon, and the present Archbishop of Toronto. There is a little episode that may be added here. The ten thousand dollar check was to be forwarded to the Suspension Bridge. It went astray, however, and every post-office in the country was telegraphed to for this letter. This gave rise to a wide-spread report that Father Lynch was receiving every day checks of ten thousand dollars, and that in fact he was going to found a second Rome on the banks of Niagara. The check had gone astray to Natchez, but it was found. Is not the finger of God here? St. Teresa used to say that a sixpence and Teresa would not go far; but sixpence, Teresa, and God Almighty could accomplish all things.

Those whom the providence of God brought together were good, generous, and pious youths, but were not all perfect. Imperfection belongs to all the children of Adam. It is an awful responsibility to undertake to educate large numbers of other people's children, generally at an age when passions are the strongest, and hearts and consciences yet to be formed. There was good will amongst them. Piety and an earnest love of the superiors and of the place, are still the traditions of this seminary. The idea was strongly impressed upon them that the house and grounds belonged to God; that they were His children, and should take care of their Father's property; that they were collected together to prepare themselves to be good citizens of the world, to save their souls at any rate—and that some were destined to become good priests to co-operate with God in the salvation of souls; that no mean eye-servers, nor hypocrites, nor immoral talkers should be tolerated amongst them, and a compact was entered into amongst the boys themselves to take means to banish any boy who was immodest in word or in deed; and that removals should be made when necessary, generally at the Christmas, summer, or Easter vacation, in order to save the feelings both of boys and parents. The students, at recreation time and on play days, took delight in working this farm, and doing many little things which saved money. The rules were few, but well kept. Silence in the dormitory and study-hall, or on entering any house in the neighborhood, was the most rigid. To banish the idea of acting only from fear of the prefect, it was agreed amongst the students that a statue of the Blessed Virgin was quite a sufficient prefect for the study-hall. Accordingly a small altar was there erected, and a statue of our Blessed Lady placed on it, and thus perfect silence and close study reigned under the eyes of the Immaculate Queen of Heaven, amongst her good and devoted children. Our

Holy Father, Pope Pius IX., of holy memory, hearing from Bishop Timon that the Niagara students, imitating those of St. Mary of the Barrens, had no prefect in the study-hall except the Blessed Virgin, the Pope, with his own hand, wrote three lines under the Brief, by which he accorded one hundred days' indulgence to the students every time they studied before this prefect.

Our first examination was held a few months after the opening at Niagara. It was not a very brilliant affair, but there was one thing very encouraging about it. A bishop and twenty-six priests honored and encouraged the infant seminary by their presence, and, most wonderful to relate, the twenty-six priests outnumbered the students by two, so that the clergy from the very beginning were the great patrons of this institution. Our very poverty was the source of future wealth. Being obliged to go round a good deal, not idly, we made the seminary known, and friends were procured. The very idea of Niagara Falls being the centre of a college or seminary of the true faith acted as a charm. The cross on the seminary building was a wonder indeed, and an attraction. An old gentleman, a farmer of the neighborhood of Youngstown, drove up one day to the house and asked what was the meaning of the cross, adding that he had passed there for forty years and had seen no such sign before. He was a stray waif from Ireland. In his early youth he had been brought to this country, and hired with a farmer, whose daughter he married. The cross brought back to his mind misty recollections of the old faith. Now a word about the immediate neighbors of the seminary. At first they were in perfect dismay when they found that a Catholic college was to be established in their midst. What, said they, if Protestant students be so bad and such a torment to their neighbors, how much more dangerous must Catholic boys be. Thus they acted, burnished up their weapons, and looked around the fences of their peach orchards, and gave warning to their children and servants. Months rolled on, and no outrage on their gardens or households; then disappointment was turned into respect, and generosity too, and they displayed them by giving the boys a ride in their wagons, and an odd basket of peaches, and it was the pride and delight of some to come to the exhibitions. It was a delight on festival days to cross over to the island of Niagara Falls and there to sing the *Magnificat* and other canticles in praise of God and His Blessed Mother. The scene was grand, and the chant soul-stirring. Before us was the mighty cataract, with clouds of incense arising at nature's high altar. The booming of the falling torrents was a solemn bass to the vocal praise of a few Catholic boys, with pure hearts and noble intentions, and resolves to serve that God, who speaks in the voice of many waters. On Ascension Thursday, all approached Holy Communion. Dinner, followed by Vespers at the Falls, was promised, but, alas, the rain came down in torrents. After breakfast, Father Lynch playfully told the boys how the Sisters of Charity always obtained from God a fine day for their Corpus Christi procession in Paris. To his surprise he heard soon after breakfast the *Magnificat* chanted in the chapel, and towards the end of it thinking he ought not discourage the simple faith of those good children, he went to the chapel and sung the prayer to the end. No wonder that a fine day rewarded their piety and child-like faith. One boy, however, a little less confiding than the others, was bringing his umbrella with him. When his companions saw this, they so laughed at him that he ran back and deposited his umbrella in the hall. The day turned out delightful. My grave and respectable audience will pardon the mention of those simple things. But has not God chosen the simple and the unwise to confound the learned and the prudent? Then there were our sacred grounds—nothing to be heard there but the rosary or pious conversations and hymns. The steep and high banks near the raging rapids were too dangerous to play near, hence there was good reason to consecrate the place to God and to prayer.

The wild project of a penniless enthusiast of erecting a seminary at Niagara Falls was not at all relished by some of the prudent and the wise of the Order. They feared a failure and hesitated to approve of the undertaking. But the smile of the new visitor, Very Rev.

Father Ryan, threw a sunshine over the cradle of the infant seminary. More hope and courage after that kind visit lit up the hearts of the humble toilers. Father Lynch, against his own judgment and will, was called off to other work in Canada, but this work of love was always very dear to him. The mother loves her child the more in proportion to her sufferings for him. To have the Church of Christ well represented at Niagara Falls, was dear to him yet, and one of his first acts on going to Toronto was to purchase two hundred acres of land on the Canada side, and there to-day is erected a magnificent convent of the Ladies of Loretto, called of the Blessed Sacrament, where he hopes the community will soon be numerous enough to have perpetual adoration of the Blessed Sacrament. God must have continual worship here. There is also a monastery of our Blessed Lady of Mount Carmel being erected on the edge of the Falls, where the weary pilgrim in search of the sublime may find, in the solitude of the monastery, a rest and retreat for the wants of his soul in a higher spiritual life.

Days of trial were in the order of Providence for the seminary. Trials purify internally and cause the externals to flourish. The first superiors of the seminary feared very much that bad boys should gain admission into the seminary. The example of the defeat of the Hebrew army on account of the sin of one of its soldiers often passed through the minds of the superiors of this seminary; but with all reasonable precaution, not, perhaps, enough, some will be admitted who should not. The fiery ordeal through which the seminary passed* proved in the end a blessing from God, though at the time it might appear as a chastisement. It arose more beautiful and grand from its purification, and, like the days of Job, the last were more glorious than the first. The Holy Father honored the resurrection of the seminary by his blessing and by a noble contribution, and a vast number of friends did honor to themselves and religion by following the noble example of the Holy Father. This fire made the

* His Grace here refers to the burning of the seminary which occurred some fourteen years after its foundation.

seminary better known, and a greater number of students than before were attached to it.   The self-devotedness of the superiors and students during and after the fire was most heroic.   One life—a precious and holy boy—whose tomb in the cemetery is a constant reminder of sacrifice and victory, was lost to earth, but gained to heaven.   The students, after the fire, had to leave the place of their love, but they were kindly and hospitably entertained by noble hearts in the neighborhood, and by Bishop Timon, the Sisters of Charity, of Buffalo, and other friends.   At last, however, the word of obedience came, and all went to their homes or to other seminaries, resolved to return as soon as their own loved one should be rebuilt.   The superiors, too, had their large share of trial, over and above the burning.   Sickness both of body and heart attacked them, but here again God was the consoler.   The heart of parents, brothers and students was the mainstay of the seminary.   At the very beginning, in a small tavern, it could no longer maintain the number of students who insisted on entering.   They put up with any scant accommodations.   There was a very large barn near the house, and this with their own hands, during the recreation hours, aided by a carpenter, they fitted up, not elegantly, but comfortably, as a residence.   It was as good as the first buildings of Clairvaux or Cluny, which sheltered the holy monks that flocked to those places in St. Bernard's time. The refitted-up barn was facetiously called by the boys the University, and it well deserved the name.   I recollect in one corner of it was the oven, where good bread was baked by the brothers.   I need not enumerate all the uses it was put to.   The noble spirit of generosity between the members of the community and among the pupils themselves, and this love of the place, I am happy to hear, reigns still; and long may all this continue, and may it fulfil the primary intentions of its founders.

Of the students who entered the seminary for the three and four years, thirty-five became priests.   The total number during twenty-five years is estimated at about three hundred, of whom two hundred and fifty were ordained in the seminary; the others, after studying their classics or philosophy, went to other seminaries and were ordained.   Was the selection to the priesthood so perfect that none of them disedified the Church or caused pain and confusion to their bishops and to their former superiors? We cannot suppose this; but we are assured, all things taken into account, the students of our Lady of Angels have as good a record as those of any other seminary in this country or of Europe.   Let me here record again what was insinuated before, that it was the primary intentions of the first founders of this institution, in the first place to have a home or seminary where the primitive spirit of the Gospel, which portrayed the lives of the early Christians, would be exhibited in the lives and morals of the inmates here, and in the second place, that sacred science and its handmaids, the secular sciences, should be brought to their perfection as far as human efforts could bring them; and here should dwell a happy family of God's chosen children, frank, open, truthful, honorable, devout, pious, and religious; no meanness, no eye-serving as slaves, but enjoying the freedom as becomes the children of Christ and His Gospel, partaking of all of the grand privileges of members of the Church, their souls frequently fed and nourished on the bread of eternal life; one heart and one soul, all for God and His Church, for our Blessed Mother and the Saints.   And as true science leads to God in searching out the wonderful workings of His Providence in the laws that govern this terrestrial and celestial world that we see, and which surrounds us, these must be studied with awe and respect.   The more the mind penetrates into the ways and workings of God in this world, the more the mind and heart should be lifted up to the great Creator and preserver of all things.   A true philosopher must be a real adorer and servant of God. The perverted philosopher assumes his own hallucinations as first principles and proofs, is led from one absurdity to another, and is confounded in his own confusion; but what is equally strange, is followed, lauded, and praised by those who should have better sense.   The grand and sublime science of God, and His laws in the moral order, called Divinity or Theology, was taught by the angel of the schools, St. Thomas, and that it should be studied deeply, leisurely, and properly was the earnest desire and ambition of the first founders of the institution. A two years' course of mental philosophy after the study of astronomy, geology, and other kindred sciences, with seven years of theology, canon law, Sacred Scriptures, homiletics, and other sacred branches, would not appear to be too long a course for a student to be thoroughly initiated in the human and Divine sciences. I say initiated, because the study of these sciences only ends in seeing the beatific vision of God. St. Patrick did not lose time whilst visiting and learning in the famous monasteries of Europe, for he was, as tradition says, forty-seven years of age when he came to evangelize the Irish nation. Large funds are necessary to attain this desired course of studies, but funds will be showered from Heaven on those who will commence the work, with a strong determination to accomplish it with God's assistance. The Catholic Church in America is in one of the freest countries of the world. It depends on the Catholics themselves to make their churchmen the most refined and cultured, and the most learned in the sciences, as they must be the purest in morals, the mainstay of society at large. It is true that at the commencement of the great Catholic immigration into this country priests were wanting, and there was a great loss in the children of the first generation, but at present the organization of the Church is very satisfactory, thanks to the sacrifices of their clergy and people. The Public School system, however, forced against the consciences of the Catholics, is a stigma on the otherwise fair escutcheon of America; but this, we hope, with the advance of education and a proper knowledge of what liberty means, to see removed. In monarchical Canada this liberty of conscience is complete. A man is not taxed for an education for his children against which his conscience revolts.

The Catholics of Lower Canada, though in great majority, with true liberality and fairness, passed a law permitting their Protestant fellow-citizens to apply their school-taxes to support their own schools; and with this example before them, the Protestants of Upper Canada passed a law also permitting their Catholic fellow-citizens to support their own schools by their own taxes. We hope to see the same fairness in the United States. The government of the country is hardly as yet a century old: it is in its herculean infancy, and we hope great things with the progress of true education. The Catholic Church in America is in one of the freest countries in the world. It depends on the Catholics themselves to make it, as far as this world is concerned, the highest in culture, the purest in morals, and the main-stay of society at large. It is in an exceptionally favored position at the present time. It is true that its first members came to the country in large numbers with the old faith of their fathers in their hearts, but not having priests to instil the true faith into the minds of the children, vast numbers of them were lost. But now archbishops, bishops, priests, and religious orders of both sexes are multiplied, and, thanks to the sacrifices made by those religious bodies, the Christian education of children and the spiritual wants of the parents are well attended to. But the first century of the real life of the Church in this country is not, as yet, completed, and if the progress in the future, with large resources and means, be in proportion to the past, a most glorious future awaits the Church of America. There is no impeding its progress; it is Christ's Church, having the promises of indestructibility, and it will conquer. Our non-Catholic friends need not be alarmed, the Catholic Church has always been the friend and protector of true freedom, not of licentiousness, the support of good government, not of tyranny, the true guide of the people towards happiness here and hereafter.

From the statistics gathered rather imperfectly, the occupations of life engaged in by the students who passed through the seminary are as follows: Priests, accurately as can be estimated, are 300, of whom about 230 were ordained in the seminary; physicians, 25; lawyers, known, 47; professors in colleges and schools, 40; editors of newspapers, 15; bankers and brokers, 25; merchants, 245; and many distinguished members of legislatures. This is a respectable record, and we trust that these gentlemen do not forget their early religious instructions and the care of the one thing necessary. I have trespassed on your indulgence too long. I will leave it now to the real orators, who will address you to give the more glorious history of the triumphs of the college and seminary in its latter years; I have simply narrated its infant history. The presence of so many of its former students and friends is an evidence of the hold which this institution has on the good will and affections of them. May they long continue to shed around them the halo of a good, sound, and religious education, and may the students of the present and the future be men that their parents, their Church, and their country may be proud of. Above all, may they rejoice always in the happiness of a good and upright conscience.

CHAPTER XI.

BISHOP OF TORONTO.

A FEW stalwart members of the " Old Guard " that forty years ago gathered at the foot of George Street to escort Bishop Power from the boat to St. Paul's Church have survived the vississitudes of time, and their bowed and venerable forms add a sacredness and dignity to the very large and vigorous congregations, that Sunday after Sunday fill the Catholic churches of Toronto. They dwell with honorable pride upon the robust and manly faith of those early days; and if, with affectionate memory, they recall the past, they will also tell you that the Catholic Church has kept abreast of the progress of the city. There is not in the broad acreage of Ontario a grander manifestation of living and sturdy religious vitality than that which in every part of the metropolitan city is offered to the eye of the observant man. Under the episcopacy of His Grace the Archbishop of Toronto, religious, educational, and charitable institutions, ministering to the wants of the soul and the sufferings of the body, have risen in stately grandeur, and with swinging doors offer a hospitable welcome to wearied man.

> "The charities that soothe, and heal, and bless,
> Are scattered at the feet of man like flowers."

And if His Grace had no higher claims to our affection than those materialized in the noble institutions which he has founded, he would go down to his honored grave amid the regrets and benedictions of a grateful people.

Previously to the year 1826 the whole of Canada was subject to the ecclesiastical jurisdiction of the Bishop of Quebec. In that year Upper Canada was formed into a new diocese, with the episcopal seat in Kingston, and the Right Rev. Dr. McDonnell was made its first bishop. In 1842 the Holy See divided the diocese of Kingston, and erected another new diocese, extending from the county of York to the Detroit River, and appointed the Right Rev. Dr. Power bishop, leaving it optional with him to fix his See wherever he might think proper. Bishop Power chose Toronto, and hence the new partition was called the diocese of Toronto.

To those Catholic citizens of Toronto who can look back over the space of forty years and remember the condition of the Church then, what a contrast Catholicity in that city to-day, with its grand cathedral, nine churches, three convents, numerous charitable institutions, a college affiliated with the university, and a Catholic population of over twenty thousand souls presents to the condition of the Church when Bishop Power first took up his residence in

Toronto, to take upon himself the administration of the affairs of the new diocese. Up to the year 1828 the Catholics had not even a church in which to celebrate mass. They were accustomed to meet for this purpose at the houses of Mr. William Bergin and Mr. Frank Collins, where Father O'Grady said mass for the few faithful who were then residents of the town. Bishop McDonnell, while Toronto was still a part of his diocese, had paid it a visit, and, as the town was the most important one west of Kingston, he had resided there for a short time, while he paid pastoral visits to the extreme western limits of his then extensive diocese. St. Paul's Church was completed in 1829, the first Catholic church built in Toronto, when Bishop Power took possession of his See in 1842. The first thing he undertook was the erection of a cathedral. In order to raise a fund for this purpose, he established a weekly penny collection at St. Paul's Church, and at once set about to secure a proper site. He finally succeeded in purchasing the ground on which the Cathedral, Palace, and Loretto Convent* now stand. It was then a large market-garden, owned by Mr. McGill, of Montreal, from whom Bishop Power bought it for the sum of £1,800, which he paid out of his own pocket.

The saintly and learned first Bishop of Toronto laid deep the foundations of the future prosperity of the Church in Upper Canada. He travelled through that extensive tract of country lying between Toronto and the Detroit River, at that time

* The Sisters of Loretto (Institute of the Blessed Virgin Mary), came to Toronto on the 16th September, 1847. They opened their first convent on Duke Street, nearly opposite what is now De La Salle Institute. The first Superior was Rev. Mother Ignatia Hutchinson. The first Mass was celebrated in the convent on Duke Street, September 24, 1847, by Rev. John Carroll.

comparatively uninhabited, preaching, confirming, and attending to the spiritual wants of the few Catholics in that region committed to his charge. He labored unceasingly to obtain priests for the new diocese. To supply even a small number of priests for such a large tract of country was a very difficult matter in those days, as may be well imagined, when it is even to-day with the greatest difficulty that the Church in Ontario can provide for the absolute wants, in this respect, of old established and largely populated parishes. Bishop Power, in the midst of his labors, was stricken down with fever while attending the immigrants sent to America by the British government after the Irish famine of 1846. Thousands of these poor starved and diseased outcasts from their own country, the victims of cruelty, oppression, and misgovernment, were thrown upon the shores of America. The greater number were sent to Canada. They were shipped from their own country like so many diseased cattle, to be got rid of as quickly and efficaciously as possible, as their emaciated bodies and hungry, glaring eyes were most offensive to their masters—the owners of the broad acres upon which these poor creatures were allowed to starve, and the marble palaces near which they dare not approach—who found it more convenient and economical to ship them off to a foreign land, raize their villages, and turn the land into grazing farms for the breeding of cattle. Thousands of victims of Irish landlordism were landed on our shores at Quebec, to die in the immigrants' sheds there, or to make their way as best they might to Upper Canada; and if there had been even friendly hands to mark the spot where their bones were laid, their tombstones, like milestones, might be seen to-day marking each step of the way along the banks of the St. Lawrence, and the shores of Lake Ontario from Grosse Isle to Toronto. The scenes at the immigrant sheds at Toronto were such as might well appall the stoutest heart. Men in the vigor of manhood, the aged and decrepit, the mother whose infant had perished at the breast for want of nature's nourishment; while upon all dread fever had laid its gaunt and spectral hand. In this hour of trial the saintly bishop did not fail in his duty. He did not stand in the rear and order his men to the front. He did not ask his priests to go where he was unwilling to lead. He was in the thickest of the fray. He himself went among the dead and the dying. Death, with all its terrors, he braved. With his own hands he ministered to the dying, and at last laid down his life a martyr to his duty, and went to receive a martyr's crown. The heroic conduct of Bishop Power and his saintly death from fever caught while attending these poor people were for many years the familiar theme of the best residents of Toronto, both Catholic and Protestant. It is well that we of this day should not forget the noble deeds of these holy pioneers of the faith in Ontario.

Two years after the death of Bishop Power his place was filled by another great and saintly man, Bishop de Charbonnel. He was the eldest son of a French count, but, following the example of many of his class in the Middle Ages who became illustrious saints in the Church, he resigned his title and estates to a younger brother, turned his back upon the world, abandoned the certainty of a successful and brilliant career which his birth and family influence were sure to secure for him, joined the Church as a simple priest, and came out to Canada as a humble missionary. He was engaged in missionary work in Lower Canada, and his eminent piety and apostolic virtues being made known to the illustrious Pontiff who then ruled the Church, Pius IX., of holy memory, he appointed him to the Bishopric of Toronto. He came to Toronto in 1850, and one of his first acts was to pay off a mortgage of $10,000, held by the Bank of Upper Canada on the Cathedral, out of his own funds. The Cathedral had been begun by the late Bishop Power, but he died before it was completed. It was continued after his death, and, although not entirely finished, was consecrated by Bishop Phalen, of Kingston, during the interval that elapsed from the death of Bishop Power and the arrival of Bishop de Charbonnel. When the latter prelate arrived in Toronto, in 1852, there was, in addition to the incumbrance he himself had paid, a debt on the Cathedral amounting to $60,000, which had been temporarily assumed by the Hon. John Elmsly. The first work undertaken by Bishop de Charbonnel was the payment of this large debt. He traversed the whole of Canada, the United States, and Europe, to procure funds. He preached in the pulpit, explaining the condition of his large but poor diocese, and appealing to the charity and generosity of the faithful, and would then stand like an humble mendicant at the church-door, soliciting contributions and receiving the donations of the charitable, as the congregation was leaving. What this noble man and holy prelate accomplished during the time he occupied the Episcopal See of Toronto, is well summed up by His Grace, the present archbishop, in a pastoral addressed to the clergy and laity of the diocese, on the eve of his departure for Rome, in

1879. Speaking of the labors of his illustrious predecessor he says: "The large diocese wanted priests and
religious orders to assist in saving souls. The great
and noble Bishop de Charbonnel embraced the work
with that confidence in God and that energy that
distinguished the early Bishops of the Church. He
traversed the whole country, the United States, and
Europe, and with his own hands procured the means
of paying off the enormous debt of the diocese. He
introduced the Basilian Fathers, who founded a
college. He induced the Brothers of the Christian
Schools* to come from Montreal to establish themselves in Toronto, and brought the Sisters of St.
Joseph's† from St. Louis to take charge of the orphan
asylum and girls' schools, and to found other charitable institutions for the care of the poor. He labored,
too, with magnificent success for the establishment
of our separate schools; he spared no labor and
hesitated at no expense for this object. This good
bishop brought from France some of our best priests.
He adorned at great expense the interior of the
Cathedral, etc. The greatest of his works was the
procuring from the Holy See the division of his
diocese, and the forming of two new dioceses, having
their Sees in Hamilton and London. For the difficulty of the bishop is not so much in governing and
visiting his diocese, as in procuring priests. Then
the good Bishop de Charbonnel, having laid deep
and well the foundations of these dioceses, retired
into a monastery, like those great saints of old, away
from the praise or dispraise of men. He interrupts

---

* The Brothers of the Christian Schools came to Toronto, May 1, 1851.
They were installed by Rev. Brother Patrick, now (1884) assistant to the
Superior General of the Order.

† The Sisters of St. Joseph opened their first house in Toronto,
October 7, 1851. Rev. Mother Delphine was the first Superior.

his quiet and holy retreat at his Capuchin monastery at Lyons, only to aid the cardinals, archbishops, and bishops of France in giving retreats to clergy and people, ordaining priests, giving confirmation, preaching the word of faith, and in performing other works of charity, which have rendered his name in France blessed. We attribute to his holy prayers, mortifications, and good works a great deal of the merit of the success of our labors in his old diocese. He still lives, now seventy-six years of age, strong and well, to labor yet in the service of our good God. To serve is to reign." *

Father Lynch was appointed by his order President of the College of the Angels, and here he expected to remain for the remainder of his life. As at St. Mary's of the Barrens, he not only performed the duties and functions of the president of a college, but he still continued, when opportunity offered, the labors so dear to his heart, the giving of missions, whenever his services were required, and whenever his health permitted him to undertake such laborious work. But the college was not to be his home and resting-place for the remainder of his earthly career. He was destined to leave his quiet retreat, to assume the dignified and responsible position of a bishop of the Catholic Church, though at that time he little dreamed of any such great and important change in his life.

In 1856, Bishop de Charbonnel being desirous of having a coadjutor appointed, recommended to His Holiness the name of Father Dowd, the zealous and beloved pastor of St. Patrick's Church in Montreal. That pious and godly man, whose modesty

* This holy and saintly prelate is still living (1884) in the Capuchin monastery at Lyons, and bears well the weight of his eighty-two years.

and humility are only equalled by his zeal and fervor in the service of God and the Church, at once refused the dignity, and even went so far as to leave Canada and retire to France, in order to avoid the honor. In the same year the bishop also went to France for the purpose of preaching in aid of the Society for the Propagation of the Faith, whose headquarters were at Lyons, and in whose work he took a deep interest, having established in his diocese in every parish what are called "circles," for the purpose of collecting funds to assist the Society in their noble efforts to preach the Gospel in heathen lands. When returning to Canada, and while passing through Paris, he called to visit the President of the Irish College in that city. That gentleman, Father McNamara, had been an old college-mate of Father Lynch, and they had for years been very warm and attached friends. Knowing that Father Lynch had established a college at the Niagara Falls, which were only a short distance from Toronto, and were indeed, on the Canadian side, at one time a portion of the diocese of Toronto, the reverend gentleman inquired of His Lordship if he had ever met the President of the College of the Angels. The bishop replied that he had not; that he had been absent from Canada for over two years, and that he had not learned of the establishment of the new college. Father McNamara then requested the bishop to call on Father Lynch and make his acquaintance. Whatever conversation Father McNamara and the good bishop may have had concerning the President of the College of the Angels, is only known to themselves; but the bishop declares that, when parting with him, he said to himself, referring to Father Lynch, "I have found my coadjutor." Very soon after his arrival home His Lordship called upon Father Lynch at the college, made his acquaintance, and invited him to Toronto to preach a retreat to the community of St. Joseph. It was his first experience in missionary work in Canada, and after giving a retreat to this religious body, the bishop prevailed upon him to remain and give a mission to the people of the city. This he consented to do, and remained for the greater part of the summer of 1858 in Toronto, engaged in this work, little thinking that he was so soon to become a permanent resident of the city. Bishop de Charbonnel had brought him to Toronto in order, perhaps, that he might, by personal observation, judge of his fitness for the position he intended him to occupy. He said nothing, however, to the humble missionary of his intentions. Father Lynch returned to his college after his labors in Toronto, and his surprise may be well imagined at receiving, in the month of September of the following year (1859), the Papal Bulls appointing him coadjutor to the Bishop of Toronto *cum jure successionis.*

To the world at large the position of a Bishop of the Catholic Church seems so exalted, it commands such a high degree of respect, its occupant can wield such a potent influence on the general course of affairs in the community in which he exercises his authority, he is so important a factor in the social economy of Christian communities, that we imagine the attainment of this dignity must be the laudable ambition of all priests of marked ability; that it is the goal to which the clever and ambitious in the Church naturally strive to reach, as the bench in the legal profession is looked forward to as the crown of a successful professional career. We look upon such aspirations of the Catholic clergy as quite natural and perfectly legitimate. Judging the priesthood by the standards of the world, we look upon such hopes and ambitions as not only natural to human nature, but even in themselves highly commendable. A bishop of the Catholic Church undoubtedly occupies a most exalted station, not only in the Church, but also in the world. He is a prince of the Church universal. In Catholic times, even in England, where the nobility were always so jealous of churchmen, the bishop ranked above the noble, the spiritual above the temporal lords. Even in such an utilitarian age as ours, and in countries as democratic in government and institutions as the United States and Canada, the Catholic episcopacy is looked upon as conferring exceptional dignity and influence on its members. But the Catholic priest well knows and thoroughly appreciates the fearful, the terrible responsibility entailed upon him when he assumes the mitre and undertakes to wield the crozier. The man brought up and educated for the Catholic priesthood, who knows what is expected of a bishop of the Catholic Church, the obstacles, both spiritual and temporal, that lie in his path ; the exceptional temptations to which he is exposed; the strict account to which he will be held before the judgment-seat of God for the Church committed to his care and the souls placed in his keeping; the dangers which surround and threaten all men of exalted positions in this world—such a man, we say, would be more than human, if he did not tremble at the very thought of undertaking such responsibilities and supporting such a burthen. Many may aspire to the dignity; few care to assume it *cum onere*. Great saints have fled from civilized life to bury themselves for years in deserts, in order to escape this dangerous honor, which seems to the eyes of the world only the much-coveted prize of the ambitious priest.

Father Lynch did not escape the mental conflict, endured perhaps by every priest, in a greater or less degree, to whom this honor has been offered. He was agitated by the conflict between his duty to God and his own inclinations. He loved dearly the work in which he was then engaged. One of the most marked characteristics of the subject of this memoir, both as a priest and as a bishop, is his affection and love for the young. This was the dominating sentiment in his mind in the founding of the College of the Angels, and accepting the presidency of it. He loved to teach the young. Next to missionary work, it was the labor dearest to his heart. To mould the plastic mind; to watch and direct the growth and development of a human soul; to educate, draw out, and develop into action the dormant powers of the young and vigorous intellect; to instill principles of truth, justice and morality into the heart of the boy just merging into manhood—this was to him congenial labor in a field he loved. As the president of a college he had ample opportunity of exercising to their fullest the peculiar faculties which he undoubtedly possesses for this kind of work. On becoming a bishop all this would have to be abandoned. Besides, he was a stranger to Canada, and comparatively unknown to the priests and people of the diocese of Toronto. He learned that the City of Toronto had —as indeed it deserved, to some extent, at that day— the unenviable reputation of being very anti-Catholic, both in tone and sentiment, and he knew that it was the hot-bed of a politico-religious society which has, unfortunately, been the chief cause of keeping alive and fanning the flame of religious strife in Canada, and keeping fresh the memories of wrongs which had better be forgotten in this new country. Then, again, a Catholic bishop is, to a certain extent, a public character, and in a non-Catholic country such as this, his every action is subjected to the closest scrutiny and severest criticism by the public at large; his acts are frequently misconstrued, or motives imputed to him which he never in the remotest degree entertained. · The student must forego his books, give up his favorite study, and bid adieu to his beloved library when he undertakes the administration of the affairs of a diocese in a missionary country like Canada, where his chief labors will be to procure priests, build churches, found schools and religious institutions, provide for the aged and poor, and undertake a hundred other duties from which bishops in the Catholic countries of Europe are in a great measure exempt. All these considerations were present to the mind of Father Lynch, yet the chief question with him was "what is the will of God in this matter?" To obtain light, he prayed earnestly and took some months to consider. He said numerous masses that God might enlighten his mind and direct his course. He consulted those whom he thought knew him best, and on whose opinion as to his fitness to undertake such an important charge he believed he might safely rely, especially Bishop Timon, of Buffalo, and Archbishop Hughes, of New York. Both of those prelates urged him strongly not to refuse the office, advancing very strong reasons, and the very cogent argument that no personal predilections or any want of confidence in his own powers or ability to assume the onerous burden involved in the acceptance of this dignity should have any weight with him, providing he was confident as were they that God was calling him to this state in life.

He therefore, placing his trust in God, and relying upon His divine assistance, which is never refused to those who humbly and earnestly ask it, finally made up his mind to submit to what he believed to be the will of God, and to obey the summons of the successor of St. Peter to become a shepherd over one of the flocks in the fold of Christ. He was consecrated in the cathedral of Toronto on the 20th of November, 1859, by Bishop de Charbonnel, assisted by Bishop Timon, of Buffalo, and Bishop Farrell, of Hamilton. There were present at the ceremony, besides the assisting consecrating prelates, Monseigneur Baillargeon, then administrator of the diocese of Quebec, afterwards archbishop; their lordships Bishops Bourget, of Montreal; Guiges, of Ottawa; Duggan, of Chicago; Smith, of Dubuque; Pinsoneault, of London; and Loughlin, of Brooklyn, besides a large number of clergy from the United States and Canada. A numerous delegation of students from the College of Our Lady of the Angels came to see their beloved president receive his new dignity, and the day was one of great rejoicing to all present.

As subsequent events proved, the saintly Bishop de Charbonnel had determined to resign his episcopal office and retire into the Capuchin Monastery at Lyons, and his anxiety to procure a coadjutor to whom he could, at once, with safety entrust the affairs of the diocese was increased by this determination. With the consecration of Father Lynch, he seems to have thought that he might at once put into execution the resolution he had so long entertained of retiring from the world, and passing the remainder of his days as an humble monk, and he at once made preparations for his return to France in the beginning of the following year. In February, 1860, he arrived at Rome, and in April of the same year, he formally resigned the Bishopric of Toronto into the hands of His Holiness, Pius IX. Bishop Lynch therefore succeeded him, *jure successionis*, and took formal possession of the See on the feast of Corpus Christi of the same year. The event of taking such possession was not made the occasion of any special ceremony, but was quietly performed without any display, and thus the subject of our memoir became Bishop of Toronto.

CHAPTER XII.

EPISCOPAL LABORS.

State of the Toronto Diocese in 1859—The Work of his Predecessor—Difficulty of Obtaining Priests—Vocations to the Priesthood—Number of Priests in Diocese in 1859—And Churches—Increase—Institutions Established—Educational—Charitable—The Priests of the Archdiocese—Their Zeal and Energy—The Bishop Visits Rome to Attend Canonization of Japanese Martyrs—Visits Ireland—Goes to Rome to Attend Vatican Council—Made Archbishop—First Provincial Council—Visits Ireland in 1879—Interview with Duke of Marlborough and Sir Stafford Northcote on the Irish Question—Presentation at Court—Visits Lough Derg—Erection of the Diocese of Peterborough—The Archbishop's Laborious Life—Bishop O'Mahony his Coadjutor.

UPON taking possession of his See, Bishop Lynch at once entered upon the discharge of his episcopal duties. His pious and zealous predecessor had labored hard and faithfully, and with much success, to bring some kind of order out of the chaos that existed in the diocese when he first took upon himself the administration of affairs. He had, in a great measure, succeeded, but much yet remained to be done. He had, to some extent, to use the language of our early settlers, made a clearance in the forest. He had hewn down the timber, logged and stumped this large spiritual farm, and left the soil ready for the plough and harrow of his successor. To this great work the bishop at once addressed himself with his accustomed zeal and energy. "Upon taking the administration of the diocese from such holy and disinterested hands," says the archbishop in one of his pastorals, "we strove to build on the foundation which he had laid, and to follow his blessed example. We had labored in the holy ministry for sixteen years, twelve of which we had spent in the United States. We were broken down in constitution and weak in body from fevers contracted in Texas and Missouri, all the germs of which still lingered in our frame, and troubled us for eighteen years. We may well say that 'the weak things of this world, and those that are not, hath God chosen.'"   He at once visited every portion of his extensive diocese, giving retreats, forty hours' devotion and confirmation, and seeing to the interests of the education of the Catholic children. He held his first synod in 1863, and framed such rules from canon laws and other sources as made a complete code of ecclesiastical jurisprudence for his diocese. The first great and urgent necessity he experienced in his new field of labor was the want of priests. This is a difficulty peculiar to America. The vine-yard of the Lord is large on this continent, but the laborers are few for the work, and, what is most to be regretted, are hard to be obtained. Vocations for the priesthood in Canada and the United States are not at all in proportion to the Catholic population, or in any way commensurate with the necessities of the Church in America. Leaving out of view the intrinsic dignity of the priesthood as a spiritual or-der, the young men of this country do not seem to have an adequate conception of the social dignity conferred by Catholic orders, and the very pro-nounced position a Catholic clergyman of education and culture is accorded by general consent, even in such a Protestant country as ours. Bishop Lynch at once chose several young men whose vocations seemed to point toward the ministry, admitted them into the palace, and with the aid of a few assistants taught them himself.

This difficulty in obtaining young men for the ministry was so keenly felt by His Lordship that a few years after his consecration he addressed a pastoral on this subject to the clergy and laity of his diocese. "In all new countries," His Lordship remarked, " difficulties have been experienced in obtaining the proper subjects for priestly ordination. A quiet and religious state of society, and a deep spiritual tone in families, hard to be found in a new country, are required for fostering divine vocations to the priesthood. At first missionaries were sent from the older Catholic countries to plant the faith and attend to its development, but when the Catholic Church commences to be established then the seeds of ecclesiastical vocations take root, and by degrees, by the grace of God and with proper ecclesiastical training, the children of the soil are prepared to become, in their own country, the spiritual fathers of the faithful, and to take the places of the old missionaries, who abandoned country, home and friends to plant the faith in distant lands, and without whose labors those young men would still remain outside the sanctuary of the Church. Lower Canada in modern times furnishes a beautiful illustration of this kind working of the holy providence of God in planting the faith. In the commencement, France supplied her new colonies with bishops and priests, and they founded colleges and seminaries with the munificent aid of the laity. The children of the country were educated. Piety flourished, and the divine vocations to the priesthood were especially fostered by holy and venerable missionaries. Behold Lower Canada, with her well-organized hierarchy of archbishops, bishops, priests, monasteries, colleges and parishes, and she has commenced already to send mis-

sionaries to distant countries, besides furnishing subjects for religious orders.   In Upper Canada the
Church has not yet arrived at the same point of
development, but through the mercy of God great
progress has been made.   Colleges have been established, and many youths of the country have become
priests.   But there are great difficulties to be overcome.   The ecclesiastical education is long and ex-
pensive. A young man must receive the education of
a gentleman before he can commence his theological
studies, so that if he does not become a priest he
loses not his time during the first years of his studies.   In olden times each bishop had an ecclesiastical
seminary in his own palace, and priests trained
young ecclesiastics in their presbyteries."   His
Lordship then goes on to advise parents how they
may distinguish such among their children as have
a vocation or may be safely trained for the ministry,
and to exhort the clergy to seek out such children
and to commence to train them up for the sanctuary.
"These children," he says, "may be easily distinguished from others, by their tender consciences,
their hatred of sin, their love for the most Blessed
Sacrament and attending at the altar, their anxiety
to lead holy lives and gain heaven.   Generosity and
disinterestedness are other marks of a divine vocation.   That young man who loves to do good to
others, who is kind, affable and obliging, without
thanks or recompense, but from the motive and
pleasure of doing good and pleasing God, is probably one whom God loves, and to whom He has given
that divine grace to spend and superspend himself
for the salvation of his brethren.   This young man
is one in a thousand, and if he be protected from
the evil of bad associations and strengthened fre-

quently with the Holy Sacrament, he will be the secondary cause of the salvation of many."

In 1859, when Bishop Lynch undertook the chief pastorship of the diocese, he found in it thirty-two secular priests and four Basilian Fathers in St. Michael's College. Of these, four retired with Bishop de Charbonnel in 1860. Subsequently, at intervals, nine left for other dioceses, or returned to France in ill health; seven have died and two have been consecrated bishops, and only ten remain in the diocese whom he found in it twenty-five years ago. The two priests who were created bishops are His Lordship Bishop Walsh, of London, and Dr. Jamot, the present bishop of the new diocese of Peterboro. Both of these prelates worthily fill the Sees to which they have been appointed, and are both an honor to the Canadian hierarchy. Of His Lordship of London it is almost unnecessary to speak, as his name is a household word among the Catholics of Ontario. Gifted with talents of a high order, which he has ever used for great and holy ends; endowed with fine administrative abilities, he has built up one of the most flourishing and prosperous dioceses in the Dominion. Possessing all those qualities which distinguish the pious and the zealous priest, joined to the courtly manners of a well-bred man of the world, Bishop Walsh has won the affection of his own people and the respect of all who have the honor of his acquaintance. His Lordship, Bishop Jamot, had been laboring for years with indefatigable zeal and energy in building up a series of parishes in the County of Simcoe, when he was recommended by His Grace to the Holy See for the newly-formed bishopric of Peterboro. When selected, he was Vicar-General of the archdiocese, and had won for himself the admiration of every man who reverences the spiritual characteristics which distinguish the priest whose life is unreservedly devoted to the elevation of his fellow-man.

In 1859 there were in the diocese forty-three churches. At present there are seventy-one churches in all. St. Michael's Cathedral has been finished, the tower and spire completed, and altogether about $40,000 have been spent upon it within the last twenty-five years. The Cathedral itself is valued at about $150,000.

In giving a short summary of the work accomplished in the diocese since 1859, we may here briefly allude to the institutions of learning and of charity, although we shall speak of them more in detail hereafter. Of institutions of learning, there are the St. Michael's College, the De la Salle Institute, conducted by the Brothers of the Christian Schools, the Convents of St. Joseph and Loretto, the Monastery of Our Lady of Mount Carmel at the Niagara Falls, and also the fine Convent of the Loretto Nuns at the same place. This last named Order has also established convents in Toronto, Hamilton, Stratford, Lindsay, Guelph, and Bellville. The convent in Lindsay, built under the personal supervision of the late lamented Father Stafford, was one of the finest educational buildings in the country. The Sisters of St. Joseph have also, in addition to their fine institutions in Toronto, established others in several towns and cities in Ontario, and have in the City of St. Catharine's by far the finest building for educational purposes in the place. The community of St. Joseph have opened a convent under the name of Notre Dame Institute, in Toronto, where such young ladies as come to

Toronto for the purpose of attending the Provincial Normal School may obtain board at reasonable rates, and where they will be protected from the dangers to which young women from the country are more or less exposed in the boarding-houses of a large city like Toronto. This noble community, in addition to teaching the girls of the Separate Schools, also take charge of the St. Nicholas Home, a boarding-house established for the accommodation of the working-boys of the city. The Sisters of St. Joseph also direct the House of Providence, a charitable institution for the aged and infirm, of which we shall speak hereafter. On the whole, this noble band of religious ladies are doing a great and holy work in the cause of charity and education, and are entitled to the respect and veneration of the whole community.

It would be unjust to the hard-working priests of the archdiocese of Toronto to overlook the very efficient help they have given to their spiritual chief in the accomplishment of such great labors, and in the building up of the vast religious edifices which we have here briefly sketched. There is not in the Dominion of Canada a body of men who have given stronger proofs of a spirit of self-sacrifice and devotion to Catholic interests—the grand characteristics of the apostolic missionaries—than those which mark the lives of the priests of the archdiocese of Toronto. If the chronically censorious and keenly-critical Catholic demand from the Catholic clergy of this new country a perfection and spirituality associated with angelic substances, he will meet with disappointment. But if he seek for a stalwart, manly priesthood—a body of men who are inured to the hardships peculiar to the territorially large and half-settled parishes of Ontario; men who are ready at all hours and in all seasons to minister to the scattered members of their flocks; who with untiring energy have built churches, schools and presbyteries —we can point to the priests of this archdiocese, and tell him that these are the men he is in quest of. We can tell him, and with truth, that the daily lives and actions of these men bear witness to their sincerity and spirit of self-denial. If we expect from them, in all cases, the elegance of manners and elaborate courtesy of the *ancien régime*, or those conventional graces associated with our ideas of modern " society " etiquette, or that æsthetic effeminacy so much aped in these days by the tender maids of both sexes, we shall be disappointed; but if we look for men who, true to their divine ideal and faithful to their sacred calling, labor with an honesty of purpose and a persistency of application to the cause of God and His Church, we shall find them among these priests. Theirs are the sterling qualities of a vigorous and sturdy manhood joined to the amenities of the scholar and the man of common sense, and these are the qualities that have won for them the love of their own people and the respect and admiration of the community at large.

In 1862, Bishop Lynch, in response to an invitation from the then reigning Pontiff, Pius IX., proceeded to Rome to attend the canonization of the Japanese Martyrs. It was the first visit he had made to Rome after his elevation to the episcopacy, and he was kindly and cordially received in his new dignity by that illustrious Pontiff, who had not forgotten the ex-President of St. Mary's of the Barrens. It was on the occasion of this journey to Rome that he paid a visit to Ireland, travelled through the country, and saw with his own eyes the wretched condition of the people. He attended, in company with the late Archbishop Hughes, who was then also in Ireland, a large meeting in the Rotunda in Dublin, and both prelates addressed the people on the condition of the country, advising them to calmly and constitutionally agitate for their rights, and especially for that most important of all rights—the right of self-government. The Canadian bishop and the illustrious American archbishop, who were both also natives of Ireland, were enthusiastically received by the large audience present on that occasion.

In the year 1869, Bishop Lynch made a visit to Rome to attend the Vatican Council, and was then made archbishop. An account of this visit will be given in a subsequent chapter. On His Grace's arrival in Toronto, a grand reception was given him, in which the most prominent citizens of Toronto took part. The first Provincial Council was held in 1873, at which were present their Lordships Bishops Walsh, of London; Crinnon, of Hamilton, and O'Brien, of Kingston. In 1879, he again made a visit to the Eternal City, being the decennial visit which all bishops are required to make *ad limina apostolorum*. On this occasion, on his way to Rome, he visited Ireland and had a long interview with the Duke of Marlborough, then Lord Lieutenant, on the political condition of Ireland, and had a special audience with Sir Stafford Northcote, principally on the question of Home Rule for Ireland, a concession which His Grace considers necessary before the permanent tranquillity of that country can be assured. On his return His Grace was waited upon by Sir A. T. Galt, then the Canadian High Commissioner, resident in London.

Sir Alexander suggested the pleasure it would give him, as the representative of Canada in England, to present His Grace at Court as a distinguished member of the Catholic hierarchy in Canada. As none of the English Catholic bishops had ever been presented, the archbishop felt some delicacy in the matter, and therefore consulted Cardinal Manning as to the propriety of complying with the kindly expressed wish of the Canadian High Commissioner. The Cardinal, however, advised His Grace to accept the invitation, and the latter was accordingly presented at a levee held by His Royal Highness the Prince of Wales, on the part of Her Majesty the Queen. His Grace was most cordially received by the Prince of Wales and also by Prince Arthur, both of whom he had previously met on their visit to Canada. The appearance of a Roman Catholic bishop at the English Court was a strange sight, as it was the first time that such a thing had occurred since the reign of James II. The Spanish Ambassador and the ambassadors of the other Catholic powers cordially greeted His Grace, the former remarking to him that now that the ice had been broken, he hoped that the Catholic prelates of England would no longer be strangers in the Court of their sovereign.

But more interesting to him than all the pomp of a royal court was his own country, her people, her churches, and her shrines. He visited Lough Derg, once as renowned for its pilgrimages as Lourdes is at the present day, but for many years previously almost abandoned. His Grace's letters, descriptive of the Lough, the island, and its pilgrims, once more drew attention to this ancient resort of pious penitents, and again pilgrims began to flock to the holy isle. When His Grace renewed his visit to the place in 1881, he was delighted to see that great improvements had been made, and that a commodious hospice had been built for the accommodation of the pilgrims. On that occasion the archbishop had the happiness and pleasure of ordaining several young men to the priesthood who were destined for the foreign missions.

The increase of the Catholic population in the growing towns and newly opened-up settlements of the large territory included in the Toronto arch-diocese, necessitated the creation of another diocese and the appointment of a bishop to the new See. His Grace, on again visiting Rome, had recom-mended to His Holiness Pius IX. Father Jamot to be Vicar-Apostolic of Northern Canada. He was accordingly appointed by the Holy See Vicar-Apostolic, with the title of Bishop of Sarepta. No-tice of such appointment was telegraphed to him, and he was requested to proceed at once to Rome to meet the archbishop. He accordingly did so, and was consecrated bishop and Vicar-Apostolic by His Grace in the Church of Our Lady of the Sacred Heart at Issouden, in France, on the 24th of Feb-ruary, 1874. At the request of the archbishop, who visited Rome for that purpose in 1882, the Holy See formed the new diocese of Peterboro on the 11th of July, 1882, and Bishop Jamot was ap-pointed as its first bishop. He was duly installed in the new See, with the usual ceremonies, on the 21st of September of the same year, by the archbishop, assisted by the bishops of Ontario and many of the clergy of the archdiocese.

The amount of labor performed by His Grace since first taking possession of his See has been something enormous. He has repeatedly visited all portions of his diocese. He has preached, confirmed, ordained priests, consecrated bishops, assisted at councils, and has many times borne the inconveniences of an ocean voyage to visit Rome, in connection with the affairs of his vast and important charge. From the day the mitre was placed upon his head to the present, he has never spent an idle hour. Age has not impaired his activity nor affected his zeal. He is as anxious for the welfare of the Church and as zealous for the salvation of souls to-day as he was when, as a young priest, he braved the hardships of a missionary life in Texas. His health, though greatly enfeebled by the many serious attacks he has suffered from disease and the ravages incurred by hardships and overwork, still permits him to do good service in the cause of religion by the indomitable will of its possessor. Although at an age when most men would rather be relieved from the labor of preaching, the archbishop preaches more frequently than any of his priests. His lectures upon Catholic doctrine and belief always attract large audiences; and it is not an infrequent sight to see the vast and spacious Cathedral filled from the altar to the doors with eager auditors, composed in a large measure of Protestants. Indeed, a large number of educated and cultured non-Catholics make it a point of regularly attending His Grace's discourses, and many have been by these means brought into the Church. During the summer of 1882, the archbishop was once more stricken down with disease—erysipelas of the most virulent type having attacked him—and for many weeks his recovery was considered extremely doubtful. He, however, recovered, and his anxious friends considered that the time had now arrived when he should give up a large part of the active labor he had been so long accustomed to perform. He has, since his recovery, however, renewed his labors, and refuses to spare himself in the service of the Lord or to take the rest to which his laborious life entitles him.

These last few years, His Grace, though still vigorous and full of zeal and marvellous vitality, has transferred to the shoulders of his energetic auxiliary, Bishop O'Mahony, a portion of the burden he has so long and so patiently borne. Nor could he have selected for this responsible and honorable position, one in whom all the sterling qualities of the bishop and the man shine more conspicuously. Bishop O'Mahony possessess in an eminent degree all the attributes of a truly great man. To a fine personal appearance and address, His Lordship adds the manner and bearing of the cultured gentleman. There is about him a strength of mental and physical texture that is only to be found in men capable of conceiving and executing grand projects, and we are of the opinion that, apart from the spirituality of his nature, much of the success which rewards his labors and his preaching may be attributed to the possession of this gift of moral and personal strength. He is a hard worker, spending himself generously and without stint in the interests of religion, and striving, with a large measure of success, to infuse into the Catholic manhood around him much of that indomitable enthusiasm and pride of faith which are a part of his very being. He is an able and scholarly speaker, impressing upon his hearers in language full of magnetism the sincerity of his convictions and the divinity of the truths he unfolds. We have barely limned the outlines of the mind and character of Bishop O'Mahony, and we have taken this liberty solely on the ground that His Lordship is now intimately associated with the archdiocese and its venerated spiritual chief.

We have endeavored in this chapter to give a brief summary of the labors performed by the subject of our memoir since he first took upon himself the administration of the affairs of the Toronto diocese. We shall in subsequent chapters enter more fully into the history of the many works he has accomplished in the cause of religion, charity, education, and the social and political elevation of the Catholics of Canada.

CHAPTER XIII.

THE VATICAN COUNCIL AND ARCHBISHOPRIC.

Departure for Rome to Attend the Vatican Council—Arrival in Paris—Visits St. Lazare—Visits Lyons—Meets Bishop de Charbonnel—A Guest of the Capuchin Fathers in Chambery in Savoy—Arrival in Rome—The Vatican Council—Its Personnel—Distinguished Members—Bishops from every Land Under the Sun—A Grand Procession—The Expansion of the Church—Its Growth since the Reformation—The Church in America—Striking Contrasts—The Oriental and the Celt—A Giant Race—Bishop Lynch made Archbishop of Toronto—Toronto's Claim to the Honor—Postulating for the Pallium—Ceremony of Conferring Performed in the Pope's Private Chapel—Ill Health while Attending the Council—Resides at Civita Vecchia—Addresses the Council on the Question of Papal Infallibility—The Sudden Adjournment of the Council.

TOWARDS the end of September, 1869, the archbishop, in obedience to the summons of the Pope, sailed from New York by the French line of steamers for Rome to attend the Vatican Council. He arrived in Paris on the 2d of October. Here he was kindly and hospitably received by the Lazarist Fathers, and in their society the memories of his collegiate and missionary days were vividly brought to his recollection in friendly commune with his early companions. From Paris he went to Lyons, where, by invitation, he was the guest of the Capuchin Fathers, and where he had the happiness and pleasure of meeting Bishop de Charbonnel, his predecessor in the See of Toronto, with whom he passed many agreeable days in visiting the churches and devotional shrines for which Lyons is famous, and in communicating to his Right Rev. friend many interesting details of his former diocese. In answer to the invitation of the Capuchin Fathers in Chambery, in Savoy, he accepted their hospitality for a week, and during his stay there visited the room in which St. Francis de Sales died, and at the shrine of St. Concordantius, an Irish saint whose relics are preserved in the church adjoining the convent of the Visitation Nuns, invoked the intercession of the saint on behalf of the people of his diocese.   He sailed from Marseilles on the 13th of November, and after spending a few days in Genoa and Florence, entered Rome on the 3d of December. Five days afterwards, on the 8th of December, he took his seat in the Council at its first session.

Never, perhaps, in the history of Christianity did a grander or more venerable and imposing body of men assemble at the command of the Supreme Pontiff.   From the uttermost parts of the earth they came with the knowledge and varied experience of men who had grown old in ministering to the spiritual wants of their fellow-men.   Among them were the giants of the intellectual world; men eminent in the Church, in science, in literature; distinguished bishops; writers whose names are familiar to the educated throughout the world; profound theologians like Perrone, the French Jesuit; the brilliant rhetorician, Duponloup, Bishop of Orleans; Hefelé, the illustrious biblical scholar and able controversialist; Spaulding, the American essayist and Catholic apologist; the venerable Cardinal Cullen, who, as a scholar and theologian, ranked second to none in the Council; Cardinal Manning, the indomitable champion of Catholic rights in Protestant England, and many others whose names are familiar to the Catholic reader.   Every man who occupied a seat in the Council had, by the force of some extraordinary talent, or by the possession in a remarkable

degree of some one of those elements which raise
an individual above the ranks of his fellow-men,
won for himself a position among the peers of the
Catholic Church.   It is not paying them too exaggerated a compliment to say that these remarkable
men represented the civilization and Christianity
of nineteen centuries.   In every department of
ecclesiastical and sacred literature, in arts and
science—in truth, in every region that lay open to
the investigations of the human intellect, they had
earned for themselves the respect and admiration of
their age.

Among the seven hundred and twenty-nine bishops who sat in the Hall of Assembly, every man
bore an unsullied reputation.   Their exalted position exposed them to the critical eyes of a censorious world.   Their actions stood boldly out from
the routine of daily life, and, examined under the
calcium light of public opinion, they have elicited
the approbation of the world at large.   Never in
any former Council was the divine unity of the
Catholic Church more strongly exemplified.   At
the summons of the venerable and aged Pontiff they
came from every quarter of the globe in obedience to
his call, thereby acknowledging and proclaiming to
all the world that they recognized him as the true
and only successor of St. Peter.   Among them was
the grave and meditative Egyptian, whose sharply-
outlined features and serious air well became one who
had first seen the light of day and had grown to manhood under the shadow of the Pyramids.   Carres-
po-y-Bautista, whose hairs were whitened by seventy-
eight Mexican summers, and whose dignified bearing bespoke the descendant of the Montezumas.
From the land of Laotse and Confucius came

Bishop Pelletier, bearing to the Sovereign Pontiff the allegiance of two million of Chinese converts. From the banks of the Ganges, from the wooded shores of America's great lakes, from the mountains of Abyssinia, and the plains of Senagambia came the representatives of the infallible church to give an account of their stewardship; to testify to the belief of their respective churches, and to bear back with them to their various flocks the love and benediction of the successor of St. Peter, and the deliberative results of the assembled wisdom of the Universal Church.

To one standing in St. Peter's and witnessing the magnificent procession of distinguished bishops and great men, as they slowly and reverently filed along the lofty nave on their way from the vestibule of the grand basilica to the Hall of Convocation, which was erected in one of the transepts of the immense building, the scene was one never to be forgotten—it was a spectacle to be witnessed but once in many ages. In that procession might be read the history of Western Christendom for the past three hundred years. Since the assembling of the last General Council of the Church at Trent, her expansion and growth has been marvellous. This increase has more than compensated for the loss sustained by the so-called Reformation. Since that important event in the history of Christianity, two vast continents, then only lately discovered by the great Columbus, have been opened up and settled, and more than a hundred bishops come at the call of the Supreme Pontiff from the land of the setting sun to testify to the allegiance of thirty millions of his children in the New World. The distinguishing characteristics of the different prelates were no less remarkable than the variety of their costumes, yet every face bore the impress of meditation and profound study; and the spiritual expression and courtly bearing of each one, as he moved with measured pace along the marble pavement of the grandest Christian temple in the world, harmonized fittingly with the dignity and sacredness of the Roman purple. Nor was there wanting that harmony and warmth of color, or those striking and picturesque contrasts so pleasing to the artistic eye; the varied style and color of the different costumes, speaking vividly of peoples so remote and so different from one.another, here brought together in the unity of faith. The contrast of faces and physique was no less striking. Side by side with the bearded and dark-haired envoy from the distant Orient walked the tall and cleanly-shaved Celt, the stout, fair-haired German, the solid-looking Englishman, or the keen and intellectual American. Nor was the disparity in height and phys-ical development between the representatives of the different nations less noticeable. The Irish and American bishops seemed like a race of giants when contrasted with the lithe yet sinewy forms of their more diminutive Latin and Oriental companions. Especially was this noticeable in the Irish bishops from Canada and the United States; indeed, the two men who were the most conspicuous for their height —towering head and shoulders above the eight hun-dred prelates, who composed the procession—were Irishmen—one the late lamented Dr. Farrell, then Bishop of the diocese of Hamilton, in the archdiocese of Toronto. Even to the finely developed Roman, the great height, breadth of shoulders, and muscular development of the Celt, excited wonder and aston-ishment. It seemed as if the Almighty had fitted to their souls frames of iron, that no fatigue could weaken nor rigor of climate destroy. Looking at them as they towered above the Oriental bishops, one could easily understand that the soil which they tilled and labored, brought forth a spiritual harvest as robust and vigorous as themselves.

The most important event connected with Bishop Lynch's visit to Rome on this occasion, was the erection of Toronto into an archdiocese and his elevation to the archbishopric of the new metropolitan See. On the 15th of March, 1879, His Lordship was appointed by the Holy See Archbishop of Toronto. On the 20th of March, His Grace appeared before the secret consistory of Cardinals to perform the ceremony of " postulating for the Pallium." He received the Pallium as Archbishop of Toronto on the 25th of March, in the Pope's private chapel, together with the Right Rev. Dr. McGettigen, who was at the same time made Primate of Ireland. The ceremony was performed by Cardinal Antonelli, the then Papal Secretary of State.

The elevation of the See of Toronto to the dignity of a metropolitan, was a very important epoch in the history of the Church in Ontario, and a matter of much importance to the city of Toronto itself. Although the city of Kingston is the oldest of the episcopal Sees in what was formerly known as Upper Canada—which now constitutes the province of Ontario—yet the central position of Toronto, the fact that it is the capital of Ontario, and the residence of the Lieutenant Governor ; its importance as a city, being in population and commercial enterprise second only to Montreal ; the further fact that it is also the seat of government and the headquarters of the legal profession, the residence of the judges and the home of the courts; the city being also the seat of the Provincial University, various denominational colleges, the Normal School, St. Michael's College, several Convents, and other important institutions; all these facts, combined with others, more important still to the interests and advancement of the Church in Western Canada, constituted very potent reasons for making Toronto the Metropolitan See of Ontario.   The wisdom of the selection has been amply justified by the result.   The Church in Toronto has grown far beyond the expectations of the most sanguine and hopeful of her members.   The increase of Catholics in Toronto in wealth and influence—not to say numbers—has kept pace with the growth and development of the city.   We have spoken in a former chapter of the strong anti-Catholic feeling that existed in the capital city of Ontario, even at so late a period as 1859, when Archbishop Lynch first came upon the scene of his episcopal labors.   We think we may with truth say that much of this feeling has disappeared; that the Protestant and non-Catholic citizens of Toronto have very little of that personal antipathy to Catholics—whatever may be their opinion of Catholicity as a system of religion —that was so common twenty-five or thirty years ago; and further, we are quite sure we do not misinterpret the sentiments of the vast and influential body of Protestants who constitute the majority of the citizens of Toronto, when we say that they feel proud of the fine Cathedral, numerous churches, schools, colleges, convents, and charitable institutions with which their Catholic fellow-citizens have adorned their beautiful city—a city which excites the wonder and admiration of our American cousins, fresh from the great cities of the United States, as well as of the European traveller, or the English sportsman, who expects to make it his headquarters while hunting buffalo in its immediate vicinity.

For several sessions of the Council, the Bishop of Toronto sat, of course, among the bishops, but immediately upon his elevation to the dignity of archbishop he took his place among the archbishops. A most interesting circumstance connected with this event took place on His Grace's taking his seat in the Council for the first time after his promotion. The duty of conducting him to the seat reserved for him among the archbishops was performed by his venerable and saintly predecessor in the See of Toronto, Bishop de Charbonnel, who was also present at the Council.

The archbishop suffered from ill health during the whole period of his attendance at the Council. The climate of the city was very trying to his constitution, and he was obliged during the greater part of the time to reside in Civita Vecchia, where he could enjoy the benefit of the refreshing sea breeze, and be at the same time within easy access of Rome. He regularly attended every session of the Council. This he could easily do, as Civita Vecchia is only about thirty miles from Rome, and is connected by rail with that city, so that he could come up, attend the sitting of the council, and return the same day. Archbishop Lynch was one of the few American bishops who addressed the Council. He and Archbishop Connolly, of Halifax, were the only prelates from British North America, who spoke on the question of Papal Infallibility. He was in favor of its formal definition by the Council, and thought that some-

thing should be said on the question by the representatives of the Church in Canada. He was anxious that the Bishop of Montreal, or His Grace of
Quebec, should address the Council, and put before
that august body the views and opinions of the
Canadian Church on this most momentous subject.
They, however, declared that it was well known
that the Canadian hierarchy were unanimously of
the opinion that it ought to be proclaimed a dogma
of the Church, and as none of the other bishops appeared willing to take upon themselves the labor of
putting their views before the Council, the Archbishop of Toronto undertook the responsibility of
speaking on the question on behalf of his Canadian
brethren. He was very ill at the time, but as the
debate was drawing to a close, he determined to make
an effort. On the morning of the day on which he
had the honor of addressing this the most distinguished and important assembly of modern times,
he arose early, said mass, and spent some time in
prayer, begging that God would give him strength
and so enlighten his mind that he might properly
and intelligently place his views on the great question before the assembled wisdom of the Church.
He addressed the Council on the same day on the
subject of Papal Infallibility, speaking in favor of the
proposed decree with certain amendments.

The Vatican Council did not finish its labors.
Soon after the promulgation of the decree defining
the belief of Catholic Christendom in the infallibility
of the Supreme Head of the Church, when speaking
ex-cathedra on matters of faith and morals, the war
between France and Germany broke out, which
ended in the total defeat of the French armies, the -
surrender of the French Emperor and his army at

Sedan, the siege and capture of Paris, the withdrawal of the French troops from Rome, and the occupation of the Holy City by the troops of Victor Emanuel. The Council was adjourned, and has never since been re-assembled. Who can tell when it shall complete its labors? Who can cast the political horoscope of Europe? Who could have imagined in 1869 that France, the dictator of Europe, would so soon be hurled from her lofty pedestal, crushed under the iron heel of the German invader, humbled to the dust, and made to drain to its dregs the bitter cup of defeat, disgrace and humiliation. Germany to-day occupies her place in the councils of Europe. Is her position in 1884 more assured than was that of France in 1869? Who may tell what is hidden in the cloud which now overshadows Europe? Is it the sunshine or is it the tempest?

CHAPTER XIV.

THE VATICAN COUNCIL.

SOON after his arrival home, after attending the Council, His Grace delivered the following lecture upon the Vatican Council in the Cathedral, before an immense audience, the greater part of whom were Protestants. It created much comment at the time, and will prove interesting even at the present day:

Truth has only one thing to fear—that is of not getting a hearing. It fears not discussion nor inspection nor length of time nor the calumnies of men. It is also said "let a lie get an hour's start, and truth will never overtake it." Let us this evening give truth a hearing and let it overtake some points of falsehood.

The Œcumenical Council of the Vatican commenced the year before last, on the 8th of December, 1869, and is only temporarily suspended. It has lost none of the interest attached to so solemn and sacred an assembly very rarely held in the church. It is yet the topic of many conversations, and many inquiries, as there is a widespread misapprehension of the Council. I hope this evening to lay before you a summary of the history of the Council, and of its internal workings. First, a word concerning a council. A council in its simplest expression is a meeting of the heads of families to consult upon matters referring to the welfare of the family or to arrange matters in dispute. A Council of State Parliament, as it is now called, is a convocation elected by the legitimate authority of the sovereign of members chosen by the people, or designated by the sovereign from various portions of the empire, to make laws for the public good, or to settle differences. A general Council of the Church is an assembly of the bishops of that church, convoked together by the supreme authority of the Sovereign Pontiff, their head and the successor of St. Peter, to consult together and to make decrees for the entire Church, concerning faith and morals. Such is the Council of the Vatican, or Church teaching, congregated together; as the bishops, in their various dioceses, are termed the Church teaching dispersed. There is a National Council composed of all the bishops of the nation, with a primate or an archbishop delegated by the Holy See to preside. There is a Provincial Council composed of the bishops of that province, with their archbishop at their head, whilst there is also a synod made up of the priests of the diocese, presided over by the bishop of that diocese. All these councils or synods can make laws and regulations for their respective provinces or dioceses only. A general council alone can make decrees binding on the universal Church.

The Œcumenical Council of the Vatican is only known to the world in general from reports of newspaper correspondents. These reports are generally very unreliable, many totally false, others containing a grain of truth in a bushel of falsehood, and cannot be relied upon. These reports generally came back to us in Rome, and amused and often surprised us, as each bishop received the leading newspaper of his city. A weekly Toronto journal kept me posted in the news of the day here and brought me news from Rome that I was entirely ignorant of. The secular newspapers, as a rule, were what we term in opposition. The Catholic journals had also their correspondents in Rome, who, though they knew nothing of what was passing in the bosom of the Council, yet published the external news and reports always favorable and just. We know what opposition papers say in reporting the doings and sayings of their opponents in political life—for instance, in reporting a meeting: "The meeting, if a meeting it may be called, was composed of a few men and ragged boys collected from the streets and paid to shout. Not a single individual of respectability dared to show himself in such a disreputable cause. The meeting was a failure in every sense, and the candidate has not the most remote chance of being elected." Hear another journal in favor: "The meeting was a grand success in every respect, in numbers, in respectability, and in enthusiasm. Our candidate is certain to be elected." Let us hear a criticism in the opposition journals on the speech from the Throne: "The speech put into the mouth of the representative of the Sovereign by his Ministry, was an old re-hash of generalities and meaningless sentences, couched in bad English, without point or statesmanship or policy. Such a Ministry cannot hold out half the session." But the ministerial organ says of the same speech: "The speech from the Throne was a rare specimen of statesmanship, comprehensive in its scheme for the public good, and must commend itself to all men of good sense and patriotism." Now let us read the journals in opposition to the Council of the Vatican: "A few old doting and decrepid men have assembled around the tottering throne of a feeble old man, whom they call the Holy Father. It is true they came from all parts of the world; but most of them to recruit their health, and to enjoy themselves. They are filled with the old hallucination that they are going to inaugurate the millennium."

Read a journal in favor: "Rome never saw in its greatest days of splendor so learned or so saintly a body of men collected together. They represent about fifty nationalities, and are the picked men from all quarters of the world, and derive their titles of Episcopacy from its most renowned cities. We have here the successor of St. Anslem, of England; St. Boniface, the Apostle of Germany; St. Patrick, of Ireland; St. Germain, of Paris; St. Gregory, of Tours; St. Isidore, of Seville; St. Lawrence Justinian, of Venice, and St. Chrysostom, of Constantinople. There are bishops of Capadocia, and of Pontus, and of Galatia, and of the Red River, and of Pekin, of New York, and of Algiers; bishops of San Francisco, and of the Sandwich Islands, of Chili, and of Calcutta, of Quebec, and of Mexico; bishops of Australia and of Scotland. Compare the Pan-Anglican Council with this imposing assembly of real bishops, representing the whole of the Christian world, and we will conceive you comparing the entire tree to the broken truncated limb.   Venerable missionaries have come from all quarters of the world; from the East bringing with them the old traditions of that portion of the Church.   The young and vigorous missionaries of the new world bringing with them their ideas of progress, allied with other eternal truths of the Gospel.   Their numbers and the variety of countries which they represent, surpass that of any other council which the Church has seen."   This, at least, announces the widespread diffusion of the Gospel throughout the entire world.   But the journals in opposition say: "Those old men have assembled to do the bidding of the Pope who overawes them.   They are manipulated by Cardinal Antonelli by presents and promises and hospitality.   This council will lose all its weight from the bishops not being free to propose decrees as they please."   A journal in favor says: "The bishops of the Vatican Council enjoy more liberty from within and have less pressure from without than any other council ever assembled.   That the discussions were free can be inferred from the fact that over 171 speeches were made in a few months, many of them lasting over an hour, and only three or four speakers were called to order by the President, who was to keep them to the subject, and not allow them to bring in extraneous matter.   There were no personalities ever indulged in, and all spoke with perfect freedom upon the subject in debate."   For my part, I must say that on hearing the strong criticisms and reflections made by some bishops in perfect freedom, I unconsciously exclaimed to myself, "It is a serious thing for the Pope to collect all the bishops of the world around him and give all perfect freedom to criticise even his administration and household."

To speak of the Council in order, we will treat of: 1st, its preparation, convocation and the members composing it; 2d, the place of the assembly; 3d, the order of the day and mode of procedure; 4th, cause of the Council, and, lastly, a word on the Papal Infallibility.

PREPARATIONS AND INVITATIONS.

Our Holy Father, the Pope, at the eighteen hundredth anniversary of the martyrdom of St. Peter, announced to the assembled bishops his intention of convoking an Œcumenical Council, and on the festival of St. Peter and St. Paul, 29th June, 1868, by apostolic letters, he commanded all the bishops in communion with the Holy See to assemble at the Vatican, to confer with him on the affairs of the Universal Church. We may remark that the apostolic letters were only sent to bishops in communion with the Holy See, as having the right, in virtue of their consecration and mission, to sit as judges in that venerable assembly. Our Holy Father, in his great charity, sent two other letters, not invitations, but rather exhortations. The one addressed to the schismatic bishops of the East to take advantage of the Council, to return to the unity of the fold of Christ. The other to non-Catholics, earnestly pressing them also to embrace the opportunity of the Council, to seek the truth of Jesus Christ, confided to the keeping of His Church, the pillar and ground of truth.

"Other sheep I have," says Christ, "which are not of this fold; these also I must bring that there may be one fold and one shepherd." Ambassadors and princes from the various Catholic countries assisted in the galleries. But no crowned head was invited to assist on the floor of the house, because all had abandoned the Protectorate of the Church, and were not required to promulgate its decrees. Preparatory congregations for this Council were held during a whole year in advance. These were composed of theologians taken from all parts of the world, both the old and new, who were to state the wants, the evils, the remedies, the·progress, and means of success affecting the Church in their own countries. About forty young men selected from the various colleges at Rome, the American, Irish, English, Scotch, German, Propaganda, Italian and French, were put under training as stenographers, to report the speeches in Latin of the Fathers—those young men were sworn to secrecy. A more talented and splendid set of young men I have not seen. I took particular pleasure in conversing with them from time to time, especially with those of the English-speaking colleges, who were, for the most part, either Irish or of Irish descent. Owing to the great facilities of communication, thanks to the telegraph and steam, prelates could assemble from the most distant parts of the world with greater facility and ease than the Bishops of France could to the Council of Trent.

The place of assembly was truly historic. Old Rome, or modern Rome, with its splendid Basilicas and palaces nestling amongst the mighty ruins of what was once the greatest city of the world; Rome that witnessed so many disasters and so many triumphs, so many nations crushed by her when Pagan, and so many people raised up and healed when she became the Christian metropolis of the world. The Vatican, as all know, was built over the tomb of SS. Peter and Paul. Nearly all the Roman Pontiffs have also their burying-place in the Catacombs there. They were situated in the heart of the early Christian quarters amongst the shanties, an unhealthy spot beyond the Tiber, not much inhabited by the wealthy Pagan Romans. Here, also, were Imperial gardens, where wild beasts for the shows were kept and fed ; where also the Christians were rolled in pitch and set on fire to illuminate the gardens, to glut the inhuman savage tastes of the Emperor and his household, and to pacify him, or pander to the prejudices of the vilest rabble, whose cry of " Christians to the beasts " was so often heard in the streets of Rome. This is the spot on which Christianity achieves her grandest triumphs.

An obelisk adorns the piazza of St. Peter, formerly brought from Egypt by Augustus and Tiberius, and placed here by the hands of Christians. It bears the inscription, " Christ conquers, Christ triumphs, Christ reigns." The Council was held in the right transept as you enter St. Peter's. It was screened off and arranged for a council-hall. It was about 220 feet by 100, somewhat larger than this Cathedral. The exterior length of St. Peter's is 727 feet by 500 feet in width. The hall at first was found too large for acoustic purposes, very strong voices alone being able to fill it. Its dimensions were afterwards reduced and other arrangements perfected, so that even weak voices could easily be heard. The hall was arranged in the form of an amphitheatre, as the Romans well know how to do. The seats arranged for the bishops were plain benches covered with carpet; ten sat on each bench, not on splendid arm-chairs covered with crimson. There were small leaves attached to each bench, which might be raised or lowered at pleasure, to serve as desks. The seats were anything but comfortable. The Pope's throne was opposite the tomb of St. Peter, or, as it is called, the " Confession of St. Peter." The Cardinals sat in a semicircle around the Papal throne; then came the patriarchs, primates, and archbishops on the higher benches of the amphitheatre; then the bishops, and lastly the generals of religious orders, who were not bishops, on the floor of the hall. At the public sessions the princes and nobles that waited on His Holiness the Pope, stood on the steps of the throne. There was a Master of Ceremonies to show the prelates to their places, which were numbered from 1 to 800; each prelate sat according to his rank as patriarch, archbishop or bishop, and in the order of his nomination to his See, not taking into account the antiquity of his See or his own personal worth. As bishop we took No. 593; being consecrated ten years, we held a place less than midway amongst the bishops. But as we were named archbishop during the Council, we then took the last place of that order. We had, consequently, on our left, the oldest bishop of the Council, a venerable prelate from Belgium, over forty years governing his See.

The day previous to the opening of the Council a preliminary meeting was held in the Hall of Constantine, as it is called, situated over the vestibule of St. Peter's, 233 feet long, where take place usually the washing of the feet by the Pope and banquet given to the pilgrims after the ceremonies of Holy Thursday. On entering the Council Hall for the first time, I was much astonished not to step upon the magnificent Brussels carpet, so much spoken of by special correspondents, presented by the

Emperor of Prussia, which was to serve as a reminder to the bishops, to respect the German Empire. The grand marble floor was covered with a plain green cloth, which reminded us of the covering of our dear mother earth. The Pope presided only at public sessions. He was represented at all the private sessions by five Cardinal Presidents, who called the name of the prelate whose turn it was to speak, and made such announcements as were necessary; in fact, they performed the office of chairman of a meeting. The prelate spoke in the centre of the hall from a pulpit whose sounding-board extended over half the hall. Hence there were no complaints of not hearing well. An altar was erected at the end of the hall opposite the Pope's throne, with candles burning as at mass, and on the centre of the altar, at a magnificent stand, lay an open Bible; all as they passed before made a reverence towards it. In the public sessions the prelates wore capes and white mitres; in the private sessions, which were held every day, they dressed in Rochet-Cape and Cross, as I am at present. The Greek prelates wore flowing robes with turbans and tiaras, some with veils—a more venerable, pious and imposing assembly could not be witnessed on this earth. The opposition papers represented the assembly as an arena of hot-headed and angry old men, quarrelling and disputing, each wearing a white dress with long white paper caps. Often did I look around the hall and admire this wonderful assembly, calling to mind the words of our Lord: "Where two or three are gathered in my name there I am in the midst of them." How must He be present in this august assembly of the successors of His apostles, collected in His name to forward the interests of His spouse the Church. This truly is the "Tabernacle of God, with men," the living, teaching Church of Christ. O, often thought I, in the loneliness and humility of my heart, is it possible, are you then here a bishop, in a general Council of the Church? And amongst such men? There is the Pope; here the Patriarchs of Jerusalem, of Constantinople, etc., etc.

The bishops, before entering the Council Chamber, prostrated themselves in silent prayer before the Most

Blessed Sacrament, and then before the tomb of the Apostles. The private sessions commenced at nine o'clock in the winter and eight in the summer season. Hence the bishops had to rise very early for prayer and meditation. Each prelate celebrated mass privately every morning; and, after a hasty cup of chocolate, proceeded to the Vatican. What a stir on the streets of Rome! The private session was opened by a low Mass of the Holy Ghost, celebrated by one of the Council in turn—cardinals, archbishops, and bishops. Mass was celebrated in Latin by the prelates of the Latin rite; in Greek, Syriac, Armenian, Chaldaic, and other Oriental languages by the prelates of the East. Here we had the unity and diversity of the Church combined; unity of faith and diversity of ritual. The Greek service appeared to us *cool Western* bishops so florid and reverential that I considered, on the other hand, that our simple Latin worship should appear to our Oriental brethren almost irreverential in comparison with theirs. We worshipped with heads uncovered, they with their mitre and crown on, but with bared feet. The main portion of the mass, in every rite, was the same. Portions of the Sacred Scripture, the epistles and gospels were read. The offering of the bread and wine, the consecration, the breaking of the form of bread and wine, the communion and invocation of the Blessed Virgin, St. Peter and St. Paul, and the saints were common to all. I had also the great happiness of celebrating mass, attended by our Vicar-General, Very Rev. Father Jamot, an event which carries with it the most sacred and pleasing recollections, and that same day I had the privilege of addressing the venerable assembly on the great subject of infallibility as the teaching of the Roman Pontiff, and to bear our testimony in its belief to this portion of the Church of God. The session lasted from four to five hours. Crowds assembled in and around the Vatican to see the prelates enter and leave the Council. I remarked that the English, American, and French bishops had many friends to recognize in the vast crowd that lined the avenue open to the bishops.

The Council was opened 8th December, 1869, by august

ceremonies. Mass of the Holy Ghost was sung, and all the cardinals, archbishops and bishops and fathers of the Council during the singing of the *Kyrie Elieson* approached the Papal throne in procession and kissed the Pope's hand, covered with his stole, as a sign of reverence and submission to the head of the Church. This ceremony lasted over an hour. The first days of the Council were employed in electing, by a free vote of the fathers, four deputations or committees: one on matters concerning Faith, one on Church Discipline, one on matters relating to Religious Orders, and the fourth concerning the Foreign Missions and the Oriental Church. These committees or deputations were charged with introducing the various dogmas proposed and of changing the words or sentences, and even the punctuation, according to the desire of the Council, and of explaining why some changes were not made, or defending the law or dogma proposed or amended. There was also a committee of cardinals and prelates from all parts of the world deputed, on the part of the Pope, to examine all projects of laws or dogmas proposed by any of the Fathers of the Council. Never was there a parliament assembled on this earth for which so much preparation was made, or whose internal management was conducted with so much talent, order, liberty, prudence and means of discussing, and finding out the whole truth. Each bishop received a manual containing prayers and ceremonies of the Council. They received also a scheme or project of decrees about to be presented for the deliberation of the Council, which was printed in large pamphlet form, on one-half of the sheet only, leaving the other blank to receive written notes and comments of the Fathers of the Council, supporting those comments by Scripture, tradition and testimony of the Fathers. Each prelate was at liberty to send those notes to the Secretary of the Council, to be handed to the deputation having charge of the matter. Each prelate, as he wished to speak on these projects, wrote his name on a book kept on the president's table. Each spoke in the order of his inscription — cardinals taking precedence, then patriarchs, archbishops, bishops and generals of religious orders. As the turn of each came his name was called out by one of the presidents. He ascended the pulpit in the centre of the hall, carrying with him his notes, and either read them or delivered his speech from memory. All spoke Latin, and we must say with considerable fluency, some with overpowering eloquence and rapidity, as though speaking in their mother tongue. But to believe the opposition papers, the Fathers spoke Latin with such a diversity of accent that none understood his neighbor. This, too, is a stretch of imagination. There was a diversity of accent, but the words were distinctly pronounced, and I for one understood the Spaniards as well as I did the Italians, and the French as well as I did the English. Even the Greek bishops were distinctly understood, many of whom were formerly students of the Propaganda College in Rome. They read their speeches, very carefully composed, but in a singing tone, according to the usages of their country, just as we hear sometimes school boys reading their early lessons. Their tone was pleasing, and relieved the monotony of the subdued European intonation. The utmost order reigned in their discussions, as should be expected from old men and bishops dressed in canonicals. Only on one occasion did I see anything approaching what might be termed, in parliamentary language, confusion or murmur. Though, to believe the opposition papers, "The Fathers nearly came to blows; their robes were torn in tatters, and the most disgraceful scenes took place." Special correspondents had no place in the Council. They reported the speeches and scenes according to the tastes of their readers, from their own imagination; the murmurs of many voices did ascend through the hall and up the dome of St. Peter's, as the Fathers addressed a few words in a low voice to his neighboring prelates after each speech, as a few moments' rest was given. The Fathers sometimes quitted their seats to take a little walk in the adjoining halls; the stenographers also changed, but such movements could not be called unseemly or ridiculous disorder. All may recollect the sensation caused by a special correspondent's telegraph that Mgr. Dupanloup, Bishop of Orleans, was assaulted in the Council, and fled from it in a rage, escaped with his life, his vestments all torn, etc., etc., hurried to his carriage and drove off to his villa. Let us pick out a grain of truth from this bushel of falsehood. Monsignor Dupanloup made a magnificent speech, in impassionate and vehement eloquence. It was a hot day in June, and in a Roman climate. He spoke for nearly an hour, and appeared to perspire profusely. Retiring from the pulpit, his rochet caught in the door and tore a little; he was surrounded by his friends, who congratulated him. There was considerable under-tone speaking amongst the Fathers for a few minutes before the next speaker was called upon, as it often happened. The bishop then quickly left the hall, sought his carriage and returned home to change his saturated garments. As all his movements were closely watched, the special correspondent had a splendid opportunity of manufacturing a sensation, and telegraphed to the world the undignified conduct, the scenes of confusion, the rude strifes, and worse than American Congress scenes amongst the Fathers; but I believe they were not charged with carrying revolvers.

When the discussion on the schema was exhausted, all the Fathers who wished to speak having done so, the committee of twenty-four bishops, chosen by the Council, having the project of the laws or decrees in charge, consulted together, read over the various charges or modifications proposed by the several Fathers, classified, then and there formed the project of decree according to the modifications and amendments proposed by the Fathers. This amended project or schema was printed and handed to the Fathers for further consideration and comment. Then one or two Fathers of the committee were appointed to ascend the pulpit and explain to the Fathers what modifications they introduced, what rejected, and the reasons that caused them. Then all were invited again to discuss the second amended project, and to hand in, in writing, any further amendments they wished to propose. A synopsis of these amendments, and reasons for them, were printed and distributed to the Fathers, and the decree was brought in again for the third time in its amended form. The decree on the Papal Infallibility was modified and amended five times before the final vote. A vote was then taken before its final passage—in three ways was the vote permitted to be given. *Placet, vel non placet, vel placet juxta modum*, which means it is pleasing, or it is not pleasing, or it is pleasing with some change or modification. Those prelates who voted "*placet*" *juxta modum* were requested to send in the changes which they wished to have made. These changes were again printed and handed to the Fathers. The deputation on the law again make the desired changes, or give reasons for not changing, and the decree is put to the final vote, which must be either *Placet* or *non placet*. As no decree of a General Council has ever been or can be repealed or amended, the utmost care must be taken to have it as perfect as human genius, aided by the spirit of God promised to abide always with His Church, can make it. What a contrast is this solemn deliberation, careful consideration, earnest prayer to the Holy Spirit of God for the composition of those decrees, with the mode of passing laws in secular parliaments. How few laws which have passed secular parliaments have not appended to them many amendments.

I defy any Parliament or Congress of this world to produce a fairer or maturer mode of deliberation, or a more exhaustive mode of discussing the various proposals of its members, or of finally voting upon laws. No personalities were ever indulged in—no appeal to passion or partisanship. It is true we heard appeals as to how the world and its governments would like such and such things; but then the answer to these observations was: "We come not to discuss how the world will like these things, but what is God's truth, and what remedies an invalid world requires for its cure. Laws are to be made for the good of all, in the light of the Sanctuary and the Holy Scriptures, and the traditions of the Church." No Father ever complained that decrees were passed hastily in the Vatican Council without due consideration, or ample and free discussion. The secular papers did raise the cry of want of liberty of the Fathers, but this false assertion never found a seconder, though silly people believed it. A great many Fathers who gave notice of their wish to speak, renounced their right when they saw the subject was thoroughly discussed and exhausted, as happened at the discussion of the project of the Decree on Papal Infallibility.

CHAPTER XV.

THE VATICAN COUNCIL—(*Continued.*)

WE may be asked what were the special reasons for convoking the Council. There are two kinds of reasons—reasons of necessity, and reasons of utility. The first reason did not exist, the Church being founded upon a rock against which the gates of hell cannot prevail. The Church can exist without a General Council. It has its peculiar constitution and government directly formed by our Lord Jesus Christ himself, who upholds, directs and governs, with His divine spirit, His own Church. The Faith which He has planted within it will last to the end of time. The craft and wickedness of men cannot change that faith. Being a divine emanation, it partakes of the attributes of God. Heresies will spring up, "*Oportet esse hereses,*" says St. Paul. They are the weeds and tares that grow up in the garden of the Lord, but they cannot choke up the good wheat. The first Council held by the Apostles at Jerusalem was not necessary for the extinction of the first formal dispute that arose amongst the first Christians after all about discipline, for the Apostles themselves were infallible; but the Council of Jerusalem was of great utility, and so were the Councils of the Church, and so the Council of the Vatican. For 300 years the Church preached the Gospel, and established itself through the entire world, even beyond the Roman Conquests. It suppressed heresies in all ages without the aid of a Council; in the first age, Corinthians and Ebonites; in the second age, Gnostics and the Marcionites; in the third, Sabellians and the Novatians and Manichians. Yes, even before the books of the New Testament were composed and distributed, the faith was established everywhere by the preaching of the Apostles. The canonicity of the Sacred Scripture, that is, what was the inspired word of God, which point was not, before the Council of Trent, decided by an Œcumenical Council. The particular Councils of Hippo and Carthage, in 393 and 397 respectively, settled the canonicity of Sacred Scripture, and finally in 494, in Rome, by seventy-four bishops presided over by Pope Gelasius, and recognized by the Church and confirmed by the Council of Trent. General Councils are most useful for instituting general laws of discipline, suppressing heresies and applying remedies to the internal evils of the Church members, and providing for the further spread of the Gospel. For these purposes the Council of the Vatican was convened. It is over three hundred years since the last Council was held at Trent, and since that time the Church has passed through an ordeal of persecutions and combats like to those she endured in the first ages of Christianity; laws the most oppressive and penal were enacted against her authority. Her bishops and clergy were put to death for maintaining the Faith of Christ. Cathedrals, churches, colleges, convents and monasteries were either diverted from their use or destroyed, and a general persecution swept over many countries of Europe, forcing the laity either to abjure their faith, and renounce all spiritual allegiance to the Successor of Peter, or to lose the right of citizenship, their lands and their estates, and even the education of their own children, and everything they held most dear.

The princes of this world arrayed themselves against Christ and His Church and pretended to govern her as they would a conquered enemy, or a department of police force; as though Christ had said to kings "Feed my lambs, feed my sheep," and not to the humble fisherman. They elected bishops, their own mere tools or creatures, rather as state officials than as the divinely appointed shepherds of the flock of Christ.

Our Holy Father took a view of the Church in old Asia, in Europe, in Africa, and in the New World of America and Australia; and what met the eyes of that vigilant and loving pastor? Society in general sick at heart, a general upheaving of the lower strata of society against the higher; and by these higher strata of society—I mean the rich and powerful, the kings and emperors, the politicians and the worldly wise—waging war against the sovereign authority of God, against His divine and sacred laws, and against His spouse the Church, subjecting the higher order of things, the spiritual, to the lower order or temporal interests. To attain this end they assumed the education of youth, to mould according to the ideas of this world the tender minds of children, made to the image and likeness of God, whose whole lives should be a preparation for eternity, worldly fitting them only for sordid gain and giving them no education to fit them to overcome the devil, the world and the flesh. Endeavoring also to break the key-stone of that mighty arch of humanity—the sacredness of the marriage tie. In fine, they wished to banish God and His laws and His blessed name from the earth.

This state of things produced the first stage of a mortal malady—indifference towards all religion, and a loathing to all restraints placed upon unruly passions. The second state of the malady has already appeared in the communistic doctrine which may be read in the lurid glare of burning palaces and the institutions of charity in Paris, and in the petroleum jets of their private dwellings. On the one side there appeared to be a mighty conspiracy to grind down the poor to that state in which life was merely tolerable, extracting from their bones and sinews the greatest amount of work to support the luxuries of the rich; on the other side the poor—the immense majority of the human family—sufficiently educated to know their degradation, and the injustice practiced on them, and not sufficiently educated, either politically or religiously, to bow with submission to the all-wise decrees of Providence, that has ordained that there should be rich and poor, and to submit to His adorable decrees in view of a more glorious and happier life reserved for them in heaven, and that there is a way of asserting their rights and obtaining them by fair and honorable and peaceful means, and not by revolution, in which upheaving of society, the poor generally suffer most. The religious condition of Europe called for serious attention on the part of the Church.

But European civilization cried loudest for redress because nearest to the centre of unity. The solid German mind was sinking back into materialism and low rationalism. French philosophy invented the subtle poison of Pantheism, that is, investing everything, even the meanest object, with portions of the divinity. This was spreading throughout high societies of so-called literary men, and a general spirit and determination obtained amongst kings and law-givers to throw from their own shoulders and the shoulders of the people, the yoke of the Gospel, declaring that the higher order of spiritual things or the Government of God, was subject in all things to the state laws, thus subjecting the spiritual to the temporal, and renouncing the kingdom of Christ, placing the material above the spiritual, subverting all order, subjecting the key-stone of society—marriage, a divine institution—to the caprice and anomalies of human law, to the state control, that wished to banish it; thus falling back again into Paganism. Though there was a little returning from that of late, when the French Assembly, with the most daring courage, acknowledged that God existed. The Russian Empire, composed principally of semi-barbarian tribes, with a large population of Polish Catholics crushed under penal laws, that disgraced the reign of Henry VIII. of England, presents to the eye of civilization a sad spectacle of despotism that hides its deformity within its own horrid boundary. The rest of the world is precluded from hearing the groans of suffering, the newspapers are not allowed to publish any deed of barbarity, and none but official papers are permitted to cross the frontiers. The Catholic Church is entirely banished from Norway and Sweden, under severe penalties, as was the case in England in days gone by. In Germany the Church endures its greatest struggles; the governments are generally hostile, and owing to the want of purely ecclesiastical seminaries, the religious education of the priests is sadly in default. We cannot educate a pious and learned priesthood amidst the turmoil and vice of large cities, and secular universities. Students of law, medicine and arts, when in large numbers, are not considered safe companions for ecclesiastics preparing for the most pure and holy altar. Hence the Church had to deplore, in those countries, a great deal of laxity and indifferentism or materialism. The governments of Spain, Italy and Austria set themselves to undermine the fabric of the Church, and divorce themselves from the salutary laws and discipline of the Gospel; the large majority of those countries are profoundly Catholic at heart. The Church of France offers at once a sad and a glorious spectacle: sad in the immorality and antagonism of the working classes of the cities and in the spirit of revolt against God and the laws of their country; glorious in the untiring zeal of their clergy, both pious and learned, in the number of religious orders who manifest a great and untiring spirit of devotedness for the salvation of souls, especially in foreign countries, though we have still to deplore a dark spot of what is termed "Gallicanism," which we shall explain further on.

England also presented a sad and glorious spectacle to the eyes of the Holy Father; sad in the immorality and degradation of the lower orders; glorious in the mighty efforts put forth by the most earnest Englishmen to throw off the prejudices of the past and return with that energy characteristic of the nation, to the old faith of their ancestors. And as the defection from the faith commences with the kings and nobles, so also is the return to it. It has been well said that if the Catholics of England were banished upon the shores of some vast foreign lands, a fully equipped society could be formed from the royal blood, nobles, commons, generals of armies, statesmen, admirals, and all the other branches of industry, and make a mighty Catholic nation, and this principally from conversions to the true faith within the last thirty years. This was effected by laborious religious inquiry and heroic renunciation of family ties, and honors and emoluments. A hundred priests stood round the altar at the consecration of Archbishop Manning, himself a convert, formerly archdeacon. These priests enjoyed benefices and honors in the established Church. Many converts, in the fervor of their zeal to return thanks to God for their happy conversion, emulated the noble generosity of their Anglo-Saxon progenitors and founded churches, monasteries, convent-schools and hospitals.

I am happy to say that the bishops governing English-speaking dioceses represented at the Council the largest portion of the present known world, and also from the most distant countries; and to the glory of the Irish nation may it be recorded, that the Irish people and their descendants formed by far the largest portion of the dioceses of English-speaking bishops, and supplied the means of travel for those bishops, together with large donations for the Holy Father.

England was always an object of particular solicitude to the Holy See, on account of the sterling character, great generosity, and talents of its people. More money has been spent, and Bibles and tracts distributed at home and abroad by that propagandist people, than would have made the world Protestant if our Lord had decreed that it should be converted by spreading the Bible misinterpreted. The earnest English conscience is not content with the church whose governing head is its privy council, composed of men who do not believe in her dogmas, or a church deprived of sacraments and sacrifice. And the English Church, though maintained by all the power and patronage of the state, is to-day in the minority, even in England, and the proscribed faith of the Catholic Church regains all its ascendancy. England was converted by the free preaching of missionaries from Rome. The Pagan, Ethelbert, gave liberty of conscience to his subjects, and to the missionaries Augustin and his forty companions. "We shall not hinder you," said the king, " from preaching your religion, and you shall convert whom you can." England, a thousand of years afterwards, was robbed of this liberty of conscience, by another, King Henry VIII., of unhappy memory, who employed the torture and the stake, the blazing fire and the scaffold. Augustin and his companions, at Christmas tide, in the year 597, converted 10,000 of the Anglo-Saxons and administered to them the sacrament of baptism in the Thames, at the mouth of the Medway, opposite the Isle of Sheppey, where now the navy of the mightiest empire of the world rides at anchor. England of the nineteenth century is being reconverted from that internal Paganism and worship of Mammon and animal passions by the free preaching of missionaries, also holding their power and missions from the centre of Unity, and their gradual conquests will soon equal those of the first missionaries. England and her colonies were to be benefited by the wise decrees of a Council. England had its morning star and its setting sun, but another day of splendor is dawning and the nursery rhymes of children are changed into canticles of Mother Church. If England continues her present race towards Roman Unity, in less than half a century she will again be one of the finest pearls in the diadem of the Church. If the defection from the Faith in Europe caused whole nations to desert the old ark of the Church and to drift about in frail vessels, tossed to and fro by every wind of doctrine, whole nations in the new and old worlds were regained to make up its losses. The Church has regained in the East, by the preaching of St. Francis Xavier and other holy missionaries, a part of her losses in Europe, and in the New World is doubling her gains. The Church in North America alone, from the coast of Labrador across to Manitoba, down to the Gulf of Mexico, if it continue the strides made in the last eighty years, will be the Christendom of the New World. One-fifth of the population Catholic, and always increasing from one in two hundred eighty years ago, to one in five at present. The Council was to consider the means of seconding this mighty increase in her numbers, especially in forming or remodeling laws of discipline to meet the new wants of the Church put into a new position with the world, deprived as she was of large revenues and benefices bequeathed to her by the piety of a thousand years in Europe.

In America the Catholic Church outnumbers all the sects put together. The Church in the East had its wants. China for 300 years was slowly but steadily receiving the gift of Faith cemented in the blood of her martyred bishops, priests and nuns. Tartary, too, had its bishops; all the Chinese Empire was divided into dioceses, with their bishops, priests, seminaries and convents. The British Empire was likewise partitioned. The Church in Africa, slowly rising from a long night of slumber, induced by the persecution of Mahomet, had no peculiar wants except that of missionaries. Ireland was the land of missions, as fervent to-day as in the days of Columbanus. The Church in Mexico had its deep sorrows which sixty years of revolution had occasioned. The States of South America were afflicted with the wound of Cæsarism; whilst France, too, was suffering from a deep sore, which was spreading into Germany and other countries, that cried for a physician—it was termed Gallicanism. It floated in the air in some undefined shape during the deplorable schism of the west, as it was called, when the Church beheld the scandal of three claimants to the Pontifical throne. It took some shape after the Council of Constance, and finally was promulgated by Jansenists, courtiers of Louis XIV. of France, in 1682. The Jansenists were condemned by two Pontifical constitutions, but they maintained their errors, saying that the Pope's condemnation had no effect, and they were not obliged to submit to it, inasmuch as the Pope himself, as head of the Church and universal doctor, was liable to error, and that a general Council alone could condemn them. This declaration astonished and scandalized the whole Church. Certain bishops of France yielded to the courtly pressure and maintained also the doctrine, but the vast majority of the teaching body of French theologians stood firm and maintained the old doctrine of the Church, that the teaching, *ex cathedra*, of the Pope is infallible, and, consequently, his teaching cannot be appealed from and must be believed. If the Jansenist doctrine were true concerning the teaching of the Roman Pontiff, *ex cathedra*, then to govern the Church and suppress heresies, a general Council should be permanently sitting, for if not, heresy might spring up in the Church and go on increasing from year to year, and ruin the Faith in many places, till an

Œcumenical Council should be assembled, a thing not at all times convenient, nay, oftentimes impossible. Hence, if there were no infallible tribunal in the Church to pronounce on the teaching of the inferior ministry of the Church, errors could not have been suppressed, for the first three hundred years of the Church's existence, when the bishops of the Church, had they met together, would have been all strangled by the Pagan emperor, and the Church would have been crushed out from the world.

This infallible teaching of the Pope, *ex cathedra*, being badly understood and much misrepresented, I must explain.

PAPAL INFALLIBILITY.

I beg your serious attention to this, and would beg you to divest your minds of your former notions of it and take in my explanations as true; I need not fear, in so enlightened an audience, to paint truth in its real colors. There is a difficulty, I know, to make truth look like truth, but it is in consequence of men's minds being clouded with error, and not because truth is not grand and beautiful.

The secular newspaper correspondents have published that Papal Infallibility means that the Pope is like unto God, Supreme, not subject to any error, and can make truth falsehood, and falsehood truth. I need hardly say that this definition is utterly false. Another journal says that Papal Infallibility means that the Pope is impeccable —cannot err—and that all his sayings and doings are infallible; that also is false. He is subject to human weaknesses, and confesses them, like every good child of the Church, and receives absolution and penance. Another writer says that the Pope can prophesy and invent a new religion as he pleases—well, that also is false. He receives no gift of prophesy by his election to the Popedom and can invent no new dogma or religion; he can only pronounce that such and such truth has been always in the Church, and has been revealed to the Church by the Holy Ghost on the day of Pentecost, according to the words of Christ, " I will send you another Paraclete who will teach you ALL truth—not truth, but ALL truth. The

Pope can make no new revelation. We need not further notice the false impressions created in the world by the erroneous idea set forth of Papal Infallibility. It means that when the Pope, acting as successor of St. Peter and head of the Church, and as such, united to all the bishops of the Church, as the head is united to the body, and in the capacity of universal teacher of the Church, after having taken all human means of knowing the truth which he judges expedient, pronounces that such doctrine is true and is found in the *depositum fidei* of the Church, and that such a doctrine is false and not contained in the deposit of the Faith. The Pope then pronounces the decision true and irreformable. I have said, as head of the Church, and not as a private individual or theologian; I have said also, as universal teacher of the whole Church, and on matters relating to doctrine and morals that affect the whole Church, and not an individual case in the Church. When the Pope has to decide *ex cathedra* on any doctrine, new and in dispute in the schools of theology, what does he do? He imitates the good husbandman who wishes to have a plentiful harvest, who prepares well his fields; he plants, he waters, and uses all human industry to help Providence, for such is the will of Providence, who does not produce fruit without seed. The Holy Father, when about to pronounce a dogma *ex cathedra*, assembles his cardinals as a congregation of theologians; they discuss the subject, in the light of the traditions of the Church, which existed before the books of the New Testament were written, and then of the Sacred Scriptures and of the piety of the Fathers and theologians, not throwing overboard reason either. Then after months, oftentimes years, of research and prayer and consideration, the Pope hears the reports of his councillors or theologians, and after mature consideration and prayer, pronounces that such and such doctrine is true, or such is false, as the case may be; then he communicates that decision to the Church, and finally the dispute is ended. Peter has spoken by the mouth of his successor. In this nothing has been added to the Faith. What proof have we from Sacred Scripture or tradition for this?—we have many. I will only mention one text, as I reserve this very important subject for another lecture for further development, as also to give a history of the discussion of this subject in the Council and the opposition to it. Christ said to Peter: "Peter, Peter, behold, Satan hath desired to sift you, as wheat; but I have prayed for thee, that thy faith fail thee not. And thou, when thou art converted, confirm thy brethren."

Infallibility is no new idea in the world, and especially in the Protestant churches, where personal infallibility is one of the primary articles of their faith. The Catholic Church holds the head of the Church infallible only in his official capacity and when speaking *ex cathedra*, after taking all precautions to find out the truth in the depository of the Church, but he can create no new truth, nor any new dogma. But in the Protestant churches every member is infallible, and his own private judgment is his infallible rule of judging even in the most subtle and abstruse doctrines of their church, although the Scripture says, 2 Pet. iii., 16: "There are certain things (speaking of the Epistle of St. Paul) hard to be understood, which the unlearned and unstable wrest (as also the rest of the Scriptures) to their own destruction." Again, 2 Pet. i., 20: "Understanding this first, that no prophecy of Scripture is made by private interpretation." Without an infallible guide, would Christ have said, "He that hears you hears me, he that despiseth you despiseth me. He that will not hear the Church let him be to thee as the heathen and the publican." It was the prerogative of the high priest in the Jewish dispensation to be clothed with infallibility, from whose decision there was no appeal. Deut. xvi., 9.

The Council has not been concluded, it has only been temporarily suspended, as many other Councils have been in past times. Meanwhile the authority enjoyed by the Pope and universally recognized in all ages in suppressing heresies, is sustained by a decree of an Œcumenical Council of the Infallible Church. The decrees issued by the Council in the public session have been received in the Universal Church, with extraordinary unanimity, by all the bishops of the Church. Those few bishops who opposed the doctrine of infallibility till the very day before its final promulgation, have all humbly bowed their heads to the decision of the majority, and on arriving in their various dioceses have promulgated that doctrine.   One of the most learned and pious of that number, the illustrious Archbishop of St. Louis, with that submission that does him honor, in thanking his clergy and people, said: "We accept all the dogmas of the Council, the decree of the Papal Infallibility alike."

We say to the Church, Our Mother, as St. Peter says to Christ, "To whom shall we go, thou hast the words of eternal life."   We are glad to see that Père Grattry, a very distinguished writer, has lately given in his adhesion to the Archbishop of Paris.   Dr. Dollinger may yet follow his example.   There are a few lay professors and some unworthy priests that we almost despair of—but the clearest water has its sediment.   Père Hyacinthe has exhibited other erratic symptoms than pride, yet we don't despair of his conversion; he was once a pious religious.   The Council has only commenced its labors, and from the index of the projected laws, which we have received, the Council has revised all the theologies of the private doctors of the Church concerning Faith and morals; has also formed a complete code of canon laws, especially those relating to letters of ordination, the improvement of the laws relating to civil and mixed marriages, abstinence and fasting.   The Council will also revise the rules of the religious orders and their peculiar discipline; the election of bishops and the government of the diocese—the See being vacant—and ecclesiastical tribunals.   We were frequently asked if the Council would make any new decree concerning the celibacy of the clergy, either of the Greek or Latin rite.   Up to the present there is no question of it, for the bishops and priests of the Latin rite. But we will take a future occasion to speak of this subject.

CHAPTER XVI.

EDUCATIONAL INSTITUTIONS.

Educational Institutions of the Archdiocese—St. Michael's College—Order of St. Basil—First Educational Establishment in Toronto—Building of St. Michael's—Success of the College—The De La Salle Institute—The Founding of the Order of Christian Brothers—Its Object—Their Success as Teachers—Are Employed in the Separate Schools—The Reasons for their Success—Why they are Preferable to Lay Teachers—Their Reputation in the Province as Teachers—Their Issue of the "Language Series" of School Books.

THE diocese of Toronto has reason to feel proud of the many educational and charitable institutions it contains—institutions built and supported by the liberality and generosity of the Catholic people, a people who are not blessed with such an abundance of this world's goods as their more fortunate Protestant neighbors. The amount of money represented by the many schools, colleges, convents, and charitable institutions in the archdiocese of Toronto is indeed something wonderful, especially when we consider that up to a comparatively recent period the wealth of the Catholic body, taken in its entirety, would fall far below that of any other religious body of the community.

The first and most important among the educational institutions in the diocese of Toronto is St. Michael's College, conducted by the Basilian Fathers. The Basilian Order was founded in the year 1800, by Archbishop Davian, of Vienne, in France, who intended that the Order should devote itself to the task of carrying on preparatory colleges and semi-

naries for the education of young men for the priesthood. As will be seen, therefore, the Order is a
comparatively recent one, and its objects somewhat
new in the annals of religious institutions, but as
noble as it is new. Its first house was established
in the parish of St. Basil, among the mountains of
the Vivarais, and from the parish the Order took its
name. For a number of years it was a free association
until Mgr. Guibert, then Bishop of Viviers, with
the help of the superiors of the Order, devised a new
constitution, which was approved by the Holy See.
The members take the four solemn vows of poverty,
chastity, obedience, and humility. The mother house
of the Basilians is situated at Annonay, France, and
they have houses in France, England, and Africa,
besides those in Canada.

The few fathers who first formed the nucleus of
the present flourishing college of St. Michael's were
brought to Toronto from France by the great and
good Bishop de Charbonnel, shortly after that saintly
prelate was appointed to the See of Toronto. The
holy man saw, at once, upon entering into possession of his See, that great difficulty would be experienced in educating such young men as were
intended for the priesthood, and of giving a thoroughly sound Catholic education to such other
young Catholic men as desired to take a collegiate
course. The beginnings of the college were
very humble, and very unpretentious. A small
building was procured on Yonge Street, for the
accommodation of the new arrivals, and at once
these zealous and energetic men commenced their
labors. That such an institution was very greatly
needed in the diocese even at that early day was at
once demonstrated by the number of students, who at

its first opening appeared in the modest study-halls to begin their college life. It was quite evident that the place was too small, and that larger accommodations would have to be procured at an early day. It was determined, therefore, to begin the building of a college on a large scale without any delay. That generous, noble-hearted man who had already done so much for the Church in Toronto, the Hon. John Elmsly, donated to the good fathers of the Order a few acres of land in the northern part of the city, on which the erection of the present handsome structure, with church attached, was at once begun, and rapidly pushed to completion. St. Michael's College and St. Basil's Church (the college chapel) are among the architectural ornaments of Toronto. The situation is one of the most beautiful in the city. The place was, in the old days of Toronto, known as " Clover Hill," and the college and church stand upon a gentle eminence commanding a view of Toronto Bay, Lake Ontario, and the surrounding country.

Within the past few years the church has been greatly enlarged, and is now the parochial church of St. Basil's parish, which has been formed in that part of the city since the building of the college. Students attend St. Michael's from all parts of Canada and the United States; and from the day the college opened in the new building until the present, the record of the institution has been one of unqualified success. The teaching staff of St. Michael's College will compare favorably with that of any other college in the Dominion. It is composed of men of varied learning and ripe scholarship, and the students of St. Michael's, whenever they have chosen to compete for any of the honors or scholarships awarded by the university, have always come off with brilliant success. A few years ago the college became affiliated to the Provincial University, and thus the students of St. Michael's are enabled to take their degree from the chief university of the province. This is a very important matter, especially for those young men who intend to study for the legal profession, as the holding of a degree shortens the period of their legal studies two years. Besides this, a degree from Toronto University has many other compensating privileges. The college being located near the university, the students of the former are enabled to avail themselves of the advantages—very great in themselves—of attending the scientific lectures in the latter institution. The affiliation of St. Michael's to the university—a Catholic college to a State university—is due to that tolerant spirit which His Grace, the present Archbishop, has done so much to foster between the different sections of the Canadian people, as well as to the mutual forbearance and earnest desire for the educational progress of the country, exhibited by the respective authorities of the two institutions in settling upon the basis of the affiliation.

Another collegiate institution is De La Salle Institute, conducted by the Brothers of the Christian Schools—an Order, which has become renowned for its teaching and conduct of the educational establishments of the Church in many countries. The following sketch of this most important Congregation is taken, with some corrections, from that excellent work, the *Catholic Dictionary*:—

The proper title is "Brothers of the Christian Schools." This admirable institution was founded by the Venerable

Abbé De La Salle, the process of whose canonization was begun at Rome some years ago. Born on the 30th of April, 1651, at Reims, where his father was a distinguished advocate and king's counsel, Jean Baptiste devoted his remarkable powers of mind and will at an early age to the divine service, and, having been ordained, was nominated Canon of Reims. Schools, called "little schools," to promote the education of the poor, had begun to be organized in the thirteenth century, after the legal establishment of the University of Paris was checked by the Hundred Years' War, which raged in France at short intervals from the middle of the fourteenth to the middle of the fifteenth century. In 1570 a society of teachers was established under the title of the Writing-Masters (*maîtres écrivains*) of Paris, whence it spread to other cities. Their aim was to teach writing and arithmetic and a little Latin, so that their pupils might be qualified to assist the clergy in the Church offices. They received many privileges, which they construed into a monopoly of teaching. About the year 1680 many good and earnest persons, both among the clergy and laity, were engaged in promoting the Christian education of the people. Prominent among these was a M. Nyel, of Rouen, who selected teachers and trained them, and then sent them to the cities or great seigneuries which offered to provide buildings and salaries. The Abbé de la Salle, who was an intimate friend of M. Nyel, had his attention thus drawn to the subject, the importance of which soon engrossed his thoughts. In his capacious mind the spirit of system was united to a sound common sense, quick perception of character, and the tenderest charity. He took charge of several of M. Nyel's teachers, and engaged others; but finding that many of these young men were anxious about their future, and dreaded to embark in a calling which the death of their leader might deprive of stability and social favor, he resolved to renounce his Church preferment, and also his private fortune, that he might be able to say to them that he, even as they, had no help or trust save in God. He accordingly resigned his canonry and distributed his patrimony to the poor. This was in 1684; in the same year he drew up the first rules for his teachers, and selected the name which they should bear; the origin of the brotherhood, therefore, dates from this time. The teaching in all his schools was to be gratuitous for the day scholars, but boarders and day-boarders were to be received. The Venerable Founder himself often taught in his schools, and, with his fine eye for organization, reformed the instructions in many large schools (*e. g.* in that connected with St. Sulpice, at Paris), the inefficiency of which had baffled the efforts of their managers. De La' Salle insisted that Latin should be no longer an obligatory subject in the schools for the children of the poor, but that the basis of their teaching, after the catechism, should be their own language; let them first learn to read and write French correctly, and then, if they had time and means, they might take up Latin. On this account the Venerable De La Salle is often regarded—and it would seem with justice—as the founder of primary schools and primary instruction, which, till his time, had been confounded with secondary. It is true that St. Joseph Calasanctius had founded at Rome, long before (1597), his admirable institution of the *Scuole Pie* or Pious Schools, in which instruction was given gratuitously, but the line was not clearly drawn in these, as regards the subjects taught, between what constitutes primary and what constitutes secondary education. Latin was not excluded, and the teachers were encouraged to aspire to the priesthood: hence the Pious Schools passed by degrees into the rank of secondary establishments. On the other hand, the Venerable De La Salle required that the Brothers who bound themselves by vow to devote their lives to teaching in the schools, and wore the religious habit, should be and remain laymen (*i. e.,* without holy orders) equally with the professors and assistant teachers who were employed under them. And this has continued to be the practice of the Congregation ever since. For the training of the Brothers, the founder instituted a *novitiate ;* for the professors, etc., a *normal school.* Founded at Reims in 1685, this appears to be the first training school for primary teachers in Europe. It was and still is a part of the rule that the Brothers should work in pairs. They take the three religious vows and two others peculiar to their Congregation. The habit gives them an ecclesiastical appearance. It consists of a long black cassock, with a cloak over it, fastened by iron clasps, a falling collar, and a hat with a wide brim.

The founder lived to see the fruit of his labors in the establishment of his schools in many of the principal towns of France. He died on the 7th of April, 1719, leaving his Congregation so firmly planted that all the convulsions by which French society has since been torn have not been able to extirpate it. It has, moreover, spread to many countries beyond the limits of France, and has been imitated by other teaching associations.

It appears from the same authority that at the end of 1880, the Brothers had under their charge 2,048 schools, attended by 325,558 scholars, of whom 286,004 were receiving gratuitous instruction. Out of this general total, France and her colonies contributed 261,000 scholars; Belgium nearly 19,000; the United States, Canada, and Spanish America, 36,000, and England upwards of 2,000. Nearly 12,000 Brothers, 5,000 Professors and 2,500 novices were employed in teaching.

Since its establishment by its venerable Founder until the present day the Order has suffered many vicissitudes and has survived them all. It was suppressed in France at the Revolution, but re-established by Napoleon, and since that time it has spread into many parts of the world. It has numerous schools and colleges in England, and has acquired a very high reputation in that country. At the late " Health Exhibition " in London, England, at which, among other things, were exhibits of the methods of teaching in the various schools, the apparatus used, books, maps, furniture, course of studies, and generally everything relating to the various systems of education, the Christian Brothers carried off the palm. They had exhibits from the Order in France, Belgium, England, Canada, and the United States, and in all departments they were awarded the highest prizes. The Inspector of the London schools, in a letter to the "Times," says that "It was generally thought in England that they knew something about schools and methods of teaching, but that they would have to go to the schools of the Christian Brothers if they wished to see in operation an almost perfect system of primary and secondary education." A gold medal was awarded to one of the Brothers for a series of maps, the first of the kind introduced into school illustration, and the merits of which their inventor explained in an address before the Geographical Society of England. A silver medal was awarded to another member of the Order for an arithmometer, by which the principles of the metric system, fractions, etc., are fully and lucidly explained. The Director of the Normal School of Malorme, of the same Order, received a silver medal for a system of illustrations simplifying the study of geometrical projections, while another Brother received a medal for designs to simplify the study of complicated figures in the higher grades of perspective and ornamental work. Besides these a Diploma of Honor— the highest prize given—was awarded to the society of the Brothers of the Christian Schools for the excellence of their exhibits in general, and for the perfection of the details furnished by their schools in the United States, Canada, and France ; in addition to this, four diplomas of honor were awarded to the Brothers' educational institutions in the United States, Canada, France, and Belgium. One of the diplomas of honor granted for school-work specially mentioned the short-hand reports, telegraphic course, and similar subjects of study.

In France, the Christian Brothers are the only religious teaching body tolerated under the Republic; a pretty strong evidence of their efficiency. In this country they have made great progress, and not only are they engaged in primary education—the special object for which the Order was originally founded—but they have several colleges for higher education in New York, Maryland, Missouri, California, Rhode Island, and Pennsylvania, besides several commercial academies in different parts of the Union.

The Christian Brothers were first brought to Toronto in May, 1851, by Bishop de Charbonnel. They were introduced and established by Brother Patrick. St. Michael's School was first opened, and in September of the same year a school composed of two classes was opened in St. Paul's Church; the two divisions being merely separated by a screen. In September, 1853, St. Patrick's School was opened in a red brick building (still standing) on the eastern side of St. Patrick's Market. It consisted of four classes, two taught by the Brothers and two by the Sisters of Loretto—Mother Joachim, of Loretto Convent, being one of the teachers. In the same year Father Fitzhenry built a school-house containing three rooms in St. Paul's Parish, at the corner of Power and Queen Streets, and the Brothers moved their classes into the new school. St. Mary's School, Bathurst Street, was opened about 1854. These original schools are now increased in size, remodelled or replaced by modern schools of the most approved style of architecture, elegantly furnished, and equipped to the highest degree of modern taste. The Brothers commenced to teach at St. Catharines in April, 1876.

The De La Salle Institute, conducted by the Brothers, is one of the principal educational institutions in Toronto, religious or secular, Protestant or Catholic. It was first opened as an Academy in 1863, on Jarvis (old Nelson) Street, by one of the most efficient and energetic members of the Order, Brother Hugh, who died a few years ago in Liverpool, England. The Academy was largely attended by such Catholic pupils as were either desirous of obtaining a first-class commercial education, or were preparing for the theological seminary, in which latter case they took the classical course. The Archbishop has always taken a deep interest in the success of these schools, and has the greatest confidence in the zeal and ability of the Christian Brothers as teachers of the young. He has given them all the assistance in his power in carrying out their various educational schemes. The Academy proving so successful, it was determined by the Order to establish an institution analogous to the Collegiate Institutes, to stand in the same relation to the Separate Schools as the High Schools and Collegiate Institutes do to the common schools. Into this project His Grace heartily entered, and measures were at once taken to procure a proper building. The Bank of Upper Canada, situated on Duke Street, was, by the timely diligence of the Archbishop, finally secured. The land on which the bank stood had formerly belonged to the church. It had been donated to the Catholic body by the government for the purpose of building a church many years previously, at the time when the government was making grants of land to the various denominations for church building purposes ; but the government desiring afterwards to establish a bank, and considering this to be the most eligible site for that purpose, gave Bishop McDonnell, in exchange therefor, ten acres of land outside the then city limits. This latter is the land on which St. Paul's Church, the House of Providence, and school buildings of St. Paul's parish now stand. The pupils of the Academy were transferred to the bank—which had been fitted up and the necessary changes made, to accommodate it to school purposes—on the 17th of March, 1870. In 1871, Brother Arnold, who was then at the head of the Institute, built a large addition to the old building. The property is now vested in the Catholic Separate School Board, and as before said, is conducted as a Collegiate Institute for boys and girls, the former under the direction of the Christian Brothers, and the latter under the care of the Sisters of St. Joseph. Pupils are admitted only after a successful examination in the subjects taught in the Separate Schools. The examination papers set for entrance are very similar to those set for entrance to the Ontario High Schools, with the addition of Christian Doctrine, Sacred History, and a few other subjects. In the boys' department, diplomas are awarded to those who pass a successful examination in the commercial course, and the same in the academic course. In the young ladies' department, the pupils are, for the most part, working for teachers' certificates, and many of those attending have already obtained second and third-class certificates, and are going on for first-class.

The Brothers, as already remarked, also supply

teachers for the Separate Schools, and there is very great doubt if the schools could be carried on under any other auspices. The amount raised by taxation in Toronto for the support of the Separate Schools would be altogether inadequate to their maintenance, with anything like proper efficiency, if lay teachers had to be employed. The salaries paid the Brothers are a mere pittance compared with those received by the public school teachers. The head-masters in the public schools are paid from $750 to $1,200 a year, and upwards, and the assistant masters from $740 to $850 a year. In the Separate Schools, the Brothers, who certainly are equally, if not better, qualified, receive only $250 a year—barely enough to pay their board. It will be thus seen what a large saving is secured by the employment of the Brothers as teachers, besides obtaining the services of a body of men who undoubtedly stand in the front rank as educators of the young—even in Ontario, where we possess probably the best State system of primary education in America. The annual cost of each pupil attending the public schools is $7.67; the cost in the Separate Schools is about one-half that sum.

It is hardly necessary to add that the Christian Brothers have been as successful as teachers in the Province of Ontario as they have been in other countries. They came into the province under a cloud of prejudice, which they have succeeded in completely dispelling. This prejudice was not confined alone to the Protestant and non-Catholic portion of the community, but prevailed very extensively even among Catholics. We had not been accustomed, in Upper Canada, to see our schools presided over by members of a religious order, and the sight was somewhat strange. Upon the establishment of Separate Schools in the Upper Province, many Catholic young men became teachers in the Catholic schools, and they very naturally looked upon the Christian Brothers as competitors in this field of labor. But the Brothers steadily won their way. It was not unusual to hear the assertion made, with all the confidence that profound ignorance of a subject begets in a certain class of minds—and this, too, by people who really knew nothing whatever of the men or their system—that the Christian Brothers were incompetent teachers, men trained in an ecclesiastical and antiquated school, and not up to standard and requirements of modern educational systems.* So far did ignorant prejudice in this respect extend, that some Catholic parents preferred to send their children to the common schools, rather than to those presided over by these thoroughly trained and accomplished educationists. The fact is, the lay teachers in the Separate Schools, in the majority of cases, were not the proper kind of men for the position. It is no doubt true, to a certain extent, that the teacher, like the poet, is born, not made; but the man who undertakes the responsibilities of an instructor of the young, without a long preparation and a thorough training, depending for success upon his natural inborn capacity for teaching "the young idea," will soon find himself reduced to the ranks of that large, but demoralized, army of disappointed geniuses who have made the grand mistake of supposing that they could conquer success in life by the

---

* It may be the proper place here, to state that the Venerable De La Salle was the founder of the Normal School system of training teachers. He also founded the simultaneous system of education—a system which obtains to-day in all civilized countries.

sheer force of brilliant talents, without the necessary preparatory training, without labor, and above all without steady and long-sustained perseverance. The reasons for the failure of the lay teachers in our Separate Schools for many years are not far to seek. Most of them were—and perhaps, it may be said, are still —young men who are preparing to enter some other profession, usually either the legal or the medical, and who have temporarily taken up the profession of teaching in order to procure the means of prosecuting their studies in that profession to which they really intend to devote all the best energies of their lives, and in which, if ambitious, they hope for brilliant success, or from which, if less aspiring but more sensible, they expect one day to derive a moderate competence. Such men, even if they possessed all the requisites of good teachers, would never become successful educators. For years, in Ontario, the weakness of our common school, and even academical teaching, was owing to this very cause. A large portion of the teachers were merely make-shift teachers—men who were engaged temporarily in the profession, merely for the sake of its emoluments and who, in many cases while so employed, were industriously reading up for law or medicine. This, of course, has all been changed under our present excellent educational system, and the teaching body in our public schools, collegiate institutes, and high schools, is recognized as an honorable profession, and placed on an equal footing with what are called, by an extreme stretch of courtesy, the "learned" professions.

On the other hand, the Brothers of the Christian Schools are men who have left the world and adopted a monastic life in order to devote themselves unreservedly to the instruction of the young. Men who do this must certainly love their profession. In order to prepare themselves for its responsibilities, they undergo many years of severe and methodical training, and they are not allowed to teach until they prove themselves, by a lengthy novitiate, capable of undertaking with success the duties and labors of an instructor. They have no object in life but to teach the young. They belong to an Order "whose members," say the statutes, "prevent them from ever aspiring to the priesthood, but they are to devote themselves entirely to their calling ; to live in silence and retirement, attached to their institution by five religious vows, so that they may be able to teach gratuitously the young, inculcating in them the maxims of Christianity, and giving them an education suitable to their condition."*

The mission of these men is a grand—a noble one, and, as a body, they fully realize the importance of the work they have undertaken, and the responsibilities they have assumed. "The instructor of youth," says Leibnitz, "holds in his hands the future of society." If the boy is father to the man, how much, then, depends upon early training? Perhaps the greatest fallacy of the day with respect to the education of youth is the common assertion, which seems to be accepted almost as a truism, that education consists wholly in cultivating the mental faculties without any reference to man's moral nature. Religious instruction has been therefore entirely omitted

* *Dictionnaire de Pédagogie et d'Instruction primaire*, quoted by Rev. J. C. Caisse in his work entitled *L'Institut des Frères des Ecoles Chrétiennes, son origine, son but et ses œuvres.* J. Chapleau & Fils, Montreal. To the reader who is interested in educational matters, or who is desirous of learning more of the origin, growth, and system of education pursued by the Christian Brothers, we heartily recommend the interesting volume of Father Caisse.

from our common school system, and this is one of
the principal ·reasons why the Catholic Church in
Canada has deemed it advisable to take exclusive
charge of the education of its own youth. Living, as
we do, in a society composed of many different religious denominations, it would perhaps be impossible to
agree upon any basis of religious instruction in our
public schools that would prove acceptable to all
parties, and therefore the present position of affairs
may be rendered necessary by the exigencies of our
religious condition. The Catholic Church, however,
attaches supreme importance to the religious training of the young, and insists that it shall be made
part and parcel of a primary education. For this
duty no body of men could be better adapted than
the Brothers of the Christian Schools. They are
men of exemplary piety and of long and varied experience in the training of youth. There is probably
no class of men in the world who understand boyish
character as well as they do, and they are marvelous-
ly successful in the management and direction of that
most difficult of all subjects—the growing boy. It
is only necessary to enter one of their schools to be
at once convinced that the relations existing between
the boys and their teachers are of a different nature
from those ordinarily existing between master and
pupil. The Brothers seem to possess a peculiar faculty for gaining the confidence of their scholars, and
thus a friendly and fatherly intercourse is established
between them which enables the teacher to exercise a
powerful influence in directing the mind and moulding the character of his pupil. It is in this way, and
for this reason, that these teachers are so well fitted
to be the moral instructors of the young, and hence
the anxiety of the hierarchy, in all countries, to pro-

cure their services; indeed, the number of members belonging to the Order is altogether inadequate to the demand made upon it for teachers. If their numbers were doubled they would still be unable to supply such demand.

The Christian Brothers have already acquired a very high reputation as teachers in Ontario. In their reports, the High School inspectors speak invariably in the highest terms of the schools conducted by members of this Order, and especially of the De La Salle Institute. The reports of the Inspectors of the Separate Schools in those towns and cities in the Province of Ontario where such schools are conducted by members of this Order are no less flattering.

The Brothers of the Christian Schools in Canada have greatly enhanced their reputation as educationists by the publication of the first volume of a series of school-books to be called the " Language Series." The design of such publication is to teach the English language, grammar, and literature by an entirely new and original method, or, as their authors say, " to teach the elements of English Grammar, Composition, and Literature from a practical standpoint." The first volume of the intended series, entitled " Lessons in English," has been most favorably reviewed by the press of Ontario, and has elicited the highest encomiums from the leading educationists of the country. So excellent and practicable does the plan adopted seem, for teaching the English language and literature to the young, that the most influential journals in Canada strongly recommend that the books be adopted in our Public Schools— this system, in their opinion, being the best yet devised for teaching Canadian children their own language.

CHAPTER XVII.

EDUCATIONAL INSTITUTIONS (CONTINUED).

*The Sisters of St. Joseph—Their Origin—First Establishment in Toronto—
Academy of St. Joseph—Their Success as Teachers—The Order of Loretto
—Its Origin—Their First Schools in Toronto—The Abbey—The Separate
Schools of Toronto—Their Success—Hamilton Separate Schools.*

IN a former chapter we had occasion briefly to refer to the Sisters of St. Joseph as a religious community largely engaged in the educational work of the archdiocese, as well as in the management and conduct of our many charitable and benevolent institutions—of which latter we will treat more particularly in a subsequent chapter.

The Congregation of the Sisters of St. Joseph originated in France, in the town of Puy, in Velay, where Bishop Henry de Maupas established it at the suggestion of Father John Peter Médaille, a celebrated missionary of the Society of Jesus. This zealous missionary, having found, in the course of his missionary labors, several young women who desired to retire from the world, and who manifested, at the same time, strong dispositions for works of piety, and especially for such works as would benefit their fellow-beings, formed the project of establishing a congregation of pious women. Accordingly he addressed himself to the Bishop of Puy, Henry de Maupas, being convinced from the knowledge he had of the sublime virtue and extraordinary zeal of this great prelate for the glory of God, the salvation of souls, and good of his fellow-men, that he would not reject the proposition. The bishop at once approved of the proposal, and invited these pious women to come to Puy and there found their first establishment. For some time after their arrival at Puy, they lodged at the house of a pious lady, who not only contributed to the utmost of her power to the formation of the establishment, but, moreover, labored with extraordinary zeal and charity for its advancement till her death. Everything being finally arranged by the bishop for the execution of so noble a design, he placed under their care the asylum for female orphans at Puy. On the 15th of October, 1650, the feast of St. Teresa, he addressed them a pathetic discourse, animating them to the most pure love of God and to a most perfect love towards their neighbor. He placed them under the patronage of St. Joseph, and ordered that they should be called the Congregation of the Sisters of St. Joseph. He gave them rules for their guidance, and prescribed for them a form of dress; finally he confirmed the establishment of the same Congregation and the prescribed rules by letters of the 10th of March, 1651, and during his life manifested great zeal for the success of the Congregation, many establishments of which he created in his own diocese. After his death his successor, Bishop Armant de Bethune, convinced by experience of the great services the Sisters had rendered to God and their neighbor in his diocese, confirmed, by letters dated the 23d of September, 1665, the Congregation and the rules observed by the Sisters since their establishment. Louis XIV. confirmed, by letters patent, the first establishments of the Sisters of this Congregation in the cities of Puy, St. Didier, and in several other places in Velay. The Order soon spread into the neighboring provinces, and before long was established in nearly every diocese in France.

In the year 1836, six Sisters of the Congregation arrived in St. Louis, Missouri, under the auspices of Bishop Joseph Rosati. Their first house was established at Carondelet, then a small village about five miles from St. Louis. This house was made the novitiate. The Congregation has rapidly extended over all the United States and Canada. They do not confine themselves alone to the performance of works of mercy and the management of charitable and benevolent institutions, but they also teach, and are generally employed in the teaching of the girls and smaller boys of the Separate Schools of Ontario, as well as in carrying on select schools and academies for the higher education of young ladies.

The educational institutions of the Congregation of St. Joseph rank now among the best in Canada for imparting the education usually given to young ladies in seminaries and female academies. As in the common schools, students are prepared for entrance into the high schools and collegiate institutes, the Order has, in several cities, established high schools of its own, into which pupils pass from the Separate Schools, after undergoing an examination based upon the standard of the government high schools.

Four Sisters of this Order were first brought to Toronto from Philadelphia in the year 1851 by Bishop de Charbonnel, for the purpose of taking charge of a small orphan asylum which he had established, and which afterwards developed into the present House of Providence. On the opening of the Separate Schools in 1852, the Sisters were employed as teachers, and a couple of years afterwards they opened their first boarding-school for young ladies in St. Paul's Parish. The number of pupils increased so rapidly that it was deemed necessary to erect a more commodious building, and to open a convent on a larger and more extensive scale. A piece of ground was kindly donated to the Order for this purpose by the Hon. John Elmsley,* on which was built the large and imposing structure now known as the St. Joseph's Convent. This institution has been remarkably successful, and it performs a large share in the education of the Catholic young ladies of the diocese. Pupils attend also from other parts of Canada, as well as from the United States, and St. Joseph's Convent has deservedly obtained the reputation of being one of the leading Catholic educational institutions of Ontario. The Order, as before stated, is employed in teaching the female department of the Separate Schools of the city, and they also conduct the High School for girls established in St. Michael's Parish. The Sisters of St. Joseph established their first mission house in Hamilton in 1852. The Order has also houses established in most of the cities and large towns of Ontario. St. Joseph's Convent never lacks recruits. It has always a large number of young ladies undergoing their novitiate, and every succeeding year sees their number in-

* We have had occasion to mention this gentleman's name more than once in the course of this narrative, and always for the purpose of chronicling some generous act—some munificent donation to the cause of religion, charity, or education. It is not necessary to tell the Catholics of Toronto or the archdiocese who the late Hon. John Elmsley was, but for the benefit of others we may here say that the late honorable gentleman was a distinguished convert to the Catholic Church, a man of considerable wealth and great social influence in Toronto, a member of the Ligislative Council in the old Parliament of Upper Canada, and at one time a member of the Government. He was a man of a deep religious nature, living faith, and practical piety. He gave largely and generously of his wealth to the Church, and his many donations of land and money to the cause of charity and education will make his name be forever held in veneration and esteem by the Catholic citizens of Toronto.

crease.   More postulants are received by this community than, perhaps, by any other religious institution in Ontario.   The Order itself is well suited to all classes, and appeals to the many and diverse phases under which the religious temperament displays itself, by offering a field of action to those who wish to devote their lives to deeds of mercy, as well as to that large class of young women to be found in every Catholic community, who feel that they have a vocation for the religious state, and desire to spend their lives in prayer, meditation, and the active duties of teaching.

Another community well and favorably known in the Archdiocese of Toronto, as well as throughout the Province of Ontario, is the Order of the Ladies of Loretto.* This society, unlike most of our modern religious orders, is of English origin.   The new and severe laws passed against English Catholics after what is known in history as the "Gunpowder Plot," caused a large emigration from England of the Catholic gentry and of the more wealthy and prosperous of the Catholic population in the larger towns. A numerous English colony had established itself in Munich, in Bavaria, and it was from among a number of English ladies thus exiled from their own country, on account of their religion, that the Order of Loretto originated, about the year 1631. They were at first popularly known as the "English Virgins," and were not finally approved of by the Holy See until 1703.   In 1669 a number of ladies of this Order returned to England, after the Restoration, and opened a convent in London.   Charles II. was known to be favorable to the Catholic religion, and

* The proper name is the Institute of the Blessed Virgin Mary.

it was, no doubt, thought that the times were ripe for the re-establishment of religious institutions in England.   This, however, was a mistaken idea, and the small religious colony of Loretto was obliged to live in great retirement and exercise extreme caution, in order to escape the vigilance of the " priest hunter," and those who made it a trade to spy out and prosecute " popish recusants."   The community finally removed from London to York, where they have remained ever since, notwithstanding the many dangers to which they have at various times been subjected, and in spite of the very general and pronounced antipathy the English people of the middle classes have to anything savoring of a nunnery.   The horrors of the French Revolution, however, and the large exodus from France of clergy and religious, worked a very favorable change in English opinion in this respect. The polished French abbé and the pious, modest, and zealous French parish priest presented a striking contrast to the vulgar, fox-hunting, hard-drinking English parson of the eighteenth century, so vividly portrayed in the brilliant pages of Macaulay.   The English, with all their faults, are generous to a fallen foe, and are more disposed to help an enemy in need than to lavish affection on a prosperous friend.   The reception given by the English people to the French priests and members of the religious orders, who, penniless, came to the shores of their hereditary enemies, seeking shelter from the political and social earthquake which was soon to engulf their own nation in a common ruin, is one of those pleasing episodes in the life of a nation, which the student of history enjoys as a delightful oasis in the dreary desert of wars, intrigues, injustice, and national selfishness.   This reaction in public sentiment in England in favor of

Catholics resulted in a greater toleration of their priests and religious, and as a consequence the members of the Loretto Convent at York began for the first time to wear the religious habit openly. A branch, or rather offshoot, of this community at York was founded in 1821 at Rathfarnham, in Ireland, and this is the Mother Home from which have issued the various colonies that have founded houses of this Order in all the most important British colonies, including Canada.

The Order of Loretto was instituted solely and distinctively for educational purposes. It was designed in England to afford facilities for the education of the daughters of the Catholic upper classes who were obliged, owing to the rigor of the penal code, to either send their daughters abroad to be educated or procure private tutors for them at home. Unfortunately for the Church in England in those days, as well as for England itself, there were very few of the lower classes in communion with the Catholic Church. Outside the Catholic aristocracy, and many of the country gentry, who still clung to the old faith—especially the old Catholic families of Lancashire—the Church had very few adherents among the lower or middle classes of the nation. Since the suppression of the monasteries and the breaking up of the nunneries nothing had been done for the education of women. The convents of England, great and small, were suppressed, the magnificent buildings handed over to the new nobility, and their revenues given to royal mistresses or servile courtiers, but none of the vast revenues of these institutions were employed in founding educational establishments to take their place. A few more public schools for the education of boys have been established in

England since the Reformation ; many new colleges have been founded and liberally endowed in the two great universities of Oxford and Cambridge, and even new universities have been established for the higher education of young men ; but from the time of the suppression of the convents in England until a comparatively recent period nothing was done for the higher education of women. So far as mere bodily wants are concerned, the poor-house has been substituted for the monastery, but as regards the religious and educational training of the girls of England, nothing has yet been provided as a substitute for the convents.

The Loretto nuns were brought to Toronto by Bishop Power, and Archbishop Lynch found them established in that city when he took possession of his See in 1859. Their numbers were, however, few at that period, and their accommodations limited. The Archbishop, with his usual zeal and energy in the cause of education, at once, as soon as the more important matters specially relating to the administration of the affairs of the diocese were settled, proceeded to place the community on a more satisfactory basis. He gave them a piece of ground near the Cathedral, on Bond Street, on which was built the Convent of St. Ignatius. The Order increased rapidly, and the large number of boarders received from all parts of Canada and the United States soon necessitated the procuring of more extensive accommodations, which resulted in the purchase of the present Loretto Abbey. The building now known as the " Abbey " had been a large, handsome private residence, owned by a wealthy Toronto lady. It is built in the style of a French *château*, and is surrounded by extensive and well-kept grounds.   On the completion of the purchase of this handsome estate, the community lost no time in taking possession ; in fact, Mass was said for the first time in the spacious ball-room before the decorations for the last ball had been removed.   Large additions have been made to the Abbey, and it is now fully equal to any of the European convents.

The Loretto Abbey of Toronto, as well as the convent at the Niagara Falls—of which we will speak in a subsequent chapter—has a reputation all over the continent of America.   The education imparted to their pupils by the Ladies of Loretto is well adapted to accomplish the true end of all female education—that is, to make cultured and well-bred ladies, good wives, mothers who will know how to properly train their children, and useful members of society.   A good deal is said about the superficiality of convent education, but for the great mass of girls who expect to become wives and mothers, and especially Catholic wives and Catholic mothers, there is something more important than even what some call a solid education.   One of the principal objects of a convent education is the religious training of young womanhood and the preservation and development of those distinctively feminine qualities whose bloom is so soon rubbed off by a too early contact with the world and society.   At that critical period of a young girl's life when she is just blooming into womanhood, there could scarcely be found an atmosphere purer or more healthy, in which to live for a couple of years, than within the walls of a convent.   There, a regular life of study, far from the excitements to which she would be subjected if she were living in the world and just beginning to enjoy the pleasures of her " first season out ;" there, quiet of mind, early hours, pleasant companionship, and the deep religious influences which pervade the place, go far to mould the future character of the young girl, or, at all events, leave a sweet and holy impression that is hardly ever in after-life entirely effaced. For these reasons our convents are much patronized by Protestants and non-Catholics, particularly by those parents among them who have had a large experience of the world, and know the dangers to which girls at this period of life are exposed. It is gravely doubted even by some of those who have had experience as teachers in our high schools and collegiate institutes, whether the intellectual advantages afforded to girls in these institutions entirely compensate for a certain deterioration of the womanly character, slight, perhaps, but at the same time very pronounced to the eyes of the keen observer.

What will be the result of the present movement for higher education of women remains yet to be seen. So far as their ability to cope with men in the various branches of learning usually comprised in the college curriculum, and especially in the higher mathematics and the mental and moral sciences, they have so far demonstrated their equality, if not superiority. But the question asked by many thinking men is, how will such education and such training, if it becomes general, affect woman in her more important social relations as sister, wife, or mother? Until this has been settled by a more extended and varied experience of the results, in these respects, of the higher education of women, our convents must, so far as Catholics are concerned, continue to be the training school of our Catholic young women.

Judging by the women in those countries where

convent education prevails, it would seem that, contrary to the general impression, women educated in these institutions exercise in after-life a profound influence on the social and even the political affairs of their country. The influence of women in French society has always been great. The *salon* is unknown in England. It could not exist in that country, because woman counts for nothing, either in the social or public economy of the nation, except as a figure-head in society. In France the *salon* presided over by the woman of brilliant talents exercises and has always exercised a most potent influence upon public affairs, and is made the centre of attraction to all the brilliant celebrities of the day, whether in politics, science, or art. And yet these women have been educated and trained in the French convents.*

The sketch we have attempted to give in the foregoing pages of the various educational institutions in the archdiocese of Toronto would be incomplete without some reference to the Separate Schools, in the establishment of which the present Archbishop of Toronto has taken such an important part. We will in another place deal more particularly with what was known for many years, in Canadian politics, as the " Separate School Question," and His Grace's connection therewith. Here it will be only

* Since writing the above, the author has come across the following extract from an article in the *Boston Transcript:* "As regards women, the most notable examples of self-evolvement have been furnished by France, as far back as we may look. No other country has produced such brilliant women in number or varied ability. In no other country have women played so notable a part in public events, nor approached them in influencing the men who shaped those events. Yet most of these women were the early product of the convent, where elegance, rather than severity of education, was the aim. But the French woman's development was largely due to the best French male minds, who made her *salon* the theatre of their thought, thus, without any elaborate theorizing, lifting her at once to their own plane."

necessary to say that the Separate Schools of Toronto, in the efficiency of the teaching staff, the excellence of the educational methods employed, and in the general proficiency of the pupils attending them, are not surpassed by the best public schools in the province. The financial affairs of the schools have been for many years admirably managed by a board of trustees elected by the people, and composed of both clergymen and laymen. The school tax has been promptly collected, the teachers regularly paid their salaries, debts wiped off, and new buildings erected, embodying all the results of the latest and most approved methods of modern school architecture. Everything in the way of interior accommodations, ventilation, and sanitary arrangements in these new school buildings has been carefully attended to, and are in these respects fully up to the standard, and in many particulars surpass the vast majority of the public school buildings throughout the province. The Toronto Board of Separate School Trustees have demonstated the possibility of successfully carrying on the Catholic schools of the city upon the money collected from the school tax levied upon the Catholic rate-payers. For many years the full tax had never been collected. The consequence was an annual deficit, which had to be made up by voluntary contributions. This necessitated periodical appeals to the generosity of those who had, as a general thing, promptly paid their own school tax, but who were now called upon to supplement this by a further contribution, made necessary by the default of others. No steps had been taken for years to enforce payment of the Catholic school tax, such as those resorted to in cases of default of payment of other municipal taxes. All this has been changed. The tax is regularly and as fully collected as any other municipal tax. The consequence is that, instead of annual deficits, the School Board has found itself in possession of all the necessary means for carrying on the schools in a proper and efficient manner, and has in addition thereto, as above stated, been enabled to expend considerable sums in buildings and other improvements. Of course it must be remembered in this connection, what we have before remarked, that the remuneration paid to the Christian Brothers, the Sisters of St. Joseph, and the Ladies of Loretto, who compose the teaching staff in the Separate Schools, is excessively small, and would be altogether inadequate to the decent support of the most economical lay teachers, even if unmarried. Indeed, the sums paid to these teachers in the Separate Schools is a mere pittance, compared with the salaries paid to even the lowest grade of teachers in the public schools. Were it not for the fact, as we have before observed, that the teachers in the Separate Schools are from the religious bodies, it is doubtful if these schools could be successfully carried on, on the proceeds of the school tax alone.

Taking into consideration all the difficulties with which the Separate Schools have had to contend, since their inception—the difficulty in obtaining good teachers, the more substantial difficulty of obtaining money, and the other and numerous obstacles encountered in first establishing them—it may now be said that they are finally successful, and have quite fully justified the hopes entertained by the hierarchy in Ontario, in their long struggle for the right to educate the Catholic children of Ontario in schools conducted under the Church's auspices. Neither has the establishment of Separate Schools had the effect so much dreaded by the opponents of Separate Catholic education—namely, that it would, in reality, break up the whole public school system. On the contrary, the public schools have the entire confidence of the great mass of the Protestant and non-Catholic population of the province, whose children attend them, and although there is a strong feeling among a small portion of the Anglican clergy in favor of denominational schools, the feeling is not shared in to any great extent by the laity of that Church.

Separate Schools are established in every town and city of Ontario, and are, generally speaking, in a very flourishing condition. When we said that the Catholic schools of Toronto are unsurpassed by any of the public schools in the province, we might have said the same of the Separate Schools of Hamilton. That city has always, from the first establishment of Catholic schools to the present time, been possessed of a thorough system of Catholic primary education. An efficient board of trustees is annually elected by the Catholic people, who have always taken good care that the Catholic schools shall be maintained at a high standard. The male teachers are laymen, and hold the same certificates as those required for teachers in the public schools. Hamilton also possesses an excellent Catholic Model School, which ranks among the best educational institutions of the province.*

* The success of the Catholic schools of Hamilton is in a great measure due to the ability and energy of Mr. Cornelius Donovan, M.A., now Separate School Inspector, who was for many years the Principal of the Separate Schools of that city.

CHAPTER XVIII.

CHARITABLE AND BENEVOLENT INSTITUTIONS.

Charity a distinctively Christian Virtue—Unknown to the Pagan Nations of Antiquity—Charity and Philanthropy—Poor-houses—The Church's Care of the Poor—The Sisters of Charity—Establishment of the House of Providence—History of the Institution—The St. Nicholas Home—Its Object—Notre Dame Boarding House—The Object of the Institution—Sunnyside Home for Orphan Boys.

CHARITY, which our great poet so beautifully compares to a gentle dew that droppeth from heaven, blessing him that gives as well as him that takes, is the characteristic virtue of Christianity —the virtue, by excellence, of the Christian religion, both in the sense of love of one's fellow-man and in the sense of almsgiving. In this latter and popular signification of the word, or rather in the sense of mitigating the evils of humanity generally, charity, in our day, has taken the form, outside the Church, of what is called philanthropy, and is doing much for the poor in the way of material comfort.

This virtue, whether as exhibited by the great benevolent institutions of the Church in all ages or by the philanthropic movements of the present age, was unknown to the pagan nations of antiquity, even to the highest civilization of Greece and Rome. Poverty was looked upon with the same contempt among these nations as it is in our own day by that large portion of the world whose religion and morality are nothing more than a refined paganism. Even among the Jews, under the Old Dispensation, poverty and misfortune were looked upon as a sort of punishment for sin, as undoubtedly riches and prosperity in this world were considered, and indeed were promised, as the rewards which the just and virtuous might expect from the Almighty.

The Saviour, however, preached a different doctrine. He preached the doctrine of love of the poor. He lived among the poor. He laid great stress on the importance of alms-giving. He taught that poverty was neither a crime nor a punishment. His whole life was spent in relieving the poor and needy. He cured the lame, the halt, the blind, and the diseased; He fed the hungry—in fact His whole active life, from His baptism till His death, is briefly summed up in the few words of the Evangelist: "He went about doing good."

The Catholic Church has never, in any age, failed to reduce to practice the teachings of her Divine Founder, and to follow His example while upon earth in loving and cherishing the poor and providing for their wants. What may be called one of the notes of the Church's sanctity is her love and care of the poor.

Philanthropists undertake the hopeless task of banishing poverty from the earth — an utopian dream they are doomed never to realize. Philanthropy assumes to lay down a theory of poverty; to bring it under the domain of certain physical laws—declares, in fact, that like all the phenomena of life, it is only a phase of the two great laws of evolution, and the "survival of the fittest." It ignores human nature; treats humanity in the mass; sinks the individual; takes no account of personal character, and expects, by an elaborate code of sanitary laws,

to legislate crime, poverty, and misery off the face
of the earth.

The Catholic Church, however, accepts the words
of our Saviour, "The poor ye have always with you,"
literally.   She knows that poverty and misery have
always existed, and she believes they will continue
to exist till the end of time.   She has no faith in
an earthly millenium.   And can any one acquainted
with the present social condition of the world deny
that she is right?   Was there ever in the whole
history of the world more debasing and degrading
poverty than there is at the present day in the dazzling noon-day of this nineteenth century?   Is it
not a fact that as the few become enormously rich,
the many become correspondingly poor?   Accepting
the principles of political economists it must necessarily be so—it follows as a necessary and logical consequence.

How then is the evil to be met?   It can only
be met now, as it was in the days of the Apostles
and the first Christians, by the efforts of Christian
charity exercised upon the individual.   We are not
disposed to underrate the great service modern philanthropy has done for the good of mankind, but
official charity is everywhere dreaded by the poor.
Who will say that the poor-houses of England provide for the poor as well as the monasteries did?   It
is a common charge made against the monasteries of
the Middle Ages that they encouraged pauperism.
On the suppression of the religious houses in England, at the Reformation, poverty was for the first
time in the history of the Christian world, declared to
be a crime by law, and the most cruel and barbarous
statutes were enacted to prevent begging.   Three
hundred years have elapsed, and to-day the poor are

more numerous in proportion to the population, and there are more paupers supported at the public expense in England than at any previous period in the history of that country.

The well-known antipathy, not to say positive dread, the poor people of England and Ireland have of the government poor-houses is well known, and in most cases, especially in the latter country, they would rather die on the highway than take advantage of those last resorts of the poor, aged and disabled unfortunates. And well may they dread them. It is doubtful if Dickens, in the wildest flights of his fancy, has really exaggerated the dreadful horrors of the English poor-houses. In our own day, in the neighboring republic, which boasts of leading the van in all philanthropic movements of the age, the disclosures made before legislative committees, as to the management of State charitable institutions, show an amount of dishonesty in the management of the finances of those establishments, a selfish disregard for the comfort of the inmates, and, in many instances, a species of refined cruelty towards the unfortunate victims of State "charity," that one is almost led to doubt the utility of such institutions at all.

Knowing well the nature of State institutions for the poor, the Catholic Church, whether in Protestant or in Catholic countries, puts forth all her resources to provide refuges for the homeless and aged poor. She believes the spiritual welfare of the poor is no better cared for by the State, in such institutions, than is their material comfort, and therefore she places her charitable and benevolent establishments under the direction and management of those good and noble women who, for pure love of God and their neighbors, have left the world with all its pleasures, and all its fascinations and allurements, to live and work for the good of their fellow men. These are the women who compose that grand army called " Sisters of Charity," and their name is legion. We have all heard and read much concerning the heroic life of Florence Nightingale, who left home and friends to succor the wounded in the Crimean War. Far be it from the writer to pluck one leaf from the laurel with which the whole world has by common consent encircled her brow in honor of her noble deeds, but truth compels us to say that in the Catholic Church of to-day, in this prosaic, money-making nineteenth century, Florence Nightingales are to be found by the score, aye, by the hundreds, among our Sisters of Mercy. These are the " saints unknown to the world ; " the ministering angels who are to be found in the hospitals when the fatal epidemic is decimating populous cities ; on the field of battle amid the smoke and carnage of contending armies, moistening the parched lips of the dying soldier ; or in our large cities passing from door to door—and these often ladies brought up amidst all the luxuries and refinements of high estate—for the scraps that fall from the rich man's table, to feed the poor and helpless whom the cold charity of the world has thrown upon their hands, yet whom these true followers of Christ look upon as their fellow creatures to be loved and succored.

If Archbishop Lynch had no other or greater claim to the respect and gratitude of the people of Toronto, both Catholic and Protestant, than his exertions in the cause of charity entitle him to, the efforts he has made in behalf of, and the deep interest he has always taken in the poor and unfortunate, should cause his name to be mentioned with respect and esteem by every citizen of Ontario's capital. The House of Providence, the St. Nicholas Home, and Sunnyside Home for orphan boys, will long stand as monuments of his zeal, benevolence, charity, and love of the poor.

The House of Providence is one of the largest institutions of its kind in America. It has accommodation for more than five hundred people, and has usually that number of inmates within its walls. Everyone is admitted to the institution without regard to creed or race. The poor and helpless, the sick and the incurables from every parish in the Archdiocese here find a home and a refuge. They are kindly and tenderly cared for by the good Sisters of St. Joseph, not in the stern and unsympathetic manner of State-paid functionaries, but with the loving tenderness and humane sympathy characteristic of these meek and lowly followers of the divine Saviour. The establishment is supported by the voluntary contributions of the charitable citizens of Toronto and the Archdiocese, supplemented by a small grant from the Ontario government.* In this charitable work it is gratifying to know that many of our Protestant fellow-citizens take great interest and give generously of their means towards the support of the House.

The House of Providence was, when opened in

---

* This annual grant, small as it is, meets with a determined though ineffectual opposition from certain members of the Legislature and from a portion of the ultra-Protestant press, as being an "appropriation of the public funds to sectarian purposes," and no doubt if it were not for this opposition the government would be disposed to grant a larger sum to such a deserving institution as the House of Providence. The opponents of the grant seem to ignore the fact that the 500 inmates of the House of Providence are so many poor cared for, who would otherwise be a burden on the citizens of Toronto, or on the people of other municipalities.

the year 1857, under the charge and direction of a few Sisters of St. Joseph, who had been brought by Bishop de Charbonnel, from Philadelphia, for that purpose. The house was a small one at first, consisting of only one wing of the present building. It was commenced at a period in the history of Toronto when the anti-Catholic spirit was very strong, and an attempt was made to destroy the building, but it was fortunately discovered in time to frustrate the design. When the good Sisters entered the building they were literally without an article of furniture, except a few chairs and tables. The institution was well named the House of Providence, for it was on Providence alone they relied for the absolute necessaries of life, and they were not disappointed.

Meagre as were their accommodations, and uncertain as were the sources of relief, the good Sisters did not refuse admittance, immediately on their taking possession of their new abode, to a number of young children who had been heartlessly abandoned by their parents, and these poor outcasts were the first inmates of the House of Providence. By the end of the year there were between forty and fifty orphan children in the institution, and it became absolutely necessary to make some sure provision for their maintenance. Food must be procured in some way, and as a last resort the Sisters set out to beg through the city, from door to door, for food and such articles of clothing as the kind-hearted and charitably disposed were willing to bestow. In those days the well-to-do citizen, coming down town to his office or place of business on cold winter mornings, comfortably clad and just after the enjoyment of a substantial breakfast, might frequently meet, thus early in the day, the black-bonnetted and veiled face of a Sister of St. Joseph, basket on arm, on her daily tour, begging for alms wherewith to feed the hungry and clothe the naked victims of poverty, disease or misfortune committed to their care; or later on might one of these angels of charity be seen in the crowded market place modestly soliciting such scraps of food as would be otherwise cast to the dogs. A reverend gentleman, who was at one time chaplain of the House of Providence, has kindly furnished the author with the following interesting details concerning this noble institution: " Since the establishment of the House in 1857, many strange circumstances happening within its walls or connected with it, show in a clear manner that the Almighty never forgets or abandons the poor or the infirm who found, and do still find, a home in this House. The laudable object for which it was founded has never been lost sight of by those under whose maternal care it has been placed, and great, too, is the anxiety and fatherly care of the venerable Archbishop, in whose diocese the House of Providence is silently but efficiently doing God's work. Under the roof of this house may be seen the poor victims of nearly every disease to which flesh is heir ; feeble and helpless old men and women, either deprived of children and friends, or ungratefully abandoned by their nearest and dearest ; widows and orphans cast on the world without the means of support, or with relations unwilling or incapable of helping them."

" Many times, for the last twenty-eight years, has it happened that the House has found itself without provisions and without money, but it was never known that the poor were a day without their regular meals.   If flour or meat were wanted at night, the fraternal hand of God brought some good charitable hand to the door in the morning, who would at once supply the House with what was most needed. At another time bills would be pressing ; they must be paid on a certain day, and no funds to meet them ; but that day never came without having the pressing debt taken off the institution by some charitable friend.

As the Protestant donations are at all times very considerable, the Sisters have no hesitation in admitting non-Catholics into the House.   Time and again has it been the case that these were refused admission into like institutions in the city and Province, but if a bed had to be made up on the floor, the Sisters would do so rather than to refuse shelter to one "whose own received them not," and invariably these poor abandoned people showed their gratitude to God and to their benefactors.   About the year 1860 the small-pox and fever raged terribly for nine months in the House, and it is a strange fact that only one or two of the children died while hundreds died outside in the city.

" The Sisters in charge of the institution relate many interesting anecdotes concerning what they consider the providential manner in which they sometimes raised provisions or money.   One morning a few years ago a Protestant farmer called at the door and said that he was on his way to the market with a load of provisions, but that his horse had balked before the gate of the House and refused to go a step further, and so he concluded to leave what his well-filled wagon contained at the institution.   He was surprised to hear that on that very morning, had it not been for his donation, the children would have been for once without their usual breakfast, as there was nothing in the House to eat and no money to purchase anything. At another time, in the year 1876, the House was in very straitened circumstances for the want of money, and the good Mother was wondering where they should be able to procure funds, when an unknown gentleman called one day and gave her $200. At another time, when in similar straits, she was handed $175 in the same manner." Very many similar instances might be told.

The House of Providence has been an object of the most anxious solicitude to the Archbishop from the moment he first set foot in Toronto as the spiritual chief of the diocese. Since 1859 the institution has been enlarged to thrice its original size; a commodious chapel for the accommodation of the inmates has been provided, and the establishment is at the present one of the largest, most extensive, and most complete of its kind in America, and all this has been done by the unwearied exertions of His Grace. He has also instituted the custom of taking up an annual collection in every church in the diocese, in November of each year, for the benefit of the House, and so anxious is he that the merits of the institution should be thoroughly known and appreciated by those to whose charity this yearly appeal is made, that he usually precedes this collection by the issue of a pastoral on the subject, to impress upon them, in a special manner, the claims which the House of Providence has upon their generosity. In one of these late pastorals he gives some very interesting particulars concerning the institution. "There are," he says, " nearly 500 inmates, by far the largest number in any charitable institution in the country. The wants of the poor in this city, always increasing, appeal to every charitable heart, especially for the coming winter. A great many poor immigrants from Ireland came out with large families. They cannot support themselves until they get work. The House of Providence receives the children for a time, till the parents are able to procure a home for them. This temporary relief has been of immense value to many of these poor parents burdened with children. Out-door relief will have to be given to a greater number than usual during the winter. There are in the House at the present time 85 sick and incurable old women, who have to be attended to like children, besides an equal number of aged and indigent persons, who were once well off. There are also 68 helpless old men, who also require care like little children ; 122 orphan girls and 130 orphan boys to be fed, clothed, bedded, and schooled. Two hundred and fifty large loaves of bread, baked by the Sisters, are consumed every day. The oven is never cool. There is no paid servant in the House; were not this the case, the expense of the establishment would be much greater.

"Another large expense had to be incurred this year and last. There was no adequate accommodation for the inmates to hear Mass, and a chapel of fair proportions was built, together with other improvements, on which there is considerable debt, but God will inspire some of His devoted servants to liquidate it. Then the roof of the main building had to be removed. It was defective and leaking in many parts, and was injuring the House very seriously. Of necessity it had to be replaced by a new roof costing over $2,000. When anything is absolutely necessary for God's home, we do not hesitate to permit debts to be contracted, as Holy Providence always manifests His care of His own children. He inspires His servants to supply His place. What would become of these five hundred inmates if they were to be abandoned? The poor to whom God has promised to be a father look to Him through you in their need of assistance. The good Sisters, who have all the trouble and anxiety of collecting funds and managing so large an institution, suffer a great deal mentally and bodily, but they act as servants of Christ, and their confidence in His mercy has been justified. Whatever you enable them to do for the little ones of Christ He will hold as done for Himself. Oh! what an honor to dress and bandage the wounds, to feed Christ in the hungry. How rich will be the reward of these Sisters and the benefactors of the poor.

" In other places committees are instituted to collect funds for such institutions as the House of Providence. This is attended with great trouble and anxiety, but it relieves the Sisters and leaves them enough to do to take care of the poor. But with us the good Sisters do all. It is edifying to see them humbling themselves so far as to stand in the market-place to receive alms for God's poor. They have done for years past the work of the ' Little Sisters of the Poor,' lately established in France. To feed, without speaking of clothing, five hundred inmates at the low sum of one dollar per week, exceeds twenty-six thousand dollars yearly. Then if clothing, house repair, and cleaning be added, together with the water-rate, which at half rate amounts to $424 yearly, the cost of keeping this large house will be seen to be very great, and great, too, is the trouble and anxiety to meet all calls. The merciful Providence of God is alone relied upon to supply all wants. The medicines, coffins, and burial expenses, too, of a great number of poor who find here an asylum where they may prepare for a happy death, amount to a great deal. We need not mention here the various sources from which help comes. They are known to the people themselves. They press but very lightly on each individual, yet all have the consolation of knowing that God's poor are cared for both in life and death. Some legacies have been received from time to time, which benefit the souls of the givers more than the poor, even independent of their continual prayers. We would exhort our good people to think more of their own souls in making their last wills. They often neglect themselves, and leave all to heirs who will very soon forget them. They send nothing, or very little, before them to weigh in the balance of divine justice against their sins. A grand funeral, with a long line of carriages, an expensive coffin, and a grand marble monument, too often minister to the pride and consolation of the living rather than help the dead. Those who give to the poor but lend to the Lord, and He will repay both principal and interest at the moment of death, when the soul is balancing between a miserable and a happy eternity. 'Alms-deeds,' says the Book of Job, 'free from death, cleanse from sin, and cause us to find mercy and life eternal.'"

We have once before, in the course of this narrative, referred to the Archbishop's fondness for boys and the great interest he has always taken in everything relating to their advancement or welfare. He sympathizes instinctively with the boyish character, and besides this natural sympathy he is profoundly impressed with the importance of giving a proper direction to youthful impulses, and thus causing the exuberant and overflowing spirits of the boy to flow on in an unpolluted channel.   Even the common and seemingly incorrigible street *gamin* did not appear to His Grace beyond the civilizing influences of a warm and comfortable bed, good substantial meals, a cheerful home, and an occasional bath, and he determined, therefore, to see if something could not be done to ameliorate the wretched condition of that class of boys from among whom is recruited the large and important army of newsboys and shoe-blacks which forms such a characteristic feature of our great American and Canadian cities.   From this belief sprang the idea of founding a home for working boys, where they would be comfortably housed and fed, their wants attended, the elements of an education imparted to them, and some endeavor made to bring them under the humanizing and benign influence of religion.   For this purpose he addressed the following appeal to the citizens of Toronto :

There are, in our rapidly improving city, many fine boys, who render good service to the community.   We must receive the daily papers, and many small and indispensable services, that boys can best afford to perform.   Therefore, these good boys ought to be protected and assisted in their present position, to enable them to work up to employments to which talent, education, and good conduct may entitle them.   It is agreed on all sides, that the present condition of many of them needs amelioration. Those boys are inexperienced, many of them are poor, some of them have widowed mothers, others are worse off with parents dissipated, and sometimes with step-mothers or step-fathers.   A great number of them, through the blessing of Our Divine Redeemer bestowed upon youth, uphold, notwithstanding all those drawbacks, the dignity of human nature — "wonderfully instituted, and more wonderfully repaired." Those youths require the kind assistance and good advice of friends to enable them to be good members of society, and inspire them with the hope of being chosen citizens of a Heavenly Kingdom.

Again, what those boys especially want is to have decent board and lodging. This luxury, at present, is far above their means, and therefore, they cannot procure it. They are ashamed to beg, they will not steal, they abhor low associations, they refuse not to work hard in the frost and snow of winter, and in the great heat of summer. But after a hard day's work, they would like to have at least a bed at night, where they would be undisturbed by drunken brawls and fights; and at least to have one good meal in the day; and, from time to time, a bath, to quench the burning heat of their blood, vitiated by over-exertion, bad food, unwashed garments, and the ever-increasing fire of youth, infused into them by the wise Creator, to sustain life and its battles. In fine, they yearn for a home and a mother's care.

To supply this great want of our youth, the assistance of the charitable and kind is needed. If we refuse it, the fault must be doubly expiated—even in this life, by supporting criminals; and in the next, the consequence will be the terrible sentence, "I was a stranger, and you took me not in; naked, and you clothed me not," etc.

We propose to place at the service of these good boys a comfortable home, on such conditions as their earnings and future prospects can easily meet, with the kind co-operation of the ever generous citizens of Toronto.

This Home will be called the "St. Nicholas," and will be conducted on hotel principles. A book of entry will always be kept; none will be admitted except the industrious, and those who strive to be good. Credit will be given to the deserving—but repayment will be expected when a boy procures employment. No lazy or dishonest boys are to be admitted—the reformatory or prison should be their place of abode. On entering the "Home," the boys will be supplied with a clean and comfortable bed and bath; kind gentlemen will see that order is observed in the dormitories, night prayers said, and proper hours kept; there will also be evening school during the winter. The good Sisters of St. Joseph will superintend the dining-room, as soon as a house is provided for them, and see that the dormitories are kept clean. There will also be attached a Clothing Store, where, with the assistance of kind ladies, clothes may be had on the most reasonable terms, and credit will be given to reliable boys, who promise to pay when they may be able. Those regulations are intended to train boys to honor, honesty, thrift, and self-reliance.

For many years we have most earnestly desired to see such an establishment in this city. The Holy Providence of God enabled us to purchase a lot at $1,050, on Richmond Street, in the rear of Stanley (now Lombard) Street School House, in order to have all facility for this work. The first difficulties of such an establishment have thereby been overcome. The ground secured is 185 ft. by 53 ft. and is situated near Church Street. There is already a large brick building, formerly used as a school. This can easily be raised to make a three-story house with a wing. All the out-offices, namely, the bath-rooms, dining-rooms, kitchen, pantry, etc., connect with the Sisters' house on Richmond Street.

From the time Our Lord blessed little children, and proclaimed that those who did not become like unto them would not enter into the kingdom of heaven, children have become the object of the dearest affection and ardent charity of all those who love God and reverence the angelic virtues. The condition of children is most suitable for little services, and their gratitude for favors is everlasting, while their resentments are not of long duration. St. Paul, speaking of children, says: "Now I say as long as the heir is a child, he differeth nothing from a servant though he be lord of all" (Gal. iv. 1). Men now say "thoughtless youth," whereas youth runs wild in superabundance of thought. To give this exuberance of thought direction and aim, and enable the mind to see heaven in the distance as the great goal of happiness, and to make them good citizens for earth, should be our earnest desire.

Christ has said "Whosoever shall give to drink to one of those little ones even a cup of cold water in the name of a disciple, amen I say to you he shall not lose his reward " (Matt. x. 42). Whilst Christ pronounces a blessing on those who assist youth, He likewise pronounces a malediction on those who scandalize them or permit them to perish — "See that you despise not one of these little ones, for I say to you their angels in heaven always see the face of my Father who is in heaven " (Matt. xviii. 10).

Even pagan philosophy forcibly recommends the proper culture of youth, and Plutarch says, children should be taught to worship God, to revere their parents, to obey the laws, to submit to rulers, to love their friends, and to be temperate in refraining from pleasure (*De Educatione Puerorum*).

We count upon the generous and hearty support of all good and charitable Christians, who have at heart the welfare of the most interesting portion of Christ's flock, for the success of our undertaking.

This appeal was generously responded to and the building referred to at once put in a condition to receive these boys. The House was named the St. Nicholas Home, in honor of that saint whose name is so dear to the boyish heart.* The Home has

---

* Rev. Alban Butler, in his Life of St. Nicholas (Butler's Lives of the Saints, vol. IV., page 646, note; Sadlier's edition, New York, 1847), says: " St. Nicholas is called particularly the patron of children, not only because he made their instruction a principal part of his pastoral care, but chiefly because he always retained their virtues, the meekness, the simplicity without guile or malice, and the humility of his tender age, and in his very infancy devoted himself to God by a heroic piety." These reasons are given in the ancient MS. Book of Festivals at Sarum, fol. 55. On the great solemnity with which it was kept by the boys at the

accommodation for about fifty boys, and there are on an average between thirty and forty regular inmates. They pay the small sum of one dollar and a half per week, providing they earn that much; if they do not, they give whatever they have made during the week, and for this they receive their lodging and their meals. The boys sleep in a large and airy dormitory; the beds are clean, the food wholesome, good and plentiful, and the accommodations, generally, as good, if not better, than are to be found in the homes of ordinary mechanics. The dormitory is in charge of a reliable man, employed for that purpose. The building is connected with the Sisters' Convent on Lombard (formerly Stanley) Street, and to them is assigned the general supervision of the Home. They clean the dormitories, make the beds, prepare the meals, and do the washing and ironing for the boys. They also mend their clothes, do all the sewing they may require, and make the most of their garments. The boys seem to like the Home very much, and nearly, if not all, the Catholic newsboys of the city patronize it. They are obliged to be indoors by eight o'clock in the evening, and during the winter months they have the advantage of a night-school, while those who desire it can have instruction at all times from the good Sisters. The St. Nicholas Home fully accomplishes the designs of its venerable founder by providing a comfortable lodging-house for these poor street waifs. The sums earned by the boys, however, would not alone suffice for the maintenance of the institution. These are supplemented by collections in the Cathedral and by the generous dona-

cathedral of Sarum, at Eton, and in the other schools and colleges of England, see the History and Antiquities of the Catholic Church of Salisbury, printed anno 1722, p. 74.

tions of charitable citizens. The financial affairs are managed by a committee of Catholic gentlemen who have kindly interested themselves in the advancement and prosperity of this charitable work. A chapel is provided and the boys who are Catholics are required to attend prayers, and are also taught their catechism. The boys living at the Home are, as a general rule, very orderly and well-behaved. Their moral feelings are appealed to, and the kindly and motherly interest of the good nuns in their personal comfort, and spiritual welfare, has a very marked effect in restraining any vicious propensities. Some boys who have been inmates of the St. Nicholas Home have already acquired honorable positions in the world, and may become husbands, fathers, and honorable members of society. If any thus succeed in life they may attribute their success to the influence of the Home, and they should ever cherish the name and bless the memory of the good man to whom they owe so much.

We would here notice the institution called Notre Dame Boarding House, though it should not be classed among the charitable institutions, as its inmates pay for the accommodations afforded. It was established by the Archbishop for the benefit of the working girls of the city, as well as for those young women who come to Toronto to attend the Normal School. His Grace felt deeply interested in the spiritual and moral welfare of the industrious and hardworking girls of Toronto who are obliged to earn their living; he pitied their isolated and lonely condition, living, as they do in a great majority of cases, entire strangers in a large city, without relatives or friends, and with no other companionship than the chance acquaintances of a city boarding-house.

He knew that many young Catholic girls came to Toronto every year to learn some trade or to occupy positions in stores; that they are friendless and unprotected, and that the acquaintances they were likely to make, or the friendship, formed, especially among the young men usually to be met in a city boarding-house, are not of a character either prudent or safe. Many of these young persons thus coming to the city are good, practical Catholics. They have been accustomed from early childhood to the faithful and regular performance of their religious duties. Coming as they do to a strange city, in which they are utterly friendless, they feel keenly the want of those sustaining religious influences to which they have so long been accustomed; and, indeed, the sudden withdrawal of these moral supports which is so often one of the consequences of migrating from their native villages into over-crowded cities, is really the one great and imminent danger to which young Catholic working girls are exposed in our large and absorbing centres of population.* Reflecting on this matter the happy idea occurred to the Archbishop of providing a boarding-house for this class of persons, where they might, at a very moderate cost, be able to enjoy all the comforts of a home, have the benefit of agreeable and congenial associates, get rid of the discomforts and annoyances of the ordinary boarding-house, and at the same time escape the temp-

---

* Some provision has been made in this respect so far as young men are concerned, by our Protestant friends, by the establishment of Young Men's Christian Associations in nearly every city and large town in the country, and if something of the same kind could be done for the benefit of our Catholic young men, it would prove a strong bulwark against the seductions of city life, and a formidable rival to the saloon and the billiard-room.

tations and dangers of city life.   For this object the Notre Dame Boarding House was established.

The old orphan asylum on Jarvis* Street was considered by His Grace a very suitable location for his purpose. A new addition of brick was built, containing rooms for the accommodation of fifty boarders. The institution is under the care and direction of the Sisters of St. Joseph, who manage the whole establishment. The sums charged for board vary according as the boarder occupies a room by herself,' or shares one with another, but in no case does it exceed three dollars per week. For this very moderate charge as good board is given as is usually obtained in the ordinary city boarding-house patronized by this class of persons. The girls are obliged to be in by nine o'clock in the evening, and the lights are extinguished at ten. Everything in the institution, as may be supposed, is conducted in the most perfect order. A large room in the building is fitted up as a chapel, and regular morning and evening prayers are recited.†
A quiet and religious atmosphere pervades the whole establishment, and the good nuns take every means to render the inmates happy and contented. The Notre Dame Boarding House is a pronounced success, and if there were sufficient accommodation twice the number of boarders could be easily obtained. Applications for board are constantly being refused for lack of room. Although the rules of the house as to being in at night and retiring are strictly enforced, yet they are cheerfully

---

* The orphans were moved from Jarvis Street in 1859.

† The inmates of this institution are soon to remove to more respectable and commodious quarters. St. John's Hall, which is now being improved and altered, will be the Notre Dame Institute of the near future.

obeyed, and are not objected to by the boarders. It is quite evident, from the success of this institution, that Catholic working girls, at least, are quite prepared and entirely willing to conform to any reasonable restrictions in order to enjoy the privileges, advantages, and domestic comforts of such an establishment as the Notre Dame Boarding House.*   It is an institution that should attract the active sympathy and material assistance of our rich Catholic fellow-citizens, as there could be no nobler work in which the charitable and philanthropic man of wealth could engage, or to which he could with better effect donate a small portion of his extensive means, than in doing something to ameliorate the condition of the working girls employed in our large cities.

It is much to be regretted that Catholics of wealth in this country display such apathy towards our charitable and benevolent institutions, show such slight interest in their success, and contribute so little, in proportion to their means, towards their support and maintenance.   The Catholic rich do not, as a body, contribute in proportion to their wealth in any degree to the same extent as the moderately well off, or even the comparatively poor do, either to the support of the Church or in the cause of charity. The Catholic Church in this country, and Catholic benevolent institutions are, in fact, supported by the

---

*The late A. T. Stewart, the well-known New York millionaire, attempted something of the same kind many years ago for the benefit of the New York working girls, but it proved a failure. He built an immense palatial structure, fitted up with all modern improvements, and capable of accommodating several hundred boarders. It was opened with great *eclat*, but the New York girls refused to be bound to any rules as to hours, and as they particularly objected to the rule prohibiting them from receiving their gentlemen friends, the great merchant prince's benevolent scheme ignominiously failed.

poor and the moderately well-to-do members of the Church. They give far more abundantly, in proportion to their means, than do their rich neighbors. Who ever heard of a rich Catholic in this country building a hospital, founding a college, establishing a scholarship, endowing a professor's chair, or doing anything with his vast wealth for the real good of society or his fellow man? This is not the case with the wealthy members of the various Protestant churches. It is no exaggeration to say that the rich Protestant gives hundreds where the rich Catholic gives tens.* It is no uncommon thing to read in the papers of Protestants who have acquired wealth giving immense sums to the building of churches, the founding of hospitals, asylums, colleges, and in various other ways testifying to their belief that the man who has acquired wealth owes something to the community in which he lives, and that a portion of a rich man's wealth ought to be devoted to nobler purposes than mere vulgar extravagance and pretentious ostentation.

The latest outcome of His Grace's zeal and interest in behalf of the poor and forsaken children is the establishment of Sunnyside, a large commodious suburban residence, surrounded by extensive grounds, situated on the lake shore, which, being for sale, he has purchased, and to which he proposes to transfer the orphan boys now in the House of Providence. A large addition has been made lately to the building. In their new abode the children will have the benefit of pure air and enjoy the invigorating charms of country life. The place is situated in the outskirts

* A well-known Toronto merchant, a member of the Methodist body, donates every year $10,000 of his income to the cause of charity and to his church.

of the city, and the few acres of land attached will be cultivated by the boys, and will no doubt be made to contribute to the support of the establishment.

We have endeavored in the last two chapters to give the reader some idea of the number and importance of the Catholic benevolent and charitable institutions of Toronto.   As we have before remarked, all these institutions owe their origin, or at least their success and their present flourishing condition, to the zeal and energy of Archbishop Lynch. No matter what might be the pressing nature of his episcopal functions — and in the Archdiocese of Toronto, embracing, as it does, the whole Province of Ontario, the duties of the spiritual chief of the Catholic Church must be many and onerous—the Archbishop always finds time to originate some new scheme, or to mature some new plan for ameliorating the condition of suffering humanity, to aid the outcast, help the unfortunate, or provide for the orphan.   For his own personal comfort the Archbishop cares very little and takes but small heed. His modest and plainly furnished apartments in St. John's Grove are hardly up to the better class of rooms in the House of Providence, while his table would most likely excite a smile of contempt in the epicure or *bon vivant*.   His is not the nature to live on the fat of the land and fare sumptuously every day, while hundreds of his fellow-creatures are suffering for the common necessaries of life.   He is a man who takes life too seriously to enjoy the happiness of this world.   He has too high and exalted an idea of his duties as a pastor of the Church, and is too profoundly impressed with the terrible responsibilities they entail, ever to enjoy that perfect repose which only the heart that is callous to the misery that surrounds it can hope to attain. If he were a man who loved the world and the things thereof, he would trouble himself very little with its miseries, or the wretched lot of the poor and unfortunate; being the man he is, with a heart capable of feeling and suffering, we have, as the results, the splendid monuments of benevolence and charity which we have attempted to describe in the foregoing pages.

CHAPTER XIX.

INSTITUTIONS AT NIAGARA FALLS.

*Establishment of Educational and other Institutions at Niagara Falls—
Loretto Convent and Monastery of the Carmelites—The Archbishop's
Pastoral—What led to the Establishment of these Institutions by His
Grace—The Order of Loretto—Their Work—The Carmelite Order—
For what Purpose the Monastery is Established at the Falls—The
Pilgrim's Reflections on Visiting the Monastery—The Future of these
Institutions.*

AMONG the many institutions established in
the diocese of Toronto by Archbishop Lynch,
not the least important are those at the Falls
of Niagara. Having so successfully founded the
College of the Angels on the American bank of
the Niagara River, he at once, on becoming Bishop
of Toronto, cast about for a suitable location near
the great Cataract where he hoped at some future
day to be able to erect buildings and establish educational and other institutions worthy of this grand
and mighty work of nature and its picturesque
surroundings. This he was happily enabled to do
much sooner than he had at first anticipated, and the
fine building of the Loretto Nuns, which now
stands overlooking the Falls on the Canadian bank,
and from whose balcony is spread out before the
spectator a scene unsurpassed for beauty and grandeur on the face of the earth, and the Carmelite
monastery opposite—a small building at present, but
destined at some future day to give place to a more
commodious structure—are the first results of a long-

cherished design on the part of the Archbishop. Perhaps no better idea of the location, the nature and object of these institutions, and the hopes and aspirations that gave them birth, can be obtained than by the perusal of the following pastoral issued by His Grace in April, 1876.

The Cataract of Niagara yearly attracts thousands of lovers of sublimity and grandeur. They come to wonder, but few, alas, to pray. The place has been to us from childhood an object of the greatest interest. A picture of it fell into our hands—we were awe-struck with its beauty, and wished that we could adore God there. The vision of it haunted us through life. The providence of God at length conducted us to it, and almost miraculously provided the means of commencing near it the Seminary of Our Lady of Angels in the diocese of Buffalo, N. Y. On our being appointed by the Holy See Bishop of Toronto, it was our first care to secure on the Canada side of Niagara Falls a large tract of land on which to erect religious establishments, where God would be worshipped with a perfect homage of sacrifice and praise, and where the Catholic Church would be fittingly represented.

It was at the commencement of the American civil war. Our heart was moved with sorrow at the loss of many lives, and the prospect of so many souls going before God in judgment, some, it is to be feared, but ill prepared. The beautiful rainbow that spanned the Cataract, the sign of peace between God and the sinner, suggested prayers and hopes to see the war soon ended; and we called the church " Our Lady of Victories or of Peace." A convent was soon erected on the grounds, and nuns of the Institute of the Blessed Virgin Mary, called of Loretto, were installed. This Order had its heroic beginnings in the reigns of Henry VIII. and Elizabeth of England. Ladies of noble birth fled to Bavaria to avoid death or the loss of religious rights in their own country. They formed a Religious Community, approved of by Clement XI., re-entered England towards the close of the last century, and subsequently came to Toronto on the invitation of its first bishop, the venerable and saintly Dr. Power. These good nuns, whilst not engaged in imparting a higher education to young ladies who assemble at the convent from all parts of the country, occupy their time in adoring God, and contemplating His overflowing sweetness and bounty in the most blessed sacrament. Their chapel windows overlook the grandest scene in the world, and holy thoughts and prayer arise to heaven as the spray ascends to form clouds that fertilize the earth with refreshing showers. The convent chapel is dedicated to the most blessed sacrament, in hopes that when the Community will be sufficiently numerous it may keep up a perpetual adoration.

We have for many years searched for a fervent congregation of men to found a monastery and a church worthy of the place and its destination. Enthusiastic pilgrims of nature's grandeur come here to enjoy its beauty; others, alas, to drown remorse. We desired to have a religious house where those pilgrims would be attracted to adore nature's God in spirit and in truth, and who would there find, in solitude and rest, how great and merciful God is. The fathers of the Order of Our Lady of Mount Carmel, the most ancient in the Church and dear to the heart of our Blessed Mother, have commenced this good work. Our Holy Father Pius IX. has been graciously pleased to confer upon the present little church plenary indulgences and other favors granted to the most ancient pilgrimages of the old world. The fathers also propose, when a suitable house is built, to receive prelates and clergy of the Church as well as laity to make retreats; and to those priests, worn out in the service of their Divine Master, a home where they can quietly prepare for eternity. Missions will be also given in parishes by the religious at the request of the bishops. A place more fitting for such an Institution could hardly be found. God Himself has made the selection. It is easy of approach from all parts of the country, and on the confines of two great nations. We have full confidence that God will finish His own good work by inspiring the hearts that love Him, and

His Blessed Mother of Mount Carmel, to contribute to the erection of a church and monastery there. Those pious souls will lay up for themselves treasures in the bosom of God, from which they will draw in their great need, when about to balance their accounts before His judgment-seat.

Let us accompany the Christian soul in his religious pilgrimage at Niagara Falls. At first sight he will be overawed by its grandeur and stunned by its thunder; recovering, he will raise his heart to the God that created it, and will presently sink down into the depths of his own nothingness. For a while he is completely absorbed, as if entranced; after a time, he gains on himself, and cries out, "*Domine, Dominus noster.*" O Lord, Our Lord, how admirable is thy name on earth!" To speak now is irksome to him. His whole soul is filled with God; he wants to be alone. Tears, with an irresistible force, will relieve his heart, and he shall soon exclaim: "What, O Lord, is man, that thou art mindful of him; or the son of man, that thou shouldst visit him." He looks upon that broad, deep, and turbulent volume of water, dashing over a precipice about one hundred and sixty feet in height, and two thousand eight hundred feet in its whole span, with a thunder echoed from the lake below with its mountain banks; and thinks of the awful power of Him who speaks on the "voice of many waters," and of his own last leap into eternity. In hope he raises his eyes and sees quietly ascending clouds formed from the spray, bridged in the centre by a beautiful rainbow. Again he cries out: "Let my prayer ascend as incense in thy sight. Let my last sigh be one of love, after making my peace with God and the world."

The water, as it sweeps over the falls, sinks deeply by its weight and momentum; and after gurgling, seething and foaming, rises again to the surface. One is reminded of that purification which takes place after death, and the troubles and agonies of the poor soul in the process of purification, to be cleansed before its rising to enjoy the brightness and glory of God's sweet countenance. The water of the lake below has also its warning lesson. It is solemn and still as death after a busy and turbulent life. Death holds many a deep secret of a good or an ill-spent life. He is aroused from his reverie by the shriek and noise of an engine, as it whirls on by the banks above, with its string of cars filled with the fashionable and the gay, some intent on pleasure, others on gain. "O," he may say, "poor mortals, how long will you hunt after vanity and be in love with lies! In a few years you will be all gone, and what will be the fate of your immortal souls for all eternity?" Let us return with the pilgrim to the monastery, and rest a little, and from the windows of his temporary cell contemplate the rapids above the Falls. It is morning. At the horizon, where the waters and the clouds appear to meet, all is calm and tranquil. Soon the river contracts; and peacefully running for a while, it meets with ledges of rock, and dashing itself into foam and whirling eddies, forms hundreds of small waterfalls, which, catching the rays of the morning sun, appear as so many white-crested billows of the sea after a storm. Joy and gladness are typified in those sparkling waves. Occasionally tiny rainbows may be seen enamelling the brows of those miniature cataracts; and as innumerable bubbles fall, pearls and jewels are reflected in prismatic colors in the foam. In these are seen emblems of the morning of life, when candor, humility, and loveliness portray the innocence of a happy soul basking in the sunshine of God's love.

Everything now is gay and joyful, and bright with hopes of wealth and pleasure, and a long and happy life. The world presents itself in all those gorgeous colors that dazzle the imagination; but the time shall come when disappointments, sorrows, and sickness will overtake him; a troubled and stormy life may be his lot; and he shall be, when the soul shall tremble on the precipice of eternity, awaiting to be ushered into the presence of his Maker. Then indeed will the pleasures and honors of the world appear as cruel mockeries, and sacrifices for Christ the only treasures worthy of man's toil. A day will arrive when this beauty will be changed. The unheeding Christian dwells on hopes of grandeur and wealth, and hurries from pleasure to pleasure; until at length the soul, writhing in remorse, is launched into an unhappy eternity, from which there is no returning. On rainy days a great change comes over the whole scenery at the Falls. The atmosphere is gloomy and the clouds heavier here than. elsewhere; the roar of the cataract, striking against the condensed atmosphere, booms like continuous distant thunder. The mind is wrapped in solemn melancholy, and is brought to think of that pall of death which daily hangs over every one, the sinner and the saint. If a clap of thunder and a flash of lightning should add their terrors to the scene, the soul must be forcibly reminded of that awful day of judgment, and of the assembled children of Adam in the valley of Jehoshaphat, and of the questions: "What hast thou done with thy own soul, and where is thy brother? What hast thou done with many graces that I have given to thee, and where are the souls that you have scandalized and ruined both by word and example?" When night comes on the soul is wrapped, as it were, in its own winding sheet, and longs for some secure repose. How sweet and consoling it will be in those days of gloom to retire to the chapel of Our Lady of Peace, where the heart, though oppressed with sadness, yet raises itself up to God in hope for mercy, and cries for pardon and grace through the intercession of His Blessed Mother.

In the midst of the rapids are seen small islands covered with cedar and balsam trees sitting quietly in the sunshine, the waves dashing around them. The pilgrim may be reminded here of the soul strong in the grace of God and calm in the midst of the troubles of the world ; and yet "In a flood of many waters they shall not come nigh unto him." (Psalm xxxi.) How many hearts, after having discharged their load of sin and sorrow in the tribunal of Penance, will look upon those islands of peace, and that rainbow of hope, and on the glorious scene around with eyes filled with tears of gratitude welling up from an humble and contrite heart! He will bless his merciful God, who, notwithstanding his many crimes, has put around him the robe of innocence, and on his finger the ring that should remind him of a father's love and of a son's gratitude and fidelity. Joy and hope will renew his youth. In this holy retreat of Niagara Falls many will find the road to heaven, and the true pleasure of serving God, and the real joy of having escaped the terrors of the world to come.

In winter time, also, the pilgrim will be taught sublime lessons. The trees and shrubs around are covered with ice, and myriads of glassy pendants hang from the branches, reflecting in dazzling brightness the rays of the sun, and by night those of the moon. May he not consider a soul encircled by the beauty of God's graces, purchased for Him through the blood of Christ? He will hear a crash. It is a branch of a tree that breaks down under its weight of icicles. Alas! how many souls break away from God, though highly favored with His special graces, and are never again engrafted on the vine that is Christ! Again, may it not remind him of the death of the young, the beautiful, and the high-born, snatched away from the caresses of friends, the splendors of fortune, and laid low in the grave? The lunar bow by night will give him hopes that in the darkest hour of sin and sorrow God's mercy-seat is always approachable.

The Cataract of Niagara has been well called "nature's high altar;" the water, as it descends in white foam, the altar-cloth; the spray, the incense; the rainbow, the lights on the altar. One must cry out: "Great is the Lord and admirable are His works! How great is thy name through the whole world! Let us adore and love Him with our whole hearts and our whole souls." As the pilgrim passes over one of the bridges that span the islands, he will see torrents of water rushing madly as it were from the clouds, the only background to be seen; and he is reminded of the cataracts of heaven opened, and the earth drowned on account of sin. Here the soul, overawed with terror, might exclaim: "Come; let us hide in the clefts of the rocks, in the wounds of Jesus Christ, from the face of an angry God." New beauties are constantly discovering themselves at Niagara. The eye, wandering from beauty to beauty, compels the soul to salute its Maker, "As always ancient and always new."

The pilgrim may cast his mind back a few centuries, and consider the Indians, encamped around the Falls, telling the simple tales about the creation of the world, and adoring God in the twilight of their intelligences, in the best manner they could; and he might vividly portray the whole tribe preparing the most beautiful virgin for sacrifice. She is dressed in white and placed in a white canoe, the father and mother, sisters and friends, bidding their last adieus and wetting her cheeks with tears as they placed her in the frail bark and shoved it off on the edge of the great precipice, that she might be a sacrifice of propitiation and sweet pleasure to the Great Spirit, to obtain pardon for the sins of her tribe, and good hunting. What sublime reflections will the recollection of this awful ceremony bring up!

God is great and powerful and just; but He is appeased with a sacrifice. "An humble and contrite heart, O Lord, thou wilt not despise." The poor Indians must have heard of the great sacrifice which God always demanded as an acknowledgment of His sovereign dominion over the whole world, and of the sacrifices which he exacts on account of sin. Perhaps they heard of the great sacrifices of Adam and of Noah, Isaac and Jacob, and of the sacrifice of the Adorable Son of God. In their simple ignorance they wished to sacrifice something themselves; the young, pure and handsome virgin is their greatest treasure. She is sacrificed. She is sent over the Falls. They are all now dead and gone, and they are before the Great Spirit which they strove to worship, and perhaps would cry with David: "Recollect not, O God, our ignorance." May not the Christian soul here say to God: "I have been endowed with knowledge, and with wisdom, and with grace, and know that my Lord was offered in sacrifice for me; and I wish to make no sacrifice myself. I have sinned, and have not sacrificed my evil passions and worldly inclinations. Come, poor Indians, teach me your simplicity, which is better than my foolish wisdom." Again he will see a bird calmly and joyously flitting across this mighty chasm, looking down fearlessly on the scene below. It is in its native air; it has wings to soar.

Thus the soul that is freed from sin has its wings also. It can look down with serenity upon the wreck of worlds, and in death it is placid in the midst of the storms of evil spirits, and when everything around is in fury and commotion, arises quietly towards its God to rest calmly in His embrace.

The Catholic Church, or, to speak more plainly, the sublime religious souls under her influence, always sought the most beautiful and romantic places to erect monasteries and churches to the service of God. Christ Himself retired to the mountain to pray, and He sought the solitude of Thabor to manifest His glory, and Gethsemani to pour forth His sorrows into the bosom of His Father. The soul, withdrawn from the din and the noise and the bustle of this world, breaks from its tension and soars towards God. The fathers of the desert sought the wilderness and the mountain-caves, there to adore their God. Our forefathers in the faith, also, peopled the islands in the Atlantic, erecting their monasteries in clefts overlooking the mighty ocean, where the monks sat and contemplated God in the fearful storms and in the raging waves that dashed over the rocks ; and admired the works of His providence in the flight and screech of the ravens and gulls. In a storm they would imagine souls in distress crying out, " Where is my God?" See them also on the islands of blessed Lough Erne. They beheld the serenity of the sky above and the peaceful waters below, and were led to sweet and calm repose in God. Again, they sought the clefts of the mountains overlooking the smiling valleys, where they could feast their eyes on the riches and beauties of God in the fertile fields below, and pity busy mortals in their incessant toil after the things that perish. Behold the lilies of the field, the birds of the air. God clothes and provides for all. He fills the soul that is empty of this world.

In Europe there are many sanctuaries, but few in this new world. Niagara will be one, and first of the most famous where God will be adored on the spot in which He manifests Himself in such incomparable majesty and grandeur. The festivals that will be most religiously celebrated in this sanctuary, besides the first-class festivals of the Church, are the ninth of July, called Our Lady of Miracles or Peace; the sixteenth, Our Lady of Mount Carmel; twenty-ninth of September, the Festival of St. Michael; fifteenth of October, St. Teresa; twenty-first of November, Presentation of the Blessed Virgin; and the tenth of December, Festival of Our Lady of Loretto.

CHAPTER XX.

THE ARCHBISHOP AS AN IRISH PATRIOT.

His Love for Ireland—Irish Success Abroad and Failure at Home—The Reasons—The Apostolic Mission of the Irish Race—The Archbishop's Pastoral—Ireland's Divine Mission—National Aptitude—Shown from the Past—Missions Abroad—In the New World—At Present—In the United States—In Canada—Providential Preparation—Persecution in Religion—Persecution in Education—Barbarous Enactments—Carried out to the Letter—Good from Evil—Improvident Emigration—The Famine—Loss of Souls—Tenacity of the Faith—Advice in Conclusion—Irish Faith and Nationality—Secret Societies—Temperance Societies—Catholic Education—Save the Children—The Spirit of the Priesthood—Mental Culture—National Societies—Love of Ireland.

NEXT to God and his Church in the affections of Archbishop Lynch comes his country. As man or boy, priest or prelate, he has ever been faithful to the land of his birth. A Canadian Archbishop, he is yet emphatically an Irish priest at heart. Nor does this conflict with his allegiance and love for Canada, the land of his adoption. On the contrary, it seems to intensify it, for he cannot help comparing the condition of his countrymen under the free governments of Canada and the United States with their position in Ireland. Well may it be said, that an Irishman succeeds in every country but his own; and why? Is it because he is lacking in any of those qualities that insure success? The fallacy of such an assertion is proved by the brilliant success of Irishmen or their descendants in foreign lands. The O'Donnells, Walls, and O'Reillys of Spain, the Taeffes and Nugents of Austria, and the McMahons and O'Neils of France, are the best refutation of the groundless assumption that the Irishman lacks the patience, industry and energy which are so essential to success in the conflict of life, and which that hybrid product of ethnological science, the modern "Anglo-Saxon," has, by dint of continued iteration of the assertion, almost led the world to believe he alone possesses.

On this continent the Irish race has already left its impress on the social and political life of the country. In Canada and in the United States Irishmen have taken a high and prominent position in commerce, at the bar, in the various other professions, and more pronounced still is their influence in politics and in the government of the country, while as soldiers, we need only to point to the fact that the son of a Catholic Irishman, General Sheridan, is to-day the Commander-in-Chief of the United States armies, while another descendant of an Irishman, General Lynch, holds the same exalted position in the Republic of Chili, and to his military abilities is solely due the success of the Chilian arms in the late war with Peru.* If, therefore, the Irish people are so successful abroad, is it not more reasonable, and more in accord with the true principles of historical investigation, to seek for the reasons of this failure at home somewhere else than in the supposed inherent incapacity of the race. As Mr. Goldwin Smith has very truly said, in combatting the assertion that there is an inherent incapacity in the French people for self-government—(we quote from memory): "These mysterious capacities and

---

* "Scattered all over Europe," says Macaulay, "were to be found Irish counts, Irish barons, Irish Knights of St. Lewis and of St. Leopold, of the White Eagle and of the Golden Fleece, who, if they had remained in the house of bondage, could not have been ensigns of marching regiments or freemen of petty corporations."

incapacities of the Celtic race, and the French branch of it in particular, are very questionable things, and will generally be found, upon closer investigation, to resolve themselves into the influences of special circumstances perpetuated through many ages." Examined in this light, the apparent or presumed incapacity of the Irish people at home, both for self-government and for material success, can be easily explained; for certainly among no people upon the face of the earth to-day has the influence of circumstances, strongly antagonistic to their national development, been more powerfully felt than among the Irish people. To reduce a nation to the lowest scale of political and social degradation by a code of laws ingeniously framed for that very purpose, and then taunt it with being unfit for self-government, is as cruel as it is ungenerous; yet this is the strongest argument the average British Philistine can urge against any scheme of local self-government for Ireland, and there are not wanting men and journals, even on this side of the Atlantic, who live, move, and have their being in an atmosphere of freedom, to adopt and re-echo an argument as absurd in reason as it is false in fact.

Archbishop Lynch is a firm believer in the apostolic mission of the Irish race to plant the faith in other lands, and particularly among the English-speaking nations of the earth. He believes that, like the Jews of old, the Irish are a providential people, and that the fearful calamities to which they have been subjected and the dreadful sufferings they have endured have been ordained by Providence to prepare them for the grand and glorious part which they are yet destined to play in the drama of humanity. What he believes to be the future of the Irish people; their divine mission to spread the Faith and to evangelize and bring back to the Church, the English-speaking races of the world ; how they have been specially prepared for such an undertaking, and how, in the providence of the Almighty, they are to accomplish it, is eloquently and learnedly set forth in a pastoral issued on the feast of Ireland's Patron Saint, the 17th of March, 1875, from which we make the following extracts:

We address ourselves to. the millions of exiled Irish people (enough to constitute a respectable State), who will hail this day with joy and sadness, and in spirit revisit the hallowed homes, the altars and churchyards, and the holy wells of the blessed land of their birth, or that of their forefathers, and pray and mourn, and say from the depths of their souls, "God bless Ireland ! God preserve the faith of her children, and her children's children,— exiles in many lands. God bless the loved island of Holy Pontiffs, learned Confessors, Monks, Hermits and Sacred Virgins, and of tens of thousands of martyrs for that faith preached to them by their great Apostle, St. Patrick,— 'that land that God hath greatly blessed, but which man hath greatly cursed.'"   It is a holy custom on the festival of the blessed Patrick for the Irish people and their children to assist at the sacrifice of the mass, receive holy communion, and listen to sermons and exhortations to excite them to love their holy faith ; to bless God for that most precious inheritance ; to encourage them to frequent the sacraments ; and to transmit to their children, and thus to future generations, that faith for which millions of martyrs have shed their blood, which has gained for Ireland in latter times the glorious title of "the nation of martyrs," as in early days she bore that of the "Island of Confessors and Virgins;" that faith for which they have been deprived of their birthrights, their lands, their education,—have been starved, and hunted, and banished. But oh! the glorious reward—they have exchanged the pains of earth for the joys of heaven; for homes that perish, they possess mansions of eternal bliss.   On this festival they will be taught to pray for their native land, that God may cause the oppression of the poor to cease; and that He may sustain the Irish clergy and Irish parents in their efforts to shield the rising generation against the most wily, determined, powerful, and unscrupulous enemy of the Church of God—the government of England (we say the *Government of England*, for millions of her people abhor the tyranny of the rulers of Ireland)—a government which has endeavored by Godless education to undermine, when it *could not* eradicate, the faith of the people; they will be taught to pray for their persecutors, that God may change their hearts and bring them to the true faith.

We feel it a consoling duty to address all our beloved people throughout the diocese, the vast majority of whom are children of Ireland, upon this Festival of Ireland.   Our object is two-fold: to encourage them to fulfill their sacred mission of preserving the deposit of the faith once delivered to the saints, and of transmitting it to their posterity; and, secondly, to warn them against temptations which, though common to all nationalities, are particularly hurtful to a highly sensitive and religious people.

Ireland has a divine mission.   In the admirable providence of God, He selects families and nations to be the agents of His holy will.   He selected Abraham and his progeny to be His people, and Aaron and the tribe of Levi to be His priests.   He has in a special way chosen the Caucasian or present European races to be the messengers of His word to the other nations of the earth.   But from time to time He has been provoked to repudiate some of His choice.   The Jewish people are no longer the people of God; Aaron is no longer His priest.   Many nations of the earth, once bright with the lustre of the true faith, are, on account of their unworthiness and sins, no longer blest with that divine light.   But through His great mercy God has preserved for a sacred purpose one people inhabiting a little island in the western ocean. Them He has tried with the most bitter earthly afflictions.   In His unsearchable providence, He has left them under the rule of an oppressor, and scourged them with many stripes of sorrow. Yet He has reserved for them the purest of all gifts, the richest of all treasures, the inheritance of a true faith which promises them eternal life for their perseverance. And such is the portion of the Irish people. And to them has God given, not only true faith, but the extraordinary mission of spreading it through all the countries of the world.

For this sublime apostleship they have been endowed with a generous and pious nature, sublime intellect, warm and tender impulses, an indomitable hatred of tyranny, and an undying love of true liberty ; a deep-rooted thirst for learning, and an unconquerable desire to impart their knowledge to others; an abhorrence of treachery and of false friends, and an unbounded love for their benefactors. In the face of these qualities, they have also their drawbacks, like every other nation since the fall of Adam. They have, too, in a greater or less degree, the vicious counterparts of the virtues here enumerated. But they have in their faith and in their Catholic instincts a remedy for these in the frequentation of the Sacraments. Apart from this, the good qualities of the majority immensely counterbalance their faults; whilst the unrestrained vices of the minority throw a lurid glare of sad reflection upon the great virtues of the majority. It has been well said that an Irishman must do twice as well as any other man to get half the credit. On the other hand, Irish defects and vices are doubly exaggerated, from the common idea of what is to be expected from an Irishman. Let him do but half the wrong of any other man, and he will get twice the blame. So high is the estimation of the ordinary virtues of the Irish. When an Irishman is not faithful and obedient to his heavenly instincts, the luxuriance of his nature makes him very vicious, and hence the disgrace of the few is the reproach of the many.

Yet the whole history of the Irish race proves its sublime mission. God has kept, as an arrow in His quiver, this little island to go forth to conquer spiritual kingdoms for Christ. " As arrows in the hands of the powerful, so are the children of the vanquished."—Ps. cxxvi. 4.   St. Patrick found the Irish, though not Christians, yet not purely idolators.   They were primitive in their habits and customs, leading a patriarchial life, with many of the noble qualities of the present aborigines of North America.   They believed in the existence of a Supreme Spirit.   They had no idols.   St. Patrick found, in all his missionary excursions through Ireland, only one object that approached idol-worship; it was a ball surrounded by twelve pillars.   It represented the sun and the signs of the zodiac; for they were not bad astronomers even in those days.   The country people, however, in their simplicity, might have worshipped these symbols with an extra reverence; but the rapidity with which the faith of St. Patrick spread, so that in his own lifetime he could ordain priests, consecrate bishops, and found monasteries of monks and convents of holy virgins, shows clearly that the religion of Christ found many disciples, and that its seed fell on luxuriant soil.

St. Patrick's bishops and priests were so ardent in their zeal that they carried the light of the Gospel into England, Scotland, Germany, France, and even into Italy, regaining to the Church many of those people who had lost the faith on account of the incursions of barbarians and the breaking up of the Roman Empire.   These holy missionaries from Ireland are invoked as patron saints in those countries.   We have venerated their relics in cathedral churches, in monasteries, in rural parishes on the continent of Europe.   We found St. Cataldus, the Apostle of Tarentum, near Naples; St. Sedulius, famous for his fourteen books of commentaries on the Epistles of St. Paul; St. Fridolin, who instituted religious houses in Alsace, Strasbourg, and Switzerland, and who is interred on an island in the Rhine in a monastery built by himself; St. Columbus, the founder of the celebrated monastery of Bobbio, near Milan; in Luxan and Fontain St. Gaul, disciple and companion of St. Columbus, Patron of the Monastèry of St. Gall, near Lake Constance, famous to the present time for its learned men and holy monks, the admiration of all travellers; St. Fiacre, the patron saint of many churches in the diocese of Meaux and through Picardy, and whose relics are the objects of pious pilgrimages to

the present time; St. Aarden, who preached the Gospel
to the Northumbrians in England, and who was the first
bishop of the See of Lindisfarne; St. Colman, who
preached the Gospel to the Northern Saxons; St. Fursey,
especially invoked in chapels built by him near Paris; St.
Arbogast, Bishop of Strasbourg, buried on Mount Michael,
where there was a monastery dedicated under his patronage; St. Maildulphus, who established the famous school
of Inglebome, now Malmsbury; St. Cuthbert, son of an
Irish prince of Kells, in Meath, Bishop of Lindisfarne,
and now invoked as an English saint; St. Killian, apostle
of Franconia, and first Bishop of Wirtzburg, who gained
the crown of martyrdom, like St. John the Baptist, for
having reproached the incestuous adulteress Geilana; St.
Virgilius, Bishop of Fiesole, preacher of the Gospel to the
Etrurians; St. Findin, Abbot of Richew, on the Rhine;
St. Buo and St. Ernulphus, who carried the Gospel to
Iceland and founded a church under the patronage of St.
Columbia, in the city of Esinberg. We have mentioned
enough of illustrious names of the Irish nation to show
how they fulfilled their mission on the continent of Eu-
rope in the early ages.

Later on, worldly men sought conquest through a newly
discovered continent. They were devoured by a thirst
for gain; and, following the instincts of their old Scan-
dinavian ancestors, their ships swept every harbor and
inlet in quest of gold and precious stones; establishments
were formed to trade with the natives and to cajole from
them their wealth; and here, as the venerable Father
Thebaud says, the Irish ascended their ships, whether
welcome or not, pressed forward to their commercial centres, crowded their cities, and at once proceeded to practice their religion. They collected together in a little
room, perhaps, at first. With heart and will they endeavor to commence a church, and there is the beginning
of the 10,000 altars from which sacrifice ascends in this
new country. The great gold fields of California are discovered. There is a rush for gold. Irishmen go there
too, and behold the California of to-day, one of the richest
gardens of the Church of God. The diamond fields of

Southern Africa are discovered. The Irish, without intending it especially, carry there also their faith. Australia is made a penal settlement where the convicts of England and Ireland are transported to do penance for their sins far from the centres of civilization. An Irishman in his poverty steals a few shillings' worth to save his children from starvation. He, too, is sent there. He carries with him his faith; the tears of his repentance water the soil; and behold, with its archbishops and bishops, another of the most flourishing churches that could adorn old Christianity.

But this is not all. At the present hour our bishops and priests and people are spreading the faith through new worlds. They are conquering back again England and Scotland, renegade to the faith since the whirlwind and vertigo of a worldly "Reformation" snatched them from Christ's fold. They are carrying the same faith through the countries where England carries the sword and commerce. The congregation of Archbishop Manning is nine-tenths Irish, or their descendants. The same holds for the dioceses of Edinburgh and Glasgow. The 2,000,000 of Catholics of Irish extraction in England have been the largest factor in the movement for the restoration of the Hierarchy; and Scotland will owe the like honor and advantages to the same cause.*

Of the work of the Irish Apostolate in the United States, we need say nothing. At the Declaration of Independence there was no bishop in the country, and but a few priests. Now there are in the United States, and British North America, eighty-two archbishops and bishops, about 5,000 priests, and 20,000 religious of both sexes. There must be at least seven millions of Irish and their descendants on this continent of America, the majority of whom are practical Catholics. They construct the railways, dig canals, buy farms, build houses, engage in commerce, and with a never-failing generosity, support the clergy, build churches, colleges, schools and convents, and fill them, too, with their children; and thus

* One of the first acts of Leo XIII., on ascending the Papal throne, was the re-establishment of the Hierarchy in Scotland.

the boundaries of the Catholic Church are extended. "Little did those laborers think, when engaged on the Erie Canal," says an eminent Irish writer and statesman, "that they were laying the foundation of five cathedrals, with innumerable churches, schools, and convents."

In Canada their triumphs are well known. The Celtic race, Irish, and French, together with the Germans, are making of this country, to the dismay of those who do not profess the true religion, a home of true faith. The Irish in Canada have given magnificent proofs of their love of religion. Fathers and mothers have brought their children to be baptized, from the head of Lake Ontario to Kingston; they have carried them to mass through the woods for many miles, when the fires lighted on the hill-tops told them a priest had come to the neighborhood. An Irishman settles in the backwoods. He is an object of suspicion, and even of dread. He does not attend camp-meetings or places of worship in which he does not believe. He tries to instruct his children in the prayers of the true faith. Another family settles near them; the priest finds them out, and behold the nucleus of a Catholic church. By this we do not approve of any Catholic unchurching himself by settling in countries where there is no opportunity for himself, or for his children, to receive the sacraments. How many have been lost by this isolation!

It has often been the boast of many villages in this country that there was not a Papist amongst them. But a servant girl is much needed. A good Irish girl comes. She brings with her an earnest love of God and preserves her faith. This is the beginning. In a few years a modest chapel is put up and the awful sacrifice offered there. There is no stopping it. The decree of God has gone forth that the Irish people, having lost all in their own country, should establish His true religion and worship wherever they turn. The Irish people are, indeed, an apostolic people. Let us, then, exclaim with St. Paul: "Oh, the depth of the riches, and of the wisdom, and of the knowledge of God! How incomprehensible are His judgments, and how unsearchable His ways!" Truly,

He has chosen the feeble things of this world to confound the strong.

My principal aim in this pastoral letter is, to direct the mind of the Irish people and their descendants to this their providential destiny, and to exhort them to fulfill it. It is the highest honor God could confer on any people, to make them His co-operators in spreading His Gospel, and in saving those that were lost.   Here I might quote the words of St. Dionysius, " The most divine of all divine works is to co-operate with God for the salvation of souls."   The heartiest blessing on the head of the preserver is elicited from one who was about to perish.   Job strongly rejoiced to feel he had such a blessing, and cried out : " The blessing of him that was ready to perish came upon me."—(Job xxix. 13.)   That blessing has been poured, a thousand times over, on the heads of the missionaries who have come to the rescue of those who were perishing for want of the sacraments.

The Irish people were prepared, as St. Patrick was, to carry the Gospel to the uttermost bounds of the earth. They too passed through the ordeal of trials and tribulations; they were conquered in every battle, but in that of Heresy against Faith, by a victorious and unrelenting enemy.   Their lands were confiscated, their churches, convents, and monasteries destroyed, their clergy put to death, banished, or proscribed.   Famine and pestilence in the wake of war reduced the population at one time to 800,000. A few Irish were kept as servants on the confiscated lands in Ulster, Leinster, and Munster—Connaught, the poorest province, being reserved as the place of banishment for the rest.   The English language became the language of the three provinces given over to the conquering race. Of necessity the Irish who were retained as servants on their own farms had to learn English, for a penalty even was laid upon their language.   Little did the Irish children foresee, when whipped for speaking a word in their mother tongue, or for being tardy in learning the English language, that the Holy Providence of God was preparing them to convert their English masters, to spread the faith in English colonies, and to gain the new world of America to the true faith. Irish zeal, Irish enthusiasm, and Irish love of the true religion, with the English language, are spreading the faith through that empire on which the sun never sets.

Let us see how our ancestors struggled to preserve the faith once preached to their forefathers, and from it let us draw a lesson for our conduct. Henry VIII. attempted to introduce into Ireland his invented religion and his new-fangled matrimonial laws. In England, unfortunately, he succeeded in inducing too many to acknowledge him head of the Church. But in Ireland this was laughed to scorn. No Irish bishop took the oath. There was, indeed, an Englishman at the time in the See of Dublin, put there by English favor. He had already apostatized in his own country. In his letters to England, he speaks of the undaunted spirit of the Irish, who held firm against the new doctrines. It is true that an English Parliament sitting in Dublin made a decree favoring Henry VIII.'s pretensions as head of the Church; but it was never accepted by the Irish. It had been a general policy of conquering nations to impose their own form of government, and especially of religion, upon the conquered, in order to make them a people united with themselves in the most important interests. Thus the Romans, with all the might and power of persecution and sword, endeavored to oppose the introduction of Christianity into their empire, because the God of Christians was not acknowledged by the State. England, in her folly, adopted the same policy in Ireland. A new-fangled faith was enforced upon the people by statutes equalling and surpassing in their atrocity the edicts of Nero and Dioclesian. Not only religion and their native tongue, but even education was denied them, except in the false doctrines of the "Reformation." We quote from a pastoral lately addressed by the Cardinal-Archbishop and the Bishops of Ireland to their people:

"Beginning with the Act of Henry the Eighth, by which, in 1537, our old Catholic houses of education were suppressed, and coming down to the year 1771, the Statute Book is full of the most barbarous enactments against everything bearing the semblance of Catholic education,

and of laws framed with the most perverse and artful
ingenuity to spread the darkness of ignorance over the
land.   As early as the year 1641, the Catholics of Ulster,
in their 'humble remonstrance' to King Charles the First,
stated, as one of the grievances which had driven them to
arms, that the 'youth of this kingdom, especially of us
Catholics, is debarred from education and learning, in that
no school-master of our religion is admitted to be bred
beyond the seas, and the one University of Ireland doth
exclude all Catholics, thereby to make us utterly ignorant
of literature and civil breeding, which always followeth
learning and arts, insomuch that we boldly affirm we are
the most miserable and unhappy nation of the Christian
world.'

"During the sad period of Cromwell's domination in
Ireland, everything Catholic was suppressed with an iron
hand ; but it was after the restoration of King Charles the
Second that the systematic enactment of laws, 'unexam-
pled for their inhumanity, their unwarrantableness, and
their impolicy,' commenced.   In the year 1665 an act was
passed forbidding any Catholic to 'instruct or teach any
youth as a tutor or school-master' under a penalty of three
months' imprisonment for the first offence; and for every
second and other such offence, of three months' imprisonment without bail, and a fine of five pounds.   Being refused education at home, our fathers sent their children to
receive it in Catholic schools abroad.   But in the seventh
year of the reign of King William the Third, 1695, a statute was passed, which, under the penalty of forfeiture of
all property and of every civil right, forbade the sending
of a child to any foreign country 'to the intent or purpose
to enter into or be resident or trained up in any nunnery,
Popish university, college, or school, or house of Jesuits or
priests.   The children thus sent, who shall be, in such
parts beyond the seas, by any Jesuite, fryar, monk, or
other Popish person, instructed, persuaded, or strengthened in the Popish religion, in any sort to profess the
same,' and even the persons sending money for their
maintenance, were rendered liable to the same penalty ;
and at home any Catholic, teaching school or instructing

youth in learning, was subjected to a fine of twenty pounds, and to three months' imprisonment for every such offence. Even the suspicion of having committed the crime of giving to his child education in a Catholic school abroad was punishable in a Catholic parent, by the like penalty of forfeiture of all his goods, and of every civil privilege, unless he could clear himself of the charge. And yet our fathers courageously exposed themselves to those dangers in order not to imperil the inheritance of the faith for their children. Our rulers, consequently, thought it necessary to make the law more stringent, and to this effect a new act was passed in the second year of Queen Anne, 1703. Even this did not suffice ; and, at length, in the eighth year of the same queen, 1709, we find the penalty of transportation, and, in case of return, that of high treason, death, with drawing and quartering, enacted against any 'person of the Popish religion (who) shall publicly teach school, or shall instruct youth in learning in any private house within this realm, or shall be entertained to instruct youth in learning as usher, under-master, or assistant by any Protestant schoolmaster.'

"These penal laws were not a dead letter, but were rigorously enforced for the greater part of the last century. * * * It was only in the year 1782—not yet one hundred years ago—that it was discovered by our rulers that the laws 'relative to the education of Papists * * * are considered as too severe' (21 and 22 Geo. III., cap. 62). In consequence, Catholics were allowed to teach, but with the proviso that they should have obtained a license from the Protestant bishop of the diocese, who had power to recall it at any time."

The penalty for denying that the King of England was head of the Church was death. No such penalty was inflicted for the denial of Christ's divinity. Schools and monasteries were destroyed. The churches were all closed up. The most minute details of cruelty were invented to crush the true faith from the hearts of the people. But the generality of the Irish people stood firm. They said, with the sons of the Maccabees and like the early Christians, "God has given you power over our bodies. Them you may torment ; but our souls you cannot touch." They had their choice, to renounce the faith of their fore-fathers, or to suffer all the pains which the most savage tyranny could inflict upon them. They chose faith and fatherland. And now their fidelity and its fruits are steadily and surely overcoming their conquerors. Christ, too, conquered when he was conquered, nailed to the cross. The Irish numbered 800,000 in Queen Elizabeth's time. So low had they been reduced by sword, famine, and pestilence. Their conquerors outnumbered them two to one ; yet by a merciful providence of God they soon outnumbered their conquerors three to one. Chaste liv-ing, healthy early marriages, and a detestation of the crime of injury to women, were amongst the Irish the fruitful causes of their increase. The Catholics, as said above, were hardly 800,000, whilst the Protestants — English, Scotch, and a few Irish apostates—were 2,000,000, with the whole island, its riches, emoluments, and offices in their hands. Catholics were banned and hunted down; yet God preserved them, and by their unalterable faith they conquered, and their children have inherited their spirit.

Ireland's nationality has all the vigor of youth, even in foreign lands; her faith is the wonder and the praise of the nations of the earth, and more especially of the illus-trious Head of the Church. God's ways are not man's ways, and He often turns the evil doings of the wicked to the greater advantage of the good. Thus, by the cruci-fixion of His Son by malefactors was the world redeemed, and the persecution and martyrdom of the Apostles caused the spread of Christianity. We have balanced those blessed truths against worldly evils, and have become consoled.

One sorrow weighs us down, and for years has caused us the most intense suffering. We find consolation only in offering up the Holy Sacrifice of the Mass to stay the evil. It is, to see and to hear of that Catholic missionary people driven from their homes in tens of thousands, in such numbers and in such poverty that their Divine mis-sion is too often thwarted, and the children who are des-tined to transmit the faith to the yet unborn generations, fall into evil associations, are picked up by proselytizing sects, and lost to faith. We have seen, with heart-bursting grief, the destitution and ruin of many children; we have heard the fathers' groans and seen the mothers' tears, as we listened to the tale of wholesale evictions as in time of war. In the depths of our soul we abhorred this wholesale depopulation, this partial ruin of vast numbers of people; and consequently, some years ago, we, in a private letter addressed to the clergy of Ireland only, and not intended for publication, raised our voice against this oppression of the poor, that cries to Heaven for vengeance. Europe, but especially Ireland, stood appalled at the statistics with which we armed our appeal; for we knew that nothing but very hard facts would strike both friends and enemies of the Catholic Church. Of these, none more earnest, wily, and powerful than the English Government, who rejoiced at the depopulation. The object we intended was partially gained; the religious conscience of the clergy and good people of Ireland was stirred up to deprecate, as best they could, the starving and evicting process that was decimating a nation.

For the last thirty years the Irish Catholic people have been subject to some of the greatest trials; but their faith sustained them, and the immense majority came forth from the fearful ordeal victorious. We refer in particular to the terrible famine, if famine it can be called. For God had blessed the land with abundance of everything, except one little root, the food to which the poor had been reduced by merciless landlords and land laws. There was enough grain and meal in the country to feed four times the number who perished in the famine. Yet by willful mismanagement the people starved. In the much maligned Papal States, by the way, a better course of policy was pursued. When the grain crop failed, the Pope forbade exportation and thus saved the lives of his subjects, as became the father of his people. And so in consequence of England's criminal mislegislation, thousands lay on the roadside as they had been dragging their emaciated bodies to the workhouse, and, as eye-witnesses testify, though dying from want of food, they would scream and cry and shudder when the " soupers," as the proselytizers were called, would approach them with food in their hand and the temptation of renouncing their religion on their lips. "Oh, mother," cried a dying child, "don't let those soupers come into the house. I am afraid I would take their food and give up my religion, I am so very hungry." These tens of thousands of martyrs to their religion, in dying rather than renounce one iota of their faith, are the most beautiful sight the world ever presented to God since the first martyrdom.

Two millions and a half died, or fled to other countries. Tens of thousands fell victims of the disease that follows starvation, and their bones have strewn the ocean's bed, and their dying breath infected the hospitable countries that received them. Heaven received innumerable souls. They died with the words, "God's holy will be done," on their lips. For those martyred souls we have no prayer. They enjoy God.

But we will speak now of the loss of souls consequent on the wholesale sweeping away of the people obliged to desert their homes and to seek foreign countries, where, from the very necessity of their condition, many of their children must perish spiritually, and be forever lost to God. They land in destitution and poverty, and are obliged to take up their abode in the lowest slums of the cities and towns. The children are put to work with Protestant masters, and must commence to earn their living without the rudiments of education. Thus in the large cities of Great Britain and America, the Irish poor, though clinging strongly to their faith, furnish too many apostates to morality. Hence the loss of those souls must be accounted for by their inhuman evictors. The sight of this misery has often furnished our mind with a reason why the oppression of the poor cries to Heaven for vengeance.

An English nobleman once said to us, that if God visits the sins of the father on the children, the English people would be sorely punished for their criminal government of Ireland. He felt consoled when we said to him that that curse would fall on those children alone who said "Amen" to the sins of their fathers, and not on those who endeavored to make some reparation for them.

Yet Christian and Catholic instincts never grow old. On tiles and bricks found in the ruins of Roman temples and theatres is found the sign of the Cross, formed by the trowel of the pious workmen—the Christian slaves. Such tenacity of the practice of their faith may be found among the Irish in America. We have found in our missionary travels in remote districts, which a Catholic priest never before visited, Irish and German Catholic families. We were often moved to tears when admiring the wonderful providence of God, who has by this means sown over the whole land seeds of Catholicity. These families had their Sunday mass prayers, when the father or the mother would teach catechism or give a religious instruction to the children. We have baptized grown-up children who had never before seen a Catholic priest, but who had been well instructed in religion by pious parents. We have sometimes been obliged to pause, during the Holy Sacrifice of the Mass, on account of the cries and sobs of the people, who had almost despaired of ever seeing a priest again. We must acknowledge, however, that all were not so fervent, or so successful in bringing up their children piously, unassisted by a priest; and again we repeat that the loss of souls from the want of priests has been very great. What we have said of America is equally applicable to all countries where the English language prevails. Nearly half the students of the Propaganda at Rome are Irishmen, or of Irish extraction, destined for the foreign missions, chiefly under Irish bishops. We were informed in Rome by a Capuchin father, who was chaplain to gangs of French workmen employed in digging the Suez Canal, that an English contractor, who had in his pay a goodly number of Irish workmen, would not allow them the use of a boat on Sundays to go to mass. "But the faithful Irish," said he, "tied their clothes upon their heads, swam from their little island on the Nile, and heard mass, to the great edification of my French congregation."

Thus, dearly beloved brethren, we have seen how at home and abroad, in the past and in the present, the Irish race has carried out the designs of God upon it. In the hands of Him who "makes all things work together unto good," who uses the "weak things of this world to confound the strong," in His hands has this great work been done. "By the Lord is this done, and it is wonderful in our sight."—Ps. cxvii., 23.

In order to draw the practical lesson from this great festival of St. Patrick, we most earnestly recommend to his spiritual children :

1st. To cherish a love of faith and fatherland. These two loves come from God. They are virtues, and their impulses are most noble.

Irish nationality and the Catholic religion go hand in hand. To break up that nationality is to do serious injury to religion. Through the great mercy of God there has always flourished in Ireland a true patriotism, betimes wild and foolish, yet intense. But it is our hope and prayer that this race of men will never become extinct. Whatever pertains to politics in Ireland is always mixed up with religion and with the preservation of the people. There are some children of Irishmen who, hardly worthy of having a father, are ashamed of their nationality because it is down-trodden. "Apostasy to nationality," says an illustrious author, "is the first step to apostasy in religion." We have in the higher walks of Irish life many examples of this truth. Tares will grow up among the good wheat. Yet, the Irish clergy, though often tempted by large bribes of worldly gains to take sides with the conquering race, never could be induced to abandon the people. They spurned the pensions offered them by the English government, and preferred poverty with their flocks to being the salaried emissaries of any government of this world. From time to time they incur the displeasure of some over-zealous patriots; but the policy of the Irish clergy has preserved the people from greater extermination and butchery.

It is true that some descendants of the Irish, when too highly favored by Providence in worldly goods, have become ashamed of the land of their fathers, because, indeed, it is under the hand of an oppressor. They will even change or disfigure their names, forgetting that the Irish race is the oldest, most respectable, and least contaminated in all Europe. But there will always be national abortions, and, as I have said, tares will grow up amongst the good wheat.*

Another means of preserving the nationality and faith of the Irish has been also providential. We have, diffused over the country, in almost every city and town, Irish societies, in which fatherland and religion are fostered, and who, on the recurrence of the festival of their patron saint, attend church and receive the Sacraments, and proclaim to the world their undying love of Ireland and of their faith. This is another of the providential dispositions of God to transmit to future generations of Irishmen the noble spirit of their ancestors. These societies, under the direction of the clergy, their best friends, form, as it were, banks to preserve this mighty flood of population from being wasted and absorbed in other and less religious people.

2d. To avoid *all* secret societies, since from their very nature they fall under the censure of the Church. Whatever hates the light cannot be good.

3d. We most earnestly recommend the formation of temperance societies, wherever there are ten Irishmen. Would to God that during the last fifty years temperance societies had been as numerous as at the present time. Tens of thousands of unfortunate Irishmen would have to-day happy homes and beautiful families.

We believe that the Irish people do not drink more than others; but their blood is so hot, and their nature so fervid and exuberant, that adding to it the fire of alcohol the Irishman becomes more unreasonable than men of other and more plodding 'temperaments. The remedy for the latter failing is, we thank God, being rapidly applied by this grand movement of temperance, aided, as it must be, by the frequentation of the Sacraments. A Cardinal said to me in Rome: "These teetotal Irishmen must be saints, since, having such splendid qualities of heart and mind, they add to them the extraordinary mortification of total

---

* We never hear of an Irishman belittling his own race or country without being reminded of Dr. Johnson's satirical remark: "The Irish, Sir, are a very candid people ; they never speak well of each other."

abstinence." Intoxicating liquors cause great crimes and misery. They are misery itself. Of all the virtues that make an Irishman happy, and make him tend to the accomplishment of his apostleship, temperance is the most necessary, after his faith.

4th. We exhort Irish Catholic parents to procure for their children a Christian, Catholic education. In mixed schools, both faith and morals are in great danger. Where there is not the restraint or the sacramental grace of confession, there must be certainly a large amount of bad example and vice amongst youth. Parents say: "I must get the best education for my children, that they may prosper in this world." My dear parents, consider that your children have immortal souls, and through all eternity they may regret that you did not think so when you were rearing them. What will it profit you or them if you gain the riches of the world and lose Heaven. If you want to have consolation in your old age with your children, train them up in the holy love and fear of God. Our ancestors have sacrificed all in this world for their faith and that of their children, and why not sacrifice a little for the same object? Do then all you can to encourage the establishment of Catholic schools, for where they have been fairly established they are generally not inferior to the others.

The enemies of our creed and country lose no opportunity of seducing our people into heresy; and the many Irish Catholic names which we begin to find amongst the ministers of the Protestant religion prove what we have said to be but too often true. The Irish heart is religious; and the mind of a child, so easily warped to heavenly feeling, can be readily influenced to what he considers the honorable work of preaching the Gospel. It is, therefore, looking upon the destruction of this race as one of the greatest losses which the Church could sustain, and as hindering the designs of providence, that we are so solicitous for the preservation of this people and of their children. We regard it as one of the greatest public benefits. For by their means the true faith will be preserved in whatever land they inhabit in large numbers.

Were the children preserved, and had there been priests enough to gather them into congregations, the Church would rejoice in additional millions of Catholics in this country. It has been the hope and aim of our life to preserve as many as we could of the children of this noble race. They fill every Catholic college, school, and convent in this country. Read the ordinations in the various seminaries, and Irish names are the most numerous. Read of the names of those holy virgins who consecrate their purity to God in the thousands of convents that bless this country, and the Irish names predominate. We are delighted with the deep faith and great wisdom of children of the second generation born in this country. Their noble character of truth and honor, their respect for their parents and their priests, their reverence in receiving the Sacraments, their charity to the orphans, and their willingness to render a service, have often charmed us. Yet there is a great deal to be done. Would to God we had some of those monasteries of Ireland in her glorious days, where students could be received gratis, that by good education they might be fitted to take a place in society, and where at the same time their eternal welfare could be cared for. The loss of one child, we repeat, is the loss of all its posterity. And hence the duty of preserving the present generation of Irish children is the more incumbent on us. It may be very well to build costly churches, but it is far better to preserve living temples of the Holy Spirit.

5th. Let Irish mothers cultivate amongst their sons the holy spirit of the priesthood. And let Irish families in this country, as in Ireland, make it their glory to have a priest of their own blood to offer up the holy sacrifice of the mass for them. And to the young aspirants to the ecclesiastical state, we would say: Be of good cheer; poverty will be no obstacle to the realization of your hopes. Preserve the purity of your bodies and of your souls. Pray; frequent the Sacraments; be devout to the Immaculate Mother of our High Priest, Jesus Christ; and God will send an angel from Heaven to teach you rather than allow your divine vocation to be lost.

6th. Cultivate the good, sound literature of the age.

You have, for instance, the lives of the Irish Saints now brought to light, from the archives especially of foreign countries, by priests and patriots of the highest order of talent and merit. For the history of this providential people is more studied in foreign countries than in their own. Their undying perseverance in faith and nationality, against the greatest odds, has challenged the admiration of the world. Read, then, the lives of your country's saints; read, too, of her heroes, raised for her by God in her adversities. Read, and learn from their example. Learn, too, the present state of your country. You can do this by hearing lectures, by reading our good Catholic newspapers. They are an immense means of instruction and improvement.

7th. We recommend to the national societies the care of the poor, of emigrants, and especially of the orphans. They bear in their hearts a treasure above all worldly riches—that is, the faith, which is our victory. Let it not be lost. For faith, to the Irishman, is his consolation in the darkest hour of affliction; his hope when the world frowns upon him. His Church is the bosom of his home and country. When lonesome in a foreign country, he seeks consolation from his God alone. His faith to him is everything, for it promises him an eternal reward in the enjoyment of God and of his friends in Heaven.

8th. Lend a helping hand to all peaceful and constitutional struggles of the Irish at home. But do not allow yourselves to be led off in this matter by feelings of resentment or by first impulse; no good can come from such inconsiderate action.

There is, in this connection, another evil insinuated by bad and irreligious men. It is to divide the clergy from the mass of their people; for what purpose is evident—to withdraw them from the prudent and religious influence of the Catholic Church, and to place them under the influence of secular demagoguism, to make them tools of a party, to be used as best suits self-interest and evil associations. The Irish clergy have always stood by the people, and by their rights; and the mass of the people in return have stood by their clergy, and followed their advice. It is true, that when the people, infuriated by crushing tyranny, were instigated to rise to assert their rights as men, the clergy strove to pacify them. They did not tell them that they had no rights to save; but they told them that the little that was left them would be wrested from them by an overpowering force, and that a rising of weakness against power would only end in sad disaster, and cause misery untold, to their families. In this they acted as prudent and patriotic counsellors, and not as abettors of tyranny. In this country of Canada, as a minority, we enjoy rights and liberties which the majority in Ireland are denied; and as we increase in numbers and wealth, *we will enjoy more.* Hence loyalty to this country is a sacred duty. As Irishmen, we need not grudge to England the little power that she enjoys here, since we make our own laws and our own government. To injure this country, is to injure ourselves. Were Ireland governed as Canada, she would be a happy country; and she would be unworthy of her existence as a nation if she were contented with less.*

* The following extract is from an editorial in the Toronto *Globe* of March 19, 1857, on the above Pastoral: "We have more than once pointed out the fact that in Ireland Roman Catholicism is not merely a religion, but a patriotism, and no better instance of how interwoven it is with Irish politics could be found than the pastoral of Archbishop Lynch, read on Wednesday in St. Michael's Cathedral. If at this moment, in every quarter of the world, thousands of British-born subjects arrayed in green celebrate St. Patrick's Day with no loving feelings for England, and no respect for the hated red which they would fain pull beneath that which they regard as a holier color, what must be thanked for this is an oppression so unjust, so complete, so galling, that it makes a Froude, with all his sympathies for rigor, stand aghast, and has arrayed the consciences of enlightened men, the world over, against a nation which saw the cogency of liberal arguments everywhere else but in Ireland and amongst Irish Catholics. What was patriotism in Poland, what was noble in Italy, what was sacred in Spain, what was justice in Germany, in Ireland was disloyalty, dishonor, political sacrilege, and unqualified treason. In all the afflictions of the people the Irish priest was afflicted, and when, in their own country, every avenue to distinction, to honor, to aught beside a species of serfdom was closed against them, the Roman Catholic Church threw open her honors to the social outcast and the officially proscribed. Her priesthood was within the reach of the Irish peasant; he might aspire to her bishoprics and archiepiscopal sees; there was no barrier between his low estate and princely rank in a society which claimed to look down on the Royal caste. The Church did for the Irish

peasant in the seventeenth, eighteenth, and nineteenth centuries what she did for the creatures of the soil in the Middle Ages, in the times of the barons, standing between him and the world's contempt and his own ; she also not only braved but suffered with him the violence of power. And it must be confessed that he has repaid her with gratitude, for in no part of the world can the traveller go without finding strong, able men, with Irish names and Irish accents, upholding a cause which no longer attracts the highest intelligence of other nationalities."

The writer, we presume, then, would not class Newman, Manning, and Brownson among the "highest intelligence" of their respective nations.

CHAPTER XXI.

ON the occasion of Bishop Lynch's first visit to Rome, in 1862, after his elevation to the episcopacy, he visited Ireland. He there saw with his own eyes the wretched condition of the Irish people in their own land ; but a greater evil, as it appeared to him, was their wholesale deportation. On this subject he, in 1865, addressed a letter to the Bishops of Ireland, quoting statistics as to the effects of such emigration, that completely astounded, not only the hierarchy of Ireland, but of all Catholic Europe. The letter was translated into French and extensively circulated among the clergy of France. His Lordship wrote this letter with much pain. It was necessary, he thought, that the people of Ireland, and particularly the Bishops of that country, should be fully informed of, and should thoroughly understand, the loss to soul and body suffered by vast numbers of these poor immigrants thrown, as they were, on the shores of America, with no provision made for their reception, and a prey to all the temptations and dangers of the great cities of the Atlantic coast. The question of improvident emigration having at last been forced upon the attention of the American government, by the action of the British government in shipping the inmates of the Irish poor-houses and the pauper population of the country, generally, to American ports— the victims of its own misrule and oppression—the indignation of the American people became aroused, and the subject at once assumed an importance it had not before possessed.   Some dissatisfaction was expressed in Ireland at the publication of the statistics contained in Bishop Lynch's letter, but His Lordship thought at the time that the truth, however unpalatable, had better be told, and that desperate diseases required desperate remedies.   Late events have fully justified the course the present Archbishop of Toronto then took.

In 1883 His Grace addressed to the Bishops and clergy of Ireland another letter on the same subject, as follows :

TORONTO, November, 1883.

We are forced again by the most pressing calls of duty towards the Church, and charity towards the Irish people, to address another letter to you on the evils of a wholesale emigration of an impoverished people.   The evils that we every day witness around us make a deeper impression than the evils which we merely hear of.   Hence our concern and deep sorrow.   The Irish question of to-day partakes more of a social and religious, than of a political, character.   We address *you*, Most Rev. Prelates and Clergy, to whom the good Catholics of Ireland look for counsel and support in their increasing and dire calamities. They have before them the history of holy bishops, an Ambrose, a Chrysostom, not to speak of saintly Irish Prelates, lately alluded to by the illustrious Bishop of Achonry, who exposed themselves to the anger of tyrants, and suffered too, whilst endeavoring to protect the poor flock of Christ.   Where shall we find heroes of charity and patriotism if not among the prelates of God's Church? We did not, we repeat, fully realize the justice of this sentence of the sacred Scripture, " That the oppression of the poor cries to heaven for vengeance," until we witnessed the social and moral degradation, and consequently the loss of souls of these victims of oppression, both at home and abroad, where many of them must necessarily sink deeper still in the scale of humanity if something be not done to relieve them.

There are occasions of vice as well as of virtue, and the Irish people, having the taint of original sin, in common with others, will fall when cast into the proximate occasion of vice. In matters of faith it is well known that they fall far less than any other people. A miracle of God's mercy is shown in them by the spread and preservation of their faith in circumstances the most trying and unfavorable. It is, indeed, surprising that a greater number of the Irish people have not lost their faith, when every means has been employed to pervert them. It is very rarely that any of the older people abandon their faith, in foreign countries. We have said before that were the Irish people permitted to emigrate as the Germans, or even the Icelanders do, with some means to make a new start in life, then, indeed, the loss of the Irish children to the faith would be far less. What signifies the great fortune of a few pounds given the Irish to begin life in a strange land? It may supply the means of support for a few days, but that is all.

We are accustomed to count with pleasure the gains to the Catholic Church in America by Irish immigration; but it pains us to consider the loss of the offspring of a Catholic people. We must acknowledge that millions of the Irish race have, from various causes, been lost to the Church in this country since its first settlement; the want of priests being the principal reason. We shall hereafter enumerate others that operate at the present time.

We presumed to send to Pope Pius IX., of blessed memory, a copy of our last letter to the Irish clergy on the loss of souls, consequent on wholesale and improvident emigration. His Holiness was deeply moved by the letter, and especially by the proofs that we brought forward. Our Holy Father designed, through the Prefect of the Propaganda, to address us a letter, thanking us and directing us "*agere cum Episcopis Hiberniæ de hac re*." We quoted statistics of jails, prisons, and the returns of Protestant societies for the protection of children, tens of thousands of whom were Irish Catholics, and were sent to the Western States and bound to Protestant farmers. In many instances their names were changed that their parentage might not be known. We have met some of those children, now men and women, staunch Protestants. Some, however, have been reconverted to the faith. We were blamed by some parties for exposing the faults of our people, but we were thanked for our courage in having done so for a good purpose, by the highest dignitaries of the Church of America.

We thought that statistics were necessary to prove a point, which simple narration would not sufficiently impress on some minds, always accustomed to look on the bright side of things.

Any people treated as the Irish have been treated would, doubtless, like the poor man travelling from Jerusalem to Jericho, have fallen in greater numbers and into deeper crime. The statistics of prisons show that the majority of Irish culprits are incarcerated for the lighter misdemeanors, especially those arising from drink and high temper. Any one who knows a little of human nature will not be surprised to find such a people as the Irish—robbed of their manhood and self-respect at home, sent adrift in this new country, abandoned to themselves, in many cases without the restraints of religion, home associations and good companions, and all the while oppressed with poverty—contributing more than their share to prisons, jails, poor-houses, and lunatic asylums.

We repeat that it is almost miraculous that so many of the Irish continue religious and faithful in these most adverse circumstances. We shall now attempt to enumerate the causes of the great loss of souls, which may in great part be remedied in future. Before doing so we must protest against all secret societies which are condemned by the Church. They are injurious in various ways—First, they exclude the members from all participation in the sacraments and prayers of the Church. Secondly, those secret political societies, being composed principally of reckless men, who will betray their companions for money to save themselves from punishment, do not gain their object. We must also protest most emphatically against the oppression of the poor, and against unjust and inhuman evictions from their homes of thousands of families in the dead of winter, to be exposed to death, homeless and foodless, to be sent to the poor-house or driven to a foreign land, often to fall into deeper misery, and for no other fault than inability to pay an unjust rent, which their farms could not yield, owing to bad seasons permitted by the Providence of God. If we condemn secret societies, we must also condemn the root of the evil—"tyranny."

There is a just God in Heaven who will hear the cry of the poor and the oppressed, and will, even in this life, punish the unjust steward. The public records of the Land Commission Court have shown to the world that the landlords of Ireland forced from their tenants, in many instances, almost double the rent they should receive; and if the bad harvests be taken into account, and the past unjust and exorbitant rents, the length of time they were paid and the improvements made by the tenants themselves, for which an increased rent was added, they in most cases owe the landlords very little; or rather the landlords owe the tenants. We speak now according to the information gained by the proceedings of the Land Courts of Ireland, and published in the public journals. Scenes of evictions, such as have been enacted in Ireland by the military and police authorities, would not be tolerated on this continent and in very few places in Europe. Evictions, according to Gladstone, England's Prime Minister, are "*Death Warrants*," which no honest jury should pronounce. Other people have allowed themselves to be massacred in their cabins rather than leave them; but then, religion, which is mocked at by too many of their enemies, saved the world the horror of wholesale slaughter of the innocent people. Let injustice cease, and Ireland and the Irish people will become a happy and a loyal people. By justice thrones are strengthened, and governments prove their legitimacy and their right to respect and loyalty.

We shall now enumerate the causes of the loss of souls in America. We have cited already—1st, the scarcity of priests; 2d, the fact that the great majority of Irish emigrants arriving in America, till very lately were so poor, that they were unable to push their way into the country and there follow their old occupation of tilling the land. Hence they were forced to take lodgings in overcrowded tenement houses, in the poorest and most unhealthy parts of the cities, infested by the lowest characters, where they and their children sicken, and many premature deaths occur. The children are forced to frequent the streets for fresh air and exercise. Many of them fall into bad company; they are hungry; they are soon taught to steal; they are sent to jails or reformatories, or are picked up by agents of various societies, get food and clothes, and are sent out "West," to non-Catholic masters. We must not forget to mention that a great many are received in Orphan Asylums and Protectories, established by the zeal of bishops, clergy, and religious in this country, and supported by the voluntary contributions of our good people.

Another cause of so many Irish orphans is that their fathers, accustomed to the fresh air of the country in Ireland, were obliged in America to work in foundries, rolling mills, gas houses, sewers, and unwholesome places. Their strength begins to fail them. They too often take strong drink to help, as they think, to keep up their strength, but it only hastens their death. This accounts in part for the number of widows and orphan children of the Irish in this country. Poor children, who with their lively faith and religious affections, might be many diamonds in the crown of the Church. Alas, the old adage "*corruptio boni pessima.*" The high, strong temperament of the Celtic Irish race, which is also talented, impulsive, generous, openhearted and open-handed, leads them into many mistakes, as these noble qualities are trafficked in by unprincipled sharpers. Their love of parents and home is proved by the millions of pounds sent annually from America to help their families to this country, or to enable them to live at home, and this money goes into the landlords' pockets. The excuse that a fine young man gave us for not going to Mass on Sundays, was that he had not good clothes. We asked him how long he was in the country. He replied, over a year. "And could you not earn enough in a year to buy a suit of clothes?" we asked. "Yes, Father," said he, "but I made a vow to God that I would not put a new suit of clothes upon myself until I sent £10 to my father to help him to pay the rent and keep the cabin over his head in Ireland." On account of the poverty of the parents, the children are sent to work very young, before they are half educated. The prevailing spirit of the young workmen of this country is independence, even of parental authority, and no wonder that many of the young Irish become impregnated with the same spirit. Many of the workmen on Sunday mornings frequently remain in bed and neglect going to church. The Catholic children who frequent the Catholic schools make their first communion, but alas! when they grow up they too often neglect, in large cities, to frequent the sacraments. In the cities and towns of England and Scotland the sad case of many of the children, we are told on good authority, is as bad, if not worse. We are meeting from time to time men and women in very good positions, who were Irish Catholic orphans, placed when young in Protestant houses and reared in the religion of their protectors. A special care was taken to instil into their minds the deepest prejudices against the religion of their parents. There is also a fallen class, who have been brought up in poor houses, and who had lost their character in their own country before coming here, and yet in the depths of their misery and disgrace, have not lost all sense of religion and shame, and will call for a priest when they are sick. Many of them retire to do penance in our Magdalen Asylums; others recover themselves and get situations. The tears and cries of these poor creatures, as they think of their happy homes, before the landlord evicted them and their parents, and they were forced into the proximate occasion of sin, must plead before a just and merciful God. The day of judgment will reveal awful crimes where they should be least expected.

Distance from church in the country is another cause of the loss of souls. Immigrants who are able to make their way into the country to get work on railroads, or where they can, or to settle down where land is cheap— and this is generally at a considerable distance from towns and villages, and consequently from any church, which may be distant from six to twenty miles, and, even if nearer Mass only once a month—find themselves at a very great disadvantage. They frequently move off and come into towns or villages to be near church. Hence even the Protestant proprietors subscribe largely to our Catholic churches in those places. It is often said that the establishment of an Episcopal See is equal to a railroad entering a town.

Another obstacle to frequenting the Catholic Church in this country is the almost impassable condition of the roads in spring and autumn ; and the heavy snow in winter for those who have no conveyances, which poverty for a long time will not permit them to have. Once or twice a year the priest may hold a " station " near them. All cannot attend it. But this good service, whilst it tends to nourish the ideas of faith and religion, yet is not sufficient to fortify the young people frequenting non-Catholic schools, and in the midst of an overwhelming Protestant population. Some, not having a church of their own religion, are often drawn, by curiosity at first, to attend Protestant churches, concerts, and prayer-meetings, become lukewarm Catholics, and drift away from the Church. Great efforts and sacrifices are being made by the clergy and people to multiply churches and schools, but it is a physical impossibility to supply the sudden and ever-increasing wants of the impoverished emigrants that come to our shores.

Common schools are another sad cause of our losses. We all know that our Holy Father, Pope Pius IX., of blessed memory, pronounced mixed education, as a general rule, to be an unqualified evil. The Catholics, where they have not Catholic schools, send their children to the common schools. Here the tone and atmosphere are essentially anti-Catholic. Catholic pupils are frequently mocked and sneered at by their companions. The teachers, when occasion offers, such as at history, or speaking of Catholic countries, or geography, often display their bigotry.   The young heart is very sensitive to ridicule, and many are not strong enough to resist.   The Catholic children, in many cases, become ashamed of their religion and the country of their parents, and become, strange to say, anti-Irish first and anti-Catholic afterwards—for the Irish come in for a great deal of abuse.   We may remark that the young Germans are as much exposed as the Irish children are.   It is well to remember, also, that the majority of the American people are unbaptized, and do not belong to any church organization.   The Irish, as a people, are naturally religious.   Even in Pagan times their Celtic ancestors had unbounded respect for religion and its priests.   If they have not the opportunities of the true religion, they must have some religion, which appears to them true.   In reading over the names of the ministers of the various Protestant denominations, we have been painfully struck with the great number of Irish Catholic names, and we are told that they are the most earnest and eloquent of ministers.   We know a Catholic priest whose two brothers are Methodist ministers.   They were reared under different circumstances.   One of the Protestant denominations held a meeting in the State of New York to discuss the subject — what could be done to convert the Catholics.   After a long and earnest disputation, the conclusion arrived at was, to make no efforts which might have the contrary effect to that intended, but to leave the Catholic children to the action of the public schools.   These schools, from official investigation leave a great deal to be desired on the subject of morality, so that the Catholic children are between two evils—the danger of the loss of faith and the danger of corruption of their morals.

Mixed marriages is another source of fruitful loss.   The Catholics in many parts of the country are as one to 5, 7, 10, and even more.   They are associating almost constantly with Protestants, and intermarriages are the consequence.   They are far from church and the influence of its teaching.   Catholic neighbors are few and far between.   The children of these marriages frequent the common schools.   No wonder, then, that if the Catholic parent be not very fervent, the children can hardly escape. In the returns of one of the dioceses of the United States, where the Catholics are very few, nearly half of the marriages were mixed.

The unprepared condition of the emigrants is another cause of loss. They scatter about in search of situations, the parents being too poor to keep them together. The children, as well as themselves, are low spirited and slavish. They cannot help it. They lived in hovels not fit for cattle. They are poorly clothed and badly fed. The people among whom their lot is now cast are comfortable and high spirited. The Irish feel keenly their former degradation, and cherish the bitterest memories of the past. Now, they begin to enjoy, comparatively, some comfort, and it is not to be wondered at that the heads of many of them should turn in this sudden transition. The children quickly surpass, in general knowledge, their parents, and if true religion do not come to their aid, they are tempted to neglect or to be ashamed of them. Shame upon any government that has been the cause of bringing its subjects to such a condition. All agree that Ireland is the black spot on the escutcheon of England. In giving confirmation, we frequently notice the fine foreheads and comely countenances of the children born in this country, where their mothers were not half starved when they bore them, and contrasting them with their parents, brothers and sisters born in Ireland, we conclude that good blood will tell, when not starved. The Poles being in a similar condition to that of the Irish, come in also for a large share of the sympathies of the American people. The success of the Irish who come to America with any reasonable share of this world's goods and education is rapid and prodigious, and the number of those who have worked themselves up to good positions from very poor beginnings, proves that the cry that the "Irish are lazy at home," is ridiculously absurd. But culprits will, to excuse themselves, throw the blame of their own misdeeds upon their unfortunate victims.

Drink is another cause of loss and of great misery and untimely deaths. The Celtic blood is so strong and hot that very little spirits, in too many cases, will set it in a blaze, and render the person half crazy. Hence total abstinence is the only preventative. Whilst drink is not the universal fault of the Irish, yet they come in for universal blame, inasmuch as many of them are noisy, foolish, and often troublesome. The world then knows all about their faults. Drunkenness is almost the only crime that leads them into jails, and their children into asylums and orphanages. Would to God that there were more Cardinal Mannings in the British Isles! There are temperance societies headed by the clergy in almost every city and town of note. Thank God, in the country places drunkenness is not the besetting sin of the Irish, or in cities either, as a general thing. Bad and insufficient food, and drinking on an empty stomach, are the chief causes of intemperance amongst the Irish. It is remarkable that even in their drunken state they respect religion and the priests.

Another cause is that the Irish come isolated, without organization, not knowing what part of the country to settle in, having no choice, their poverty forcing them to accept the first chances of work which are offered. Hence they become scattered all over the country, as it is not to be supposed that they can get employment as soon as they land. Many suffer a great deal of hardship and want before they get settled down. We must now speak of the young women and girls who, in great numbers, come unprotected; God alone knows how much they suffer and combat. We wish to speak of them with great respect. The immense majority of them obtain situations very soon and succeed well in life. That they preserve their virtue and religion in the midst of dangers and difficulties is due to the special protection of God and to the intercession of the Blessed Virgin, to whom they are singularly devoted. Some that might have been saved by ordinary precautions are allured by the wily efforts of the agents of iniquity, and are lost; but we hope not eternally. Young men and boys are scattered through the country, on railroads, canals, steamboats, farms and workshops, and are lost sight of in too many instances. In sickness, however, they do not forget their early training in the true faith. Married men also leave their wives and families in Ireland to acquire means to bring them out. Alas! some of them fail and fall miserably.

We repeat again, that what could not be effected in Ireland by religious persecution, loss of land and homes, social disabilities and starvation, has been accomplished here in too many instances by the enemy of all good and his agents. The forced immigration of an impoverished people into a new country whose inhabitants are overwhelmingly non-Catholic, has effected it. What was the conduct of the Hebrews, whilst yet the people of God, when they were transported from their own country without their prophets and priests? Did they not fall away in vast numbers from their religion? And should the Irish people be expected to surpass all other nations in religion and virtue in circumstances the most unfavorable, when no pains were spared to proselytize them. What was the conduct of the English and Scotch people under persecution?

From all that we have said above, we look with deep and religious anxiety at the efforts made in Ireland to ameliorate the condition of the people. Religion and patriotism demand these efforts, nay, even more. Patriotism is a God-given virtue, and the people of a country are bound to, and do, give up their lives to preserve their altars and their homes. We often remark that when the French bishops speak publicly of their country they invariably call it their " dear " France. Is patriotism in an Irishman to be considered criminal?

It was sad to notice in the days of slavery in the South, that the slave mothers dare not call their children their own. The masters claimed them as their own property, and could barter and sell them as they pleased. Our venerable brethren may ask us to suggest a remedy for the evils mentioned above. We have too much respect for their better judgment and patriotism to suggest any. They know best the condition of their country, and we the condition of ours. The salvation of tens of thousands of souls for whom Christ died is at stake, and the account which we must give of those confided to our care is terrible.

With the most profound respect and reverence we beg to subscribe ourselves most reverend and revered brethren, your humble servant in Christ.

JOHN JOSEPH LYNCH,
Archbishop of Toronto.

CHAPTER XXII.

IN every movement for the welfare and elevation of his fellow man, Archbishop Lynch takes a deep and permanent interest, and in no work does he more actively sympathize than in that now being done all over the Dominion of Canada in the cause of temperance. One of the preliminaries required by His Grace from all applicants for holy orders, as a condition precedent to their ordination, is that the young aspirant to the priesthood shall take a pledge to refrain from all intoxicating liquors for a certain number of years after ordination, so that, at all events, the young man may be entirely free, during the early years of priesthood, from the peculiar dangers and temptations, in this respect, incident to youth and inexperience. He is also a strong advocate of temperance societies, and is incessant in his appeals to his spiritual children, old and young, to the temperate as well as to the drinker, to join these organizations, whose object is to fight the demon of intemperance, which is the great and overshadowing evil of the English-speaking races all over the world. Such organizations, in his opinion, formed for such a noble end, and placed, as they should always be, under the direction and control of the lawful pastors of the Church, cannot fail in accomplishing much good, must exert a powerful influence in the cause of temperance, religion, and morality, and are deserving of the recognition and active support of the bishops and priests of the Catholic Church. Convinced of the good these temperance societies have done in the past, and the great results that are likely to be realized by them in the future, His Grace, on the occasion of a public meeting of the various Catholic temperance societies, held in Toronto in the year 1866, addressed to them the following pastoral :

There never arose any great evil in the Christian world but what a remedy for it sprang up in the Church of Christ. In the middle ages, multitudes of Christians were reduced to the most cruel slavery by the Mohammedans. Their galleys, even up to the commencement of this century, swept the Mediterranean, and all Christians captured were brought to Africa and sold as slaves. One of the most remarkable of these was St. Vincent de Paul. They were obliged to work in the mines and in the fields under a burning sun ; during the night they were confined in loathsome prisons and dungeons to prevent escape, badly fed, scantily clothed, and inhumanly whipped to extract from them the greatest amount of work or to gratify the base passions of their brutal masters. Vast numbers died from cruel treatment, others were tortured and put to death for giving signs of their Christian faith. On the other hand they were proffered liberty, wealth and honors if they renounced Christ and embraced Mohammedanism. Some Christians in their dire distress forgot to call on God for help, yielded to the temptation and apostatized ; but the greater number, after lingering years in the most excruciating tortures and sufferings, ended a life worse than death by receiving the martyr's crown for their fidelity and constancy in the faith of Christ. God raised up for their succor holy men, among whom was St. Peter Nolasco, who, under the inspiration of the Blessed Virgin, founded a religious order for the relief of those cruelly oppressed Christians. It was called "Our Lady of Mercy for the redemption of Captives," and was instituted in

1218, and approved of by Gregory IX. The members, besides the vows of chastity, poverty and obedience, made a fourth vow that when they should find captives in danger of losing their faith they were to exchange places with them. This was the most heroic act of charity, equal to martyrdom. Many of the members of this order gave up liberty, country, domestic comforts, and all that they held dear in life, and embraced the chains of "Slaves" to gain them to Christ. Our dear Lord redeemed them with the price of His blood, and these noble, religious, men brought back again those souls to Christ at the price of their own lives.

Monasteries of this celebrated order were scattered all over Europe. England and Ireland possessed many of them. The order was divided into two classes: 1st, knights who were to guard the coasts against the attacks of the Saracens, but were obliged to attend the offices of the choir when not on duty, and 2d, strictly religious men with the solemn vows mentioned above. They travelled all over Europe collecting alms to pay the ransom of the captives, and brought the sums to their Mohammedan masters, and scattered themselves amongst the poor slaves, to administer to them spiritual and temporal consolation. They brought considerable numbers of the purchased slaves to their monasteries in Europe, and supplied others with means to carry them to their families and homes. Thus many thousands were saved from the most degrading slavery, and others from a worse fate, that of apostacy and spiritual death.

In these latter times a more cruel and deadly enemy of the human family exists among us, and lies in wait for its victims in every street of our cities, and in every hamlet and village, and on the roadsides. Hundreds of thousands of Christian people are led captive, not by any external force, but, by yielding to the weakness of immoderate thirst for poisonous drugs, become voluntary victims of intemperance, and are more degraded than the slaves of the Moors and the Saracens. They are excited to the commission of a thousand crimes, against which, in their more sober moments, their souls would recoil in horror. To combat this dreadful evil there arose in our own time, in the Church, an humble priest, Rev. Theobald Mathew, of the Order of St. Francis of Asissium, who, under the protection of a merciful God, instituted associations of self-sacrificing religious men and women who, without making vows of religious perfection, have banded themselves together in solemn compact to refrain from all intoxicating drinks. These men are doing for the worse than Turkish slaves, the poor drunkards, what St. Peter Nolasco, St. Raymond Peneforte, James, King of Arragon, and others did for the enslaved Christians under the Moors. Members of our Temperance Associations are not bound by any religious profession, but they take a Temperance pledge to refrain from all intoxicating liquors themselves, and to use all their influence to break the chains of those who are under the dreadful captivity of the demon of intemperance. They are the sorrow, shame, and ruin of their families, and unfortunately belong to the higher, middle, and lower classes of society. They beget children having the germs of the most fatal vice in their constitutions, and propagate a degrading progeny with a sad legacy of constitutional infirmities. Temperance Associations are effecting as much good in their way, and are preventing as many evils as did the religious men of the Order of Mercy amongst the Christian captives of the Turks. We look upon those men who have made the sacrifice of not touching any intoxicating liquors, in order that they might be more free and have more authority in redeeming their brethren from the captivity of the vice of drunkenness, as standing on a higher grade of perfection than ordinary Christians. We wish to address you some words of encouragement and advice, and to lay down a few additional rules that, it appears to us, would greatly advance the cause of Temperance. We recommend the example of the members of the Order of Mercy as your model. This Order consisted of three classes of workers, regular monks, knights and sympathizers who subscribed means for redeeming the captives. Therefore let every member of your association consider himself as specially called upon and delegated, in virtue of his Temperance pledge, to go into whatever house he may have reason to know intemperance reigns, and entreat and beseech, in season and out of season, the victim to renounce his dreadful sin. If your neighbor should fall into a pit, would you not immediately draw him out? The fishermen that sit by their nets and receive only the fish that enter them will not be rewarded with that abundance which they might secure by trawling and compelling, as it were, the fish to enter their nets. Holding weekly or monthly meetings, without searching after the drunkard, will effect but a small amount of good. Lectures are very good for those who are not convinced of the evil of intemperance. Alas, few are in this ignorance, and none more alive to its evil than the drunkard himself. Visiting and endeavoring to cure the drunkard, who more frequently requires medicine from the doctor to overcome a deranged system, will often do more good than long lectures. People who voluntarily attend your meetings are generally convinced of the evil of intemperance. The sick only have need of a physician. Christ came to save that which was lost. The healthy need not a doctor.

It is a mistake to suppose that the seeking after the lost sheep is the exclusive duty and privilege of the ordained ministers of the Church, who, in this country especially, have more work to perform than their constitutions are well able to bear. The laity have also the duty of co-operating in the saving of souls, parents especially. God has given to every one a commandment concerning his neighbor (Eccles. xvii. 12).

1st. Christ has expressly said to all His followers, "But if thy brother shall offend against thee go and rebuke him between thee and him alone. If he shall hear thee, thou shalt gain thy brother, and if he will not hear thee, join with thee, besides, one or two ; that in the mouth of two or three witnesses every word may stand; and if he will not hear them, tell the Church, and if he will not hear the Church let him be to thee as the heathen and the publican" (Math. xviii. chap. 15, 16, 17 v). If therefore the drunkard will not listen to three of you, go and inform the priest.

2d. That all temperance workers should consider that

it is from God alone must come that health and strength necessary to draw the sinner from the depths of vice, especially that of intemperance. Prayer is absolutely necessary, and the frequentation of the sacraments and avoiding the occasions of sin. There are some constitutions like powder, that will explode by one spark of fire; so when these persons take the first drop of liquor they are hurried on, and will not stop till they become intoxicated, and, when once in this deplorable state, will continue drinking until they become crazy. Many die in this madness; and, oh, what a lamentable condition it is to enter into the presence of a just God, in such a condition, to be judged, and have their lot settled for eternity. Persons with such constitutions should never touch the first drop of intoxicating drink; the moment they do so they throw themselves into the immediate occasion of grievous sin, which is as serious a crime in itself as one would commit, who should put fire to inflammable matter which would necessarily cause a great amount of destruction, whether he intended it or not.

3d. We recommend that there should be paid organizers or knights whose express calling will be to go to seek after the captive drunkard, and to try to recover him, having him in charge, as a doctor, till he is in his sound state. I will most gladly subscribe a yearly sum for this purpose, and there are many, both inside and outside the temperance organization, who will cheerfully do the same. Organizers must be able to live and pay expenses that they may do good. The monks had always sufficient allowed them by their superiors for food, clothes and expenses.

Now, many men who are not strictly of your association ought to be brought in to co-operate by subscription, and other encouragement, in order to help you to place the redeemed drunkard in a position in which he might be preserved from relapse, and enabled to earn his living.

I am pleased to know that there are benefit societies for the relief of the sick attached to your organizations. The reward which you will have for saving these souls will be the salvation of your own; for St. James, in his

Catholic Epistle, says, " My brethren, if any err from the truth, and one convert him, he must know that he who causeth a sinner to be converted from the error of his way shall save his soul from death, and shall cover a multitude of sins" (C. v., 19, 20 v.).

Trusting in the mercy of God, and in your co-operation with His holy grace, we have every reason to hope that by following those admonitions your blessed organization will increase more and more, and that you will be enabled to do a larger amount of good.

May the blessing of our Lord Jesus Christ be with you all to assist you in your great work.

CHAPTER XXIII.

THE ARCHBISHOP AND POLITICS.

His Grace not a Politician—The Catholic Church in her Relations to Governments—The Catholic Hierarchy in its Relations to Political Parties—The Archbishop's Views as to the Proper Functions of the Church and the State—Condition of Canada when His Grace became Bishop of Toronto—The Country in a State of Political Transition—Both Provinces Dissatisfied with the Union—Causes of this Dissatisfaction in Upper Canada—Political Parties in Canada—George Brown—His Character—His Influence in the Liberal Party.

IT would hardly be possible, even in the most cursory review of the life of Archbishop Lynch, to omit some reference to his supposed connection with the two great political parties of Canada, or some mention of the course he has seen fit to take on matters usually considered as lying exclusively within the domain of politics. Very few men rise to eminence in any path of life, without making some enemies more or less pronounced. In the administration of the affairs of the Catholic Church in Ontario, and in his performance of the duties appertaining to the Episcopal office, no one, either within or without her pale, has ever, so far as we are informed, found any fault with His Grace; but with regard to what has been erroneously called his " political conduct," or rather his attitude on certain questions which are generally assumed to be purely political questions, considerable difference of opinion exists.

In the first place, then, it may be desirable to say at the outset that the Archbishop disclaims the imputation of being a politician in any sense of the word. As a bishop of the Catholic Church he looks upon both political parties, so far as their general principles and policy are concerned, and in so far as such principles and such policy do not affect the interests of the Church, with perfect indifference. The Catholic Church is universal. She is to be found in all countries and under all forms of government. She accommodates herself to all. She flourishes as vigorously under a republic as under a monarchy. As a Church, she commits herself to no particular form of government, and in those countries where government by party prevails—as in Canada—her members are found in the ranks of both parties. The only case in which the bishops of the Catholic Church feel bound to interfere in political matters, is where they believe the interests of the Church to be involved. It is generally considered a reproach against the Catholic hierarchy, that they place the interests of the Church before those of the State. They admit the accusation, and assume the consequences. They cheerfully admit their Church is not Erastian. If they place the Church above the State, it is only the logical result of their belief in her divine origin and her sacred mission. They believe, therefore, that the spiritual order is above the temporal, and, if the two conflict, they prefer to obey God rather than Cæsar. Substitute God for the Church, and Protestants must assume the same position, if they would be consistent, or if they would conform their practice to the maxims of the Gospel as they themselves interpret it.

The Catholic Church and her Bishops view

governments and political parties, therefore, solely as they affect their people as members of the Church. So long as political questions do not involve any matters of Catholic doctrine or morals, the hierarchy are neutral. But the moment any question arises, even as a purely political one, in which such matters are involved, or where the rights of Catholics, as Catholics, are in question, then the hierarchy are not only justified in interfering, but it is their bounden duty to interpose, and use their power and influence as Bishops of the Church in such manner and to such extent as they may deem most effectual.

There have been, or are, few, if any, prelates of the Catholic Church in America who hold broader or more liberal views, as regards either religion or politics, than those entertained by the present Archbishop of Toronto. Even his most determined opponents, those who are the most dissatisfied with what they choose to consider his "political action," must admit that, at all events, he has never used his episcopal *authority* to influence the political conduct or opinions of Catholics. In a short sketch of his life written not long since by a Protestant gentleman for a prominent Toronto daily paper, in the form of an open letter addressed to His Grace, the writer, in referring to the charge made against the Archbishop that he has had, as a Bishop, too much to do with politics, very justly and very fairly says : " It is not a great matter, even if the charge be well founded, and I believe it has only been put forward by those whose political bias prevents them from looking at the question with perfect disinterestedness and impartiality. The simple fact I take to be this : that taking your circumstances and your creed into consideration, the texture of your mind is exceedingly, almost phenomenally, liberal. While holding fast by the tenets and traditions of your faith, you are disposed to exercise a free discretion as to matters especially pertaining thereto. Recognizing the fact that your lot has been cast in a land where the majority of the people are Protestants, you have never assumed to direct the theological belief of those beyond your pale, or to meddle with secular affairs with which you have no manner of concern. If you have at times held the balance of power between Mr. Mowat and the Ontario Opposition, it has been because your own rights and those of your Church were in some way involved."

Of course it would be absurd, as well as untrue, to contend that Catholic bishops, as individuals and citizens of the Commonwealth, have no political opinions—or perhaps we might better express it— opinions on such questions as do lie exclusively within the domain of politics, and do not affect Catholicity or the Church. To assert this would be to deny that they take an interest in the material or social welfare of their country — would be to say, in fact, that they are lacking in patriotism. But certainly the Catholic hierarchy in all countries have ever, in the time of trial, proved themselves as true to the interests of their native land as any other class of its citizens. In our own day we have been witness to the loyalty of the Catholic bishops of Germany to the cause of father-land, in the Franco-Prussian war, even when they well knew that the success of the German armies meant the crushing of the great Catholic power of Europe, and the destruction of the only support on which the Holy See could rely for the maintenance of its temporal power; while on the other hand, in France, we saw the

French bishops, though entirely disapproving of the war, yet when their country was invaded, among the first to rush to her defence. The teaching orders of the Church, in this dark hour for France, closed their schools, and sent their members into the field. In the late civil war in the great republic—our neighbor—the loyalty of the Catholic bishops of the North, and their efforts to preserve the Union, are too well known to require more than a mere reference; indeed, at the most disastrous period of the conflict, when it was thought by many that the success of the South was but a question of time, the most illustrious of the prelates of the Catholic Church in America, the late Archbishop Hughes, of New York, was entrusted by the American Government with an important mission to Europe, and there can be no question that the valuable services he rendered his government at that critical juncture of affairs, prevented the recognition of the Southern Confederacy by the European powers. In the South, the Catholic bishops, in accordance with the practice of the Church in such cases, gave a loyal and hearty support to the *de facto* government which the people had established. As to the patriotism of the Catholic bishops of Canada, no one doubts it. There is no class or order in the Dominion more loyal and devoted to the laws and institutions under which they live than the Catholic hierarchy, and perhaps none of its members more so than the distinguished subject of this memoir.*

* In answer to the assertion that the Catholic Church is inimical to republican institutions, and that a good Catholic cannot be a true citizen of the American Republic, the Fathers of the late Plenary Council of Baltimore say : "We repudiate with equal earnestness the assertion that we need lay aside any of our devotedness to our Church to be true Americans; the insinuation that we need to lay aside any of our love for our country's principles and institutions, to be faithful Catholics. To argue

With reference to the relations between Church and State, and the respective powers and functions of each, the Archbishop holds views exceedingly broad and liberal. In a lecture delivered in the Cathedral in June, 1876, on the subject of Church and State, he thus speaks of the jurisdictions and powers of each: "The question *in limine* is, which is the higher power, Church or State? As regards the source of their power, both are equal, because both derive their authority from God. It is not from the Church that the State has its power, but directly from God, and it is not from the State that the Church has its power; she derives it from our Lord Jesus Christ himself. As regards the aims of the Church and the State, the Church has the higher, for she aims at securing the eternal happiness of the people; the State only claims to aim at a lesser good, the temporal welfare. Both Church and State are each supreme, one in the supernatural order, the other in the natural order. * * * When I say supreme, I do not mean infallible. The State does not claim infallibility for its decisions, for, to be infallible, it should be under the directive influence of an infallible guide. As the Church and State are ordained of God for the spiritual and temporal welfare of the people here below, there should be no clash of au-

that the Catholic Church is hostile to our great republic because she teaches that 'there is no power but from God;' because, therefore, back of the events which led to the formation of the republic, she sees the Providence of God leading to that issue, and back of our country's laws the authority of God as their sanction—this is evidently so illogical and contradictory an accusation that we are astonished to hear it advanced by persons of ordinary intelligence. We believe that our country's heroes were the instruments of the God of Nations in establishing this home of freedom; to both the Almighty and His instruments in the work, we look with grateful reverence: and to maintain the inheritance of freedom which they have left us, should it ever—which God forbid—be imperilled, our Catholic citizens will be found to stand forward as one man, ready to pledge anew, 'their lives, their fortunes, and their sacred honor.'"

thority; each, keeping within its own bounds, should, like the captain and pilot of a ship, be of one mind, that the passengers may happily arrive at their destination. We speak now of a State Church whose government and people are Christian. No Christian king or ruler can say I am above all law and not subject to any Church or organization, which Christ left on earth to do His work. Popes, kings, presidents of republics, and rulers are all subject to the law of the Gospel. With pagan governments we have now no concern. Were I to substitute the Bible for the Church, Protestants would all agree that the Bible, or rather the teaching of the Bible, is above all State laws, and that Christian statesmen are obliged to conform to its instructions in and out of the council chamber."

As before remarked, whatever influence the Archbishop may have used in matters usually considered purely political, he has never attempted on any occasion whatever to use his episcopal *authority* to influence the political action of Catholics. The most he has ever done in this direction, has been to give to one or other of the two political parties the weight and influence attaching to the dignity of his office —a weight and influence which derives its power and importance from the opportunities a bishop of the Church is supposed to possess—in fact does possess, to an extent not attainable by the great majority of the laity—of knowing and deciding as to what particular matters, within the domain of politics, injuriously, or otherwise, affect the interests of the people in general or the Church. To use such power and influence, the result of opportunity and large experience, in a perfectly lawful and legitimate manner, in favor of a party or policy he may deem most favorable to the interests of his Church, or against a party or policy he' may consider antagonistic thereto, is one thing ; to use the priestly or episcopal *authority*, or to resort to ecclesiastical censure to attain such an object, is altogether another affair. The latter course Archbishop Lynch has never taken. On the contrary, he is strongly opposed to any such interference by the clergy with the political liberty of Catholic laymen.

When Archbishop Lynch succeeded Bishop de Charbonnel in 1859, the country was in a state of political transition. The union of Upper and Lower Canada, recommended by Lord Durham, and which was consummated by the Imperial Act of 1840, had not proved satisfactory to either province. The political union of the two provinces, with one executive and a common legislative body, was a measure whose practical utility was very much questioned even at the time of its accomplishment. It was a political necessity precipitated by the rebellion of 1837–38, and never had the sympathy or support of the people of Lower Canada.* Even in Upper Canada opinion was divided as to the benefits to be derived from a legislative union of the provinces. It was agreed to by the Parliament of Upper Canada as an inevitable necessity, and because it was believed by the people of that province that they would be the gainers by such union. It was hoped and confidently expected that by thus uniting the two provinces the English element would soon become dominant and would in the end succeed in

---

* The question, of course, was not submitted to the people of Lower Canada. The constitution being then suspended, there was no representative body in existence. As far as Lower Canada was concerned, Mr. Poulet Thompson (Lord Sydenham) had only obtained the consent of the " Special Council of Lower Canada."

absorbing and assimilating the French portion of Lower Canada, and measures were taken to embody such provisions in the Act of Union as would, in the opinion of their authors, secure this result.*   Their hopes and anticipations were to a certain extent realized. Upper Canada did eventually become the more populous and influential of the two provinces. But the French population in Lower Canada, instead of being absorbed by the English speaking races—English, Scotch, and Irish—have increased in a greater ratio than have all the other races combined, and far from abandoning their national customs or giving up the use of their own language, the national spirit was never stronger than it is to-day in the Province of Quebec, and the use of the French language is as prevalent as ever among the natives, while its use has become almost a necessity to the English-speaking portion of the population.

Upper Canada, however, soon outstripped her sister province in population, wealth, and general progress. Already in 1858 the population of Upper Canada stood 1,300,000 to 1,000,000 in the Lower Province. As the representation was equal, practically 300,000 Upper Canadians were without repre-

---

* In the address to Her Majesty in favor of a union of the provinces, moved by Mr. Cartwright, it was recommended that the seat of the Provincial Government should be in Upper Canada ; that the use of the English language in all judicial and legislative records should be immediately introduced, and that at the end of a definite period after the union all debates in the Legislature should be conducted in English. A strong party in Upper Canada was also opposed to giving Lower Canada equal representation in the new parliament, although at that period the population of the latter province was larger than that of Upper Canada. A minority in the House of Assembly would only vote for the Union with "conditions" which, Mr. Sullivan declared, would, if carried out, have the effect of disfranchising the French Canadians. He declared further that such a scheme of a union would never be agreed to by the British Parliament. It would seem that the great mass of the Tory party in Upper Canada of that day hoped, by the union, to reduce the Lower Canadian French to a condition of political vassalage.

sentation.   Besides this, many questions were of
great importance to the people of Upper Canada,
on which public opinion had been for years strongly
pronounced, and which, had Upper Canada been
alone, would very soon have found a settlement
satisfactory to the majority of the people—such, for
instance, as the question of the clergy reserves. But
notwithstanding that this question affected Upper
Canada only, and although the people of that province, by the result of the general elections of 1847
and 1848, had strongly pronounced in favor of the
secularization of these reserves, the Baldwin-Lafontaine Government were unable to give effect to the
people's verdict, owing to the opposition of the
Lower Canadian members of the cabinet, as well as
to the apathy, if not actual antagonism, to such a
measure, displayed by the Lower Canadian section
of the Reform party.

Year by year, however, as Upper Canada increased
in wealth and population, her people became more
dissatisfied with the union. They believed they had
grave reasons for this dissatisfaction. They complained that, although the more populous and
wealthy of the two provinces, and although contributing the largest amount of the country's revenue, yet, practically, by means of certain political
combinations between the leaders of the Conservative party in Upper and Lower Canada—a party
which represented only a small minority of the people of the latter province—Upper Canada had in
reality the least share in the government of the
country. The Lower province being almost entirely Conservative, a political leader who could
manage to secure a small following from Upper
Canada was able to retain power, although having

an overwhelming majority against him in that province.

The two great political parties were then, as now, the Conservative or Tory and the Liberal or Reform. From 1851, however, the Liberal party had become practically divided into two camps which, if not actually hostile to each other, were, at least, sufficiently antagonistic in principle to greatly weaken the influence of the organization. The new party—which was, in reality, only the radical or extreme wing of the Reform party—obtained the name of "Clear Grits."* They were dissatisfied with the course of the Baldwin-Lafontaine government, who, in their opinion, had failed to grapple with, and settle, the questions which had been agitated and discussed at the general elections of 1847 and 1848, and on which, they contended, the Reform party had gone to the country, and obtained an emphatic verdict in their favor. It is unnecessary in this work to discuss the events which led to this split in the Reform ranks; it will be sufficient for our purpose to say here that the Clear Grit party demanded the secularization of the Clergy Reserves, representation by population, were strongly opposed to Separate Schools in Upper Canada, and were violently anti-Catholic. They were led by Mr. George Brown, and their mouthpiece and chief organ was the Toronto *Globe*, of which Mr. Brown was editor.

Of the late Hon. George Brown not much need be said here. His name will always be intimately associated with the early politics of Canada, and he

---

* The name "Clear Grits" was first applied to this section of the Reform party by Mr. Brown, in the *Globe*. In an editorial in that journal he denounced the originators of the movement as " a little miserable clique of office-seeking, buncombe-talking cormorants, who met in a certain lawyer's office on King Street and announced their intention to form a new party on clear grit principles."

himself will go down to posterity as one of Canada's greatest men. That he was, however, more responsible than any other man in the province for the violent anti-Catholic prejudice which was, for many years, so important a factor in the politics of this country, is unfortunately too true. In reading the *Globe* from 1853 down to near confederation, one is amazed at the uncalled-for abuse, the scurrility, and, in many cases, the lack of even common decency, which characterized his articles against the Catholic Church, her clergy and her religious institutions. In the present day such language would not be tolerated in the columns of any respectable journal against the worst or most insignificant political opponent. Yet great allowances must be made for the man, particularly for the journalist, who is obliged to speak out his mind from day to day to the public. There were, perhaps, many men in public life, in those days, who agreed with Mr. Brown, and who whispered in private what he, as a journalist, was obliged to say to the public at large, and yet who were not considered by their Catholic contemporaries as either fanatical or bigoted. Born and educated in the Scotland of seventy or eighty years ago; possessing a thoroughly Scottish intellect, keen and penetrating as it is narrow and one-sided; add to this all the dogmatic intolerance of the Scottish character, and it is not at all surprising that he should have displayed, in all their intensity, the inherited prejudices of his country and race against the Catholic Church. His temperament was enthusiastic, his nature impulsive. He had not the sympathetic faculty of placing himself in the position of an opponent, and viewing a subject from his standpoint. In his opinion his antagonists were

perversely in the wrong, and he himself undoubtedly
in the right.   He despised half-measures and com-
promises—in a word, he was a violent and an un-
compromising adversary.   But no one ever doubted
George Brown's sincerity.   Cardinal Newman, while
yet a minister in the Anglican Church, greatly dis-
turbed the decorous placidity of the Broad Church
section of the establishment by declaring that what
they wanted in the English church of that day was a
little more intolerance.   This shocked British culture, as well as British philistinism, but the assertion
was justified by the nerveless inactivity and the evident lack of faith in their professed principles and
doctrines, exhibited by the great mass of the Anglican clergy of that period.   Mr. Brown used language
against the Catholic Church, her clergy and her institutions, which is still resentfully remembered by
many Catholics of an elder generation.   But it must
be remembered that, from his point of view, there
was great provocation.   Upper Canada, he contended,
was being practically ruled by Lower Canada.   Lower
Canada was Tory, French, and Roman Catholic, and
against these combined influences it seemed hopeless
for Upper Canada to contend.   Mr. Brown lived to
regret, if not the political course he pursued in those
days, at least the language he allowed himself to use
against Catholics and the Catholic Church.   The
antipathy thus created in the mind of a large portion
of the Catholic population against him and the *Globe*,
his organ, was one of the chief causes that led to the
large defection from the Reform party of life-long
Catholic liberals—men who had fought and suffered
for the party in the days when Reformer and rebel
were synonymous.   In thus alienating the Catholic
vote from the Reform party, Mr. Brown committed

what, in politics, is considered worse than a crime—
he committed a blunder. This defection of the
Catholic vote was the principal cause of the weakness of the Reform party in Upper Canada for many
years, and it is almost certain that, without the aid
of that vote, the party could not have come permanently into power in the province of Ontario.

CHAPTER XXIV.

THE SEPARATE SCHOOL QUESTION.

The Separate School Question—What Catholics Demanded—Protestant Separate Schools in Lower Canada—The Principle of Separate Schools always Recognised in our School System—Sketch of the Ontario School System—The School Bill of 1850—The Bill of 1853—Catholics of Ontario not Granted by these Measures the same Rights as are Enjoyed by Protestants of Lower Canada—Rev. Egerton Ryerson—His Opposition to Separate Schools in Ontario—Efforts of Bishop de Charbonnel to Obtain a Separate School Bill—Succeeds in Obtaining the Bill of 1853—Objections to the Bill—Bishops Petition Parliament for a New Bill—Government Promises to Pass a Satisfactory Measure—They Fail to do so—Mr. Bowes' Bill—It is Opposed by the Government—Reasons for Archbishop Lynch Supporting the Conservative Party when he first came to Canada—The Conservative Party Defeated—Liberal Party Come into Power—Mr. Scott's Bill—Defects of the Bill of 1863—The Archbishop's Attempt at Confederation to have the School Question Settled—The First Parliament of Ontario—Advent of the Liberal Party to Power in Ontario—Mr. Mowat's Government—Its Liberality to Catholics—Reasons for the Archbishop's Support of the Mowat Government—Conclusion.

WHEN Archbishop Lynch assumed the government of the Toronto diocese in 1859, the principal subject affecting the rights of the Catholic body was the Separate School question. The Catholics of Upper Canada had been for many years agitating for the right to educate their children in schools under their own control, and supported by the taxes they were obliged to pay for the support of the common schools to which they felt they could not conscientiously send their children. It is irrelevant to discuss the question as to whether the Catholics of Upper Canada were right or wrong in their belief that the faith of their children would be endangered in these schools. They, at all events, or their spiritual directors, thought so, and still continue so to think. In the Catholic province of Lower Canada, this right had been already freely and generously conceded to the Protestant minority of that province, and all the Catholics of Upper Canada demanded was that, in this respect, they should be placed in the same position as their Protestant fellow-citizens of the Lower Province. This was only a fair and reasonable demand, and yet for years it was persistently refused, nor was full justice ever obtained by the Catholics of Upper Canada in this matter until the advent to power of the present Liberal Government of Ontario.*

* It was constantly asserted by the opponents of Catholic Separate Schools that by the Upper Canada School Act the Catholics of that Province were given all the rights and privileges in respect to Separate Schools, enjoyed by the Protestant minority in Lower Canada. To prove that such was not the case we will here cite a few provisions of the two acts, to show how very materially they differed from each other, and in how much better position the Protestants of Lower Canada were placed, in this respect, than the Catholics of the Upper Province. 1st. By the Lower Canada School Act, *any number whatever* of Protestant inhabitants, by merely giving notice to the School Commissioners, had power to establish a Separate School, and constitute themselves trustees. These trustees had all the powers of the Commissioners of Common Schools. In Upper Canada it required *twelve heads of families*, either householders or freeholders, to form a Separate School ; nor could any Separate School be established in any school district except where the *teacher of the Common School was a Protestant.* This, of course, practically put it in the power of the Protestant majority to prevent the establishment of a Separate School in any district, by merely appointing a teacher who happened to be a Catholic. No such analogous restriction is contained in the Lower Canada School Act. 2d. The Trustees of the Protestant Separate Schools in Lower Canada had the right to constitute their own school districts independently of the school districts established by the Commissioners of Common Schools. In Upper Canada the Separate School Trustees had not this power. It was the duty of the Municipal Council to provide the limits of the divisions or sections of Catholic Separate Schools—a very important difference, when it is remembered that these municipal bodies in Upper Canada are Protestant, and, in the large majority of cases, were intensely hostile to the establishment of Catholic Schools. 3d. In Lower Canada "no priest, minister, or ecclesiastic shall be entitled to visit any school belonging to any inhabitants not belonging to his own persuasion, except with the consent of the Commissioners or Trustees of such school." In Upper Canada "all clergymen of whatever denomination" were constituted school visitors of all schools in their districts. This is perhaps not of much importance, except as showing

The principle of Separate Education for those who considered that they could not conscientiously send their children to the schools provided by the State, had been admitted from the very inception of the School law, and had been practically carried into effect by the establishment by the Protestant minority of Lower Canada of Separate Schools for the education of their own children.*   By the Lower

the determination of the Protestant minority of Lower Canada that no clergyman of the Catholic Church should have free access to their Separate Schools, while in Upper Canada the working of the Catholic Separate School Act was placed in the hands and under the almost absolute control of a minister of a Protestant denomination—Rev. Dr. Ryerson, the Chief Superintendent of Education.   4th. By the Lower Canadian School Act the Protestant Separate School Trustees were authorized to *communicate directly* with the Chief Superintendent of Education, and receive from him, *direct*, their share of the School Fund.   In Upper Canada the Trustees of the Catholic Separate Schools were obliged to address themselves to the Local Superintendents.   These gentlemen were appointed by the Municipal Council, were independent of the Government, were in many cases Protestant ministers, were usually opposed to Separate Schools, and, as a general rule, felt not indisposed to do all in their power to hamper the free action of Separate School Boards.   In fact, most of the difficulties with which the Catholic supporters of Separate Schools had to contend against, were caused by the opposition of the Local Superintendents and Local School Boards.   As a case in point: In the year 1853, the Catholics of St. David's Ward, in Toronto, desired to establish a Separate School.   Application was duly made, under the provisions of the Act, to the Local Board, but the application was rejected on the ground that the teacher in the Public School in that Ward was a Catholic, and the election of Catholic School Trustees refused.   The case was one of such flagrant injustice, that the Government was obliged to interfere and direct the Chief Superintendent to order the Board to comply with the demands of the Catholic Trustees.   Many other instances might be cited to show that the Separate Schools in Upper Canada were not as favorably treated as the Protestant Schools in Lower Canada, but the foregoing will be sufficient for our purpose.

* Attorney-General (afterwards Chief-Justice) Richards, in introducing the Supplementary School Bill of 1853, in the course of his speech said: "How is it in Lower Canada? The Protestants are not compelled to pay for Catholic Schools—why then should Catholics be called upon to pay for Protestant Schools in Upper Canada. I do not believe it is a safe or a sound policy to render the large patriotic Catholic population of Upper Canada dissatisfied with the legislation of the country, especially when that population can turn to Lower Canada, and see the Protestant minority there treated with more respect than themselves." He further remarked that "the history of the Common School System in this

Canada School Act the Protestants of Lower Canada were allowed to establish Separate Schools, maintain them out of their own school tax, and were exempted from supporting the general Common Schools of the Provinces. This was all the Catholics of Upper Canada claimed for themselves.

Before entering upon the subject of the Separate School agitation in detail, it may be well to give a short sketch of the history of our Ontario School System.

In Canada, the first step taken by the Legislature in educational matters, was the Act of 1807, authorizing the establishment of District Grammar Schools. The idea of establishing a general system of primary education for the benefit of the masses had not then entered the minds of our rulers, although such a system had been in operation for many years in the neighboring Republic. All these early movements in the direction of education were for the benefit of the rich, or more wealthy portion of the community, or more particularly, perhaps, for what was in those days considered as the "upper classes": that is, the professional element, the ministry, the official class, and such like. The prejudice against educating the masses, which in England exists even to this day, seems to have prevailed among the ruling classes in Canada in the early part of the present century. As early as 1798, the Crown had set apart 500,000 acres of the public lands for the purpose of endowing Grammar Schools, and establishing a Provincial University; but as land was at that time worth only

country shows that, from the first, the principle of Separate Schools had been established—that is to say, that Separate Schools might be established by any considerable number of the inhabitants of the country who might think the religious faith of their children would be interfered with by their attendance at the Common Schools."

a shilling an acre, the amount realized from their
sale was found inadequate for the purpose, and the
scheme was abandoned. In 1816 a commencement
was made towards a general system of elementary
education, and the first Common Schools were established. The legislature set apart the then very large
sum of $24,000 for their maintenance. The measure
seems, however, to have been merely a tentative one,
and the experiment would appear not to have proved
satisfactory, for in 1820 the grant was reduced to
$10,000 a year, and the teachers' salaries from $100,
to $50, per annum. The Grammar School teachers
were receiving a salary of $500 per annum. In 1823
Sir Peregrine Maitland, the Lieutenant-Governor,
obtained permission from the Home Government to
establish a Board of Education. This Board made
some very important improvements in the administration of the educational affairs of the Province,
and succeeded in exchanging 225,944 acres of the
most inferior of the school lands for the better and
more valuable Clergy Reserve lands. In 1827 the
House of Assembly proposed to appropriate $18,000
per annum for the support of eleven free Grammar
Schools, and $26,400 per annum for the support of
Common Schools in all the townships of Upper
Canada. In 1839 the large amount of 250,000 acres
of land was set apart as a permanent endowment
for the Grammar Schools. The government was
empowered to appoint five trustees to manage each
of them—a bonus of $800 was also granted to any
county which should raise a like sum for the purpose
of establishing a Grammar School. Such were the
principal measures affecting education passed by the
Upper Canada Government previous to the union.
In the Parliament of 1841, the first after the union,

an act was passed, establishing a school system for the whole Province of Canada, and fixing for its support an annual grant of $200,000. In this act the principle of Separate Schools was embodied, chiefly because the Protestants of Lower Canada objected to sending their children to the Common Schools, as these schools would of course be composed mainly of Catholic children, and presided over by Catholic teachers. The Act of 1841 was repealed in 1843, so far as it affected Upper Canada, and a new law for that Province was passed, in which the principle of Separate Schools was still recognized.

In 1844 the Rev. Egerton Ryerson was sent to Europe to examine the several educational systems in operation there, especially the common school system of Prussia. He also visited the United States to examine their system. The result of his inquiries was embodied in his very interesting "Report on a System of Public Elementary Education," accompanied by the draft of a School Bill, which was passed in 1846. The new school system of Dr. Ryerson was very severely criticised, and had many opponents. It is unnecessary to go into the details of the arguments used *pro* and *con* the common school system. The dispute was bitterly carried on for several years, and finally resulted in the total repeal of all the School Acts. In 1850 a new bill was submitted to the Baldwin Lafontaine Government by Dr. Ryerson, who was the Chief Superintendent of Education, and passed the same year.

By Section 19 of the Upper Canada School Act of 1850, the Catholic minority of Upper Canada were also allowed to establish Separate Schools, but the Act was so clogged with restrictions, and burdened with conditions, that it was impossible to work it satisfactorily.   The Catholic minority were not by the Act of 1850 placed upon the same footing, in regard to separate education, as the Protestant minority of Lower Canada.*   The agitation carried on for so many years about Separate Schools had no other object than to obtain for the Catholics of this Province the same rights, as regards the education of their children, enjoyed by their Protestant fellow-citizens in the Catholic sister-province.   Any one who shall impartially study the history of the Separate School agitation will, however reluctantly, be forced to the conclusion that the Protestant majority of Upper Canada were not prepared, and for years refused, to concede to the Catholics the same rights and privileges in educational matters possessed by their own co-religionists in the Lower Province.

The agitation continued after 1850.   The Bill was found to be unworkable, and in 1853 a " Supplementary Bill " was introduced by the Government.   Among the questions in dispute after the passing of the Act of 1850, was the question of the right of Separate Schools to share in the portion of the Clergy Reserve Fund likely to be appropriated by the municipalities to educational purposes.   The Act of 1853 was intended to settle this question, and also to make such amendments in the School law as would render the establishment of Separate Schools more practicable.   Still, Parliament was far from conceding the same rights to Upper Canadian Catholics as were enjoyed by the Protestants of Lower Canada.   Conditions and restrictions were still retained, that greatly marred the efficiency of the Act.   The principle of Separate Schools was admitted by a majority of the

* See note, page 283.

people's representatives, but there seems to have been a strong inclination to prevent its practical realization.

The chief difficulty in establishing Separate Schools was caused by the antagonism of the Chief Superintendent of Education, Rev. Egerton Ryerson. This gentleman for many years practically directed the policy of the Government in educational matters. The dictatorial and autocratic tone he assumed towards the Bishops of the Catholic Church who were merely demanding what they conceived to be their rights, was most offensive.*   He was strongly opposed to the establishment of Separate Schools. Although he was obliged to admit that the Catholics of Upper Canada had, in principle, the same rights in the education of their children as those possessed by the Protestants of Lower Canada, and that, equitably, they were entitled to Separate Schools, yet he thought that by rendering their establishment difficult, the idea would, in time, be abandoned.† Mr.

---

* Writing to Bishop de Charbonnel on one occasion, taking that venerable and saintly prelate to task for his efforts to obtain for the Catholics of Upper Canada equal rights with the Protestants of Lower Canada, Dr. Ryerson says: " I feel that I am not exceeding my duty in speaking plainly on this point, since the educational interests of all classes have been entrusted to my care. I am bound by official duty as well as by Christian and patriotic considerations to do all in my power to prevent a single child in Upper Canada from growing up in ignorance, and therefore in a state of vassalage and degradation in our free country." One is less inclined to smile at the Rev. Doctor's conceit, than to wonder at his assumption of the character of an educational Messiah, for he had evidently convinced himself that he was the only man in Canada who knew how to educate its youth, both Protestant and Catholic.

† In his Report for the year 1853, he says (page 21): " Religious minorities in school municipalities in Lower Canada have the protection and alternatives of Separate Schools, and these members being chiefly (entirely?) Protestant, attach much importance to this provision. Religious minorities in Upper Canada, whether Protestant or Roman Catholic, cannot be fairly denied that relative protection of right which, under the same legislation, they enjoyed in Lower Canada." With glaring inconsistency, however, in the very next paragraph he advocates the retention

Ryerson considered himself the father of the Common School System of Canada. He believed that Separate Schools would prove destructive to the entire school system. It was with this gentleman that the Catholic bishops were obliged to contend for years; it was against his powerful influence that every amendment to the School Act had to be carried; it was in his hands that the whole administration of the School Law was placed, and upon him depended, in a great measure, the successful operation of the Separate School provisions of the Upper Canada School Act. Every government was obliged to reckon on his influence or opposition, before it might dare to introduce any measure affecting education, and by the tone and manner he assumed, it was evident he considered himself the dictator of the educational department of the government.*

of the onerous clauses in the U. C. School Act, in reference to Separate Schools, because, he says, such retention is "the only effective method of causing *the ultimate discontinuance of Separate Schools.*"

* In 1865, in giving his version of the negotiations preceding the passage of the Separate School Bill of 1863, he writes as follows : "At length Mr. Scott called upon me, to explain some personal matters and to know my specific objections to his bill. I replied that I objected to the very principle of a private member of Parliament doing what the Government alone should do, namely, bring in a measure to amend (when deemed necessary) a system of public instruction for the country, but Mr. Scott wished to know what objections I had to the bill itself. I then showed, and at his request lent him a copy of the amended bill with my erasure of objectionable clauses and notes on others requiring modifications to assimilate them to the Common School Law. In a day or two Mr. Scott called upon me again, stating that, having consulted his friends, he acceded to my objections, and would propose to amend the bill accordingly. I replied that I still objected to any other party than the Government conducting a measure of that kind through the Legislature; but as he removed from the bill what I considered objectionable, I would waive my objections on his proceeding with the bill, and would aid him to get it passed on two conditions. First, that it should be assented to on the part of the Government, and therefore passed on their responsibility; and, secondly, that it should be accepted by the authorities of his Church as a final settlement of the question." This has the true ring of the dictator. What possible difference could it make to the Chief Superintendent, in carrying out the provisions of the Act,

It could not be expected that, from such a man as Dr. Ryerson, Separate Schools should have fair play, or have even a fair chance of success. Looking now calmly back on the whole history of the Separate School agitation in Upper Canada, one is driven to the conclusion, as we before remarked, that the Protestant majority in Upper Canada were not prepared to extend the same rights to Catholics, in the education of their children, as were enjoyed by the Protestants of Lower Canada, nor can it be doubted that Dr. Ryerson, assisted by the powerful influence of Mr. Brown in the *Globe*, were the two most important factors in moulding public opinion against the whole system of Catholic Separate Schools.*

whether it was passed on the responsibility of the Government or not? Or why should the fact that the bill was introduced by a private member affect its principle or its merits? The demand that such a bill should be a final settlement, that it must never be altered, amended, or improved, is so monstrous and so absurd as to hardly require an answer. And yet in every concession on the Separate School question granted by the opponents of the measure, they wished to make it a condition that it should be a "finality." No measure passed in this enlightened age of representative government is considered a "finality" on the matter effected by such legislation. A law is final only so long as the people desire it to be so. Apply the principle of finality to the School System of this country, and where should we now stand? There is hardly any subject on which there is more legislation in Ontario than on education. Many radical changes have been made in Dr. Ryerson's School System itself, which never could have been effected if his School Bill had been considered final.

* Notwithstanding this, Mr. Brown never really had a very high opinion either of Dr. Ryerson's principles or of his fitness for the position of Chief Superintendent of Education. In September, 1853, he says of him, in the *Globe*: "There are four reasons why Dr. Ryerson should not retain his office, any one of which ought to be sufficient. First, because his appointment to the office was one of the most vile jobs that ever disgraced a country. He did so much work for a stated price, and, to give him his payment, a gentleman was taken out of the office Ryerson wanted, and put into a Professorship for which he was utterly unfit. Second, because Dr. Ryerson is an unprincipled man, in whom the public have long ceased to have any confidence; and it is not creditable to the country that the education of the youth of the province should be entrusted to such hands. If there is an office that should be filled by a man of high moral character, it is this. How fearful to think of such a

The episcopacy of Bishop de Charbonnel had been one continual struggle to obtain for the Catholics of Upper Canada the right to educate their children in their own schools. All that that zealous and energetic prelate demanded, was equal rights with the Protestants of Lower Canada, and nothing more. At first, he did not ask even that much, knowing how very deep and strong was the prejudice in Upper Canada on this question, and besides being himself a new-comer and, as the Chief Superintendent of Education was accustomed to call him, a "foreigner."* By his unwearied exertions a Separate School Bill was introduced by the Hincks Government in 1853, known as the Separate School Bill of 1853, or the Supplementary School Bill referred to above. It was the intention of the Government, or at least they led Bishop de Charbonnel to believe so, to give the Catholics of Upper Canada, by this bill, all the rights and powers, in educational matters, enjoyed by the Protestants of Lower Canada.† But the bill was so amended in com-

---

man as Dr. Ryerson being looked up to by the teachers and scholars of our country, as their great example! Third, because the Superintendency is a non-political situation. Dr. Ryerson may tell us he has forsaken politics—but who will believe him? Fourth, because, were Dr. Ryerson as pure as the driven snow, his system, however well adapted to Prussia, is not suited to the atmosphere of Canada, with a Liberal ministry at the helm. The educational department is one of the highest trusts which the Ministry have committed to them. If they feel that they can discharge that responsibility with Egerton Ryerson at the head of the department, we will deeply regret it."

* "When in May, 1851," writes Bishop de Charbonnel in 1853, "we solicited a law intended to free the Separate Schools from some of the fetters in which we found them shackled in 1850, the Hon. A. N. Morin, then in Toronto with the Government, found us so moderate in our demands that he expressed his astonishment at it, adding that he himself would not be satisfied with so little; but we were newly arrived, and we wanted to proceed slowly and surely."

† On the 11th of January, 1853, the Archbishop of Quebec writes Bishop de Charbonnel: "I am happy to tell your Lordship, in answer

mittee that, as finally passed, it failed in its objects. It was violently opposed by Mr. Brown and the Grits on the Reform side, and as violently by the Orangemen on the Conservative side. It did not give the Catholics of Upper Canada anything like the same rights and privileges accorded to the Protestants of Lower Canada. Catholics were still liable to be taxed for Common School purposes. The provisions of the Bill were in some very important particulars indefinite, and in the hands of the Chief Superintendent and his subordinates might be interpreted contrary to the intentions of its authors, and against the rights of the Catholic minority. A Chief Superintendent who believed in the retention of the onerous provisions in the Separate School Law, because such provisions would, in his opinion, cause the "ultimate discontinuance of Separate Schools," was hardly the man to put a construction on the new Act favorable to Catholics, nor were the various School Boards throughout the country any more likely to give effect to the intention of the Legislature, by a large and liberal construction of the Act in favor of Separate Schools, as was very soon quite apparent.*

to your letter of the 1st inst., that Mr. Morin, who has taken the trouble to come and see me, with your Lordship's letter to him, assured me that himself and his colleagues were in the firm resolution to give the Catholics of Upper Canada the same advantages which the Protestants in our part of the Province enjoy." On May 30th, Attorney-General Richards writes to him: "My Lord, I hope that the provisions of the bill will be such as to prevent future disputes and differences. As I said to you personally, I have endeavored to give the Separate Schools in Upper Canada the same rights and powers that the dissentient schools in Lower Canada have."

* On August 3, 1853, Mr. Hincks writes to Bishop de Charbonnel: "My Lord, I have learned with much regret from your letter of yesterday, that a fresh difficulty has arisen regarding your schools in Toronto. Believe me, my attention will be promptly given to the subject of the grant, with a view to find a remedy, if there be any attempt to obstruct a

There is hardly any doubt that the Hincks Government were anxious to do full justice to the Catholics of Upper Canada in the matter of separate education—to give them, in fact, all the powers and facilities possessed by the Protestant minority in Lower Canada.* The School Bill of 1853, although not going very far in this direction, would still have been a great advance on the former law, and would have placed the Catholics in a much better position with respect to their schools, had it been liberally interpreted, and its provisions construed in a broad and generous spirit. Such, however, was not the case, and on the re-assembling of Parliament in the session of 1854, Bishop de Charbonnel took measures to have the Act amended. A memorial signed by the bishops and archbishops of the ecclesiastical province was presented to his Excellency, Lord Elgin, then Governor-General, in June, 1854. In this memorial the petitioners declare that the Catholics of Upper Canada "do not ask exclusive privileges; they demand simply that the law which regulates Separate Schools in behalf of Protestants in Lower Canada should be extended to the Catholics of Upper Canada. It is a right

law honestly intended by the Government to heal up wounds which were most injurious to the peace of society. I regret my inability to call on your Lordship and express to you, personally, my great respect for your worth, which I had much pleasure in doing on the floor of Parliament." On the 18th of August, Vicar-General Cazeau writes to Bishop de Charbonnel: "My Lord, I have seen Mr. Hincks. Your school question vexes him very much. He will write strongly to Mr. ——— to make him interpret the law in such a way as to do justice to Catholics. If the law is not interpreted as necessary, a new one shall be enacted in order to require imperiously that the Catholics of Upper Canada shall be treated with the same liberality as the Protestants of Lower Canada, and thus justice shall be obtained."

* On September 4, 1854, Hon. Mr. Morin writes Bishop de Charbonnel: "As to your great question, Mr. Hincks is all disposed to cause that the law that authorizes Separate Schools should be a truth."

which we trust they will not ask in vain from your Excellency."

The ministerial complications which resulted in the resignation of Mr. Hincks, and the formation of the Mac Nab Government, prevented the passage of any school bill during the session of 1854. The new ministry promised, however, to pass a Separate School Bill, satisfactory to the Catholics of Upper Canada, and it was on this understanding that the Lower Canadian section of Mr. Hincks' cabinet consented to remain in the Government.* The new Government, early in 1855, prepared a School Bill to be submitted to Parliament at its next session.† This measure, as originally prepared, was very acceptable to the Upper Canadian bishops, although it did not give them all they demanded.‡

---

* On September 11, 1854, Vicar-General Cazeau writes his Lordship of Toronto: "My Lord,—All the Lower Canadian ministers will be maintained in the Cabinet. I do not deceive myself in telling your Lordship that they agreed, as a condition to their alliance with Sir Allan, that justice should be done to your Catholics about Separate Schools." The Bishop of Kingston wrote, on November 10, 1854: "My Lord,—I have a letter from our Attorney-General (Hon. John A. Macdonald), in which he promises that he will pass a bill that will be satisfactory to us all. Notwithstanding all his promises, I still feel anxious to see that some action should be taken on our School Bill." On December 28, Vicar-General Cazeau again writes: "My Lord,—It has been resolved in Council that justice should be done to the Separate Schools. Sir Allan hastens to tell me that he had always been favorable to them, and I replied that your Lordship always relied on him."

† The Bishop of Kingston writes, on January 8, 1855: "I have delayed writing you until I had an interview with the Attorney-General, who assures me that he has a bill prepared for us in Upper Canada. He says he gave it to Mr. Morin, as a Catholic in communication with Right Rev. Dr. de Charbonnel. The Chief Superintendent read it attentively, and said nothing against its provisions.

‡ The bishops demanded—1st. A Special Superintendent for Separate Schools, *not being a Protestant clergyman;* 2d. One trustee by ward, and one board for the different wards in cities; 3d. Free circumscription of Separate Schools, as enjoyed by the Protestants of Lower Canada; 4th. Equal share in the public school funds to which Catholics contributed their share of taxes, or at least free disposal of their own municipal taxes, as

It was submitted to the Chief Superintendent of Education, who, at first, made no objection to its provisions. Still, those who knew Dr. Ryerson were not inclined to conclude that his silence gave consent.* Parliament met in February, and although the Government had promised to bring in a Separate School Bill, up to April they had made no move in the matter, and it became the opinion of the Upper Canadian bishops that they did not intend to do so during that session. In April the bishops of Toronto, Kingston, and Bytown pressed the matter upon the attention of the Hon. John A. Macdonald, the Attorney-General.† They demanded that the

enjoyed by the Protestants of Lower Canada ; 5th. Repeal of the clause of the School Act by which Catholics were compelled to contribute to the building of public schools and the establishment and support of public school libraries ; 6th. Repeal of the onerous provision requiring a supporter of Separate Schools to make an annual declaration. They asked that a ratepayer, having once made a declaration that he was a Separate School supporter, he should always be rated as such unless he gave notice to the contrary. All of these demands have since become law.

* On January 16, 1855, the Bishop of Kingston writes the Bishop of Toronto : "I assure you I have my misgivings about the new School Bill, as unobjectionable to —— [Dr. Ryerson], and therefore I earnestly requested the Attorney-General to send us a copy of it, that we might send it back to him with our remarks on the margin of it."

† On April 16, 1855, Bishop Phelan, of Kingston, wrote the Hon. Attorney-General : "Hon. Sir,—Although you informed me in your last letter that it is, and always was, your object to enable the Catholics of Upper Canada to educate their youth in their own way, it does not appear, however, at present, that you intend making, at this session, any of the amendments in the present School Act which you required me to communicate in writing to you. If this was the case, what was the use of asking me for my views on the subject of Separate Schools? I am aware of your difficulties on this point ; the Chief Superintendent of Schools for Canada West, especially, being opposed to any measure that would be favorable to our Separate Schools, and consequently determined to prevent, if possible, the amendments we require. But I trust that neither you nor the Ministry will be prevented from doing us justice by your allowing us the same rights and privileges for our Separate Schools as are granted to the Protestants of Lower Canada. If this be done at the present session, we will have no reason to complain, and the odium thrown upon you of being controlled by Dr. Ryerson will be effectually removed. If, on the contrary, the voice of our opponent upon this sub-

Government should keep its promise to introduce a School Bill, giving the Catholics of Upper Canada all the rights and powers enjoyed by the Protestants of Lower Canada. This remonstrance had its effect, and a bill was accordingly introduced, notwithstanding the opposition of the Chief Superintendent. This gentleman still had a potent influence in the Educational Department, and was supported in his opposition to the measure by the Clear Grit members in the House, the *Globe* and Mr. Brown out of the House, and even by the Orange supporters of the Government. The bill, as introduced and passed on its second reading, was a fair measure of justice as far as it went, but it yet did not give the Catholics of Upper Canada the same rights conceded to the Protestants of Lower Canada. Even such as it was, it was emasculated in committee, and a very important clause declaring that "all provisions of this act, and, generally, all the words and expressions thereof shall receive such large, beneficial, and liberal construction as shall best attain the objects thereof, and the enforcement of its enactments according to their true intent, meaning, and spirit," was stricken out. This undoubtedly was the work of the Chief Superintendent. Whatever law was passed respecting Separate Schools in Upper Canada, he was determined that, so long at all events as he was at the head of the Educational Department, it should not

ject of Separate Schools is more attended to and respected than the voice of the Catholic Bishops, the clergy, and nearly 200,000 of her Majesty's loyal Catholic subjects, claiming justice for the education of their youth, surely the Ministry that refuses us such rights cannot blame us for being displeased with them, and consequently, for being determined to use every constitutional means to prevent their future return to Parliament. This, of course, will be the disagreeable alternative to which we shall be obliged to have recourse if full justice be not done us at this session with regard to our Separate Schools." This letter was sent to the Attorney-General, with the concurrence of the other two bishops of Canada West.

have a "large, beneficial, and liberal construction."
This was a very important provision, for, as we before pointed out, even the Separate School Bill of
1853 might have proved a great advance on the old
law, and would no doubt have been found practically
beneficial, with all its shortcomings, if it had received
a broad and liberal interpretation at the hands of Dr.
Ryerson and the local School Boards.* The new
bill, as it was introduced and read the second time,
was satisfactory, as far as it went, to the Upper
Canada bishops. When, however, they saw how it
had been tampered with in committee and finally
passed, they were greviously disappointed, and the
venerable Bishop of Toronto, in disgust at the Government's duplicity, resigned his position as a member of the Council of Public Instruction, and went
to Europe. The bill, among other great defects,
left it indefinite, and subject altogether to what
interpretation was put upon it, whether Separate
Schools had or had not the right to share in the
funds thereafter to accrue from the secularization of
the Clergy Reserves, to be handed over to the Municipal Councils, and by them set apart for school
purposes.

In the session of 1856 an application was made by
the bishops of Upper Canada for an amendment to the

* Scarcely had the new School Bill been in operation more than a few
weeks before trouble arose, owing to a strained interpretation of the
clause entitling the Separate Schools to share in the Legislative
grant according to the attendance. Dr. Ryerson contended that this
should be the *daily* attendance. On July 11, 1856, Bishop Phelan, of
Kingston, writes to Bishop de Charbonnel : "I see that Dr. Ryerson
gives his own interpretation to our new School Bill, stating that the
amendment of 1851 is repealed, but it is our Attorney-General's opinion
that it is not repealed. The doctor reads in our daily reports the 'daily
attendance,' instead of the 'average attendance.' Now our Solicitor-
General, Mr. Smith, has blotted out the word 'daily,' and authorizes the
Rev. Mr. Dollard to hold to this."

Separate School Bill of 1855. The Government, fearing the opposition of the Grits, and dreading still more their own Orange supporters, who, as the Parliament was now sitting in Toronto, were able to make their power and influence felt, were not prepared to introduce any measure in favor of Separate Schools. It was tacitly understood, however, that a private member should introduce a bill, and that it should be left as an open question to be dealt with by the House as a private measure. Accordingly Mr. Bowes, a supporter of the Government, introduced a bill to amend the Separate School Act of 1855, early in the session. Nothing was said, either for or against the measure by the members of the Government on its first reading. However, such opposition was at once developed to any legislation in favor of Separate Schools, by the *Globe*, the religious journals, and the organs of the Orange Society, that, on the second reading of the bill, Hon. Mr. Spence moved, in amendment, that it was "not expedient to make any change in the present School Law." As the Lower Canada section of the Cartier-Macdonald Cabinet had promised to introduce a Separate School Bill at that session, this amendment was considered rather too strong, and another amendment was carried, postponing the second reading of the bill for a period of five weeks. When the time had elapsed, and the bill was reached, in its regular course, Mr. Bowes said he did not think the measure could pass, and therefore he would move to discharge the order. Mr. Felton moved that the bill be now read a second time, which was lost on a division. The bill was then dropped, nor was anything ever done afterwards by the Cartier-Macdonald Government to redeem the pledge they had given to introduce and carry through a Separate School Bill satisfactory to the Catholics of Upper Canada.*

Notwithstanding the treatment received by the bishops of the Catholic Church at the hands of the Conservative party on the Separate School question, they still continued to give their support to that party. It was a question of George Brown and the Grits on one side, and the Tories and Orangemen on the other, and they seemed to have preferred the latter. Thus, when Archbishop Lynch came to Canada, it was very natural that he should have adopted the opinion entertained by the whole episcopacy—namely, that it was to the Conservative party that they must look for a Separate School bill, as they could not hope for any measure of justice at the hands of Mr. Brown and his followers. His Grace, on his arrival in this country, found the Liberal party, dominated by the influence of Mr. Brown and the *Globe*, strongly opposed to Separate Schools. Roughly speaking, it may be said that the Grits were composed chiefly of the Scotch Presbyterian portion of Ontario, and a large number of Methodists. There were many other religious denominations represented in

---

* Attorney-General Cartier and Hon. Mr. Couchon both voted in favor of Mr. Spence's amendment, and against Mr. Felton's motion. The *True Witness*, of July 25, 1856, says; "In February, 1856, before the session which has just closed, application was made to the Governor-General and to ministers for an amendment to the iniquitous bill of 1855, and at as early a period of the session as possible. Mr. Bowes introduced a motion for its amendment, only, however, *in part*. It was considered as an open question, to be voted upon according to the conscientious convictions of the members of the Legislature, but, to our astonishment, the Ministry stepped forth and opposed its passage with menaces and threats, and so effectually as to prevent its being brought forward. This bill, which was so unwarrantably thrust aside, received the sanction of Bishop Phelan, the holy and zealous bishop of Kingston, who wrote to the Attorney-General West (Hon. John A. Macdonald) in its favor. For its rejection, and the degrading shackles which the bill of 1855 imposes on the Catholics of Upper Canada, the Ministers and their creatures are responsible."

the party, among what our High Church friends would call the " dissenting churches," but undoubtedly the bone and sinew of the party were the Scotch Presbyterians. These, of course; were intensely hostile to Separate Schools. On the other hand, the backbone of the Conservative party in Ontario was then, as it is now, the Orange Society. Its members were still more determined that their hereditary enemy should be granted no concession in Canada, either religious or political, if they could prevent it. There can hardly be any question but that the leaders of the Conservative party would have granted a full measure of justice to the Catholics of Ontario in the matter of Separate Schools, had they not been deterred by the fear that their Orange supporters would desert them. Unlike Mr. Brown and his followers, Conservatives were not opposed to the *principle* of Separate Schools. Besides this, their whole strength lay in the Catholic Province of Lower Canada, whose bishops were unanimous in demanding such legislation as would place the Catholics of the Upper Province in the same position in respect to education as the Protestants of the former province. The Conservative leaders would have been glad to meet the views and accede to the legitimate demands of a body on whose aid they were obliged to depend for the maintenance of their power in Lower Canada. But they could not do so without losing their Orange support in Upper Canada, and they seem to have been quite satisfied that the Catholic hierarchy would never give their support to the Liberal party in Upper Canada so long as Mr. Brown was its ruling spirit.

For several years after Archbishop Lynch's elevation to the episcopal See of Toronto, he believed, with his brethren, that sooner or later the Conservative leaders would introduce a satisfactory Separate School Bill. They had every reason to believe so. That party was in power, was strong in the country, could have carried such a measure, and, as we said above, the leaders would no doubt have been willing to do so, had it not been for fear of their Orange allies. Having the almost entire support of Catholic Lower Canada, and of the hierarchy of both provinces, and Sir George Cartier (himself a Catholic) being at the head of the Government, and the party, even in Ontario, possessing at that time the support of a large majority of Catholics who had been driven out of the Reform ranks by what they considered the bigotry of Mr. Brown and the *Globe*, it was a hope that might be reasonably entertained by the Catholics of Ontario, that the Government would do something for them on the Separate School question. Still nothing was done. There was no chance of any Government carrying a Separate School bill while the Parliament sat in Toronto. The majority of the Catholic electors of Upper Canada, however, continued to support the Conservative party. Of two evils they chose what they considered the lesser. They preferred the Orangemen of the Conservative party to "George Brown and the *Globe*", and the few Catholics who could not give up their Reform principles and abandon their party, were subject to considerable odium from their co-religionists for continuing their alliance with a political organization having Mr. Brown for its leader and the *Globe* for its organ. Still there were not wanting strong indications that the question of Separate Schools would be made a test question for candidates of both parties seeking the suffrages of Catholic electors, and that all such aspirants to Parliamentary honors would be made to declare their opinions, and the course they would pursue on this question in case they were elected.

At length in 1858 the Catholics obtained definite promises from prominent Conservatives on the question of Separate Schools. In the general election of 1857 the Hon. Mr. Cayley, a member of the Conservative Government, was defeated in several constituencies when offering himself for re-election. There is no doubt that the Catholic vote had a good deal to do with these defeats. It was finally arranged that the member elect for the county of Renfrew should resign in favor of Mr. Cayley, as there was a fair prospect of his election, provided he could obtain the solid Catholic vote. To secure this, Mr. Van Koughnet went to Ottawa and called a meeting of Catholics of both parties. A resolution was passed, promising the support of the Catholics of Ottawa to Mr. Cayley, providing the Conservative Government would undertake to introduce and carry through a Separate School Bill satisfactory to the bishops of Upper Canada. Mr. Van Koughnet agreed to this, and gave a written pledge on behalf of the Government to that effect, and on this understanding Mr. Cayley received the almost united Catholic vote of Ottawa.

The pledge given, however, was not kept. The Conservative Government were retained in power, but, though they had a good working majority, they failed to introduce the promised measure. In 1862 the Conservative Government were defeated, and gave way to a Liberal Government. At once the new Government was urged by those staunch Catholic Reformers who had remained true to the party when most of their co-religionists had gone over to the other side, to bring in a Separate School measure, and thus remove one of the obstacles that stood in the way of Catholic support of the Liberal party in Ontario. But the Reform Government found themselves placed in much the same position, on this question, that their opponents, the Conservative Government, had been. They were as sure to be opposed by the extreme or Grit wing of their own party, on the Separate School question, as were the Conservative party by their Orange supporters. The most the Liberal Government could promise, was that they would support a bill brought in by a private member, but they declared that they could not undertake to introduce a Separate School Bill as a Government measure. Early in the session of 1863, in accordance with this arrangement, Mr. Scott prepared a bill. Like all the former measures in favor of Separate Schools, it was opposed by the ultra-Protestant press. It had also to be made acceptable to the Rev. Superintendent of Education, Mr. Ryerson, and what would be acceptable to him was not very likely to be fully satisfactory to the Catholic body of Ontario. However, Mr. Scott's bill was the best and most satisfactory measure that had been introduced up to that time in favor of Separate Schools, and was a great advance on all preceding measures affecting the educational interests of Catholics. The bill was passed in the session of 1863, with the support and entire concurrence of the Liberal Government. It was, of course, opposed by the Grit wing of the Reform party, and also by many Conservative members who had pledged themselves during the elections to support such a measure if introduced.

Archbishop Lynch was very active in promoting the passage of the School Bill of 1863, and was very successful in his endeavors, but still the bill, as a whole, fell very far short of giving the Catholics of Ontario the same rights and powers as those granted to the Protestants of Lower Canada, in the matter of separate education.   It was, however, the best that could be obtained at that time.   Prejudice was still too strong against Separate Schools, and the hierarchy and the Catholic body could only possess themselves in patience, until this prejudice had sufficiently abated to allow more just and equitable sentiments to prevail.   When it was found that neither of the two political parties could govern the country, and that the only remedy for the political evils of Canada lay in a confederation of all the British North American provinces, his Grace of Toronto considered the time opportune to have the School question in Upper Canada satisfactorily settled.   As, under the contemplated scheme of confederation, educational matters were to be relegated to the Provincial Governments, and as the Protestant minority in the Lower Province had had all their rights in this respect fully guaranteed, the Archbishop thought it was only just that the Catholics of Upper Canada—thenceforth to be called Ontario —should be placed in the same condition of security. It was, of course, expected that, educational matters being once placed in the hands of the people of Ontario, Catholics might give up all hope of ever having justice done them in the matter of Separate Schools, and so efforts were made by the Archbishop and the other bishops of Upper and Lower Canada to have such provisions embodied in the Act of Confederation as would secure to the Catholics of this province the same privileges as those enjoyed by Protestants of

the Province of Quebec.*   In making this demand,
they were met by the answer that the Separate
School Bill of 1863 was a "finality," and had been
accepted as such by the Catholic hierarchy.   This
was the ground assumed by Mr. Ryerson, and persistently maintained by him.   The same argument was
taken up and re-echoed by the press throughout the
country.   Archbishop Lynch denied that he had ever
accepted the act of 1863 as a finality, or that he ever
considered it as such.†   He said that it was consid-

* In New Brunswick the Catholics by trusting to the good faith of their
Protestant fellow-citizens, failed to make provision for Separate Schools
at confederation.   They were never able to obtain them from a Provincial
Government afterwards.   Mr. (now Hon.) John Costigan, the present Minister of Inland Revenue, the Catholic representative from that province,
struggled in vain for many years to obtain justice at the hands of the majority on the School question, and even went so far as to introduce resolu-
tions into the House of Commons at Ottawa on the subject.   A general
election was carried on and fought out on the Separate School issue in New
Brunswick·after confederation, but the Catholics were overwhelmingly
defeated.   Mr. Stewart, in his " Canada Under the Administration of the
Earl of Dufferin," says of this opposition: " The Catholic portion of the
community asked permission to spend their own money—that is, the sum
they were to pay for primary education—in support of Separate Catholic
Schools.   They did not seek to compel the assistance of Protestants in
any way in furthering this object.   The school-law advocates (*i. e.* the
opponents of Separate Schools) did not consider the justice nor the injustice of such a claim.   They contented themselves with simply denying
in a round-about way the possibility of dividing the fund set apart for
educational purposes.   This view was extremely fallacious and ridiculous, and none but the veriest bigots and the most savage and unreasonable controversialists in the universe would entertain the justness of the
plea for a single moment.   The Catholics asked merely for the exclusive
benefit of their own contributions.   They wished to be relieved from
contributing to a common fund from which they sought no aid or benefit."

† Bishop Lynch wrote to the Toronto *Leader*, on March 2, 1865, while
the question was under discussion: "You will confer a favor on me by
giving space to the following remarks, which I write with a view of cor-
recting a mistake concerning my acceptance of the Separate School Bill
of 1863.   When earnestly pressed to accept the bill as a finality, I studi-
ously avoided the term, and was taken to task by a city journal for so
doing.   The term savored too much of the perfection of human progress,
and seemed to place a bar to the claims and exigencies of the future.   I
said I was content with the bill, as were also my brethren in the episcopacy, as far as I knew their sentiments.   But since B. N. A. provinces
wish to take a consolidated form (and, we hope, a form that will last for a

ered final merely so long as the two provinces remained in their then anomalous political condition. The bishops, however, were not successful in inducing Parliament to accede to their demands, and the scheme of confederation was perfected and carried through without making any provision for the Catholic Separate Schools of Upper Canada, although, as we said before, Lower Canadian Protestants had been guaranteed all the rights and privileges they had demanded in this respect.

It seemed for some time after confederation that the Ontario Catholics would be obliged to make the best of the imperfect act of 1863, as there appeared but small prospect that any legislature elected by the people of that province would be prepared to do anything towards making the measures more effective. The coalition Government of Mr. Sandfield Macdonald, the first government of the new Province of Ontario, did not feel disposed to grant any concessions to the Catholic body in the matter of Separate Schools. A better feeling, however, soon began to prevail among the Protestant majority towards Catholics, which we are bound to say, the present Archbishop of Toronto was largely instrumental in bringing about. The people of Ontario at last realized the injustice of admitting the principle of Separate Schools, and yet preventing, by burdensome and onerous restrictions, their full and free development. The consequence and the result

long time), and as the important question of education is to be placed on a permanent basis, I consider that we should be wanting greatly in zeal for the good of posterity were we to content ourselves with anything less than the Protestant minority of Lower Canada have. I therefore rejoice that I did not use the word *finality*, which, even had I used, could not certainly be interpreted to mean *final* under any and all circumstances, but final only so long as the position of the two provinces remained unchanged."

of this change in public opinion, and in the better and more liberal sentiments of the Protestant majority of Ontario towards their Catholic fellow-citizens, is, that the present liberal Government of Ontario have been enabled to grant to the Catholic minority of this Province all the amendments to the Separate School Act, necessary to carry out the spirit and intention of the law. What other governments could not or would not grant in this respect, has been fully and generously conceded by Mr. Mowat's administration. For this reason, and for the further and most important reason that the present Liberal Government of Ontario have always shown themselves prepared to treat the Catholics of this Province in a fair and equitable spirit, and have recognized the claim of the Catholic minority by giving an important portfolio in the cabinet to a representative Catholic,* the present Archbishop of Toronto has felt it his duty to give Mr. Mowat's Government such support as a Catholic bishop may, consistent with his position as bishop of the Church, and without compromising himself by merely political entanglements. For giving such assistance to the Mowat Government, His Grace has been accused of deserting the Conservatives and going over to the Liberals. We think we have shown that he never belonged to any political party, and therefore cannot be accused of having deserted any. We have shown why, on first coming to Canada he naturally gave his support to the Conservative party. We believe that even at the present time, His Grace is in accord with the Dominion Government in their general policy— at all events, he is known to be a strong advocate of the national policy. In the Province of Ontario, how-

* Hon. C. F. Fraser, Commissioner of Public Works.

ever, His Grace believes that at the hands of Mr. Mowat's Government, Catholic interests will always receive a fair consideration. For the ground that that gentleman's administration has taken in favor of conceding to Catholics all the political privileges enjoyed by their Protestant fellow-citizens, he has drawn upon himself and his Government the ill-will of the extremists even of his own party. Under these circumstances His Grace considers that it would be not only ungenerous but it would be even ungrateful to refuse his support to a Government that has been the first in Canada to do justice to Catholics. For pursuing this course he is accused of being a politician. How far such a charge is well-founded we leave the unprejudiced reader to judge.

CONCLUSION.

In the foregoing pages we have endeavored to give an account of the most important events in the life of the present Archbishop of Toronto. It will be seen that not only as a bishop of the Catholic Church, but also as a private citizen, he has closely identified himself with all the movements of the day having for their object the welfare of his fellow-men, and that he has always taken a deep interest in the advancement and prosperity of Canada. Indefatigable in promoting the interests of the Church in this country, he has been no less active in everything tending to the mutual development and social well-being of the whole community ; and he has on all occasions, both at home and abroad, by pen and voice, endeavored to make known to the world the advantages possessed by Canada, and particularly the happy freedom the Catholic Church here enjoys. The great influence His Grace possesses has always been wisely and judiciously exercised; and since his assumption of the Episcopal office and his first coming to Toronto, whatever view may be taken as to his general course in affairs, either religious or political, few will deny the integrity of his motives, or that his action has ever been dictated by other than unselfish motives, or any desire other than the advance of the Christian religion and the general good of society. During the past twenty-five years the Catholic Church in Ontario has made rapid strides, and has more than kept pace with the material development of the Province and the increase of population. The Catholic body has everywhere throughout Ontario maintained a steady advance. New sees have been established, and Toronto has been elevated to the dignity of a Metropolitan. The Church in Western Canada holds at the present day a position which twenty years ago would hardly have been dreamt of by the most sanguine of her children. Old prejudices are gradually dying out. Any one who can recall the political and social condition of the Catholic body in this country even twenty years ago cannot fail to recognize the vast improvement which has taken place in these respects. The practical exclusion of Catholics from all the offices of state no longer exists to the same extent that it formerly did, and both of the great political parties in Canada have come to realize the fact that the Catholic body is a very important factor in the political affairs of the Dominion. Even the feelings of Protestants and Catholics towards one another have greatly improved in Ontario, and there is now a social mingling of the two classes, and such a general absence of the prejudices that formerly separated the two bodies as argues well for the future of our country, and leads us to hope that, in the next generation, the people of Canada, of all creeds and countries, will be welded into one homogeneous nation, and that whatever may be their political or religious differences, they will at all events be animated by one common national senti-ment.   The present happy condition of the Church in Ontario, and the disappearance of much of that religious and race prejudice which formerly existed, to the great injury of our social relations and the inevitable detriment of our national development, is, we believe, largely owing to the exertions and in-fluence of Archbishop Lynch.   The position of the Church in a democratic and self-governing country like Canada or the United States is quite different from what it is in the older Catholic or even Protest-ant monarchies of Europe.   Bishops in missionary countries, like America, must of necessity be permit-ted a larger margin for the exercise of their Episco-pal functions than in the older countries of Europe, where the canon law prevails.   By reason of such latitude, necessary to the efficient administration of ecclesiastical affairs in this country, a peculiar tact, the application of sound common sense, and a more than ordinary knowledge of men and things are more in demand.   That the Catholic Bishops have nobly fulfilled their duties and have fully justified the wisdom of their selection for the important trusts confided to them by the Holy See, the progress of the Church in Canada and in the United States amply proves.   The very difficult and delicate task has devolved on the bishops of America of advancing the Catholic cause, and preaching the doctrines of the Church—doctrines which are so much disliked, and to a certain extent dreaded, by the Protestant majority—without wounding the susceptibilities of the non-Catholic portion of the community or unnecessarily alarming their prejudices. That they have been successful in this respect to a very high degree, the general attitude assumed by the great mass of the Protestant laity of America towards the Catholic Church is the best testimony. No bishop, in the ecclesiastical history of Canada, has, we believe, displayed more admirable tact in his general management of affairs than the subject of this memoir. He has been eminently successful in conciliating the good will of the Protestant community of Ontario, without in the slightest degree compromising his position as a bishop of the Catholic Church. He has done a great deal towards softening down and smoothing away the political and religious asperities that were formerly so common. He is liberal—not in the offensive sense of that word, but in the sense of a broad and comprehensive charity that would seek to minimize, as far as possible, the differences that exist between Protestants and Catholics, in the interests of peace, harmony, and Christian brotherhood. His efforts in this direction have been fully appreciated by the whole community, Protestant and Catholic; and the magnificent tribute paid to his personal worth as well as to the dignity of the office he fills, by all classes and all creeds, on the occasion of the twenty-fifth anniversary of his consecration, is sufficient evidence of the high esteem and admiration entertained for His Grace by the people of Ontario.

APPENDIX.

THE ARCHBISHOP'S JUBILEE.

(From the Toronto Globe of December 11th and 12th, 1884.)

THE reception accorded to Archbishop Lynch last evening was such as might have been expected from the esteem in which he is held by the people of his archdiocese. For more than an hour before the time announced for his arrival men, women, and children were gathered on Yonge Street, from King Street to the Esplanade. In half an hour the street from Wellington street south was so thronged with people that the marshals had difficulty in keeping the passage clear. Good-humored though eager, the crowd kept increasing until the bell announced the arrival of the train. There was a rush for the train, and for a few minutes it seemed as if the crowd were in danger of being trampled under the feet of the carriage-horses and the spirited animals ridden by the marshals. As the train drew up, loud cheers rent the air; the band struck up "Yankee Doodle" to welcome the visiting bishops; rockets, Roman candles, and other fireworks hissed and blazed, and pierced the darkness with lights of many colors.

While the Archbishop and the visitors were being seated in the carriages the procession was forming for the march, and the blazing torches which had been scattered among the crowd were blending into a thin line. Here and there were seen three-sided transparencies bearing words of welcome to the Archbishop and the visiting ecclesiastics. They read as follows:

May the Archbishop live for his golden jubilee.
We love to honor our clergy.
The Queen City honors her beloved Archbishop.
The Emerald Benevolent Union greets the visiting bishops.

The Emerald Benevolent Union welcomes the Archbishop.
Long live our Archbishop.
Toronto delights to honor its Archbishop.
The Irish Catholic Benevolent Union greets its great patron, the Bishop of Philadelphia.
Toronto welcomes the American bishops.

The procession being formed, moved off in the following order, with bands playing and fireworks blazing:

Band of I.C.B.U., 20 members.
I.C.B.U. Society, Martin O'Rourke, Marshal, 500 members.
St. Vincent de Paul, and members of Holy Family, P. Curran, Marshal, 200 members.
St. Nicholas Newsboys bearing torches, J. Carbury, Marshal.
Maple Leaf Band, E. McCartney, leader.
Emerald Association, in regalia, Grand Marshal, G. M. Vincent; deputies, J. Shehan, Michael O'Brien, W. J. Patterson, Michael Carroll, John Fahey, Henry O'Brien, M. Matthews, 600 members.
Archbishop's carriage surrounded by mounted escort, followed by carriages containing citizens and guests.

Among the citizens in carriages were Messrs. B. B. Hughes, Patrick Hughes, Peter Ryan, Benjamin Hughes, Welsh, M. Dissette, C. Cashman, Cornelius O'Connor, W. A. Lee, C. P. Higgins, and others.

The Archbishop's carriage was surrounded by mounted men bearing torches. The crowd kept pressing in upon it, until the driver was obliged to whip his horses into a run.

The procession moved up Yonge Street to Front, and then turned west to the Queen's Hotel, where there was more cheering, and the discharge of fireworks increased. The same performance took place in front of the Rossin House, which was reached by way of York. At this point the procession turned eastward along King Street, and the crowd which lined the sidewalks or kept up with the procession greatly increased. At the corner of King and Yonge Streets the throng was dense, and from this point Yonge Street was thickly lined, the crowd extending beyond the sidewalk into the roadway. Yonge Street, from King to Shuter, presented a brilliant appearance with its rows of brightly lighted shops, the long line of torches, and the scintillations caused by a constant discharge of fireworks. Soon the procession reached the Cathedral. The square was packed with a dense mass of human beings, and the crowd extended for a considerable distance along Shuter and Bond Streets. A large crowd also gathered in the garden adjoining the church, and adventurous men and boys occupied the fence, and even the trees. The procession halted, and those who composed it mingled with the crowd for a short time. A sudden movement denoted the approach of the Archbishop. The crowd was pierced by the long thin line of torches; the bells of the Cathedral rang; the bands played lively airs; rockets flew up towards the lofty spire, and at length the Archiepiscopal carriage arrived at the gate, and cheer after cheer arose.

The exterior of the Cathedral presented a stately appearance. A large arch of evergreens was erected over the façade of the Cathedral.

Four large electric lights lit up the tower at the base of the spire, one light being suspended from each corner. From the upper louvres of the spire floated the Papal and other flags, while from the four corners of the tower floated respectively the British, French, American, and Austrian flags.

The first thing to strike the observer upon entering the Cathedral was the beauty of the Altar illuminations and the profusion of festooned flags and evergreens. A closer examination was required to fully appreciate the design shown in the decorations. From the lofty gothic ceiling red and white streamers were festooned to the principal pillars. On the face of the gallery before the organ was a large silk banneret of green and gold, in the centre of which was a medallion representing His Grace as administering the extreme unction to a member of the society of which His Grace is patron. On the right of the banneret was the British ensign and on the left the Stars and Stripes. From pillar to pillar were hung festoons of evergreens, with white pond lily enrichments, while the Roman letters XXV., representing the twenty-fifth anniversary of His Grace's consecration, were placed on the front of each pillar and all around the side of the church. White shields, 24 x 18, with gold edges, were placed around the church, bearing inscriptions relating to the different epochs in the life of His Grace. The shields were arranged according to date, the inscription recording his birth being on the right of His Grace's throne, and the epochs progressing around the sanctuary and into the body of the Cathedral. The inscriptions were as follows:

> Born 6th February, 1816, near Clones, county Monaghan, Ireland.
> 1833 to 1845, Clondalkin College and Castleknock.
> Ordained priest in Maynooth by Archbishop Murray in 1843.
> Missionary in Ireland from 1844 to 1846.
> Mission in Texas, 1846.
> Professor St. Mary of the Barrens Seminary from 1848 till 1856.
> Founder and President of the Seminary of Our Lady of the Angels, Niagara Falls, 1856.
> Consecrated bishop at Toronto, November 20, 1859.
> Archbishop in 1870.

On similar shields, near the lower part of the Cathedral, were the following inscriptions representing the works accomplished during His Grace's archiepiscopate:

> Loretto Convent, established in 1862.
> St. Joseph's Convent, established in 1863.
> St. Michael's tower and spire, built in 1865.
> Loretto Abbey, Wellington Place, extended in 1867.
> St. Nicholas Home, established in 1869.
> Attended Ecumenical Council in 1870.
> De La Salle Institute, established 1871.
> Consecrated Bishop Crinnon, Hamilton, 1874.
> Consecrated Archbishop Taschereau, Quebec, 1874.
> Consecrated Bishop O'Brien, Kingston, 1875.
> Convent of the Precious Blood, established 1874.
> Magdalen Asylum, established 1875.
> Convents of St. Joseph, established in St. Catharines, Thorold, Barrie, and Oshawa.
> Forty parish churches and thirty presbyteries established.
> Seventy priests ordained for the diocese.
> St. John's Grove and House established.

The right front pew was reserved for His Honor the Lieutenant-Governor and suite. Upon the door of the pew was emblazoned the emblem of Ontario, while upon the pillar immediately in front of the pew was a silk banner bearing the arms of the Dominion. The left front pew was reserved for His Worship, the Mayor, and suite.

Upon the door of the pew was emblazoned the crest of the city, while a white silk banner bearing the arms of the city was placed upon the pillar immediately in front of the pew. There was upon each of the pillars a small white banner having upon it the picture of a saint with drapery of gold. Under the windows were banners containing the following inscriptions:

Salvation and happiness of the people my first aim.
Suffer little children to come unto Me.
Detestation of oppression of the poor.
Glory only in the Cross.
Love of country—native and adopted.
Loyalty to legitimate Government.

All the banners and decorations were skilfully arranged so as not to interfere with the view. An auditorium was erected on each side of the sanctuary and immediately in front of each of the side altars for the accommodation of the visiting priests, while the crimson covered seats were placed in the sanctuary opposite the throne for the visiting high dignitaries of the Church. The pulpit was newly draped with velvet and gold. The Archbishop's throne, chair, and canopy were magnificent, being of maroon plush and bullion gold, the gifts of Mrs. John McGee, of St. Michael's parish. But the grandest sight was the altar with its candelabra and illuminations. Over the altar were traced in gaslight a bunch of shamrocks surmounted by a cross and the Roman figures XXV.

A great many people had assembled in the Cathedral when His Grace entered, leaning on the arms of Vicar-General Laurent and Vicar-General Rooney. His Grace was met at the door by about a dozen little boys, who were the guard of honor for the occasion. They wore crimson gowns and presented a very pleasing appearance. His Grace knelt before the altar for some minutes in prayer and then walked through the sanctuary and to the palace. There followed a large number of prelates. The reception at the palace was altogether an informal one. His Grace received the personal congratulations of all present. Among those present were noticed Archbishop

Ryan, of Philadelphia, Pa.; Archbishop O'Brien, of Halifax; Archbishop Taschereau, of Quebec; Bishop Ryan, of Buffalo, N. Y.; Bishop Fabre, of Montreal, Que.; Bishop de Goesbriand, of Vermont; Bishop Shanahan, of Harrisburg, Pa.; Bishop Duhamel, of Ottawa; Bishop Wadhams, of Ogdensburg, N. Y.; Bishop Gilmour, of Cleveland, O.; Bishop Sweeny, of St. John, N. B.; Bishop Cleary, of Kingston; Bishop Walsh, of London; Bishop Gross, of Savannah, Ga.; Bishop McNeirney, of Albany, N. Y.; Bishop Loughlin, of Brooklyn, N. Y.; Bishop Burgess, of Detroit, Mich.; Bishop Fitzgerald, of Little Rock, Ark.; Bishop Jamot, of Peterboro'; Bishop Carberry, of Hamilton; Bishop La Rocque, of St. Hyacinthe, Que.; Bishop Lorrain, of Pontiac; Bishop O'Mahony, of Toronto; Bishop Wigger, of Newark, N. J.; Mgr. Bruyere, of London; Mgr. Farrelly, of Belleville; Rev. Father O'Dowd, of Montreal; Vicar-General Heenan, of Hamilton; Dean O'Connor, of Barrie; Dean Harris, of St. Catharines; Mgr. Hamel, rector of Laval University; Vicar-General Rooney, Toronto.

His Grace partook of refreshments, and an hour was taken up in billeting the prelates upon citizens who wished to entertain them during their visit in Toronto. His Grace Bishop O'Brien, and His Lordship Bishop Shanahan, of Harrisburg, Pa., are at Government House. His Lordship Bishop Ryan, of Buffalo, and Rev. Father Erey are stopping with Mr. Patrick Hughes. His Lordship Bishop Sweeny, of St. John, N. B., is at the residence of the Hon. T. W. Anglin. His Grace the Right Reverend Dr. Ryan, Bishop of Philadelphia, is staying with his friend, Mr. B. B. Hughes, "Glenhurst." His Grace Archbishop Taschereau, of Quebec, is at the residence of Mrs. Crawford. His Lordship Bishop Fitzgerald will remain at the residence of Mr. W. A. Murray during his stay in Toronto, and Bishop Loughlin, of Brooklyn, N. Y., is at the Palace, Church street. Bishop Cleary, of Kingston, went home with Bishop O'Mahony, Power street.

The celebration of the twenty-fifth year of the episcopacy of Archbishop Lynch was continued yesterday. Pontifical high mass was celebrated in St. Michael's Cathedral and in the morning addresses were presented to the Archbishop by the various parishes. The admission to the cathedral was by ticket, and long before the hour for opening the service the wisdom of adopting this course was proven. People flocked into the cathedral, and by ten o'clock not only were the seats all taken, but the aisles were lined with people, and at the head of each, and in front of the pews just without the sanctuary, people were crowded, some fortunate enough to secure chairs, but the majority standing. Lieutenant-Governor Robinson and Mrs. Robinson, and Mayor Boswell occupied pews. Many other prominent citizens also were present: among them, Hon. T. W. Anglin, Messrs. Patrick Hughes, B. B. Hughes, E. O'Keefe, Foy, Dr. Cassidy, and Dr. Travers, St. John, N. B. The nuns of Loretto and St: Joseph sat on either side of the church near the sanctuary. The Sisters of the Precious Blood and the Sisters of our Lady of Charity were also present. The bright light of the sun toned down and varied into a hundred shades by the stained glass windows added greatly to the beauty of the interior, already made beautiful by the elaborate and handsome decorations. The choir for the occasion was entirely of male voices, the students of St. Michael's College and those of De la Salle Institute having joined to make up what proved to be a truly effective choir. The musical direction was entrusted to Rev. Father Chalendard assisted by Rev. Brother Odo Baldwin. Mr. J. H. Lemaitre, the organist of the cathedral, occupied his customary place. At ten o'clock the organ began playing the introduction to one of the solemn Gregorian Chants, and shortly afterward the procession of Acolytes, Priests, Bishops, and Archbishops, which had started from the palace entered, and proceeded slowly up the main aisle, the choir breaking forth in full chorus. When the whole procession had entered, it extended from the sanctuary to the end of the aisle. The moment was the grandest and one of the most solemn and impressive of the occasion. The procession, beginning with little boys, and followed by young men but lately entered upon the sacred duties of the priesthood; after these, men who had seen years of earnest service and quiet self-sacrifice in the interest of their fellows; then the grey-haired reverend dignitaries who had won honors and distinction in their high calling, and last of all, the loved and honored Archbishop, who is the central figure of these rejoicings; the crowd of people, some bowed in devotion, some turning to gaze, but all hushed and awe-struck, the beautiful "half-lights" admitted by the stained glass windows, the gorgeously lit altar, the solemn pealing music, all went to make up an occasion which those who were present will not soon forget. Arrived at the sanctuary the celebration of the mass proceeded, the celebrant being Archbishop Lynch himself. His voice, though not strong, was heard in every part of the church, for, as he intoned, stillness fell upon the people, and no sound was heard save the voices proceeding from the sanctuary. · The music by the choir was grand and solemn and in full keeping with the occasion.

The musical service was "Dumont's Mass of the Second Tone," one of the most beautiful of the Gregorian compositions. The singing proved that the choir had been carefully trained, and that it was led by one who had it under perfect control. The "Kyrie Elieson" was especially fine as rendered. The number of priests and dignitaries about the altar also gave additional importance and solemnity to the occasion. The deacon of honor of the day was Very Rev. Father Rooney, V. G.; and the sub-deacon of honor, Very Rev. Father Vincent, V. G. The deacon of the mass was Very Rev. Dean O'Connor, Barrie; and the sub-deacon of the mass, Venerable Archdeacon Cassidy, Dixie. The assisting priest was Very Rev. Father Laurent, V. G., and Rev. Fathers McEntee, of Oshawa, and Hand, of the Cathedral, officiated as master of ceremonies. The following were the visiting prelates: Archbishops Ryan, Philadelphia; O'Brien, Halifax; and Taschereau, Quebec; also Bishops Wadhams, Ogdensburg; Loughlin, Brooklyn; Fabre, Montreal; Fitzgerald, Little Rock; Ryan, Buffalo; Goesbriand, Vermont; Sweeny, St. Johns, N. B.; Lorain, Pembroke; Duhamel, Ottawa,; Walsh, London; Jamot, Peterborough; Cleary, Kingston; Gilmour, Cleveland; Shanahan, Harrisburg, Pa.; Carberry, Hamilton; and McKierney. All agree that the services of yesterday exceeded in impressiveness and grandeur any other that has ever taken place in St. Michael's Cathedral.

ARCHBISHOP RYAN'S SERMON.

The sermon was preached by Archbishop Ryan, of Philadelphia, who chose for his text words taken from Psalm cx. 4—" Thou art a High Priest forever, after the order of Melchisedech." "Twenty-five years ago," he said, " some of his hearers had witnessed in the sanctuary of the church, the consecration of their chief pastor. After twenty-five years they were assembled, in the first place, in a spirit of thanksgiving to God for the graces and favors bestowed through his ministry upon his people, and for the preservation of that chief pastor with increased experience and wisdom still to discharge the high functions of his office to the glory of God and the salvation of human souls. The great duty of thanksgiving to God was too often neglected. We were constantly coming to Him, extending our hands as beggars for alms, and forgetting the great duty of thanks for mercies already received. He pointed out that in the model prayer the first petition was " Hallowed be Thy name," and the " Gloria in Excelsis " sung that morning was wholly thanksgiving and rendering of glory to God, while it contained only two petitions. And in the second place, they were to do honor to the great priest. For although without God they could do nothing, though the grace of God was omnipotent yet grace would not interfere—grace would not oblige us to accept it. Hence the man who accepted grace, who labored for salvation and prayed for his people, deserved credit and honor. The reception accorded to the Archbishop on his arrival, and the multitudes assembled in the church, were the exterior marks of the interior feelings of gratitude and respect toward the chief pastor. It was not necessary to give a detailed account of the life of the archbishop, as the daily press had already done this, and most of his hearers had themselves witnessed his devotedness and perseverance in his work. Those who were not of the Catholic faith must have felt the effects of the mission of such a man, independently of religious considerations, though they were really wrought through its agency. Even from a merely human standpoint they were ready to do honor to the man whom God had employed to effect such works of beneficence—to wipe the tears from the cheek of sorrow—to aid the orphan, the outcast, and the immigrant, and to promote the welfare of the race by the various institutions of mercy which he had founded and fostered. Every man, whatever his belief, must honor the Christian man who, for twenty-five years, had done all in his power to alleviate the distress, not only of his own people, but irrespective of creed or nationality, by those constitutions which spring from the Church and are fostered by it. As appropriate to this occasion he wished to speak some words on the office of the Christian priesthood, of which the episcopacy was the plenitude. The office was all divine—there was something in it consecrated and supernatural. There were two ways in which God showed Himself to man. First, directly. They had felt the influence of an inspiration, when the Divine Spirit came down to the human spirit and communed with it. But God ordinarily communicated with man through the agency of man, and especially through the priesthood and the episcopacy. Now the office of the chief priest was to represent man to God, and to represent God to man. As God ordinarily communicated with man through man, so man would communicate with God through man, and preeminently through the priesthood and the episcopacy. The priesthood, without taking away the direct communication between God and man, stood in the presence of God as the representative of humanity, and also stood in the presence of humanity as the representative of God. As the representative of man he offered to God sacrifices for the sins of the people, and in the name and with the authority of God he spoke to the people. When the Jewish priests spoke to the people they did not say, "This is my opinion, here are our reasons," but, "Thus saith the Lord." The great high priest, the bishop of our souls, Jesus Christ, came to the people with the double office of sacrifice and of teaching. He was to enter the sanctuary at once as the priest and the victim. The hand of man had plucked the fatal fruit from the tree, and the hand of Jesus was pierced with nails. The feet of man had walked in evil ways, and the feet of Christ were nailed to the cross in agony and suffering. Man had lifted his head in rebellion against the Father—and behold the head of the Son crowned with thorns. So as the spirit of man had wandered away from God, Christ, at the supreme moment of sacrifice, cried out, " My God, why hast thou forsaken me ? " The second priestly office of Christ was to teach man. Some of the great moral philosophers had declared that the religion of God could never be taught with certainty until God should appear upon this earth ; and the idea of such an incarnation was made familiar to even the classic Pagan nations by their traditions. There was nothing absurd in the idea that God should come to the earth in the form of His most glorious creature, the being that He had made in His own image and likeness. See how much beauty there is in humanity—take the gentleness of one, the strength of another, the talent of another, the perseverance of another, the beauty of another—combine together all the good qualities of humanity in one being and you have Jesus Christ. The double office by sacrifice and teaching assumed by the Lord Jesus Christ, was continued in the episcopal and priestly office unto this day. The priest-hood of Jesus Christ, continued in his church, as the representative of humanity, offering sacrifices before God, as the representative of God teaching humanity. The office of the priesthood was a high and important one. How could a man believe unless he heard the Word ; how could he hear the Word without a preacher ; how could a man preach unless he be sent ? Salvation depended on prayer ; prayer on faith, faith on preaching, preaching on mission. So that in the Church of the living God we have faith, ministry, sacrifice, and teaching, continuing in the communicated priesthood of Jesus Christ. Hence the wisdom and the vitality of the Church were allied with the consciousness of this mission. The latter portion of the sermon had special reference to the Archbishop of Toronto. The preacher expressed the hope that he who had labored so long and so successfully might be blessed with length of days and continue to speak the words of truth with the authority of an ambassador of God, with the consciousness that what he says God says. He hoped he might still continue to speak to his separated brethren, and especially as he had spoken in recent lectures, calmly, gently, and truthfully declaring that Roman Catholics do not believe the doctrines that were popularly attributed to them, and on account of which they were stigmatized as irrational and absurd. He approved of the plan of proclaiming first of all what Catholics do not believe, for the world was not opposed to the Church so much as to something which the world wrongly conceived to be the Church; and authoritative declarations, such as those made by the Archbishop, were, he believed, the best method of bringing men to understand and appreciate the real doctrines of the Church. No matter how much churches or individuals might differ in their interpretation of texts, there was one text which all could understand, "Love one another." When our Lord was asked by the Jewish lawyer, "Who is my neighbor?" he replied with the beautiful parable of the good Samaritan. The good Samaritan was a heretic in the eyes of the Jews—and it was the stranger and the heretic who lifted up and cared for the poor wounded traveller. Christ showed by this parable that he was a friend of liberty—though not that false liberty which said that truth was as good as error. Without relinquishing one iota of the truth, Christ would be tender to the unbeliever. He would take the stranger and the errorist, and treat them so as to create an example of fraternal charity, and show that the heart of Christianity was as broad, as grand, as tender, and as all-embracing as the heart of humanity. Addressing the Archbishop of Toronto the preacher said: "So continue bishop of the Church, until the crozier that you received twenty-five years ago is changed into the palm of eternal victory; until the mitre that you wear shall be changed into the crown of eternal justice, not losing the mark of your episcopacy, not losing the mark of your priesthood, for in God's hierarchy, even as on earth, you shall bear the eternal mark of that priesthood, for 'thou art a high priest *forever*, after the order of Melchisedech.' "

The following address was presented from the clergy of the Diocese :

To His Grace the most Rev. the Archbishop of Toronto:

MAY IT PLEASE YOUR GRACE: It is now twenty-five years since you were summoned from the retirement of the Seminary of the Holy Angels, over which you presided ably for many years, and in obedience to the voice of the Supreme Pontiff, assumed the burdens and the responsibilities of the Diocese of Toronto.

Many of those who then loyally grouped themselves around you and solemnly pledged their obedience to your commands, have been called to their reward ; those of us who have survived the vicissitudes of time are here to-day, and with the younger generation who have been honored with a call to the ranks of the sacred priesthood, tender to Your Grace the expression of our affectionate attachment, and the assurance of the happiness with which we assemble in the temple of the Living God to thank Him for the length of years and blessings He has bestowed upon you.   Nor will we weary you by dwelling at greater length on the very great progress the Catholic Church has made under your able administration.

You have proved your zeal for the best interests of the holy religion in the ceaseless and unwearied attention you have given to every detail in your exalted office, and that this has been recognized by the Supreme Pontiff is evidenced by the pallium which to-day so fittingly marks your Archiepiscopal dignity.   There is not in the broad extent of Ontario a grander manifestation of living and sturdy religious vitality than that which in every part of your metropolitan city is offered to the eye of the impartial observer.

Under your fostering care, religious, educational, and charitable institutions, ministering to the wants of the soul and the sufferings of the body, have risen in stately grandeur, and with swinging doors offer a hospitable welcome to wearied man. If your Grace had no higher claims to our respect than those materialized in the noble institutions you have founded, they alone would entitle you to our reverence and affection.

Every parish of this large archdiocese bears the impress of your guiding hand, in the seats of learning, presbyteries, and churches that rise up as monuments to tell unto future generations the great works that have been accomplished under your active administration.

Here, as elsewhere, the great struggle of the day is against free thought in religion and secularism in education. Your pastorals and sermons are convincing proofs of the vigor with which you combatted the one, and the number of Separate Schools you have established in your archdiocese is sufficient evidence of your hostility to the other.

The sympathy of feeling and cordiality that binds together priest and people under Your Grace's paternal rule is the strongest proof of the unity that cements the head and members of the Catholic Church in the Province of Ontario.

The presence here this morning of the Right Rev. Prelates in affiliation with this Metropolitan See, and of the illustrious Archbishops and Bishops who have come from the distant parts of our Dominion and the United States to tender to Your Grace their congratulations, and publicly testify their high appreciation of the virtues which adorn your life, is, to us and to the people of Canada, an edifying example of brotherly love that unites the Catholic Episcopate.

For the last quarter of a century you have unreservedly devoted yourself to the service of Almighty God and the spiritual care of your priests and people.

The strength of your manhood and the wealth of your intellect were truly and generously at our call.

We are here to-day to bear witness to your unselfish devotion to our interests, to renew the pledge of our obedience and loyalty to you as our ecclesiastical head, and to express the affection and veneration we owe you as spiritual sons.

(Signed), F. P. Rooney, V.G., St. Mary's; J. M. Laurent,

V.G.; R. A. O'Connor, Dean of Barrie; Edward Cassidy, Archdeacon; W. R. Harris, J. J. McCann, and Wm. Bergin.

The following address from the parishioners of St. Michael's was then read to His Grace by Mr. Patrick Hughes, who had had the honor of being present at His Grace's consecration:

To His Grace the Most Reverend John Joseph Lynch, D.D., Archbishop of Toronto, etc., etc.

MAY IT PLEASE YOUR GRACE:—The parishioners of your Cathedral Church of St. Michael, some of whom had the happiness to be members of the first Catholic congregation formed in this city, tender Your Grace their heartfelt congratulations on this the twenty-fifth anniversary of your Episcopal consecration.

They devoutly render thanks to God, the Giver of all Good, for having bestowed upon them, and upon this Diocese a ruler so pious, so zealous, so able, and so wise, and for having guided and sustained Your Grace during all these years in the discharge of the trying and onerous duties of the Episcopacy.

The great work accomplished during Your Grace's administration, and the many services rendered to religion and the Catholic people by your administrative ability and unceasing labors, are manifest in this your metropolitan city, and in all parts of the diocese committed to your charge. New parishes have been created to meet the ever-increasing wants of the people. The number of zealous, devoted priests, carefully educated and trained to the proper discharge of the duties of their sacred office has steadily increased. Many new churches have been built, and others have been commenced where, even a few years ago, it seemed that Catholic churches would never be needed.

The religious orders introduced by Your Grace's predecessors have grown and flourished under your fostering care, and others have been added. The House of Providence, in which so many orphans are sheltered, and so many old and infirm persons are tenderly cared for, is an institution which would do honor to any diocese in the older countries.

To Your Grace's solicitude for the spiritual welfare of all committed to your charge we are indebted for the introduction into this diocese of the Orders of the Carmelites and of the Redemptorists, whose labors in the service of their Master are so fruitful of good; of the Order of the Precious Blood, whose members, spending their lives in recollection and prayer, give glory to God continually, and bring down His choicest blessings upon the people; and of the Order of the Good Shepherd, whose members, leading the erring from the paths of sin to the ways of virtue, render inestimable service to religion and to society.

To Your Grace we are also indebted for the establishment of the St. Nicholas Home, in which so many who might have been lost are trained in virtue and self-respect, as also the Notre Dame House for servants out of employment.

On the success which has crowned the wise and zealous efforts of Your Grace in the cause of education, the handmaid of religion, we also sincerely congratulate you, likewise, St. Michael's College, the Loretto Abbey, and the Convent of St. Joseph, that give ample opportunities for the education of the children whose parents can afford to pay the moderate fees necessary for the support of these noble institutions.

Your Grace, ever solicitous for all classes of your people, and watchful especially over the young of your flock, has, by unremitting efforts, succeeded in bringing our Separate School system to such a degree of perfection, that a sound Catholic education is now within the reach of every Catholic child in this city, and in the greater part of this Archdiocese. And so excellent is the secular education imparted in these schools, that, in all the competitive examinations which have been held, our pupils take a large share of the honors. The glory of Your Grace's administration in this respect, we may be permitted to say, was the securing, for the purpose of Catholic education, of the buildings of the De La Salle Institute. Thanks to the efforts of Your Grace, the ground first granted to the Catholics of Toronto for church purposes, and the buildings erected at such cost by the Brothers of the Christian Schools, assisted by the people, are dedicated hereafter and forever to Catholic education.

To Your Grace we owe the completion and adornment of this your Cathedral Church—the splendor of the sacred ceremonies by which glory is given to God, the religious aspirations of the people are satisfied, their zeal and piety are quickened and strengthened, and many who are yet without the one fold are irresistibly attracted. To you also we owe the ministration of priests, whom we revere for the sanctity of their lives and admire and love for their zeal and devotion.

Your Grace's labors for our instruction and enlightenment have been fruitful of much good. Your frequent exposition of the Catholic doctrine, and your clear, conclusive refutation of the slanders and calumnies by which the enemies of the Church seek to destroy it, have not only enlivened and strengthened the faith of Catholics, but have carried conviction to many who, wandering in the mazes of error and encompassed by the darkness of unbelief, sincerely sought the truth.

Although we know that you desire not the thanks of men for having faithfully and zealously discharged all the duties of the high position in His Church to which you were called by God ; yet, we feel that we would be most ungrateful did we not give to Your Grace the thanks which we owe to you because our every spiritual want is supplied, the means of salvation are placed within our reach, and because our children can receive a full intellectual equipment for the battle of life, without danger to the faith which is above all treasures.

We thank Your Grace for all that you have done in our behalf—we congratulate you again upon this happy anniversary, and we earnestly pray to God that He will grant you many years to serve Him, and to enlighten and guide those whom he has entrusted to your care.

Be graciously pleased to accept the accompanying testimonial as a token of the love and esteem enshrined in the hearts of your parishioners.

T. W. ANGLIN,
Chairman.

J. J. CASSIDY, M.D.,
Secretary.

P. HUGHES,
M. O'CONNERS,
M. J. MACNAMARA,
Members of Committee.

After reading the address, Mr. Hughes also presented His Grace with a testimony on behalf of the Lieutenant-Governor of Ontario, the Ministers of the Crown, members of Parliament, and the merchants and bankers of the City of Toronto.

Mr. Matthew O'Connor, of the Address Committee, and Mr. Cassidy, father of Dr. Cassidy, Secretary of the Committee, had also the honor of being present at His Grace's consecration as Bishop.

Addresses were then presented from each parish in the archdiocese, together with presentations from the congregations. His Grace made complimentary remarks regarding the progress of the different parishes. He adverted especially to the vast growth of the Catholic Church in the diocese, as evidenced by the great increase in the number of churches and presbyteries. He complimented in eloquent terms the laity for the munificent assistance they had given himself and the clergy generally in beginning and perfecting the various religious works to which the addresses had referred. The proceedings terminated about two o'clock, when the prelates and priests adjourned to St. Michael's Palace for lunch.

The complimentary banquet given by His Grace Archbishop Lynch to his friends, to the clergy of his archdiocese, and to the visiting prelates, on the occasion of his silver jubilee, took place at the Rossin House in the evening. The banquet was a grand success, the large dining parlor at this hotel was handsomely decorated with flags and evergreens. The Union Jack and Stars and Stripes were unfurled together across the north end of the dining hall, just behind the chairman's seats, and the seats of honor. At the southwestern end of the hall, on a raised balcony, was placed a splendid string band, which furnished good music for the occasion. At eight o'clock His Grace Archbishop Lynch, accompanied by about two hundred and fifty friends, assembled in this beautifully decorated dining hall. His Grace was attended by a dozen pages, who wore crimson sashes with lace collarettes. They acted as the guard of honor for the evening.

The chair was filled by the host of the evening, the Archbishop himself. At the head table beside him were Lieutenant-Governor Robinson, Archbishop Taschereau, Hon. Oliver Mowat, Archbishop Ryan, Philadelphia; Mayor Boswell; Archbishop O'Brien, Halifax; Chief-Justice Wilson; Bishop Loughlin, Brooklyn; Bishop Cleary, Kingston; Bishop Goesbriand, Vermont; Hon. Charles Clarke, Speaker Ontario House of Assembly; Lieutenant-Colonel Gilmour, Dalton McCarthy, Q.C. The vice-chairs were filled as follows: Bishop Walsh, Bishop Jamot, Bishop Fitzgerald, Bishop Fabre, Bishop Carberry, Bishop Wadhams, Bishop Duhamel, Bishop Shanahan, Bishop O'Mahoney, Bishop Lorrain, Bishop Ryan, Bishop Conroy, and Bishop Gilmour. There were also present, seated at the different tables: Hon. John Costigan, Hon. John O'Donohue, Hugh McMahon, Q.C., J. J. Foy, Rev. W. Flannery, St. Thomas; Rev. F. Ryan, S.J., Chicago; W. A. Murray, Toronto; Dr. Sullivan, Kingston; J. Eustice, Grimsby; Rev. P. McMahon, Streetsville; H. H. Cook, M.P.; Rev. R. A. Campbell, Orillia; Rev. L. A. Lambert, Waterloo, N. Y.; James Way, Rev. Mr. Bergin, Toronto; Rev. T. J. Morris, Brockton; Mr. Justice O'Connor, Wm. Gormaly, Alex. McCarthy, Barrie; Thos. Kennedy, Barrie; H. C. McKeown, St. Catharines; James A. Sadlier, Montreal; Brother Tobias, De La Salle Institute, Toronto; Rev. J. S. O'Leary, Friellton; J. F. Egan, Hamilton; W. G. Falconbridge; Hon. T. B. Pardee; Col. G. T. Denison; Hon. A. M. Ross; Rev. Father Allan, Uxbridge; C. E. Caron; Patrick Hughes; Rev. Father Finan, Merritton; Rev. Father Beausang, Pickering; Rev. Father O'Malley,

Niagara Falls; Rev. Father Power, House of Providence;
Rev. Father Cronin, Buffalo, N. Y.; Dean Harris, St.
Catharines; Prof. Herchfelder, Rev. Father MacBride,
Penetanguishene: Mr. Thomas McCrossen, Penetangui-
shene; Mons. Bruyere, London; Rev. Father Laboureau,
Penetanguishene; J. N. Leclere, St. Joseph's Church,
Montreal; James Ryan, Edward McKeown, Jas. Cooper,
Jas. Mason, E. O'Keefe, H. P. Dwyght, J. H. Gilmour,
J. Hamilton, M. J. Stack, Rev. Father Davies, Rev.
Father Duffy, Dixie; Patrick Whitney, Newmarket;
Rev. Father Moyna, Mr. C. Burns, Rev. H. G. Gibney,
Alliston; Rev. P. S. Dowdal, Pembroke; J. J. Monkle,
Streetville; Dr. B. Travers, St. John, N. B.; Rev. F. F.
Murphy, Halifax, N. S.; Rev. M. E. O'Reilly, Leslie-
ville; Rev. Alex. Klander, Rev. J. Kilcullen, Port Col-
borne; John Herbert, Very Rev. C. Vincent, V.G., Su-
perior St. Michael's College; Wm. Mulock, M.P., Hon.
G. W. Ross, Minister of Education; Mr. P. D. Hughes,
Rev. M. Mulcahy, St. Michael's College; Very Rev. Dean
O'Connor, Barrie; Rev. J. E. Crinnon, Brantford; John
Kells, Edward King, Rev. T. G. McEntee, Oshawa; Rev.
Jas. Allziri, Suspension Bridge; Rev. J. J. Corcoran, Tees-
water; Rev. P. C. Kenny, Rev. W. J. McGiully, Schom-
berg; Rev. P. J. Gavan, Joseph Bandidler, W. A. Lee,
M. Kielty, Rev. J. Pallier, Ottawa; Rev. D. Morris, Rev.
Father Teefy, Toronto; Thos. Coffey, London; Dr.
O'Sullivan, Peterborough; Capt. Law, R. N., Dr. Gra-
ham, Rev. Father Gwinane, St. Michael's College; Rev.
Father McCann, Toronto; Very Rev. N. G. Heenan,
Hamilton; Rev. Father Dougherty, S. J., Guelph; Rev.
Father Kiernan, Collingwood; Rev. Dr. Funcken, St.
Jerome College, Berlin; Rev. Father Harold, Niagara;
L'Abbe Gagnon, Secretary to Archbishop Taschereau,
Quebec; Rev. Father Waller, Dr. Sweetman, Mr. J. J.
Withrow, M. O'Connor, Capt. Geddes, A. D. C., Dr.
O'Reilly, and Defoe, W. G. McWilliams, D. Hayes, James
Brady, Ingersoll; Rev. Father Brady, Woodstock; Robt.
M. Keating, J. J. Mullon, T. Delaney, D. Nelly, Very
Rev. Father Laurent, V.G., Rev. James F. Wagner, Dean
of Windsor, Ont.; Rev. A. P. Dunouchel, St. Michael's

College; Rev. Father Bauer, of Sainecourt, London; Rev. P. Ray, Uptergrove; Rev. Dr. Kilroy, Stratford; Geo. S. Crawford, Toronto; J. A. Macdonell, Toronto; Sir Melville Parker, Bart., Cooksville; Ven. Archdeacon Cassidy, Dixie; Rev. Father Keogh, Chancellor, Hamilton; Very Rev. V. G. Dowling, Paris; Wm. Neill, Osgoode Hall, Toronto; Dr. J. J. Cassidy, Toronto; Capt. W. F. McMaster, Toronto; Dr. D. Wilson, President Toronto University; Rev. Father D. J. Sheehan, P. F., Bradford: Edward Stark, Mimico; John Mallon, J. P., Toronto; John A. McGee, Toronto; M. McConnell, Toronto; L. J. Cosgrove, Toronto; E. A. O'Sullivan, L. Bolster, J. H. Lemaitre, J. D. Warde, M. J. Macnamara, W. Guinane, J. J. Franklin, Toronto; Right Rev. Mgr. Farrelly, Belleville; Hon. T. W. Anglin, Toronto; Rev. Father Kerr, Brooklyn; Rev. Father Kavanagh, Our Lady of Angels College, Niagara; Rev. Father Moran, Brooklyn; Rev. Father Griffa, Oswego; Rev. Father Jeffcote, Secretary to Archbishop Lynch; Rev. Father Twohey, Kingston; Rev. Father O'Connell, Mount Forest; Rev. P. Lennon, Brantford; Rev. Father Brennan, St. Michael's College; Rev. Father Corduke, Toronto; Rev. Father Conley, Rev. Father Sullivan, Thorold; John Battle, Thorold; James Church, Toronto; Alex. Thomson, Toronto; B. Ingoldsby, Lockton; Rev. Father Sloan, Ottawa; Rev. Father McSpiritt, Adjala; Rev. Father Gallagher, Caledon; Rev. Father Shanahan, St. Catharines; Rev. Father Frayling, Rev. Father Hand, Toronto; Rev. Father Lynett, Midland; Rev. Father McCabe, Caledon; and Rev. Father Gearin, Flos.

The Lieutenant-Governor rose to propose the first toast of the evening. He said: Your Grace, My Lords, and Gentlemen,—Having been requested by some of my friends to propose a toast, I rise with great pleasure to fulfil that request. The interesting ceremonies of this day are brought to a fitting conclusion in this sociable and hospitable gathering. As I looked upon this scene I could not but think it an evidence of the generous spirit of an Irishman—(loud applause)—the doing of one who was unwilling that this, one of the greatest days of his life, should pass without the presence of his friends, Protestants and Catholics alike, to share with him the remembrance of this day twenty-five years ago. (Loud applause.) Few of us, perhaps none, can expect to equal the grace and magnitude of the hospitality which has called us here to-night, but there is one thing, Protestants and Catholics alike may well try to emulate—the noble and liberal spirit which has prompted it. I remember that when Bishop Jamot was installed at Peterborough some three years ago, a prominent newspaper stated that at the banquet given on that occasion as many Protestants were present as Catholics. That evidence of good feeling is renewed here to-night. (Loud applause.) The Archbishop of Toronto, in the discharge of his great duties, has preached the gospel of peace and good-will and mutual respect. A noted historian has said that the savage nature of man occasionally breaks through the thin coating of civilization, but thanks to the good feeling encouraged by His Grace, this savage nature of man does not break out in discussion here where the interests of the Dominion are concerned. (Applause.) It may break out occasionally in exhibitions in the press when the characters of our respective leaders are discussed—(laughter and applause)—and it would be well for the leaders of the press if they followed the example which our Protestant and Catholic Bishops are only too glad to set them. It would ill become me to speak of the duties of the Archbishop's high office, but no one needs to tell me of the ardent efforts he must have made as a missionary, what talent, what zeal, what force of character, what administrative ability he has shown in his present high office. These characteristics, combined in him, sufficiently account to me for the position he now occupies, and of which he is so great an ornament. I am only too glad that it falls to my lot to propose the health of the Archbishop of Toronto. It gives me all the greater pleasure because I have here an opportunity to acknowledge the many personal kindnesses and courtesies which for more than twenty years have been extended to me and mine by the distinguished gentleman who presides over us this evening. I give you, gentlemen, " The health of

Archbishop Lynch, wishing him health, prosperity, and success."

The toast was received with enthusiasm. The orchestra played a few bars of "The Maple Leaf," followed by "St. Patrick's Day," "Yankee Doodle," and "Rule Brittania." As the music ceased three hearty cheers and a couple of "tigers" were given for the Archbishop.

Archbishop Lynch said: Your Honor, Most Reverend Prelates, and my noble guests: It is a very trite saying on such an occasion as this that words will not suffice at all to adequately express one's feelings. In this case those words are really true. I would be glad to coin my ideas into words to give them to you and to His Honor the Lieutenant-Governor, for his very kind speech in proposing this toast. If I have done anything to rouse up the people of my adopted country, to increase brotherly love and affection one for the other, if I have done anything to advance the interests of the country, I have followed the dictates, not only of my own feelings, but of my conscience. (Applause.) I thank His Honor very much for his kind words. I take only a small portion of the praise, because his good feelings have translated many of my common doings into virtues. I rejoice very much, indeed, at the good kindly feeling which exists amongst, I may say, the *élite* of Toronto, of all nationalities and all creeds. We are here as brothers on this earth of ours, not to harm one another, but to honor and reverence and respect one another, and especially to respect the conscientious feelings of our neighbors. (Applause.) I return thanks most heartily, indeed, to those most reverend prelates who have come, some of them, more than twelve hundred miles to do honor to this occasion. But for the long-protracted Council—a week more than was expected —we would have had at least ten more prelates here. But, as they had made appointments in their own dioceses, they could not very well pass them over. I have received expressions of the kindest feeling on the part of these very reverend and right reverend prelates. I wish then to propose a health. It will be a very large and complex one indeed—the health of our guests, commencing with the

Lieutenant-Governor. While away I often thought of him and his most estimable lady. He has education and culture, but more—he is a gentleman, and when I say that I mean a great deal. In this toast I include also his Honor the Mayor of Toronto. He also is a gentleman. It is a great thing to have the city and the Province represented by gentlemen of culture, education, and broad views. With a succession of such Mayors, I think our city will prosper in every respect. I desire to include in this also the health of those reverend prelates who have come from long distances, especially those from the neighboring Republic. (Applause.) We have with us to-day the youngest of the prelates of the United States in the person of the illustrious prelate near me on my left, the Most Reverend Dr. Ryan, Archbishop of Philadelphia. You know him by reputation, and I know that you are now convinced that what public opinion says of him is true. He is a born orator. (Applause.) There is no true orator who has not a large heart and cultivated mind, both of which His Grace, the Archbishop of Philadelphia, has. We also have the senior Bishop of the United States in the person of the Most Reverend Dr. Loughlin, Bishop of Brooklyn. We have also others, so many that it would take too long to even mention their names, but we thank them very much for their condescension and kindness in coming to do honor to this occasion. I feel this honor, not personally—personally, I am nobody; but as Archbishop of Toronto I am somebody, and, therefore, gentlemen, the honor of the presence of these prelates is to you far more that to me. I also am glad to propose the health of many of my old friends and pupils who, after the lapse of about thirty years, come to do honor to this occasion. I am very happy to propose the health, or as an old and very good toast has it, "Our noble selves." I say noble, because nobility does not consist only in money, nor, perhaps, in education. Nobility consists in the possession of a charitable, generous heart. Many such a heart beats beneath a rough exterior. I propose the health of all my guests, hoping that the good feeling which has been spoken of will continue. I should not forget to mention in this connection the Premier of Ontario, Hon. Mr. Mowat. (Loud applause.) Sir John Macdonald (applause) writes a very kind letter indeed, expressing regret that he cannot be here because he has but lately returned to the country. I am quite sure that if it were in his power at all he would be here. He is a particular friend of mine. (Applause and laughter.) True friendship flows above all political considerations. I would have a very poor opinion of a man who would not love a friend because he was of another way of thinking. We should not allow our politics or religion to interfere with our friendships. (Applause.) Friendship is too holy a thing to be interfered with by outside-world considerations. Hence I say that our friends are of no particular politics—they are our friends, and that is quite enough. (Applause.) I have received a great many telegrams from friends who apologize for not being present, but as this is a family dinner we shall not read them. I must apologize to a great many gentlemen who do not occupy, on this occasion, seats which their high position in Ontario might entitle them to. We have done the best we could. The right reverend prelates who are here, not only those of Canada, but those from the United States, were kind enough to represent my humble person at the head of the several tables, and hoping that the guests would consider me with them, I'm extremely obliged to those most reverend prelates who have done us the honor to occupy these places. Let me ask you to drink the health of all, including besides those I have named, my friend the Archbishop of Quebec, Archbishop O'Brien, of Halifax, the Bishop of Montreal, and Chief Justice Wilson. Gentlemen, from my heart I wish you all prosperity in this life, and glory in the next.

The guests rose, and with their host, loyally drank one another's health.

The Lieutenant-Governor, in response to the toast, said he would not weary His Grace with another speech, and would give way to the reverend prelate on his right. However, he might say that they all welcomed the distinguished prelates from the neighboring country. (Applause.) He thanked His Grace for the compliment, which was a great reward for the little which he had done. He was glad that he had been able to exercise his duties satisfactorily to the mass of the people of the Province of Ontario. He hoped they would all be here to enjoy such a celebration twenty-five years hence with His Grace in the chair. (Applause.) In conclusion he said he appreciated the compliments which had been tendered by His Grace to himself and Mrs. Robinson.

Bishop Loughlin, of Brooklyn, said His Grace Archbishop Lynch had styled him the senior bishop of the States. In a sense he might admit it, but there were others who were his seniors in some ways. For instance, there was the born orator of the day. (Loud applause.) He (Bishop Loughlin) was not a superior speaker, as they all knew. They had all listened with unspeakable delight to the sentiments expressed by the Lieutenant-Governor and His Grace. Long acquaintance with His Grace had perhaps been the cause of his calling upon the speaker to say something. He had known His Grace before he was raised to the episcopacy. His Grace had been a great worker for his Divine Master, and he had done a great deal to advance religion. The speaker was at his consecration twenty-five years ago, and all who witnessed his manner of living since that time would say that he had been loyal to his country and loyal to his God ever since he took charge of this see. (Applause.) The scene in the Church to-day was most gratifying no doubt to His Grace, and there were present gentlemen of intelligence who were doing him honor. He closed by expressing his gratification at being present.

His Grace Archbishop Ryan, of Philadelphia, who had been alluded to by the last speaker as "a born orator," was loudly called for. His Grace is without doubt a natural born orator. He spoke as follows: "His Grace of Toronto assured me to-day that I had spoken enough, and I should not be called upon this evening for a speech. As you have been kind enough to call upon me, I shall not detain you, for I understand from His Grace we shall have some excellent songs. I shall simply express, as the junior Archbishop, my very great gratification in coming to Toronto under these circumstances.   For over thirty years I have known your Archbishop.   I knew him in Missouri, the scenes of his missionary labors, and have marked his career ever since, always with the greatest gratification and pride in my old friend of thirty years ago.   The reception last night, the scene at this banquet, and the many kind things said by the Archbishop and by the Lieutenant-Governor, were all evidences of the kind feelings towards the visiting bishops of the United States, and lead me to fear that between His Grace, though he is not a politician (loud laughter and applause), and between the Lientenant-Governor, the Mayor, and civic authorities, there must be some hidden conspiracy (laughter) to annex the United States to Canada. (Laughter.)   You have already annexed the hearts of the prelates of the United States to you (applause), and I trust these cordial feelings will ever continue, and that not only in the Catholic Church, which is the same everywhere, but also those friendly feelings of which His Grace has spoken, which are above political and national considerations ; that the same cordiality will ever exist, that the same two great countries will progress together, and we will be always found with those feelings of affection that are evidenced here to-night.   It is a delightful thing to see an assembly like this of various nationalities and various religious denominations bound together in the catholicity of social intercourse.   (Applause.)   And there is a catholicity when people looking in each other's faces could see warm hearts beneath.   This is the stronger evidence of affection, no matter what their differences may be.   They meet on a common ground.   Then it is that the religious or national or political differences will more or less disappear.   Then social intercourse destroys these asperities."   The speaker closed by thanking those present for his kind reception.

Archbishop Taschereau said he had come here, a long distance, after a long voyage from Europe, to show his gratitude to the Archbishop of Toronto, who was his consecrator, and also because he (Bishop Taschereau) represented the old church of Quebec, which had under its charge at one time the whole country as far west as the Pacific Ocean.

The Church of Quebec had always maintained good relations with all her children, and he hoped that the bonds which bound this and other dioceses to the old parent diocese would become closer than before. (Applause.)

Archbishop O'Brien, of Halifax, said that when a child he had been told by his mother, "Now, my boy, don't rise to speak until you know what you are going to speak about, or you will make a fool of yourself," but as he found that he made a fool of himself anyway he had failed to keep that rule of late. (Laughter.) He had understood that there would be only two speeches this evening and he had never thought that His Grace would go back on his word after twenty-five years of episcopacy. (Laughter.) He returned thanks on behalf of the guests of the evening, of whom he was glad to be one. If this was a sample of the way guests were received in Toronto they must consider Toronto not only the Queen City of the West, but also the Queen City of social intercourse. Coming from the far east of the Dominion he was glad to meet so many friends in the west. Here in the Dominion the people had worked out many social problems more completely than in any other country. This Dominion was the one country which would see the end of the world. (Great applause.) Down by the sea they were glad that this celebration was taking place, and in congratulating His Grace he spoke for many. He bore especially the good will of Dr. McIntyre, Bishop of Charlottetown, P. E. I., who, but for the difficulties of navigation at this season, would have been present.

Mayor Boswell made a few remarks commenting with expressions of pleasure upon the good feeling which existed between all classes of the community. He congratulated the Archbishop especially upon his broad-mindedness, and said that he hoped that if the present bishop of another denomination should see the twenty-fifth year of his episcopacy, and celebrated the anniversary, he would follow the example set to-night and invite Catholics as well as Protestants to be present. (Applause.)

Hon. Oliver Mowat, on rising, was greeted with loud applause. He said: "I would have been glad on this occasion to 'hear the Church' instead of speaking. At the same time, I have great pleasure in expressing my thanks to His Grace for having invited me to be present. The experience of to-night is a new one to me. I never saw so many bishops as I have seen to-night. The very air seems Catholic to-night, but I have not felt that it does any harm to a Protestant appetite. (Laughter.) From what I have seen of the right reverend prelates here I could wish they were all Protestants, and not only all Protestants, but all Presbyterians. (Laughter.) I have been delighted, sir, with the observations you have made to-night. I share with all my heart in the sentiments you have expressed regarding the desirability of harmony among all classes of the community. I rejoice to know that there is so much good feeling between the Protestants and Roman Catholics of my Province. (Applause.) There never was a time in the history of the Province in which there was so much unity between the two great sections of the community as at this moment. I rejoice to know that we are all glad of this. We know it is a good thing for the temporal welfare of the community, and I apprehend also that no evil will result to the eternal welfare of the population either. I apprehend, sir, that not a little of this good feeling is due to Your Grace. (Loud applause.) During the twenty-five years you have lived amongst us, and in your high position, we have learned to know something about you. We know that amongst your own people you are loved and admired, and that you deserve to be. We have learned also the esteem and respect which were due to your character. We have found you, sir, to be a man of most genial nature, of most kindly disposition and most generous character. We have found you always interested in whatever was for the benefit, especially of the poor and suffering. (Great applause.) We have found you anxious to promote what you considered to be for the public advantage, and while we Protestants cannot join in the religious congratulations you have received this day, we can at all events congratulate our Catholic fellow-citizens upon having such an Archbishop as you are. I can only wish in an especial manner in regard to you what I have wished in regard to the other prelates, that instead of being a good Catholic you were a good Protestant. (Loud laughter.) The good feeling which prevails amongst us is manifested in many ways. I rejoice to know that of the seventeen years which have passed since Confederation, for five of those years a Catholic Lieutenant-Governor has presided at the Government House. In our population Catholics are only about one-fifth as numerous as Protestants. In the younger Province of Manitoba, which has not been so long a part of the Dominion as Ontario, a Catholic Governor has presided for five years. I might recall many such facts, but it would be tedious to do so. I rejoice at them all and am glad to have this opportunity of expressing the great esteem and respect with which the Protestants of this country regard you, sir, and my hearty wish that you may live long, and that what remains to you of life may be full of comfort and happiness." (Loud applause.)

Bishop Ryan, of Buffalo, was received with applause. He was born in Almonte, in Canada. (Loud applause.) He hoped the good sentiments expressed would be carried out, and they would always live together as warm friends. He was glad to see that Archbishop Lynch had been so justly honored. Archbishop Lynch had done a great deal in the way of harmonizing the society in which his lot had been cast. (Applause.)

Bishop Walsh, of London, protested against the serious attempts of Mr. Mowat to make a Protestant of the Archbishop of Toronto. (Loud laughter.) The Bishop replied in a happy speech, which was loudly applauded at intervals.

Bishop O'Mahony, of Toronto, was received with applause. He spoke in high terms of a friend who had differed from him in religious principles. He had endeavored to cultivate friendship wherever he was, no matter what a man's religious opinions might be.

Bishop Cleary, of Kingston, had joined with those who had presented His Grace with addresses. He objected to a saying which he has heard, that Toronto was "the Metropolitan See." Kingston, he held, was the parent of Toronto. (Applause.) He gave a brief history of the birth of the bishopric of Kingston.   He protested against stating that his bishopric was "affiliated" with Toronto. (Laughter.)   He referred to the grand reception to His Grace on his arrival from Baltimore.   It looked as if all Toronto had turned out to pay their respects to a man whose religion did not cover one-fifth of the population. This showed a great spirit of hospitality.   It was an honor to Toronto to have these American prelates present.   He wished "God speed" to Toronto, because Toronto was his child. (Laughter.)   The Bishopric of Toronto was from Kingston.   The Bishop closed with a speech in a comic strain, which might well be called the speech of the evening.   His Lordship possesses wonderful powers as a public speaker.   His words are witty and he speaks with great force.

Captain Geddes, A.D.C., then sang in fine style, " Then You'll Remember Me."   Mr. I. F. Egan, of Hamilton, followed with " Nil Desperandum," which was loudly applauded.

The proceedings then terminated.